TO UNLOCK HER HEART

LINEN AND LACE - BOOK TWO

ROSIE CHAPEL

~

To Unlock Her Heart
Linen and Lace - Book Two

~

First printing 2016
ISBN: 978-0-9954303-2-7 (e-book)
ISBN: 978-0-6451116-0-6 (paperback)

Ulfire Pty. Ltd.
P.O. Box 1481
South Perth
WA 6951
Australia

www.rosiechapel.com

Cover artwork by JF Holland
Cover Images Courtesy Period Images and Deposit Photos

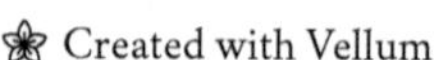 Created with Vellum

~

To Helen
For graciously and enthusiastically sharing your vision
(and time and a lot of patience).
This book is dedicated to you with all my love!

~

ACKNOWLEDGMENTS

My deepest thanks to Janet and Jane,
for being brave enough to edit my work!
I am eternally grateful.
Heartfelt appreciation to Julie for generously
creating the beautiful new cover for this book.

Although I recently updated the covers on my Regency
series, I remain forever grateful to my sister, Helen, who
created the gorgeous originals.

~

~

The Linen and Lace Clan

An exclusive club, only accessible to the fortuitous few.
Those who - no matter their differences in money, titles,
background or position - marry for love.
In an era when status, influence, and wealth are bolstered
under the guise of marriage, you are like rare gemstones -
admired and envied.
Let your mutual respect and true affection for one another
be the beacons by which you navigate the rough and the
smooth of life's journey.
Whether your clothing be of the cheapest linen or the finest
lace, may the blend of either or both bring the richest and
happiest union.

~

PROLOGUE

SUMMER 1816, LONDON.

ot again, she begged mutely, no please not again, not here. Hadn't he taken enough? There was nothing left, she was merely a shell. She couldn't even find the strength to fight.

He used to like it when she struggled to escape, when she tried to scream and thrash, attempting to free herself, it spurred him on, but he had quashed even that.

Inside a tiny pocket within her soul, locked away and buried so deeply she wasn't sure she would ever find it again, lay her heart. It was the only thing he could never reach.

While he took his pleasure, she closed her mind, letting everything become blank, the cold stone of the wall seeping through the delicate material of her gown.

She no longer felt his hands on her as, crudely, he tugged her clothes out of the way. Nor she did hear his grunts of satisfaction.

His insults about her lack of looks or her statuesque figure or her ugly hair. Even his threats against her family —

should she ever utter a word of what he did — had no effect anymore, she had long given up on anyone caring.

It was inconceivable to her that he had never been caught. Why had no one come when she cried for help? She suspected her family already knew. That they allowed him to use her. That she had been traded for something more important. Something only he could either give or deny them.

For what seemed like an age, this had hurt. Their betrayal like the last knife to her soul, yet through it all, she held her peace, unable to inflict on them the same pain. The anguish she suffered knowing her family, whom she trusted and believed loved her, would allow anyone to treat her this way, nearly destroyed her.

Didn't they realise she was ruined for all time? She might as well be dead! No decent man would ever want her. She was tainted. She used to cry for hours after he left. Constantly coming up with new and ingenious ways to cover the bruises on her body. Panicking in case she had to explain those marks.

Now, she rarely left her room, so it didn't matter.

Now she had no feelings at all.

Unable to sleep — for he stalked her dreams turning them into nightmares — she went through her days like a spectre, a pale shadow of who she once was. Occasionally, she visited her close friends, but she lost the ability to gossip aimlessly and forgot how to laugh, and the invitations dwindled.

If she went to a ball, he would be there, watching her every move, never acknowledging her, which was both a blessing and a curse. He took malicious satisfaction in hunting her down and taking her in the gardens or along a balcony. Triumphing in the fact he could do so, virtually in full view of the *ton*, yet no one ever noticed.

He loved the challenge, the risk of exposure, because he had his excuses ready. Whatever happened, he would not be shamed.

So, she remained silent and slowly lost herself in a pit of darkness.

Tonight was no different. She had tried to cry off, saying she was suffering from a debilitating headache and please might she be excused. Her mother ignored her entreaty. The ball was in honour of some marquis or other's engagement and everyone would be there.

Her heart had sunk. She knew what that meant. There would be no avoiding him — again. Wearily, she had allowed Peggy to dress her and style her hair, and by sheer force of will looked to be enjoying herself. That worked until about fifteen minutes ago.

He had appeared out of nowhere, hooked her arm under his and, holding her hand as though he might like to break it, while nodding and smiling to the guests they passed, drew her out onto the terrace.

Here she was, desperately praying no one came through those doors. He didn't speak to her. He never bothered. He unbuttoned the fall of his trousers with one hand and dragged up her skirts with the other. Cruel fingers digging into her soft skin.

When he began to thrust, he pressed one hand over her mouth, banging her head against the wall and silencing her whimpers of pain. His fetid breath in her face making her want to gag. *Let it be quick* she entreated, silently, *for once let it be quick.*

Regrettably, this time he wasn't quick enough. A movement along the terrace distracted him. Several, fashionably attired, people drifted out through a set of French doors at the far end, laughing and chattering, glasses in hand. The wide shaft of light illuminated the couple against the wall, and she heard him curse under his breath. He dropped her clothes, quickly righting his own but it was too late.

The group had seen sufficient to form their own opinion and a horrified gasp went up from one of the women, while two of the men strode along the terrace.

She was more humiliated than she ever thought possible, but maybe now someone would help her.

"Please, my Lord," she gasped, recognising one of the men. "Please, you have to help me. I-I... didn't ask for this." Beseeching them, frantically hoping someone, anyone would believe her. She could feel the marks from his hand already bruising her face. Her distress must be obvious to these people. Her tormentor somehow looked abashed and shocked all at the same time.

One of the men hesitated, an expression of distaste flickering over his features, but whether it was directed at her or him, she couldn't tell. As always, *he* took control.

"Say nothing, Hardacre. This silly chit cornered me, threw herself at me begging me to kiss her. Seems she's had three seasons and no offers. I think she wanted someone to come upon us, so I would have to marry her."

Her jaw dropped. Surely, this deceived no one. Her dress

was torn, her face and arms bruised. She must look as though he had forced her. His next words were like a death knell.

"She is no innocent."

There were mutters of consternation, and she was certain she heard the words 'strumpet' and 'whore'.

The world receded. There was a loud roaring in her ears, then blessed oblivion.

She regained consciousness in a carriage. She had no clue whose it was, and she was lying along the seat. *He* was sitting opposite her and there was no chaperone. Her head was groggy and, when she tried to sit up everything spun. Groaning weakly, she lay back down. On the brink of darkness, she heard his voice, dripping with malevolence.

"I told you not to speak of it. Now you will pay the price for your foolish tongue." And she knew no more.

She did not know how long she slept, it seemed like forever. In fact, she would have been content never to wake again, but one day she became aware of movement and opened her eyes. Peggy was pottering about doing whatever housemaids did. Her curtains were open, as was the window, and the air felt fresh and warm.

"Now then, miss, how are you feeling? I was wondering whether you was ever coming back to us."

She glanced around. Nothing had changed and she was in her own bed. *How did she get here?* She looked at Peggy, questions in her eyes, questions she didn't dare ask. Peggy came and sat in the chair next to the bed.

"You were dumped on the doorstep, miss. There was a knock and when Mr Gregson opened the door there you was in a heap. We got you up to bed but couldn't wake you. Then your parents and brother came home, all in a flap. Something about an incident at the ball and how terrible it was."

The maid looked at her mistress weighing up whether to tell her, deciding there was no longer any reason not to. She took the thin fingers in hers. "We all know, miss. We know what he does and are so sorry we could not stop it."

She stared at her maid. Tears spilled down her cheeks. *How odd, she didn't think she had anything left to cry.* "Oh, Peggy. What will become of me? He said he would ruin my family if I didn't..." she paused, unwilling to say the words, finding better ones she finished "...allow him such liberties.

"It seems it was all for naught. I was already ruined, he knew that, but to blame me, to declare it so in front of society..." she trailed off, the enormity of his actions threatening to engulf her.

Peggy sat with her until she drifted back to sleep, knowing there was yet more sadness to come for her distraught mistress.

By the time she felt able to leave her bedroom, her world had altered beyond recognition. Her parents and brother had departed for their country estate, leaving strict instructions she must not follow.

Shunned by society, her life contracted to the house with the odd visit to the bookstore, museum or art gallery. People she had thought her friends refused to acknowledge her.

She had to face those of her class who believed his claims and, eventually, she stopped trying to convince anyone she was innocent. He was a duke, she a baron's daughter. Social climbing was the norm.

It was easier to accept a giddy girl of the lower nobility seduced one of higher rank in order to trick him into marriage; it was not unheard of. Curiously, many seemed pleased he refused to bow to expectations.

Worse was to come. A couple of months later, she discovered she was increasing. Was there no end to the shame he had wrought on her? Previously he had spent himself into a cloth or on her clothes. How typical, this last time, by avoiding one indignity, he committed another just as, if not more, harrowing.

Alone, save for the few household staff, she struggled through the months, with no idea of what to expect. Apparently, her family were informed but no one came.

The birth was traumatic, and she was beset by infection and fever. It was several weeks before they deduced her well enough to be told the child had not survived and it was unlikely she would ever be able to bear another.

She knew she ought to feel sad, but all she could summon up was relief.

The *only* good thing to come out of all this was, she never saw or heard from *him* again. He did not call, and she was comforted by the knowledge that if he had, Mr Gregson the footman, would have sent him away with a flea in his ear.

For a while she was at peace.

CHAPTER 1

TWO YEARS LATER, VILLAGE OF OAK
STANTON, HAMPSHIRE

It was over. An interminably long day accepting condolences from, and being courteous to, people she didn't know. Her face hurt from smiling. She was standing in the front garden of a substantial property.

People milled around her, sharing stories about Beatrice Montgomery, which on any other occasion would have made her chortle with mirth. She could not bring herself to do that today. It was too much of an effort.

Everything was happening as though from a distance. Her head felt muddled and all she wanted to do was collapse in a chair and sleep. The funeral had been solemn and dignified and it was clear by how many attended, her great aunt had been well loved in these parts.

What was *not* clear was how she came to be her beneficiary. Her, Grace Alde… no it was Fitzgerald. She must remember she was Fitzgerald now, not Aldeburgh. Black sheep of the family, of several families. She was still coming to terms with her surprise inheritance.

Hands clasped neatly over her stomach, Grace let her mind wander back to that meeting, scant days before, at

Handley and White's Solicitors. She could still recall the smell permeating the suite of rooms, parchment and cigars with a hint of leather, a comforting kind of smell. Maybe that was the point.

~

Mr Handley, the senior partner, ushered her into his office. A room so haphazardly piled with books and papers, she failed to comprehend how he ever knew where anything was.

He seemed wholly unaware of the chaos and pulled several sheets of parchment covered with flowing cursive script, from a file, while explaining her great aunt, Miss Beatrice Montgomery, left everything she owned to Grace.

This included a house — somewhere in Hampshire — a portion of land, a carriage, and an annual stipend. Grace, impolitely she fancied, goggled at the solicitor unable to take it in.

Grace remembered her Great Aunt Beatrice — who was far too young to be a 'great aunt', barely older than her own mother — as an unfailingly cheerful sort of person who made every visit so much fun.

Never a care about how many tasty treats were enjoyed, and someone who didn't mind when you came home covered in mud and dirt from playing in the stream or rolling in the grass. Her memories of staying with her great aunt were of long sunny days filled with laughter. It was an eon since she had laughed.

Great Aunt Beatrice lived in the tiny village of Oak Stanton, attached to the estate of the Earl of Winchester — wasn't he the earl who married fairly recently? Grace thought there might be a whisper of scandal surrounding his bride. It wouldn't come to her, and who was she to talk anyway? Making sure she was thinking of the right relation, Grace asked whether it was this aunt.

Mr Handley nodded, concerned about this pale, quiet lady who outwardly seemed so poised, yet was obviously flustered over the news. He rang for his secretary and, when the young man poked his head around the door, requested he bring a strong cup of tea.

Grace dragged her attention back to what the portly, whiskered man was saying to her, and apologised for seeming baffled. "It's just I do not understand why she left anything to me. I'm sure she has nephews and nieces who are closer to her. I haven't seen her for oh, at least five years. Was there a letter, or anything, which might clarify her reasons?"

Mr Handley shook his head. "Not in any formal document, my dear. Your great aunt came here about two years ago, specifically to draw up this will. She said everything was to go to you and we had to ensure it could not be contested."

Two years. Grace stiffened. Two years ago. Now it made a little more sense, but why on earth would her aunt want to give her a house? She couldn't take it in. After all she had endured, suddenly there was a glimmer of light. She had somewhere of her own, somewhere she could remove to, where it was unlikely anyone would know or, for that matter, care who she was.

She nodded absently, accepting what Mr Handley was telling her, without grasping the import of his words. He was explaining the funeral would be held this coming Thursday at Oak Stanton and he had made arrangements for her to attend.

"B-b-but, how can I attend? I don't even know where this village is. I have never had to find it on my own. Anyway, I have things to organise here, I can't just up and leave." Grace stuttered in her panic. Everything was running away from her. She needed to regain some control.

The solicitor raised an eyebrow. "Miss Aldeburgh, your great aunt apprised me of your…" delicately voiced, "…situation. She felt you might require a place where you could be yourself without fear of, how shall I put it, consequence. A refuge if you will. Circumstance has been unkind to you, my dear and Miss Montgomery wished to save you from further distress."

Grace struggled to meet his eyes, as his kindly face wrinkled in a gentle smile. She didn't know whether to be mortified he knew so much about her, or grateful for his sensitivity. She was not accustomed to such care.

"T-thank you, Sir. I do appreciate it, it's just…" she faltered again.

"All rather overwhelming?" He finished for her.

Grace let out a huge sigh and nodded again, blinking away sudden tears. She would not cry. She was stronger than that. Straightening her shoulders, she took a deep breath.

"Right, Mr Handley, tell me everything."

Someone was asking her a question. Grace forced her attention back to the line of people waiting to speak to her. A petite young woman was pressing her hand.

"Please accept my heartfelt condolences for your loss, Miss Fitzgerald. Please do not hesitate to ask if there is anything, anything at all you need."

Grace heard the words but couldn't form any of her own. She tried again, but nothing came out. Helplessly, all she could do was stare, feeling like a simpleton.

The woman looked anxious and motioned to the tall and exceedingly handsome man at her side. "Giles, I think Miss

Fitzgerald might appreciate some time on her own. Please would you deal with these people, I'll take her indoors."

The man nodded and turned, addressing the crowd in a deep, yet quiet voice, his words reaching effortlessly to the furthest person. Grace had no idea what he said. Whatever it was had an effect, because there was a kind of collective murmur and everyone moved away.

Grace allowed herself to be ushered into the house, through the hallway to a comfortable parlour whose windows looked out over an overgrown, but attractively colourful, walled garden.

"Please just rest, Miss Fitzgerald and I'll make a hot drink."

Grace gaped at the woman, who winked mischievously.

"I do it all the time. Giles has given up worrying about it. I cannot expect the staff to be at my beck and call at random times of the day or night. They have enough to do and Sarah, our cook by the way, suffers me being in her kitchen as long as I don't get under her feet."

Grace thought her jaw must be somewhere near the floor, and the tiny woman gurgled with laughter.

"I do beg your pardon, I forgot to introduce myself. I'm Billie Trevallier, and my husband is Giles, the tall man handling crowd control." Waving her hand in the general direction of the front garden. "Now, you just stay there, and I'll sort out the drinks. I've been here many times and know where Miss Montgomery kept everything."

Billie disappeared through into the large kitchen. Grace heard the sounds of what she presumed to be a pan being put on the stove to boil, and crockery being piled into the sink to soak. Billie chattered away, while she worked obviously not requiring any reply, and Grace let the sound wash over her.

She rarely saw anyone. In fact, other than her one friend and her domestic staff, she couldn't remember the last time anyone had just talked to her and it made her feel very welcome.

Listening to Billie's lilting voice, Grace laid her head against the back of the chair and did what she wanted to do for the last hour. She shut her eyes.

~

Grace roused and for a moment could not work out where she was. Then it all came flooding back. She was in Oak Stanton. She owned a house, there had been a funeral and a tiny woman was talking to her.

Someone had covered her with a soft, fringed blanket. The days were warm, but the house had cooled in the late afternoon air. People were talking quietly in the kitchen, their voices blending together as they chattered about this and that, and she could hear the chink of china.

Pulling herself together, and folding the blanket tidily, Grace followed the sound of the voices. When she entered the kitchen three people turned and smiled. Billie and Giles were there along with another man, nearly as tall as Giles, but without the aura of authority exuding from Billie's husband.

Billie introduced both men, adding, with little sign of the respect due to his station, her husband was the Earl of Winchester — so this was the woman about whom the rumourmongers whispered — and the other gentleman was Theodore Elliott; retired soldier, doctor and all-round excellent friend.

Grace dropped a curtsey saying it was her pleasure to meet them all.

The two men studied her without appearing to.

The severe black attire, demanded on such occasions, somehow suited Grace's unusual colouring. Her lustrous hair, in no way disguised by the tight bun into which it had been scraped, was a vibrant shade of auburn. Dark eyes closer to amber than hazel and far more expressive than Grace was aware, sat in an oval face. Creamy skin, paler than it should be, was powdered with a sprinkling of freckles across her nose and cheeks.

Theodore Elliott knew all about this young woman. He had been her great aunt's doctor for several years and doctors encourage all manner of confidences. Also, he had seen Grace at the occasional ball he attended in London, under sufferance, at the request of his mother, not long before the scandal broke.

There had been something about her then. Her poise, elegance and hint of vulnerability, stirring in him emotions long forgotten.

At the time, he could not understand why she always seemed to be trying to blend in with the furnishings. Now he knew. Then she disappeared, and even as he contemplated calling upon her, he knew her family would refuse admittance.

When Miss Montgomery had revealed the truth, he was aghast. Not because of how society treated Grace, to shun those judged to have flouted the rules was not uncommon, but that they believed this quiet, unassuming beauty capable of such guile. By the time her great aunt was in the last throes of her illness, it was nearly two years since Grace had been seen in public.

Once he knew about the legacy and, without breaking a trust, Dr Elliott had discussed the matter with Giles. At the request of his friend, Theo had refrained from mentioning anything to Billie, who would have immediately taken the woman under her tiny wing.

Giles was concerned his wife already had enough on her plate. What with running the little school, supporting him with matters concerning the estate, cultivating her herb garden, occasionally helping in Whiteoaks' kitchens and assisting Theo when required, using her traditional remedies in conjunction with the doctor's modern treatments, her days were full. Giles also knew it was a losing battle. Even in the short hours of their acquaintance, he sensed his wife already liked this newcomer.

Before long she would gain the woman's trust and Miss Fitzgerald would tell Billie all without even realising she had. For reasons best known to himself, he just wanted to delay fate for as long as possible.

These things passed through the minds of both gentlemen, while Billie plied Grace with a cup of fragrant tea and a plate full of tempting sandwiches. Grace heard her stomach rumble and remembered she had not eaten since her meagre breakfast at the inn that morning. *Had it been only that morning? It seemed a lifetime ago.*

Grace had arrived in Oak Stanton a little before eleven and was directed to her great aunt's home, otherwise known as The Gables, by a friendly villager. She was expected. Mrs Weatherspoon, a local lady, had aired the house and everything was cleaned and polished within an inch of its life, the whole place fairly sparkling.

That good lady was there to meet Grace, who pronounced her heartfelt thanks at such kindness, and who in her turn blushed, assuring the new owner it was nothing.

The garrulous Mrs Weatherspoon nattered away happily, commenting that Miss Montgomery had been a delightful soul. Everyone was so pleased a family member had inherited the house, and they all hoped Miss Fitzgerald would be staying on.

~

Now it was late afternoon, the funeral was over, and three people she didn't know were tidying up her kitchen.

"I do beg your pardon. I did not mean to fall asleep. I fear the last few days must have caught up with me unawares. Please…" noticing they were clearing away her pots, "…leave them for me. You should not be washing up." Nonplussed a peer of the realm, and doctor, were not only lounging in her kitchen, but also drying her china.

Billie laughed merrily. "We are quite capable of helping out here and there, just because Giles is an earl doesn't mean he cannot wash a few pots. He is a dab hand at hot chocolate too." She smiled wickedly at her husband grinned back.

Grace nearly gasped at the depth of emotion which passed between them in so simple a gesture. How remarkable. To have someone care so much. She bent her head for a moment, biting her lip and refusing to dwell on what would never be hers.

Theo watched her curiously, but said nothing, content to bide his time.

· · ·

Back in control, Grace thanked them prettily and asked whether they would like to join her in a glass of something stronger than tea. She had spotted a tray with glasses and decanters alongside a fine-looking Cognac and a ruby port all standing invitingly on the walnut sideboard in the parlour.

"By way of appreciation for all you have done," she explained in her quiet way. "Everything happened so quickly, I did not think it probable I should arrive in time, and certainly I would not have been able to arrange so beautiful a wake. My great aunt must have been well liked."

"Miss Montgomery was a pillar of our little community. Most people did not realise she was a woman of status. She lived a conservative life but was always the first to offer her services for all manner of events," Theo said, his tone one of deep respect. "Her nephew is a friend of ours. He will no doubt call on you in the next few days. He was at the funeral but left not long after because he had call on his time."

"Would that be Mr Ralph Montgomery?" asked Grace.
Billie nodded.

"The solicitor told me he still lives in the area. I hope he is not upset Aunt Beatrice left me the house. He deserves it more than I." Back in the comfortable parlour, Grace moved to pour the drinks.

Theo was ahead of her. "Please allow me, Miss Fitzgerald. Just you take a seat."

Grace inclined her head and returned to the chair in which she had fallen asleep. Billie brought in cups of tea for Grace and herself.

Theo poured two glasses of the dark golden spirit, handing one to Giles, before continuing, "Ralph has known you were to have this house for some time. He has his own home at the other side of the village and was growing concerned about the extra upkeep should he have inherited this property.

"I know Miss Montgomery discussed her reasoning with him at length, and he was both relieved and happy it would come to you. He said he remembered you when you visited as a girl, something about pushing you in the stream."

Unexpectedly, Grace laughed, the golden sound rippling around the room as, unbidden, images of those carefree days flooded her mind. Her gangly cousin, whom she had worshipped, always tripping her up or pulling her hair and — yes — tipping her into the stream.

"I must have been such a pest to him," she smiled. "When I look back on it, I was always there, under his feet, an annoying brat of a child who constantly interrupted whatever he was doing. It will be most agreeable to see him again."

She chattered on for a few moments, regaling them with amusing tales of her childhood. The room fell quiet. Three faces watched her intently while she talked.

Abruptly and, surmising Ralph would likely not want to be associated with her, Grace stopped speaking and, to those in the room, it was almost as though she physically withdrew. Her whole countenance stilled, and the light left her eyes.

Out of Grace's line of sight, Billie glanced at her husband and raised an eyebrow. Giles nodded imperceptibly and turned the conversation to much more mundane matters, allowing the young woman to compose herself.

When the three guests took their leave, Billie demanded Grace come over to Whiteoaks the next day, to discuss Grace's staffing problem.

Currently there was no one. On Miss Montgomery's death, her staff was let go, their employer bequeathing each an annuity to keep them comfortable for the rest of their days. Well past retirement age anyway, all had refused to leave the woman, for whom they worked most of their lives, until she had no more need of them.

Capitulating, Grace agreed to call in the early afternoon, giving her time to explore the house and surrounds in the morning.

After they had gone, and not caring it was unseemly for a woman to take strong liquor, Grace poured herself a glass of brandy and took it out into the garden. The long summer evening was beautiful.

She wrapped the rug around her shoulders and found a convenient bench on which to sit, watching the evening fade to night and the blanket of stars twinkle into existence across the inky blue of the sky.

It felt like home.

CHAPTER 2

For once Grace slept without dreams, waking shortly after dawn to the sound of birds who obviously decided no sane person could possibly stay asleep on so glorious a morning. Expanding their lungs to capacity in an attempt to remind all and sundry not to waste a moment of it.

Grace stretched, and snuggled back under the thick comforter, enjoying the morning chorus. Fresh air, scented with the honeysuckle, growing in riotous abandon up over the wide front porch, wafted in through the open window.

Grace mulled over the events of the past week. Everything happened so quickly, and she still found it hard to believe all this was hers. She expected a knock on the door and two officious looking men notifying her the whole thing was a mistake and she must go back to London.

Departing the solicitor's office, Grace returned to where she had been living — nay, existing — for the last two years.

Once it was a cheerful house full of fun and laughter, where she was loved and cosseted, but one, which became a virtual prison. Her parents were dead; she didn't even know the cause, since nobody bothered to inform her until long after their funeral.

Her brother, Anthony — now Lord Hawkesworth — rarely visited, preferring to live at their country estate and, when he did, it was merely a formality. He told her what he thought she should know and, in tones which could scarcely be described as cordial, passed on any pertinent family information. She couldn't remember the last time he made eye contact with her or smiled. It was too painful. She pushed it aside, bringing her thoughts back the here and now.

She had wandered the empty rooms of the grand town house, soaking in the details. The furniture, the paintings, the ornate candelabra, and the meticulously tended garden, wishing she felt grieved at the thought of leaving this place, her home for so many years, but she didn't.

What she *did* have was a bubble of relief so huge, it threatened to manifest itself in a bout of reckless spontaneity. To skip along the hallways as she had when a child. To shatter the unnerving quiet with hysterical laughter.

Decorum, as always, reasserted itself and Grace contented herself with a small whoop of joy while dancing up the stairs to her bedchamber.

Ringing for her maid, Grace opened drawers and armoires, flinging clothes onto her bed, deciding what to take and what she could feasibly leave behind. A quiet knock announced Peggy; a pretty young girl of ten and seven who had assumed the role of Grace's personal maid when the rest of the family abandoned her.

Wiser than her age suggested, Peggy loved her mistress who was never anything other than kind and respectful to the skeleton staff left to tend her needs. Most of the household was now domiciled at Hawkesworth Manor — the Aldeburgh family's country estate — save the few whom Lord Hawkesworth determined would suffice. He allowed his sister a footman, a cook, a maid and a groom, Grace accepting his directive without comment or complaint.

When Peggy entered the bedchamber, Grace invited her maid to sit down and, doing the same, explained what the solicitor told her, adding she would be leaving for Oak Stanton Village in four days.

"I would love for you to accompany me, Peggy. Unfortunately, I do not think Lord Hawkesworth will allow it. I intend to write to him, outlining my plans, and if he is agreeable, I shall send for you." She grasped the girl's fingers. "I do not wish to lose you, for you are a great support to me, and how I will cope in a big, old house on my own is anybody's guess. Until I hear from my brother, my hands are tied."

Peggy nodded, understanding completely. "Do not fret, miss, things have a funny way of working out. I will be sorry to see you go, as will the others."

"I shall tell everyone shortly, first I need you to help me work out what to take. It is a small village attached to a large estate. I cannot imagine there will be many balls or society functions, but I think I ought to pack one or two evening gowns just in case. Mostly morning and walking dresses, oh and my riding habits I think."

Grace tapped her chin in concentration. "Maybe if you lay out some clothes while I speak to the staff, then we can go over them later."

Leaving Peggy to get on with things and knowing her maid would have everything sorted in a jiffy, Grace went to address the rest of the household. She would miss Peggy, who had become almost a friend, and one of only four people with whom she chatted with any regularity.

Making her way to the domestic quarters, Grace pushed

through the green baize door, calling a 'hello' when she entered the kitchen. She loved this room and had taken to eating breakfast here initially for want of company; eventually it became a haven.

It pleased her to note the others were all there — even Cecil, the groom — meaning she could get this over with in one go. Apologising for interrupting their day — something they smiled at — and, as she had with Peggy, Grace explained her change of circumstance.

They pronounced themselves pleased for her, although Jane — the cook — was tearful at the thought of her mistress leaving. None liked the way Grace was treated by her family, doing everything they could to make her life less uncomfortable. Jane went out of her way to create flavoursome meals, and the others always had a smile and a word for the young woman who, to them seemed unutterably lonely.

Many was the night they discussed the Baron's neglect of his only sibling. Mutterings that, had anything untoward happened to Lord Hawkesworth, might have made them highly suspect.

Glad to have that off her chest and answering their many questions about her great aunt as best as she could, Grace soon left them to their day. She returned to where Peggy was fast disappearing under a pile of frothy nonsense.

"Peggy, I cannot possibly take all these," she grinned, pulling three voluminous ball gowns off her maid who did not want her mistress to arrive with anything less than the pomp she felt was appropriate.

"But miss…"

Grace hushed her and perched on the edge of the bed, fingering the soft silk of her favourite gown, an eye-catching creation in the most divine sage green.

"I know you want me to have the best, but I do not know what room there is at Aunt Bea's. It is years since I visited and cannot recall many details about the house. I will not need ball gowns and frippery.

"We will pack these away. Should there come a time when they are required, I shall send for them. Once I am gone, Lord Hawkesworth might stay in the city more frequently, and may prefer to have this as an extra guest room."

Peggy stared at Grace, unable to fathom how a family could be so close one minute and in the blink of an eye become strangers. That Grace expected her brother to turn her bedroom into guest chambers, leaving her no real chance of return, hurt Peggy's sensitive soul.

Grace watched these emotions cross her maid's face and said gently, "Do not feel sorry for me, Peggy. I accepted long ago I am on my own. Now I have somewhere I can live where gossip is unlikely to follow. Try to be happy for me."

The young girl nodded and turned her attention back to the task at hand. By the end of the day they had sifted through the pile, choosing an adequate amount of clothing, and Grace believed she had covered all possibilities.

After Grace had gone downstairs for dinner, Peggy slipped one or two extras into the luggage. Gowns which looked stunning on her mistress, including her favourite, which Grace set aside considering them an indulgence.

The next day, Grace went through the house making sure everything was left in the way Anthony would expect. All her books and trinkets, and anything special to her, were either stowed away in boxes for storage or placed next to the trunks ready to be packed.

She drafted letters to send to the few people she felt ought to be advised of her change of situation. Mr Handley had generously agreed to deal with what little mail Grace received and would forward anything requiring her personal attention.

She had one dear and loyal friend, who she wanted to tell personally and on whom she called the next afternoon.

~

Grace had met Jemima Withers quite by chance. Both were enjoying the new exhibit at the British Museum, featuring the Parthenon sculptures and fell to chatting. Jemima was married to Major Lucas Withers, latterly of the British army, now retired.

He had loose connections to the Bow Street Runners and was often called upon to investigate matters necessitating more than a modicum of discretion.

At the outset, Grace was reserved, expecting Jemima to be warned off by her husband, who surely knew of Grace's misfortune. It never came. Either Major Withers knew and kept his counsel or neither had any idea or, if they did know, it made no difference.

Over time, Grace began to trust in this burgeoning friendship and the two ladies treasured their occasional afternoons together.

Jemima, with her open, sunny disposition and genuine affection for her new friend, broke through Grace's barriers, keenly aware she was not altogether happy.

Grace was too composed and, although she smiled, it never reached her eyes. Jemima only saw her laugh once in the year or so they had known each other, yet Grace Aldeburgh seemed like a woman with the capacity for boundless joy and vivacity. Jemima just needed to ferret out why it had been obliterated.

Little by little she had wormed it out of Grace, who acknowledged it was better coming from her than for Jemima to find out from someone who cared little for the truth; telling her friend the whole sorry tale, expecting Jemima to shun her also.

No fair-weather friend, Jemima was appalled by the treatment dished out to Grace by her family and so-called friends.

Society was a fickle mistress and Grace knew what it took to be accepted back into her fold, something she had long given up desiring. She was more upset by the reaction of her family, never imagining for one second they would believe the scandalous accusations. Although if, as she suspected, they knew all along, this could be their only response.

That was behind her now.

There was light at the end of the long and very dark tunnel.

Arriving at the Withers' residence, Grace was escorted through to the parlour. Jemima was deep in conversation with her husband, but they broke off when their guest entered. Major Withers greeted Grace in his amiable way, gave his wife a quick hug and a kiss, and excused himself, hurrying out to attend some urgent business.

Jemima patted the space next to her on the sofa, demanding to hear all her latest news. Grace sat with her friend and detailed everything the solicitor told her, finishing up by saying she would be moving to the village of Oak Stanton two days hence.

Surprised but pleased for Grace, Jemima remarked that she knew the earl and countess of Winchester, whose country seat, Whiteoaks, adjoined Oak Stanton. Jemima gave a glowing description the estate and the couple who met under the strangest circumstances and who wed the previous Christmas.

"She too had the rumour mill running hot," Jemima finished up. "Do you remember the fire at Ashbourne House?"

Grace nodded, vaguely recalling something about it.

"Everyone thought the countess set it, the fire I mean. Lucas was the one who proved her innocence. It was very exciting, involving foreign agents and missing family members. The countess even lost her memory. Quite a mystery for a while. Still she found her prince, well, earl, and they are ridiculously happy."

"I doubt I'll meet them," Grace interjected, diffidently when Jemima, eventually, took a breath. "I won't be mixing in such exalted circles."

"Oh, I think you might find they don't stand on ceremony, Grace," Jemima replied. "They are the most relaxed couple and are wholly involved in their local community. You'll see."

Grace shook her head, smiling at her friend's optimism. Jemima had already made up her mind to write to the countess and apprise her of their new inhabitant. She knew Lady Winchester would not allow Grace to be left out in the cold.

Also, she had been ruminating over the possibility of asking Lucas to make some subtle enquiries into what happened with Grace, believing there was more going on than even her friend knew. Once Grace had left the city it would be easier for him to investigate.

The two friends spent the remainder of the afternoon discussing the upcoming move. Grace hoped Jemima and her husband might see their way to visiting once she was settled. She explained the current lack of staff but anticipated being able to organise someone to assist with domestic chores when she got there. Again, Jemima was troubled by how alone Grace really was. The daughter of a baron left to fend for herself because of another's duplicity.

At the end of the afternoon, Grace thanked Jemima for everything and promised to write as soon as she was able. She blinked away sudden tears and hugged her friend, looking back once to wave when the carriage rolled away.

Another day of frantic packing and planning followed. By the fourth morning after Grace visited Mr Handley's office, she was as ready as she could be. She had said goodbye to her staff the previous evening, intending to set off at first light.

Her appreciation for everything they had done for her expressed in individual gifts, thoughtfully chosen and beautifully wrapped, to be found long after her departure. Needless to state, her gesture touched their hearts and, even Mr Gregson, the gruff footman, was heard to mutter he 'oped she'd be 'appy.

Grace took advantage of the Aldeburgh carriage. It was large enough to stow away her luggage and she decided it was the least her brother could do, not that she told him she was doing it. Her driver, Cecil, was happy enough; it gave him several days away from London, which was uncomfortably hot at this time of year. There would be only the two of them journeying to Oak Stanton.

Once society had turned its back on Grace, she forwent a chaperone. As far as she could tell, it no longer mattered whether she travelled on her own; her reputation was in tatters regardless. It was actually liberating to be released from certain constraints and was the only good thing to come out of the whole debacle.

The journey was uneventful, if rather dusty. She was able to secure a decent room in a coaching inn, arriving in the village the following day just in time for the funeral. Cecil had carried her luggage into the house, tipped his cap, refused her tip, wished her all the luck in the world and left.

Now she just had to get on with the rest of her life.

CHAPTER 3

Not wanting to let such a perfect morning slip away, Grace stopped ruminating about how she ended up here, in this peaceful little backwater, and got out of bed. Treating herself to a thorough wash, she found a modest, light cotton morning dress in dark green.

Altogether suitable, especially for someone likely to get reasonably messy from sorting out things. The preferred fashion this season was pastels or white, but it was hard to keep clean and, worse, made her look washed out. Graced avoided them whenever possible.

Making a list in her head, Grace noted she had to unpack her luggage, currently strewn around one of the other bedchambers, explore the rest of the house — she only saw one or two rooms yesterday, too tired after everyone left to do anything other than drag herself to bed — take a good look around the garden and, later, visit the countess.

She would change into something more appropriate for *that* encounter. Oh, and work out how to engage some help, along with the costs entailed.

Heading downstairs to the kitchen, Grace helped herself

to some breakfast. She could not cook to save her life, so made do with some of leftovers from the wake, and brewed herself a cup of tea. Smiling, in the knowledge Billie, a countess, was more accomplished in the kitchen than she — it was really quite mortifying.

Taking her cup of tea into the garden, she sat on the same bench where the previous night she admired the stars, and from where now she admired the garden. It was a riot of colour and, at first glance, appeared haphazard.

To her relatively experienced eye, she fancied there was a method behind its original layout. It simply required time and effort to tidy it up. Her aunt must have lost interest or been too ill during the past few months. Grace recalled her being proud of her garden.

Sauntering along what looked like pathways although she couldn't be certain, Grace spent a pleasant hour exploring. A high wall surrounded this rear garden, which was extensive. At the end, a solid wooden gate opened into a large meadow. Mostly grass, there were also several stands of trees offering welcome pockets of shade.

Mr Handley had explained this was part of her inheritance, and Grace mulled over the possibility of using it for horses. There was a stable attached to the house, where the carriage was kept, which was fine when it was inclement. This would be far better, providing any horses the freedom to wander at will. She might even be able to afford a shelter for them.

Grace loved horses and until... well... until things changed, she had ridden frequently, either through the city parks, or across the open fields of their estate. She did have her own mare; a good-natured creature given to her when a foal, but she doubted Anthony would agree to send the animal to his sister.

Trying not to let sadness for that which she could no

longer access, swamp her, Grace straightened her shoulders and continued her inspection of the property. Coming back into the house, she placed her cup on the kitchen table and investigated every room.

It was a pleasing home, all the formal rooms one might expect to find in a house of this size, including the elegant parlour, her guests and she had availed themselves of the previous night.

Continuing her tour, a cosy room tucked away at the back of the house, caught her attention. Set a little apart from the main rooms along an almost hidden hallway adjacent to the parlour, it sported a neat fireplace surrounded by a marble mantelpiece.

Walls lined with books, as well as three large and comfortable looking leather chairs currently circling the hearth. Not a large room, the high ceiling, and glass doors opening onto a flagged terrace, gave it an airy quality and the most inviting aspect.

The homely ambience reminded Grace of the snug at the inn where she stayed overnight, and she decided there and then, this was her favourite room. From that day on it became known as the Snug.

Flanking either side of the building were two wings. One housed the kitchen, scullery and laundry, above which were the domestic quarters. Across in the other wing she discovered three more nicely apportioned rooms, presumably for grooms or stable hands, given the stable and carriage house were underneath.

Upstairs, in the main part of the house, were six bedrooms, all of a reasonable size. Grace was currently sleeping in the largest — the one her aunt had used — and, because this was now her home, resolved it was only fair she keep that one for herself.

The rest would be used for guest chambers, on the off

chance she ever entertained visitors. Her brief perusal suggested all the rooms would benefit from new bed linen and, if the stipend allowed, new curtains. Despite their superior quality, the silk window furnishings were badly faded.

The main bedchamber was at one end of the hall, which along with its dressing room stretched the width of the house.

The dressing room, connected by a short passageway, contained two chests of drawers, two armoires, a bathtub and a delicately ornate dressing table. In fact, the dressing room was bigger than the whole of her bedchamber in London, something Grace found oddly amusing.

All the rooms had large windows and Grace went through the house opening them. The gentle breeze drifted through, pushing out stale air from rooms long closed up.

~

Satisfied she was beginning to understand the layout of her new home, Grace turned her attention to the gargantuan task of unpacking. Entering the room where Cecil set them down, she saw her whole life reduced to a pathetic collection of trunks and baskets.

Not even Peggy's obvious care in the manner everything was folded and wrapped in tissue, nor the sprigs of dried lavender scattered throughout to keep everything fresh, alleviated her grief at what she had lost.

For the first time since Mr Handley told her about the bequest, Grace permitted herself to remember what her world, what her life had been, before — before everything came crashing down around her ears. If only she hadn't been so gullible, if only she recognised the signs, if only… if only.

She had spent hours, days, going over the 'if onlys' and to what end? Even then would it have made any difference? He seemed determined to have her, and she couldn't change anything, for no matter what she said, nobody believed her. Now, all she had was a few clothes and a house in the middle of nowhere.

It *was* marvellous having her own home, even though she had no idea how to run one, or how to look after herself. In fact, the more she comprehended what her life now was, the more Grace felt absolutely and completely useless.

What was the good of being a baron's daughter, if you didn't have all the extras expected of such a station in life? She had no staff, no horse, no driver and no clue.

Grace flopped down on the floor next to the first trunk. Lifting the lid, she fingered the dresses within, and succumbed to a moment of unadulterated panic.

A voice broke through her consternation, forcing her to come to her senses. Calling out she would be down in a moment, Grace stood, smoothing her dress with trembling fingers and patting her hair to make sure it was still confined to its tidy bun. A calming breath and she went downstairs.

Standing in the sunlit doorway was the Countess of Winchester. A little confused, knowing she was to visit Whiteoaks that afternoon, Grace nevertheless dropped a deep curtsy, welcoming the elfin-like lady into her home. Inviting the countess into the parlour, Grace asked whether she would like a cup of tea or a glass of lemonade.

The morning, even at this early hour was already warm, and the countess replied the latter would be most refreshing. Grace found the beverage and poured it into two slender glasses. Discovering some biscuits left from the previous day, arranged them neatly on a plate, and carried everything through.

The two sat in comfortable silence for several minutes

enjoying the cool drink, then the countess became business-like.

"I know you are coming up to the house this afternoon but, when we got home last evening, I realised there are certain things which ought to be organised with some haste. You require domestic help. You need at least one horse, and someone to tidy up the garden.

"Please let me help you sort these out. I have lots of people who would appreciate a position." The countess leant forward to grasp Grace's hands, almost as though it would be Grace doing her the favour, not the other way around.

"That is exceedingly generous of you, my Lady," Grace replied in her soft voice. "I was just wondering how I would cope. I fear I am little prepared to look after myself."

The countess chuckled. "I believe you will find yourself more than capable, Miss Fitzgerald," she countered, "and please do call me Billie. I dislike being so formal with someone I know is going to be a friend."

Grace gazed in amazement at the diminutive woman sitting across from her. This woman who, on the two brief occasions they met, made her feel gladly received. "T-thank you," she stammered before pulling herself together and continuing, "and, you must call me Grace."

The two smiled at each other, and suddenly relaxed. Grace felt her lips twitching at the same time as Billie's nose crinkled. Without warning, they both burst into laughter, the sound echoing through the house.

"So, now that's settled, let us turn our heads to you," Billie said, amusement still playing around her mouth. "Giles has one or two retired army friends who are a dab hand at gardening. They love it and I imagine this garden would present them with a perfect challenge," she nodded towards the open French doors.

"Ralph knows them too, so you have reliable references.

As for a maid, my cook has a large family hereabouts and, she mentioned recently, two of her granddaughters hope to come into service. I would love to take them on up at the house, but we have no need of extra staff just now. I believe they would be eminently suitable as a lady's maid and kitchen maid. Then all we need is a cook and a driver, although your driver could also be your butler."

Grace put out a hand to stem the flow of generosity. "Please, my La… Billie. I will not need all this help. I only had four staff in London and the house was much bigger than this one. Perhaps a cook and a maid will suffice." Thinking of the cost and whether her stipend would cover it.

Billie studied the woman, taking in her pale features, rigid posture and a jaw which seemed overly tense, understanding there was more going on than she knew. Acquiescing for now, she grinned winsomely.

"Grace, my dear Grace, you shall have no more than necessary. I must point out The Gables is a large house and, if you are anything like me, have no idea how to manage it."

Grace blushed. The words almost a repeat of those which had run through her head less than an hour ago. "You are correct. I do enjoy gardening, it was my solace in the city," this was a confidence too far, and she hurried on, "but admit, I cannot cook. Neither do I have any idea how to care for my clothes, or what to use to clean and polish, although I'm sure I could learn…"

"What is it Grace? What concerns you about this?" Billie asked gently.

Grace sighed, deciding however uncomfortable the subject, she might as well be honest. "I am not sure whether the allowance is enough to pay for staff. I have never had to deal with the financial side of running a house. Since the death of my parents, Anthony, he's my brother, has took care of staff wages and domestic expenses."

She stared at the floor wishing she didn't seem so help-less. She hated it. Relying on others was not something she could abide but accepted in this instance she had little choice.

Billie cocked her head as she contemplated this. "Who would know?" she asked.

Grace surmised Dr Elliott or Ralph Montgomery might have some inkling. She explained the solicitor had not given her any paperwork regarding the monetary aspect of the bequest.

"I am so sorry. I hate to be a burden. I am used to handling things on my own." As she said this, Grace acknowledged she wasn't.

Even with everything that had happened, there were always people who looked after her, and saw to her needs. Nobody to love her or worry about her, but she had not been left destitute. Was there any chance at all Anthony still cared a little?

Unable to go there, she shoved that thought aside and looked back at Billie who was watching her quizzically. "Forgive me, my mind wandered for a moment. Do you know where I might find Dr Elliott?"

Billie said she did and would be happy to show Grace, adding, if she had no objections, she would like to accompany her, a walk being most beneficial on such a sunny morning. Gladly, Grace agreed, for she was not certain she would find her way back to the house; unfamiliar with the area after so long away.

The two women gathered themselves together and, foregoing wraps on such a warm morning, set off to the doctor's house.

CHAPTER 4

The dazzling summer sunshine presented the village to Grace in an almost magical light. The cottages and small houses dotted along the main, in actuality, only street, which ran through the village were built of the same soft red stone as The Gables.

Most nestled in neat gardens delineated by stone walls or wooden fences, bordered by all manner of flowers and bushes. Heady fragrances tickled Grace's nose as they passed, and she longed to lose herself in them.

Billie pointed out who lived where and what they did. Many were in their front gardens, or enjoying a morning constitutional, greeting the countess and by extension Grace, with a curtsy and a kind word.

Billie knew everyone's name and asked after family members in a manner indicating she cared about their answer. It was clear the countess was dearly loved, even though, as far as Grace knew, she had lived here less than a year.

· · ·

Dr Elliott's home wasn't far. Along the main road and down a quiet path. Billie walked around to a side door, and after knocking, opened it, calling out, "Theo? Theo, are you here? It's me."

An answering shout came from the bowels of the house. Billie ushered Grace into the room and through a door at the opposite side. Theo came out of a doorway along the hall wiping his hands on a cloth.

"Come in, come in. This is a nice surprise."

Billie smiled and, leaning up, planted a kiss on his cheek, while Theo drew the diminutive woman into a brief hug. Grace was astounded, she had never witnessed such close friendship between a man and a woman yet, strangely, it fit what little she knew of Billie.

Billie was chattering away with the doctor explaining the situation, asking whether he knew anything of the stipend.

Glancing at Grace who was standing awkwardly to one side, Theo was again taken by her classical features, puzzled she seemed to be trying to hide rather than embrace them.

Shaking his head at his thoughts, the doctor replied, as far as he was aware the stipend was generous, more than enough to cover the usual domestic costs, with some to spare for any extras which might be required.

Theo, recognising Grace was bemused, ushered the two ladies into his drawing room. He sat them down, rang for coffee and told them everything he knew.

Great Aunt Beatrice had been a canny soul with her money. An only child, she had inherited an appreciable sum from her father and later, when she decided to sell her large London house and move to Oak Stanton permanently, sought the proper advice on managing the profits from the sale.

She had invested wisely, and Theo believed Grace's

annual income would exceed two thousand pounds. Grace's jaw dropped. It sounded like an enormous sum of money.

"S-surely not… that is… I won't… I couldn't… how on earth?" Shocked, incoherence got the better of her, Theo and Billie chuckling at Grace's expression.

"I *told* you it would be fine," giggled Billie patting Grace on the arm. "Now please may we arrange some staff for you?"

Despite their levity, Theo saw Grace was becoming emotional. He guessed the last week had been bewildering for a young woman, who although might be nearly five and twenty, suddenly had a move, a house and an income to contend with.

Even with what Theo knew of her circumstances, Grace had lived a sheltered existence, and most gentlewomen were never required to be concerned with such things.

Theo had also known Aunt Beatrice very well, and she had been of the belief this change, this need for Grace to stand on her own two feet, would be the making of her great niece. Theo held in his possession a letter written by Aunt Beatrice a few weeks prior to her death.

She had handed it to the doctor with strict instructions to pass it on to Grace only when he felt the time was right. Theo was not entirely sure he would know when that was, but Miss Montgomery trusted his instincts, so he hoped not to let her down.

Watching Grace, a peculiar sensation swept through him. He yearned to comfort her, to tell her everything would work out and she would have a good life here in the village. Presuming it to be pity, he brushed it aside, bringing his attention back to their conversation.

Billie was in her element talking about staff and horses and goodness knows what else. Grace, looking less troubled, was being carried along on a tide of enthusiasm.

. . .

Theo interrupted their flow of chatter asking whether either would like another coffee. Billie accepted with alacrity, but Grace declined, thanking him in her gentle way. Her eyes held his for a split second longer than normal and Theo was sure the ground underneath him trembled.

Swallowing, certain he was imagining things, Theo pulled the bell and, muttering something about paperwork, hurried out. The women, deep in conversation, barely noticed his odd behaviour, but as soon as Theo was out of the door he leant against the wall, resting his head on its coolness, his heart beating erratically.

What the deuce was wrong with him?

He was smart enough to acknowledge Grace affected him in a way he did not expect. For a long time, Theo had harboured a secret admiration for Lady Helena, Giles' youngest sister. He knew it wasn't an earth-shattering passion, but they muddled along well together and for a time he hoped she might consider his suit.

Theo, although the second son of a marquis, lived the simple life of a village doctor. Not something of concern to Giles who, as Helena's brother was the person to whom Theo would need to approach for permission to court her, but her mother might be less agreeable.

Then the war intervened, and he returned a changed man. No longer interested in the hedonistic lifestyle embraced by so many unmarried men of the *ton*. Further, once he saw Grace, even though it was only from a distance, and the woman in question was wholly unaware of his existence, he recognised his feelings for Helena were more those of a brother.

He was pleased to learn Helena was being courted by

several young bucks, who had pronounced themselves enamoured with her, not to mention her very desirable dowry.

Theo also accepted he was too old for Giles' sister. He supposed himself to be staid and maybe a little boring. Time on the battlefield had convinced him excitement was not all it was cracked up to be, content with his life in this quiet village.

A little under a year ago, when Miss Willow — Billie — Caswell appeared under their noses, with no memory of who she was or how she came to be there, Theo was witness to the birth of a love so deep, those around them could well have fallen into it.

Billie and Giles shared a connection few were lucky enough to experience, and Theo concluded he would prefer to do without than settle for anything less.

Thus, this weird tingling sensation and the strange tripping of his heart, threw him off guard. He was doctor, a man of science and, talking himself out of what should have been obvious, strode down to his surgery. Ostensibly to check on something, in reality to find anything to divert his mind.

Billie and Grace were absorbed in their plans, so much so they didn't register the passage of time. Grace glanced up at the quaint little clock on the mantle and gasped when she realised it was coming up to midday.

"Oh, my Lad… Billie, I do beg your pardon. I have kept you talking far too long. What will your husband think of me? Please apologise to him if I have delayed you."

Billie chortled with amusement. "Not Giles. He is buried in estate business this morning and informed me, somewhat rudely I thought, since I intended to hound you this morning and then host you this afternoon, he would probably spend the day with his stewards."

Billie's face softened, and Grace knew her words were in no way a censure. More she was amused her husband felt the need to escape two gossiping females.

"You still wish me to call this afternoon?" Grace asked, shyly, certain Billie would have had enough by now, and this morning's discussions made the afternoon visit moot.

"Of course, why not. In fact, come with me now. We can have lunch and enjoy our afternoon. I can show off Whiteoaks, and you can respond by ooh-ing and ahh-ing, and acting suitably awed, declaring how dazzled you are by my home."

The countess had assumed a haughty expression, then ruined it by winking and grinning in the most mischievous way. The pair burst out laughing and, as Billie was not to be put off, Grace capitulated.

Billie yelled for Theo, uncaring it was not particularly ladylike. Doctor Elliott appeared, and while Billie was explaining they needed to leave, he bowed to both women. Grace dipped a curtsy, thanking him for his kindness and the excellent coffee, unconsciously reaching out to press his hand in her gratitude.

A trickle of warmth ran up her arm, and she snatched her hand away, perplexed by her reaction. Confused she tried to cover it up, but when she raised her face to Theo's, she noticed his eyes crinkling in a smile which seemed just for her. Heat coiled through her and, unnerved, she hastened from the house apologising for taking up his time.

Observing this little scene, and surprisingly for her, Billie made no comment, merely stored it away to discuss later with her husband.

Theo found his gaze drawn to the tall newcomer, as Grace and Billie wandered down the path. She was a bit of a mystery, hidden under many. Unexpectedly, he thought how wonderful it would be to peel them all away.

Grace had no idea what was going on in Theo's head and, truth be told, it might have panicked her somewhat. In light of her experiences, it would take a considerable time for her to trust another man to get close both emotionally and physically. Neither did she wish anyone to be caught up in the scandal still clinging to her name.

Billie's coach was standing outside The Gables and Billie thanked the groom, whose name was Jake, for his patience. He grinned, informing her, his brother had been down for a chat and he'd had a fine morning catching up on what his large and madcap family were up to.

Billie chuckled as he regaled them with one of his younger siblings' exploits and Grace was astounded by the friendly relationship the two shared. It was rare for servants to be treated with such cordiality. Billie spotted Grace's confusion and explained.

"Last year, I arrived here in a sorry state, and for a little while had no idea who I was. The household staff was most accommodating, especially as I gave them the odd fright — which I'll tell you about one day.

"If not for Jake here, the end of my story might have been quite different. I believe a house is only as good as those who run it, and our staff is exceptional. I love them like family and believe we enjoy a special friendship. One, few others would understand, but it works for us."

Assisting Grace up into the seat, Jake dropped a cheeky wink, giving her such a surprise, she reciprocated. The young groom waited until she seated herself next to the countess before climbing into the driver's seat.

It was an open carriage and, once they started moving, the light breeze helped cool their skin, a tad over-warm under the mid-day sun.

~

During the short journey to Whiteoaks, Billie was the perfect tour guide, pointing out all sorts of interesting things on the way. They trundled through a set of huge wrought iron gates, up a long driveway and, as Jake turned the carriage towards the courtyard, Grace got her first proper view of Whiteoaks. She was transfixed. It was one of the most spectacular houses she had ever seen.

An expanse of warm red brick softened at the corners by creamy quoins and alleviated by windows — so many great big windows — reflecting the endless sky, giving the impression the whole building was floating.

Several tall chimneys, one or two with white smoke curling out of them, were scattered across a red tiled roof. It was the sort of home she dreamed about as a child, one to where the handsome prince would whisk his princess.

She glanced at Billie, who was inordinately pleased with her new friend's reaction, realising Billie's prince had done precisely that. "Billie, what a gorgeous home you have. I am in awe, and willing to ooh and ahh until you are heartily sick of hearing it. You are very fortunate to live in so magnificent a place."

Billie smiled and thanked Grace, as they came to a stop in the courtyard. "This is the domestic entrance. I hope you don't mind. We rarely use the front doors. It is much more convenient this way."

Grace shook her head, saying she didn't mind, adding she

always preferred going into her home through the back door, on the off chance she could beg something tasty from cook as she passed. Billie giggled, agreeing this was exactly what she did.

The two women walked into the house and Billie opened a door along the passage, calling a 'hello' to those inside, and mentioned there would be one extra for lunch, as she assumed Giles was eating with his stewards. There was a rumbled reply and Billie thanked whoever spoke, saying they would eat in the library.

The countess walked briskly through the house. She never seemed to do anything slowly. Grace, with her long legs, was almost running to keep up. Billie opened a door on one side of the spacious hall.

Grace stopped as she reached the threshold, held in thrall by the charming character of the room. The library was not, as most would expect, the typical square; it was octagonal, and everything was on a large scale.

Flanked by bay windows, French doors dominated one wall, looking out over neatly manicured gardens and beyond to the Great Park in the distance. Opposite the doors, an enormous fireplace, logs stacked ready, under an exquisite marble mantelpiece.

Then there were the books — oh the books!

Never in her life, outside of a circulating library or possibly a bookshop — and even then, it was a close thing — had Grace seen so many in one place. The remaining walls were covered, floor to ceiling with books. It was perfection. A desk, a couple of side tables, several comfortable-looking, leather wing-backed chairs, and a huge world globe, completed the room.

Billie grinned at Grace, suggesting she might like to come right into the room. Lunch was about to be served and she would not be able to eat from so far away. Grace blushed, but said nothing, walking over to where Billie indicated she should sit. Minutes later a tall man in uniform knocked and entered, carrying a tray of something which had the most mouth-watering aroma.

He placed the tray on the small table between the two women, saying he would return shortly with some tea. Billie thanked him, Grace registered his name was Thomas, as the man smiled and withdrew.

After lunch, Billie showed Grace around Whiteoaks. They toured the house and the stables, both of which Grace loved, popped into the schoolroom. The point of which Billie clarified, and which was of great interest to the newcomer.

They spent a reasonable amount of time in Billie's herb garden. Grace unable to help herself, wandered along the rows of plants, noticing how well they were or were not growing. Billie explained what she was trying to cultivate and why.

This was something dear to Grace's heart, and the two started an animated discussion, which lasted well into the afternoon. They ended up in the formal garden, sitting on the grass, chattering as though they had known each other for years.

It was here, Giles and Theo found them, an hour or so later, just as the light began its subtle change, heralding a balmy evening. The two men had finished their respective days and Giles, as always, missed his wife.

The men strolled around the corner. Grace saw Billie's face light up and, with complete disregard for etiquette, she scrambled to her feet to be wrapped in a bear hug by the tall earl. He dropped a kiss on her forehead, and entwined her hand in his, while she told him about her day. He smiled at

Grace, saying he hoped she was starting to settle in and find her feet.

Grace nodded, thanking him for allowing Billie to spend the day with her.

"Oh, I have no control over my wife, Miss Fitzgerald," he chuckled. "She generally does as she pleases and as long as she's content, that's all I need to know."

Billie attempted to look contrite but failed dismally Leaning into her husband, she kissed his cheek. Unexpectedly, Grace felt lonely. She had to leave. It was too hard watching such a loving relationship.

"Err… I do beg your pardon, but I believe 'tis time I said my goodbyes. You have been more than generous today, my Lady, and I do not wish to outstay my welcome. It must be near your evening meal. If you could direct me to your driveway, I will be able to find my way home."

Billie's brow creased at the hurried words, sensing something had changed. Her friend looked sad again and they were having such a pleasant afternoon. Billie was determined to get to the bottom of whatever was going on. Giles, catching his wife's expression, nearly groaned aloud knowing exactly what she was thinking. Before either could speak, Theo stepped forward.

"Permit me to be of service, Miss Fitzgerald. I have my carriage here and would gladly escort you home."

Billie was about to remind Theo he was expected for dinner, when Giles pressed her hand. With tacit understanding, she remained silent while Grace contemplated the offer, torn between whether she should accept or try to work out how to find her way back to The Gables on foot. Common sense won out and she smiled at the doctor, saying she would be most obliged not to have to walk.

Grace turned back to Billie and Giles, curtsying as was proper, thanking Billie for one of the loveliest days she had enjoyed in a long time, unaware how telling was her comment. Theo offered Grace his arm, and the two headed around the outside of the house to the courtyard, watched by the earl and his wife.

"Something's not right, Giles." Billie muttered. "Something has demoralised that girl to such an extent, she doesn't know how to cope with happiness." Blithely ignoring the fact, 'that girl' was three years older than she. Giles squeezed his wife's hand, debating whether or not to reveal what Theo told him, knowing she would ferret it out of Grace anyway.

Maybe it was better to be out in the open. Billie was a perceptive soul, and she would want to nurture Grace, to bring her out of her shell, to try to help her overcome whatever haunted her.

Surrendering to the inevitable, Giles sat his wife on the bench and in the golden light of evening shared what he knew.

CHAPTER 5

*B*lissfully unaware of what was unfolding not far from her, Grace and Theo chatted quietly while they made their way around the house to where Theo's carriage waited.

Jake reappeared to assist Grace, while Theo hopped up with fair agility to take the reins. Grace settled into the leather seat and relaxed. The evening was warm and, even though past the height of summer, would be light for several hours yet.

The noise of the carriage made any further conversation pointless, and Grace found it nice not to talk. The woman who left London four days previously, rarely spoke more than half a dozen words to anyone during her day.

The last forty-eight hours had proved quite the challenge. She had to admit it had been fun though. Not once during the last two days had it been necessary to fend off sly digs, or pretend she had not heard some outrageous comment. She had forgotten what that was like.

. . .

Too soon they arrived at The Gables. Unwilling to relinquish their camaraderie, although not sure why, Grace invited Theo in for a drink and, as the doctor had nothing pressing, he accepted. It did not occur to Grace, by entertaining a single man in her home without a chaperone, she opened them both up to gossip because, as already noted, she had stopped worrying about such things long ago.

The house was cool, even after such a hot day, and Theo asked whether she would like him to light the fire. Grace nodded, gratefully... yet another thing she didn't know how to do. Pointing him in the direction of the Snug, she made her way along the hall into the kitchen, intent on finding something — anything — to offer the doctor in the way of sustenance. In the carriage, she realised he was probably supposed to have dinner with Billie and Giles, touched by his thoughtfulness in suggesting he escort her home.

Thanking the stars, she was capable of boiling water, Grace made a hot drink, and prepared a platter of food left over from the previous day. Slices of game pie and beef, a selection of cheeses, pickles, and some bread. It wasn't much, but it was all she had. She definitely needed to buy a supply of food and a cook.

Piling everything onto a large tray, she returned to the Snug to find Theo crouching in front of the now crackling fire, making sure the logs caught. Placing the tray on a small table which stood between the chairs and the hearth, Grace asked Theo whether he preferred brandy or port. Once the drinks were poured — Theo opting for brandy and, Grace, a small port — they settled back into easy conversation while they ate.

Grace started to apologise for Theo missing out on what, doubtless, would have been a far more sumptuous repast. He wouldn't let her finish, assuring her the food was delicious, adding that he ate with the Winchesters more often than not, so this made a refreshing change.

They chatted through their meal, over another drink and a cup of tea, Theo finding himself comfortable with this self-possessed young woman. She was well educated, had a reasonable grasp of the current political situation and, during their conversation, he discovered she spoke French and Italian, the latter a result of spending a year in Rome with her family.

Theo found himself admiring the way the firelight caught the glossy highlights in her auburn hair, long strands falling out of the severe hairstyle into which it had been twisted. He was enchanted by her impish expression, and how expressive her slender hands were when describing an amusing linguistic misunderstanding, which occurred during her time in Italy.

The evening flew by and it was late by the time Theo stood to take his leave. Grace repeated her gratitude for everything he had done for her that day.

"You have been so gracious, Dr Elliott. I'm sure I would continue to be baffled had you not explained everything so precisely this morning. Hopefully the next time you visit, I will have food in the house and someone who can actually cook a decent meal."

Theo chuckled, assuring her it was his pleasure to be of assistance, anything she needed etcetera, etcetera. Grace walked with him to the door and a little way along the garden path, at the end of which stood the carriage, with the doctor's very patient horse.

As they said goodnight they paused and, for no reason either could think of, stared at each other. Grace took in

Theo's dark blonde hair, and his deep brown eyes resting in a rather sombre face. She wanted to smooth her hand over his cheek and see his lips curve in that sweet smile.

At the same time, Theo was struggling not to pull her against him and hold her close, to entwine his fingers through her lustrous hair, undoing the pins and letting it fall around her shoulders.

Theo broke eye contact first. He dragged his gaze away and, bowing quickly, almost ran to his carriage. He clicked the reins and glanced back to see Grace silhouetted in the doorway, her fingers lingering on her mouth.

Did she want him to kiss her, as much as he desired to?

Theo knew it was vital he take this slowly, to let it unfold naturally. He didn't want to scare her; neither did he want to involve either of them in something which wasn't real. He had to be sure of his feelings first and, despite what his instincts told him, he was not ready to admit to what his heart had already recognised.

Grace stared after Theo until he disappeared in the waning light, disconcerted by her awareness of him. Unable to do anything about it then, or maybe ever, she determined the best course of action was to pretend it never happened.

Lifting her gaze upwards, she watched the first few stars appear as the last of the daylight faded. She was safe, had a full stomach and, although possibly a teeny bit tipsy from indulging in two glasses of port, was sober enough to know she might actually be content.

Going indoors, she tided everything away, washing the china and glasses, leaving them to drain on a cloth suited to the purpose. Making sure the doors and windows were secure — although she imagined she was probably the only person doing so in the whole village — Grace found a candlestick with which to light her way and went up to bed.

Whether it was because emotions, long suppressed, had begun to simmer Grace didn't know, but the dream came again. It was always the same; she was in a maze, trying to get out before he found her.

It was dark, the only light came from a weak moon, not bright enough to see properly but if she kept turning left, she should come to the exit. The sound of his footfalls, heavy on the damp ground, were gaining on her, she hoisted her skirts and ran as fast as she could.

He was so close she could hear his breathing, she was too tired, her strength was gone, he would catch her, he always caught her and then…

Grace jolted awake; her heart thumping so hard she thought the neighbours must hear it. She listened. No sounds, nothing disturbed the peace, except the few birds chittering at the false dawn.

Unable to settle, she shrugged into a dressing gown and went downstairs needing to check the house, needing to prove to herself he hadn't found her, although why he should want to, was beyond her.

Satisfied all the locks were still in place, she made a hot drink and huddled up in one of the chairs in the Snug, tucking a rug around herself, savouring the delicate flavour of the tea.

She refused to let him in. He would *not* spoil this for her. This was her chance at a new start. He had destroyed her other life; he was not destroying this one. Watching the true dawn break in luminous pink and gold to the chorus of what sounded like hundreds of songbirds, the panic began to dissipate. She stayed in the chair relishing the notion that she didn't have to move.

She dozed, waking two hours later with a crick in her neck. The rays of sunlight pouring through the glass doors, illuminated the cosy room and went a long way to banishing the horror of the dream, but she was wary now. She must not lower her guard, not let anyone in. It was not worth the fear of losing it all again.

Refreshed, following a proper wash, she dressed in a light muslin gown of pale blue. She ate more leftovers, resolving once and for all, to stock up the pantry this day. Sipping another cup of tea, she made a list.

Checking she had some coin, Grace worked out she might be able to buy the basics — having no idea what the basics were or where to buy them or their actual cost. She was jotting down the last few items, when she heard a quiet knock at the door. Grace knew who it was before she opened it, not surprised to see Theo on her doorstep.

"Dr Elliott. How may I be of assistance?" she asked politely.

"It is I who have come to offer you mine," replied the doctor. "I have one or two calls to make first thing this morning, but later I thought you might appreciate a walk around the market. It is held every Saturday and the produce is local. There is also a stall which sells the most delicious cakes and I imagine after a hectic week, a slice of one might not come amiss."

He held her eyes while he spoke, and she felt that same warmth coiling through her stomach. She must not let this happen. He was just being friendly. Straightening her shoulders, she accepted his offer and smiled.

Theo noted it did not reach her eyes and wondered what had changed.

"You are too kind, Dr Elliott. I am in dire need of real food and with no knowledge of where to buy any of it, would be grateful for your assistance." Her tone was cool, and Theo studied her expression, mildly perturbed, but determined not to let it bother him.

He inclined his head. "Until later then. Good day to you, Miss Fitzgerald." He walked back along the path and, using the rung of her fence, hoisted himself up onto his horse.

Grace watched him trot off along the road, smiling slightly when he raised his hand in farewell, wishing things might be different. Pulling herself together, she went back into the house and spent a busy couple of hours unpacking several pieces of luggage.

When Theo returned, she was pleased to note she had arranged the majority of her things. She invited the doctor into the parlour, while she located her wrap and reticule.

A last check to make sure she had coin enough for what she might buy, and they set out. Theo offered Grace his arm. After hesitating a moment, she took it, enjoying for a little while, the feel of his arm through hers.

They meandered along the stalls, inspecting all manner of wares. Grace did not really know what to buy, but Theo proved helpful, suggesting this and that, until in the end she had everything a person might need to produce all manner of appetising dishes. Not that there was much chance of Grace doing so — cooking being a skill beyond her — but it looked the part.

Theo organised for a boy to ferry the goods to The Gables, then steered Grace towards the cake stall. Grace's eyes nearly popped out of her head when she saw the multitude of luscious treats displayed. She was unable to choose, asking Theo to pick something. He purchased two slices of sticky ginger cake, which they devoured while continuing to explore around the market.

Grace was fascinated to discover you could buy farm animals too. An open field to one side featured chickens, piglets and lambs, presented to prospective buyers in several small enclosures.

When she realised, they would be fattened up for eating she was horrified and tried to persuade Theo to let her buy some, telling him the creatures would do well in her garden and meadow.

Amused, Theo asked on what would she feed them. That stumped her, but she countered by saying someone would know, it couldn't be too hard.

This conversation kept them going, and Theo noticed that somewhere along the line, Grace forgot to be formal. Her face was animated and her eyes alive with mischief as she stated her case for having several chickens, at least three piglets and half a dozen sheep. She was stunningly beautiful. In fact, she nigh on took his breath away.

Grace registered the passage of time and wondered whether Theo had somewhere to be. He didn't seem to be in a hurry, and since she was enjoying their conversation, she invited him back to The Gables, adding she would welcome his advice on one or two things at the house.

The doctor agreed willingly, and the two wound their way back through the stalls. Grace paused here and there to inspect ribbons or some of the hand-stitched napkins or lace, admiring the delicate work.

The boy must have been watching for them for, because when they turned in through the gate, he appeared with his little cart, laden with goods. Grace was shocked when she saw how much she purchased but Theo assured her they were all essentials.

The lad hefted everything through to the kitchen and, after Theo flipped him a coin, skipped away down the street, the cart banging behind him.

Adamant Theo would not see how helpless she was, Grace simply stacked everything tidily in the larder and offered her visitor a drink. She poured two glasses of cool lemonade and carried them through to the Snug.

Opening the French windows, she breathed in the delicate perfume of the flowers wafting in from the garden. Sinking onto one of the chairs and waiting for Theo to do the same, she began to talk about her plans for the meadow beyond the wall.

"'Tis clear I need at least two horses. How else will I be able to use that carriage? I thought it might be nice for them to have the run of the field. If I can find someone who would build a shelter for me, they wouldn't need to be stabled except in bad weather. What do you think?" She raised her eyebrows expectantly at Theo who was listening carefully.

"I think it has potential. There are several men in the village who would no doubt be able to build a shelter.

"Do you know of anywhere I can purchase a horse? I love them. I can ride well and know how to muck out a loose box…"

Something Theo did *not* expect to hear,

"…but, although I know how to look after horses and would recognise a good mount, I am not sure I would be able to pick a decent carriage horse."

Something he *did* expect.

He suggested talking to Giles and Billie, Giles being a good judge of horseflesh and likely amenable to organising the purchase of a mare or two.

Thanking the doctor, Grace closed her eyes for a minute, eminently satisfied with her day thus far.

CHAPTER 6

Theo and Grace were so engrossed in their discussion, neither heard a knock, nor the sound of a voice calling Grace's name. Nothing until a head covered in chestnut curls peeped around the doorway into the Snug.

"I'm sorry to intrude, Grace, but I have one or two people here whom I believe might be of use." Grinning wickedly, Billie winked at Theo who smiled back, his slow sweet smile, making Grace's heart do weird things. Shaking her head, Grace followed the countess into the hall to find what looked like an army of people waiting for her.

"My Lad… Billie, goodness what am I to do with so many?" Grace gaped. "There is only me."

Billie chuckled and ignoring her friend's expression, introduced them one by one. "These three admirable ladies are Agnes, Becca and Polly. Your new cook and maids. These two fine, upstanding gentlemen are Gibbs and Evans, driver and butler respectively. Finally, this young whippersnapper is Matt, your groom."

With earnest smiles, everyone either curtseyed or bowed.

Grace could not help but smile in return. They all looked happy to be there.

"I am very pleased to meet you all. Thank you for agreeing to help me. I am afraid I am next to useless when it comes to anything domestic and would be honoured if you would join my household." Grace aimed for a balance between formality and encouragement.

She seemed to have hit the right note, because they all started talking at once. Thanking her in return for this opportunity, they were keen to begin working for her, they wouldn't let her down, and so on.

In the midst of the clamour, Theo appeared from the Snug, and smiled at Billie, knowingly, inclining his head in tacit approval of her efforts. Billie returned the gesture, pleased with the result of her morning's efforts.

There were plenty of people in the village and outlying farms, whom the young countess knew would appreciate extra income. Handpicked, they were not only reliable, but also would be sensitive to Grace's situation. A young woman on her own was unusual, and Billie didn't want anyone in her new friend's employ predisposed to gossip.

Billie suggested the ladies might like to acquaint themselves with the house, especially the kitchen. Grace interjected saying she had just bought a large amount of food but was unsure of the best way to store it.

Agnes chuckled and, patting her new mistress' arm, said she would get on to it right away. The two girls shot off up the stairs to check out the bedchambers. Evans asked whether she would mind if he got to know the layout of the house, and Gibbs took Matt off to explore the stable and carriage house.

. . .

Grace felt as though a whirlwind had just passed through her home and abruptly sat down, needing to let things settle for a moment or two.

"Thank you, Billie. I cannot begin to imagine how you achieved this, but I am in your debt. They seem so kind and amenable. How did you find them on such short notice?"

"I am the Countess of Winchester, my dear. I know everyone on our estate and in this village. I know who needs work and what type of work they can undertake. I know who can be relied upon to be discreet and who has a tendency to chitchat.

"I already had a mind for who would be suitable to help. I have been planning this since I knew of your arrival. I wanted to meet you before I spoke to any of them, so I could be fairly certain you and they would be compatible."

Billie tried to sound imperious, but her eyes were brimming with amusement, heartened by the relief she saw in her friend's demeanour.

Being able to do this for Grace had made Billie's day. After what Giles had told her the previous night, she had been ruminating over how to help Grace without it being obvious she knew about her past.

Grace took Billie's hand and squeezed it gently. "You have no idea how much this means to me. I was starting to worry about how to go about engaging staff."

"It has been my pleasure and my joy to do this for you. Now, I must go. I have some children arriving soon for their lessons and 'tis my turn this afternoon. Grace, Theo, please come up to Whiteoaks for dinner this evening, I think Giles wants to talk horses. Any time after five would be perfect."

Without waiting for their reply, she sailed out of the house, calling a flurry of goodbyes to all those within, her gay tones echoing around the hallway.

. . .

Grace was exhausted, and she hadn't done anything. Theo laughed, as she remained seated still unable to get her head around what had just happened.

"Is she always like this?" she asked, faintly.

"Always," confirmed Theo, "but you wouldn't want her any other way." He paused. "If you would allow me, I should like a quick word with Evans, Gibbs and Matt, then I will leave you to get to know your staff. May I call on you this afternoon to escort you to Whiteoaks?"

Grace was hesitant. Part of her, well all right, most of her, wanted to get to know this man who seemed so grave and quiet, yet whose eyes could twinkle and smile making her feel warm and safe.

The other part of her suspected, even in so brief a time, he was becoming too close. The sensible part overrode her qualms. It was only a carriage ride, and how else was she supposed to get there?

She acquiesced and agreed, smiling shyly. "Thank you, that is most kind. I will see you later."

Theo bowed over her hand and, calling for Evans, headed for the stable.

Evans hurried after him and, when they reached the comparative seclusion of the carriage house, Theo spoke seriously to the three men, explaining some of why they were chosen to work at The Gables.

Giving them the briefest outline of what had happened to Grace, without stepping beyond the bounds of trust, he finished up by saying, "Suffice it to say, I cannot guarantee this man will not find her and if he does, she will be vulnerable to his predilections. You three were chosen to work here, because the countess believes you to be reliable and trustworthy and will protect Miss Fitzgerald at all costs.

"However, and this is important, please give no indication we have spoken of this and should you, at any time feel she has been threatened, I want you to inform myself or the earl with the utmost expediency."

The three men accepted Theo's directive without question. A request of this nature would not be made unless necessary. Neither the earl, nor the doctor, were given to flights of fancy. If either man was concerned about their new mistress, it was enough for them.

"Begging your pardon, Doctor, but is there any chance we know the man involved?" Matt ventured.

Theo named the man responsible. Gibbs and Matt looked blank, but Evans frowned, something teasing at the edge of his mind. He let it roll around for a few minutes and while the other three chatted, it came to him. He snapped his fingers.

"I thought his name sounded familiar," he said. "Miss Fitzgerald is not the first woman who has suffered at his hand. Somehow, he seems to be able to get away with it, insisting the women are after his title and his money.

"Me cousin's wife, before they were married like, used to work for a family whose daughter got tangled up with him. Terrible it was, can't remember for certain, but I think she might have taken her life.

"It was strange though. Hetty, that's our Bill's wife, always believed the family knew what was happening but were unable to stop it."

Theo stared at Evans. This was a development he could not ignore. "Evans do you think I could meet your Bill's Hetty?"

Evans nodded. "Certainly, Dr Elliott, they're over Nether Stanton way. They have a farm now. Our Bill took over when his Da passed."

Nether Stanton was less than five miles from where they stood. Theo decided a visit was in order and, after asking Evans to accompany him when he did go and talk to Hetty, as a way of introduction, thanked the three for their time, and left them to their duties.

~

In the main house Grace was beginning to feel more or less in control of everything — or maybe it was that everyone else was in control, so she didn't have to be.

Agnes was bustling around in the kitchen, happily arranging everything to her own satisfaction. The new cook asked whether Grace had anything she preferred not to eat, which she didn't, then hustled her mistress out, telling her not to fret, lunch would be served shortly.

Unwilling to disturb the rest of the staff, Grace took herself off to the Snug and curled up with a book, assuming, if she was needed, they would come and find her.

Evans brought her a light lunch about half an hour later. Agnes had concocted something involving potatoes, bacon and cheese, accompanied by sliced bread — liberally buttered, and a pot of fragrant tea.

Grace hadn't registered how hungry she was, and fell on it, polishing off everything on the plate. Returning the tray to the kitchen, she thanked Agnes, complimenting her on so tasty a meal. About to leave the warmth of the kitchen, another thought occurred to her.

"I'm new to this Agnes. I know you are entitled to time off, and you each might have days which work better for you. Perhaps you and Evans between you could come up with some kind of roster, making it as fair as possible. And please do not hesitate to talk to me if there is anything you need, which I haven't thought to provide."

"Bless you, miss." Agnes replied. "I think we will get along just fine. Now you go and take a load off, while I set about making some bread. I hope those giddy girls are getting on with things proper like. Hearts are in the right place but sometimes their heads are in the clouds."

Chuckling to herself, Agnes brushed a piece of invisible fluff off her apron and turned her attention to the flour.

Grace sought out Becca and Polly. They were upstairs in her dressing room. Becca was re-organising all the dresses into order of requirement — day dresses, walking dresses, riding habits, and evening gowns. Polly was sorting out her delicates and underthings.

The dressing room was perfectly tidy, but now looked more familiar. Somehow, they made it hers. The bedchamber looked different too. Grace could not see what had changed but again they had made it appear as though she had always slept here.

Stunned, she thanked them profusely, almost brought to tears by their obvious care. The two girls blushed prettily, saying it was their pleasure and, finishing up, turned to the next room.

Grace called after them. "Would you prefer to go along to the domestic quarters and sort out your own rooms? Arranging guest bedchambers isn't a priority."

The two glanced at each other, clearly desperate to see where they would be sleeping.

Grace shooed them off. I will tell Agnes and Evans where you are. Come and find me later."

The two scurried away, chattering nineteen to the dozen.

Grace smiled; it was nice having so much activity around her. She wandered back down the stairs and, after informing Agnes and Evans what the two youngsters were up to, went to sit in the garden.

CHAPTER 7

Grace had been sitting a matter of minutes when she heard a knock. About to answer it, she heard a rumbled conversation and, for a moment couldn't work it out, then remembered — she had a butler. She giggled, not only a butler, but also several staff.

All at once the utter incongruity of her situation seemed hilariously funny. Swallowing her mirth, she tried to get hold of herself, realising there was a chance she was ever so slightly hysterical and stood, brushing her skirts. Evans came through the Snug and into the garden.

"Miss Fitzgerald, there are two men here to see you. A Mr Ralph Montgomery and a Mr Duncan Barrington."

Grace nodded and asked Evans to invite them in, unaccountably nervous. It was well over five, probably closer to ten, years since she last saw her cousin, and so much had happened between. A deep breath calmed her somewhat, but she could feel hectic colour washing up her cheeks as she steeled herself for more censure.

. . .

Her two visitors came out onto the terrace. They looked tall even to her and she wasn't short. One she recognised immediately and the other seemed vaguely familiar also. One of them spoke, a rich baritone voice laced with amusement.

"Grace, my goodness me look at you, all grown up. Where's that pest of a cousin who used to push me into the mud?"

Grace spluttered indignantly. "Excuse me! I seem to recall you were the one doing the pushing. How many times did I have to get washed in the stream before I came back here because of your antics?"

She caught his eye. He was shaking with suppressed merriment. Grace took a step and then hesitated, uncertain. Not so her cousin who strode forward, wrapping her in a bear hug. She stiffened, panic tickling at her consciousness. Then she remembered who it was here in front of her and relaxed, resting her head on his shoulder briefly, she returned his hug.

"Grace, my dear girl. How are you?" Pushing her away from him. "You look…" he paused and frowned, scanning her features, "…too thin and too pale. What the dickens has been going on?"

She smiled, a mite sadly he thought.

"Nothing to concern yourself about, cousin. Just life in London."

Ralph was about to make further comment, surmising there was more to this than met the eye, but something in her expression stopped him and he held his tongue.

What had the butler called her — Miss Fitzgerald? Well that wasn't right.

He would get it out of her eventually; he always had in the past. Letting it go for now, he turned to the other man hovering in the doorway and motioned him over.

"Grace, please allow me to introduce my friend, Mr

Duncan Barrington. Duncan, this is my cousin, Miss Grace Fitzgerald." Duncan bowed and Grace dropped a curtsy. The man grinned engagingly. His smile pulled at her memory. He was definitely familiar.

"Have we met before, Mr Barrington? Your face, you seem…" She stared at him, forgetting how rude that might appear, as flashbacks from her childhood poured into her head.

"Duncan! I know you. *You* were the one who made me climb the tree to rescue that kitten, which if I recall, as soon as I reached it, jumped down and strutted off happily without a care in the world. Then I was stuck and by the time I got myself down — with no help from any of you I might add — my dress was torn, and my hair was full of sticks and leaves.

"You lot just sniggered. Aunt Bea was not pleased. She sent me to bed without any supper," Grace tried to sound offended.

Duncan did not look in the least chastised and chortled with glee. "I am astonished you remember that. It was years ago. You were only about ten and two. I am sure missing out on supper wasn't so bad. I am reminded we usually stuffed our faces with apples, and Ralph's mother always gave us a bread roll."

Both men were laughing openly now as they continued to share recollections of their childhood. Halcyon days filled with fun, the three of them along with several other children from the village played happily all day and, during the summer, well into the evenings.

Grace giggled at the picture their words conjured up. For a little while they lost themselves in those idyllic times before life interfered and stole their innocence. Ralph and Duncan saw action in the recent wars and, as with so many returned servicemen, were far more subdued than once they had been.

This is not to say they weren't able to enjoy life and, as could be seen from this exchange, laughter was not forgotten, but there was a seriousness about them, a gravity only time would lighten.

Grace asked after Tessa, Ralph's wife — another childhood friend — pleased to hear she was fine and expecting their first child in the not too distant future.

"I am thrilled for you both, Ralph. That is the best news I've heard in a sixth month. I hope she would not mind if I called on her."

Ralph assured her Tessa would be elated, and to pop around any time.

Eventually, the two men came to the reason they were there. Ralph, obviously, wanted to reacquaint himself with his cousin but, more than that, they had been speaking with Giles, and wanted to discuss the garden and the meadow.

Duncan assured her he was a dab hand at carpentry and believed three of their friends would be glad to spruce up the garden and help with the shelter. Ralph remarked that he knew these men and they were good solid workers. Grace listened to their plans with interest, agreeing with their suggestions.

"Thank you both so much. It is a relief to know all these people are willing to help. Lady Winchester has arranged my staff, and now you two have organised my garden. All I require now are two, maybe three horses and, if Dr Elliott can be persuaded, some chickens, piglets and lambs."

Ralph and Duncan gaped at this, unsure whether she was jesting.

She chuckled at their expressions. "I know, I know, it sounds ridiculous, but I saw them at the market this morning, and cannot bear the thought of them being eaten."

Her cousin did feel moved to comment that how else did she expect to have meat on the table, but she was not to be distracted. If these men were going to help, not only would she need a shelter for the horses, but also somewhere for the chickens, lambs and piglets. She had an inkling the latter would destroy the meadow if not properly restrained, and thus it was imperative the fencing surrounding the property was secure.

s she wound up, she noticed they looked resigned, and Duncan was nodding, not necessarily with enthusiasm but accepting it was her decision.

"I realise, to you, this seems frivolous. You are men, practical beings, but this is my life and I want to nurture something, to watch it grow. I know I will need advice, lots of advice, on how to look after them, but I want to see whether I can do this."

There was a wistful quality to her voice, and it pulled at Ralph without him understanding why. He gave up trying to dissuade her, acknowledging she was correct, it *was* her life.

He said they would bring the other three the next day and they could get down to business. It was crucial they build the shelter up as soon as possible. Yes, it was still summer, but autumn was around the corner and they wanted things completed before the weather turned.

Grace thanked them again when they took their leave. Ralph, troubled by his cousin's apparent frailty, was determined to get to the bottom of whatever plagued her, wondering whether he might wheedle anything out of Theo or Giles.

Friends with both for many years, Ralph was sure they would confide in him, should they deem it appropriate. Pushing it aside for now he happily agreed with Duncan's suggestion they finish their afternoon off by a visit to the Cross Keys for a refreshing beer.

~

Grace went to find Becca and Polly. The girls had completed their inspection of the domestic quarters, ably assisted by Evans who had calmly pointed out the two single rooms would be for Agnes and himself. Becca and Polly sharing one of the double rooms.

The bedchambers were amply appointed. The two maids each had a wardrobe, a chest of drawers and a chair. All the rooms were spacious, and everything, including the generous supply of bedding and towels, were of good quality.

It seemed Aunt Beatrice had spared no expense for the comfort of her staff. Grace was pleased when she had seen this the previous day, when exploring the property. It fitted with her recollection of her Aunt, and something she meant to uphold.

Asking Becca whether she and Polly might draw a bath for her, Grace climbed the stairs to her bedchamber. A bath would soothe her and, all of a sudden, she wanted to wash her hair, which after her conversation with her cousin, felt scruffy. It was all that talk of mud and leaves. Once the tub was filled with lightly perfumed hot water, Grace indulged in a long soak.

It seemed an age since she enjoyed a proper bath, and she felt much better when she got out, dried and began to dress. Polly assisted her, suggesting a rich forest green gown, which complimented Grace's distinctive colouring.

The young girl rubbed her mistress' long hair dry and brushed it until it shone, curling it up into an intricate style, the like of which even Peggy might have struggled to accomplish.

"Polly, you have magic fingers," breathed Grace when she saw herself in the mirror. Somehow Polly had woven deep green ribbon through her hair, the ends interlaced with several loose strands of auburn ringlets and allowed to trail effortlessly down the back of her neck.

Grace struggled to recall the last time she looked this fine, and when she did, wished she hadn't, because it brought back very bad memories. Doggedly she shoved that aside, refusing to let *him* mar her evening. He was of no consequence anymore.

Shortly thereafter, Theo was admitted. He looked dashingly handsome in pale grey trousers and dark charcoal tailcoat over a crisp white shirt and a waistcoat of silvery grey. As before, Grace felt her heart do the oddest leap, almost like a hiccup when she came down the stairs to greet him.

He glanced up when he heard her footsteps and smiled… *there it went again…* her lips curving upwards in response.

Drawing a controlling breath, she made it to the bottom step without tripping. Theo took her hand and bowed over it, his mouth brushing her fingers, so lightly she wondered whether she imagined it, and the quiver it evoked.

"You look enchanting, Miss Fitzgerald," Theo, still holding her hand, murmured quietly, unwilling to break the peace, which descended over them.

Grace thought she replied but could not be sure, distracted by his gaze, his dark brown eyes beguiling her. A subtle cough brought them back to reality as Evans appeared with Grace's shawl and bonnet.

Colouring a little, she dropped her eyes and gently extricated her fingers from Theo's, allowing Evans to lay the soft material around her shoulders but refused the bonnet, uncaring this flouted etiquette for she detested hats with a passion. Thanking her butler and telling him not to wait up, she smiled a goodbye and took Theo's proffered arm.

The drive to Whiteoaks didn't take long and, for some strange reason, Grace felt shy. Theo tried to make polite conversation, but she was at a loss to answer with any form of intelligibility, so gave up and admired the scenery. It was a balmy evening. The sun was halfway to the horizon, the harsh brilliance of earlier in the day softening to a more mellow hue.

The dappled light through the trees sending all manner of intricate shadows dancing over the ground. Birds zipped about, brimming with song, catching the bugs lifted on the warm air currents. The undulating landscape in shades of green and gold stretched unbroken by anything man-made as far as the eye could see.

Grace breathed in the fragrant air — so different from the smells of the city, here it was like champagne — and sighed in contentment. Unaware of the sunlight glinting off her hair, or how her expressive face indicated her enchantment in their surroundings, Grace was about to settle back against the seat, when the carriage turned into the long driveway leading up to Whiteoaks.

"Oh, we're here. That was quick," she said, admiring the grand house. "I don't think I'll ever get tired of seeing this house. It is remarkable."

Theo grinned. "I agree. There is something unique about Whiteoaks. I have been coming here since I was a boy and it still takes my breath away. I think this is not only because it's a magnificent house, but also because it is, and has always been, loved by all who live and work here. I believe buildings absorb emotion and return it one hundred-fold, which is why Whiteoaks seems to welcome you every time you visit."

Grace gaped at Theo, and the doctor felt unaccustomed heat flush his face. He rarely spoke this way, for fear of sounding addled, but he was unable to help himself. This woman sent his nicely ordered thoughts into chaos.

Grace leant towards him, touching her hand to his. "Perfectly put," was all she said, but her smile said so much more.

As ever, when Grace was close to him, Theo wanted to drag her into his embrace and hold her close. Yes, all right, he desperately wanted to kiss her until she cried out his name, but it would be enough just to hold her. He did no such thing and, as the carriage rattled to a halt in the courtyard, they both sat back, to all appearances as though little known acquaintances.

Will emerged from the stables to drop the step, helping Grace down and greeting Theo like the old friends they were. Again, Grace noted this lack of formality with those of the earl's household, and it continued to intrigue her. She had enjoyed a relaxed relationship with the four staff in London, but this was a whole other level of camaraderie, and she liked it.

Theo led Grace through the back door, pausing to shout a quick 'hello' into the kitchen. Grace heard a cheerful response and then Thomas appeared to escort them to the library, where they found Billie and Giles sitting on a bench on the terrace outside the open French doors.

The earl and his diminutive countess jumped up when Thomas announced the guests, coming into the room, faces wreathed in welcoming smiles. Grace dropped a deep curtsy as Giles greeted her; while Billie lifted her face for Theo's kiss, before catching Grace in a warm hug.

Giles nodded to the doctor. "Elliott."

"Winchester," Theo returned and, as the two men fell into discussion about the estate, Billie dragged Grace over to the bench she just vacated asking a dozen questions about her friend's day. Grace answered as succinctly as possible, including that her cousin and his friend had also visited during the afternoon.

"What with going to the market, being introduced to my staff — who by the way have settled in so well it's as though they've always been there — and seeing Ralph and Mr

Barrington this afternoon, I have been so busy. It is an age since I spoke with so many people in one day."

Reducing Billie to gales of laughter when she described how she wanted to rescue all the baby animals from the market and everyone's reaction to her decision.

"I think it is an admirable plan, Grace," Billie gurgled. "I should be honoured to join you when you eventually purchase said creatures."

Grace grinned, replying she would like that very much. Their conversation turned to other, more mundane matters until dinner was announced.

Giles offered Grace his arm and Theo did the same to Billie and they walked through the library and across the hall to one of the most elegant rooms Grace had ever seen.

CHAPTER 8

The dining room at Whiteoaks was a study in classical refinement. Billie had noticed this the first time she was invited to dine with Giles and Theo and, nearly eight months later, the room could still take her breath away.

Evidently, it had the same effect on Grace, much to the amusement of the two men. Grace actually stopped on the threshold and had to be drawn into the room by her host, whose lips were twitching with mirth at her expression.

Aware she must look like a gawking idiot, Grace apologised. A gesture Giles waved aside, gratified by her reaction.

"My Lord please, I do beg your pardon, but this is exquisite. It surpasses every other dining room I've been in, without a doubt." She longed to be able to spend time here on her own, to run her fingers over the beautiful soft furnishings and stroke the glossy wood of the table and chairs and the marble mantelpiece.

Sighing in delight, she was escorted around to her seat, from where she admired the polished silverware and ornate candelabra, to the continued entertainment of the other three.

"I'm glad you like it. We are rather partial aren't we Billie?" Giles turned to his wife who agreed fervently, "...and please call me Giles," her host grinned.

"Now, I realise business talk is not usually preferred dinner conversation, but I believe we four are beyond such conventions. I for one, would prefer to engage in a proper discussion, than prattle on about the weather and all its foibles." Giles glanced around the table eyebrows raised and received heartfelt 'yeses' in response.

Thomas and Jane served the first course, a light artichoke soup, which looked very appetising. Grace felt her mouth watering and savoured the dish, listening to Giles and Theo who had begun to discuss horses.

The meal continued. Several courses and multiple dishes, all delicious, finishing off with the most luscious dessert. No longer used to such elaborate fare, Grace was concerned she would not be able to get up from the table after so sumptuous a meal and was relieved their conversation became so involved, everyone stayed where they were.

Giles knew of a breeder whose stud farm was about ten miles distant and who always had horses for sale. Most were bred for racing, but he usually had several suitable for riding and others for drawing carriages. The earl had done business with this trader before and knew him to be an honest man.

He clarified that carriage horses were not always the most comfortable to ride, so Grace may need to consider two separate breeds. Grace was not aware there was a difference, never having had to worry about such things, so the two men explained the types of breeds for riding and those for carriages.

Apparently, Cleveland Bays or Norfolk Trotters were especially suited to carriages, whereas Arabians and Thoroughbreds were better for hunting and everyday riding. The former being the foundation bloodstock for the latter and thus substantially more expensive.

Grace became confused by terms like hot-blooded and warm-blooded but, since she intended to rely on Giles' expertise, let much of it wash over her. It was thrilling though. She had missed riding and here, in the middle of nowhere, she should be able to do so to her heart's content.

The plan was to visit the stud two days hence. Giles asked Grace whether she might like Billie to accompany them, mentioning his wife had a knack with animals.

"I guarantee she can tell good from bad tempered creatures just by stroking their noses."

Grace looked in amazement at Billie who was trying to look nonchalant at such praise, to no avail.

"My husband is prone to exaggeration," she giggled. "That said, I do believe, I can sense whether an animal might be skittish, something you do not need when riding or driving. I would love to come along, if you don't mind."

Grace smiled in relief. "I would be most appreciative," she replied. "That way I don't have to organise a chaperone and your husband won't have to worry about being seen with me."

She clamped her lips together, forgetting they didn't know; aware such a statement might warrant querying. Thankfully none at the table appeared to notice, and the conversation moved smoothly into other matters.

The rest of the evening flew by and Grace was surprised by how much she enjoyed it. It was nearly two years since she had mixed with any company, other than servants, and was anxious she might have forgotten how to behave. Seemingly, some things were ingrained and, as she managed not to commit any more verbal faux pas, all the better.

Too soon, it was time to leave. Billie's maid, Sally, brought Grace's shawl. Ever the gentleman, Theo draped it over her shoulders. The brush of his fingers felt like a caress through the lightweight material, sending a frisson down her spine. Not wanting anyone to see the blush creeping up her cheeks, she thanked Billie and Giles, and hurried out without waiting for Theo.

"Hmmm... now, I wonder..." murmured Billie to the two men, as though she already knew the answer. Giles glanced down at his wife, who was grinning mischievously. Theo looked puzzled and, after hugging Billie and saying he'd see Giles on the morrow, followed Grace out to the carriage.

Seated opposite Grace, Theo tried to work out what was going on in her head. Grace in the meantime was trying to breathe steadily and banish the sensation Theo's touch — slight though it was — elicited. She was unnerved by how this man affected her. She barely knew him and, while she trusted him to be a kind and thoughtful man, to wish it could be more was pointless.

If by the slimmest of chances, he felt the same, they had no future. His family would never agree to his courting someone with her reputation, and she could never expose someone she cared about to scandal. It was just, for a brief moment, she really wanted to feel loved.

Theo tried to read these emotions as they flickered over her face. Given what he knew, he imagined some of her confusion related to her past, which would, in her eyes, prevent her from ever having a husband and family of her own. Also, given what he knew, he realised he wanted to be the one to bring her back to life, to show her not all men were cads.

He had only known her for two days, yet her face haunted him. He wanted to release the free spirit he believed lurked beneath that composed façade, to see her eyes light up when she saw him, to catch her smiling spontaneously, and he still wanted to remove all the pins from her gleaming hair and tangle his fingers through it, while he kissed her.

He registered she was asking him a question and forced himself to concentrate.

"…how would I pay him?"

For the life of him Theo couldn't recall what she said, so apologised and asked her to repeat the question.

"If his Lordship and Billie think this man has satisfactory horses, would I be able to bring them home with me and if so, how would I pay him, the breeder I mean?" repeated Grace, frowning a little. Theo seemed distracted. *Was she boring him?*

Theo explained how purchases such as this worked, and that Giles would handle all the financial transactions. When everything was finalised, her solicitor would arrange to transfer the payment directly from the stipend into the Winchester bank account.

By the time Grace understood the complexities of business dealings they had reached The Gables. After Adam, his driver, had helped Grace down, Theo thanked him telling him to take the carriage home, as he would walk from here. Adam smiled in acknowledgement, and the carriage rumbled off down the street.

All was quiet and it was as though they were the only two abroad. Grace glanced up at the velvety blackness of the sky, scattered with millions of pinpricks of twinkling light, the moon following its time-honoured trail across the universe.

"Dr Elliott, look at the stars," she breathed. "Here, away from the city they seem so much clearer, and close enough for me to pluck them out of the sky. So beautiful."

"Quite stunningly beautiful." Theo agreed and, as Grace brought her gaze back to him, she realised he wasn't looking at the stars at all.

Her heart thudded. He was staring at her as though hypnotised.

"D-Dr Elliott?" She stuttered, her breathing going a little haywire. "A-are you…? Is everything…? Err…" her throat was dry. Words refused to form.

Theo, unable to stop himself, cupped her cheek with a gentle hand, his thumb grazing her bottom lip.

Grace gulped. Her whole body trembled as heat flared along her veins. Her hand fluttered towards the tall doctor, then fell back to her side. She wanted to touch him, to lean against him, but didn't want to shatter the magic of this moment. This moment when everything seemed poised on the brink.

Captivated by the darkening depths of his eyes, Grace remained as though frozen, while Theo's finger traced her jawline before coming to rest under her chin and, holding her gaze, bent to kiss her. His lips no more touched hers when he lifted his head, and smiled his slow, sweet smile.

"Forgive my boldness, Miss Fitzgerald," he murmured, looking in no way contrite. "I found I was unable to help myself. You take my breath away."

Grace mumbled something incomprehensible, trying to get her own breathing under control as Theo opened the gate and ushered her through. The front door opened as they reached it. Evans, ignoring her orders, had stayed up and was watching for her.

Grace felt colour wash up her face at the thought of her butler witnessing that kiss. To her relief, Evans showed no indication of any such thing, merely asking whether she would like a hot drink before retiring and whether the doctor would be joining her. Grace requested a cup of hot chocolate. Theo declined.

"Much as that would be welcome, it is late, and you have had a busy day. Another time perhaps?" He smiled at Grace and held her eyes, his hand warm on her elbow. She felt the slight pressure of his fingers when he gave it a gentle squeeze. "If I have some time tomorrow, might I call on you?"

Grace nodded and whispered a goodnight, watching him stride back along the path to her gate. Evans reappeared to secure the door, saying a hot chocolate awaited her in the Snug. She walked slowly through the house; her mind awhirl. Her reaction to Theo's touch and that hint of a kiss surprised her.

For the longest time she had not been able to bear any form of physical contact. Something as inconsequential as inadvertently rubbing shoulders with someone in the street would cause her to stiffen and recoil, beset by an anxiety of the most irrational nature, her head buzzing with images of which she could not seem to rid herself.

Even with Jemima, her trusted friend, it took almost the whole of the year or so they had known each other for Grace to feel comfortable enough to accept even the briefest hug.

She supposed her responses weren't without merit but coming to terms with them hadn't been easy. Until three years previously, Grace had been a light-hearted, carefree and affectionate personage, never thinking twice about fleeting moments of contact between female family members or her friends.

Once *he* began to pursue her, the most innocent of

touches, even the clasp of hand during a dance, became abhorrent to her.

Hot chocolate in hand, Grace relaxed in the huge chair, watching the shadow play across the walls created by the candles guttering in the light breeze drifting through the open doors.

It was soporific and, realising it would be easy to fall asleep in the chair, finished her drink, thanked Evans who was hovering in the hallway and trailed upstairs to bed. Polly, who had also ignored instructions to have an early night, met her at the bedroom door, helping the tired woman her out of her finery and into her nightrail, then quickly tidied the room.

Grace was asleep before Polly closed the door.

Grace slept without dreams and awoke, refreshed. Polly, who seemed to have assumed the duties of personal maid, appeared to help Grace dress, then spent some time brushing out her hair, which had become tangled. Perhaps she hadn't slept as well as she thought.

When Polly was satisfied her mistress looked presentable, Grace went down to the kitchen calling a 'good morning' to Becca and Agnes as she entered the sun-filled room.

The two women greeted her with warm smiles, as they bustled about preparing breakfast. The aroma of baking was mouth-watering, and Grace sent up a silent prayer, thanking whoever might be listening for Billie and her intuition.

Agnes asked whether a plate of freshly poached eggs on some crispy toast would suit, or would she prefer something more substantial? Grace nearly laughed; such an offering was more than she had eaten at breakfast in years.

She normally had a small bowl of porridge, or just some

fruit. Jenny, her cook in London despaired of tempting Grace to eat more. Nodding her approval and, after confirming she would prefer tea by way of a beverage, Grace left them to it, wandering out into the fresh air and sinking onto the bench near the French doors.

Despite the fact it was Sunday and she probably should be attending the service at the little village church instead of doing the gardening, she found she didn't care to. Maybe she would go to church next weekend; she wasn't ready to face lots of people she didn't know.

This day was for her and here was a garden in dire need of taming. Ralph must have forgotten it was Sunday, when he indicated they would start today, deeming it more likely they would delay until the morrow.

It was of little matter. Whenever they arrived, Grace intended to be involved, to be part of the transformation, of which she was prepared to begin on her own.

The thought of wrenching out weeds, irresistibly inviting.

CHAPTER 9

$\mathcal{B}$reakfast was served, after which Grace took her tea and strolled through the garden, trying to distinguish plants from weeds. As she surmised when she first inspected this space, the garden had been properly laid out.

Here and there she discerned what appeared to be paths and hedges delineating garden beds. Everything was terribly overgrown, but she didn't think it would take very long to get it into some semblance of order.

While ruminating on this, she heard voices in the house and turned, startled to see Ralph, Duncan, and three other men, walking out through the back door. Ralph called over to her and she made her way back through the neglected flowerbeds to where the five men waited.

"Grace, good morning, cousin. These are the three I mentioned, Nate, Owen, and Harry. This is Miss Al... Fitzgerald," Ralph tripped over her name. He corrected himself quickly, and the others did not appear to have noticed, to Grace's relief.

She greeted them warmly and thanked them for giving up

their time to help her, making a mental note to ask Theo the going rate for labour and materials. The three strangers grinned cheerfully and stood aside while Ralph and Duncan organised their tasks.

Duncan had arranged for a huge quantity of wood to be delivered which, unbeknownst to Grace, arrived late the previous day and was piled up in the meadow. This was for the shelter. Nate, Owen and Harry had brought with them all manner of gardening implements, and since Grace was fairly certain she had none, was fortuitous.

After receiving assurances, they really were willing to undertake manual labour on a Sunday, Grace asked Ralph whether it would be acceptable for her to work alongside those who would be clearing the garden.

She explained she wasn't a horticultural novice, having spent many hours tending both her family's garden in London, and the one on their country estate. The three in question readily agreed, with Owen remarking one more set of hands would be welcome, and they all moved to begin their day.

Entering the house through the kitchen, Grace put her cup on the table and thanked Agnes for her delicious breakfast. She hurried upstairs to change into a dress more suitable for spending the day getting dirty.

Fastidious Polly was horrified Grace wanted — nay was excited — to mess about amongst smelly weeds but made no comment when Grace found one of her oldest gowns; a well-worn plain brown poplin.

Laying her morning dress on the bed, Grace shrugged into the poplin, then dug out a despised bonnet to cover her hair, acknowledging its wide brim would protect her pale skin.

Rooting through her chest of drawers, she retrieved a pair of gardening gloves. Dropped into her luggage at the last minute, Grace never expected to use them again but was unable to throw them away.

Her happiest times had been devoted to their gardens. She could lose herself amongst the plants and bushes, forgetting everything except tending to herbs and flowers, trying to cultivate new varieties of this, that or the other.

She almost skipped down the stairs, enthusiasm clear in her merry smile, as she rushed to join the three men already tackling the huge patch of weeds at the back of the garden near the stone wall.

"Where do you want me to start?" she queried. "Do you have a plan?"

The three men looked at each other. Despite Grace's request to help, they were unsure of etiquette here. Gentle-born women didn't normally engage in this type of chore. They were saved by Ralph, who, upon hearing her question, stuck his head over the wall and suggested she start near the house and work towards the other three.

The weeds and undergrowth were much thicker up at the back and would require a good few days' toil, whereas those in the beds closer to the house were far less dense.

While she worked, Grace could hear the rhythmic bang of a hammer and the occasional sound of a saw and she liked it. It was the sound of something being created, in contrast to the necessary destruction the four in the walled garden were wreaking.

Evans appeared an hour or so later with cool drinks and a plate of biscuits, which they inhaled. At some point, Matt and Gibbs joined them, arguing, since they had no horses to tend to, they might as well make themselves useful.

The group chatted light-heartedly and worked solidly until Becca called them to stop for luncheon. Agnes had made pies and pasties, followed by slices of rich fruitcake. Everyone wolfed the food and downed several glasses of lemonade.

They did not pause for long and were soon back to it. By the end of the afternoon, Harry, Owen, and Nate had made great progress. The pile of weeds, deadwood and briar was higher than the wall. Grace, Matt, and Gibbs hadn't been slacking either; the patch of cleared garden growing with a rapidity none expected.

When Duncan and Ralph appeared through the gate in the wall sometime around four in the afternoon to apprise Grace on the progress of the shelter, the remaining six were standing in a loose group, conferring over what was left to do, while stretching their backs, trying to ease aching muscles. They looked pleased with their efforts.

"Goodness, Grace. I'm astonished at how much you've achieved today!"

Grace smiled at her cousin, her bonnet awry and her auburn hair, somehow full of twigs and grass, tumbling out of its neat bun. She had been rubbing her face, for there were streaks of mud along one cheek and across her forehead.

The Grace leaning against the wall fanning herself with a random leaf, her face flushed and happy — albeit smudged, was in striking contrast with the pale and pensive young woman with whom he had become reacquainted only the previous day. This was the Grace he recalled from their childhood and, once again, he wondered what happened to quash that vitality.

"It wasn't anything I did," she demurred. "Once Matt and Gibbs joined in, all I did was pull a few weeds, and rake the beds as they cleared them."

The five men gawked at her. They knew she had worked as hard as they — testified by the state of her clothing, filthy from where she knelt on the ground to dig up recalcitrant weeds — and were amazed she took no credit. Not once did she complain about being tired or hot, carrying piles of debris to the ever-growing stack.

Knowing they were coming to assist a member of the nobility, they had expected a fragile, somewhat incapable female, who would float about the garden getting in the way and achieving nothing. That Grace turned out to be the polar opposite boosted their estimation of her tenfold.

Ralph and Duncan chuckled. They remembered Grace, and how she refused to let being a girl stop her from joining in everything the boys did, usually to her own downfall. Young ladies should not climb trees or ride horses bareback or jump over hedges or into ponds, but she did not care, and her Aunt Bea never chastised her for having fun.

Even though this often involved trying to explain why so many of Grace's dresses magically disappeared every time she visited. Miss Montgomery believed there was a time and a place for her niece to learn decorum and it was *not* while staying at Oak Stanton.

"Would you like to see how far we've got with the shelter Grace?" Ralph asked. Grace beamed at him, and nodded, almost tripping over bits of rubbish in her haste, making the others laugh.

Suppressing a childlike impulse to stick out her tongue at their mirth, Grace ignored them and followed the path they had uncovered. She took Ralph's proffered arm, as Duncan led them through into the meadow.

The two men had made great progress. A skeleton frame stood at the edge of the meadow in line with the garden wall, but not too close.

It looked huge but, as Ralph talked Grace through their design, she realised it was exactly what was required. There would be room inside for four spacious stables. Duncan assumed Grace would end up with at least three horses, two for the carriage and one for riding.

There would be the usual shelves and hooks, and the fourth stable would provide an additional area to store tack and food. Because Grace had intimated, she wanted to purchase other animal stock, it also offered a suitable place for extra fodder, negating the necessity for a dedicated shed.

The loose boxes would stand two together facing each other separated by a wide passage. Ralph and Duncan had decided to tile the roof, arguing that although it was only a shelter — the main carriage house being for stabling in inclement weather — if they were going to build something this substantial, they might as well build it to last.

Grace was thrilled, thanking them profusely, her mind spinning with possibilities.

The three ambled back into the garden, Duncan latched the gate when they passed through it. Grace saw Theo had arrived. She glanced down at herself, realising she must look an absolute mess; the heat in her cheeks nothing to do with her exertions of the day.

Lifting her head, she locked eyes with the doctor who, by the wicked twinkle in his eye, knew exactly what she was thinking.

"Good afternoon, Miss Fitzgerald. It looks as though you have had a most productive day," Theo grinned at her across the garden, amused at her discomposure.

"I… err… mmm… well…" Grace's voice died away. *What could she say?* There was no hiding the fact she needed a bath, and some clean clothes.

She pulled off her gloves and yanked the bonnet from her head. Her hair — which had been slowly unravelling itself from the neat style Polly had taken so much time on — gave up, and spilled around her shoulders, tangled up with all manner of detritus.

"You might leave one or two flowers for the garden, Miss Fitzgerald," Theo chuckled, reaching out to pluck a lavender stalk from her locks.

Grace held her breath. The others hadn't seen the doctor's gesture, engrossed in a discussion about their plans for the following day — standing slightly to one side of Grace and Theo — pointing out which areas required further attention.

Theo handed Grace the stalk, their fingers catching, making Grace tingle. Trying to ignore the sensation, she rolled the lavender in her palms crushing the tiny florets and inhaling the delicate fragrance before raising her eyes back to his.

Theo was entranced and, when he thought about it later, this was the precise moment he finally stopped fighting his heart, recognising he was irrevocably in love with Grace Fitzgerald. She looked as though she had lost a fight with a haystack.

There was scarcely a single part of her not covered in dust and dirt. The heady scents of lavender and rosemary with just a hint of damp earth clung to her yet, despite all this, and the exhaustion etched on her face, her eyes were sparkling, and she exuded happiness.

"I think all this fresh air might be just what you need after the confines of London," he commented. Grace grinned and showed him what they had done, explaining how far Ralph and Duncan had got with the shelter, her elation infectious.

Evans came out carrying a tray laden with tall glasses full of ale for them all. Theo wasn't sure it was fair to accept one, having done none of the hard work, merely turning up to admire their achievements. Grace, who had lemonade instead of ale, pooh-poohed that, so he acquiesced and sipped the cool liquid gratefully.

All five men confirmed they would return the next day, and Gibbs and Matt said they would like to assist once any chores for the day were completed. While they were enjoying their beverages, Grace thanked them for their generosity in helping her, adding even though she had to be somewhere on the morrow, she hoped to see them on her return and would be back to helping them the day after if required.

The men smiled. They would likely finish the next day but acknowledged her appreciation.

She excused herself, trudging into the house calling for Becca and Polly who, anticipating their mistress' needs — or, more likely, primed by Evans — had already started drawing a bath.

Theo followed Grace, catching up with her as she reached the bottom of the stairs.

"May I beg a moment of your time, Miss Fitzgerald?" he asked.

Unaware of his approach, his deep voice startled her. Grace spun around, her foot snagged the bottom stair, and she tripped. Theo caught her; steadying her with his body, before carefully standing her on her own two feet.

His nearness sent her heart rate thrumming, and it was all she could do not to lean against his chest. Her legs seemed to have lost their usual strength, which she put down to tiredness, determining the doctor was just doing what any self-respecting gentleman would do to prevent a lady from making an idiot of herself.

"How may I help you, Dr Elliott?" she replied, pleased her voice sounded normal.

"I was wondering whether you had any objections to my accompanying you and the Winchesters tomorrow, to the stud? My mother is on the hunt for a new carriage horse, and some of the horse traders near the city can be less than scrupulous. I am hoping this chap may have what she needs."

"For my part I think that would be agreeable, but what of Billie and the earl?"

"They will not think it untoward, more likely they would think it strange if I did not go along." He smiled his slow smile, and her legs turned to jelly. She had to stop letting him affect her this way; he was just being friendly.

Ahh, but those words last night, his kiss, that was a tad more than 'just friendly,' she argued with herself, forcing her attention back to the doctor who was watching her, an odd expression on his face.

"Please, forgive me. I… something… that is… I. What did you say?" Flustered, she forgot what Theo had said.

He repeated it gently, his eyes still holding hers. "I hoped you might be agreeable to my calling for you in the morning to drive you over to Whiteoaks? From there, we will travel together in the Winchester coach, and my groom can spend the day with Will and Jake, which he will relish."

Theo made it sound as though she was doing him and his groom a huge favour. Well, she certainly did not want to be the one to spoil their fun.

"I should be pleased, Dr Elliott, and look forward to tomorrow. I believe his Lordship wishes to be on the way no later than ten."

"I shall be here at nine thirty, my dear. I too am looking forward to it." He bent over her hand, his lips giving it the briefest caress, his cool fingers lightly stroking along her palm as he straightened his back. "Until tomorrow."

Grace suppressed a sudden urge to smooth her skirts and brush the mud off her face, as Theo stepped towards the door. Evans miraculously appeared, bowing as the doctor took his leave.

Theo turned at the last minute and tipped his head. Grace

felt a smile curve her lips in response. What *was* it about this man? She couldn't help it, he made her want to smile all the time, and even more so when he was near.

Shaking her head at such nonsense, she continued up the stairs to the bath her two maids had filled, the hot water perfumed with a relaxing kind of fragrance and tried to put it out of her mind.

CHAPTER 10

Their well-laid plans were thwarted. Overnight the long spell of hot, dry weather broke and it was pouring with rain. Giles sent word it was too wet to contemplate a journey to inspect horseflesh, but would Miss Fitzgerald like to spend the day with Billie at Whiteoaks?

Grace was delighted and confirmed she would be glad to accept such a kind invitation. She was unsure what to do about Ralph and the other men who were supposed to be coming over to continue their work on the shelter and in the garden presuming they would not be crazy enough to work in such appalling weather.

She fretted until Evans — knowing all the men well — assured her they would return on the next fine day and not to worry.

Theo arrived at nine-thirty. In her concern about the change to the day's plans Grace had all but forgotten he was to have accompanied them to the stud. The doctor didn't seem perturbed, and offered to drive Grace to Whiteoaks, arguing his carriage was already outside, and both his driver and his horse were already wet.

Since Grace didn't have any other way to get there, other than on foot, she was easily persuaded.

The two hardly spoke on the drive. Theo seemed preoccupied, and Grace did not feel she knew him well enough to ask what bothered him. Suddenly awkward, she was out of the carriage almost before it pulled to a halt, barely giving Will the chance to drop the step.

Theo stared in consternation. He had started to unfurl his umbrella to cover them as they walked across the courtyard, but it was too late. Grace was already dashing over the slippery flags. The rain was torrential. She would be saturated before she had taken two steps.

Thankfully, Thomas appeared with a large umbrella, holding it over the young woman protecting her as she hurried indoors, before turning to do the same for Theo. The doctor waved him back indicating he had brought his own.

Confounded by her odd behaviour, Theo walked slowly into the house, shaking the rain from his umbrella. He placed it upside down in the stand designed for the purpose, water running off to drain away, creating little rivulets along the stone floor of the outer passageway.

Grace's cloak was hanging on one of the huge hooks, Thomas having shown her through to the library, where Billie was waiting. Theo stuck his head into the kitchens shouting a 'hello' to Sarah and the other staff, before following in their wake.

When he entered the handsome room, a fire already lit to banish the chill which accompanied the rain, Theo was relieved to see Giles was there. Billie and Grace were chattering nineteen to the dozen about goodness knows what.

Theo was momentarily distracted by Grace's lively countenance, and the way the fire caught the reddish highlights in her hair. He turned to greet Giles, who grinned at him know-ingly, suggesting they remove to his private study, adjacent to the library, where Thomas would bring them coffee.

When the two men left the room, Grace relaxed. A tension she did not know she was holding, evaporating.

Billie was eyeing her new friend curiously. "Is everything all right Grace?" Her tones solicitous.

For a split-second Grace was tempted to confide in Billie, believing she could trust the countess, but it was hard to share anything of herself. "Thank you for asking, but 'tis naught to concern you." Summoning up what she trusted was a reassuring smile.

Billie watched the doubt flicker over her new friend's expressive face and, while she imagined she knew its cause, wasn't about to press the issue. She would wheedle it out of her eventually. Grace just needed time.

Recalling what Giles had told her, Billie's heart ached for this fragile-looking woman, whose composure seemed to be hanging by a very slender thread.

The moment passed and the two began to discuss the school-room. Grace was interested in helping Billie and, by exten-sion, Giles. She could speak Italian and French with fluency, had a smattering of Latin and Greek and, as she read anything she could get her hands on, had a fairly good grasp of the classics, as well as geography, history and mathematics.

Billie explained the simple timetable and the days on which the lessons were held. Grace listened intently, asking questions here and there until she understood how it worked, and offered her skills, such as they were, for any days Billie thought she might be useful.

Billie was ecstatic. In the not too distant future, she would need to reduce the number of hours she spent around the estate although, currently, only she and Giles knew the reason why.

This kept them occupied until Thomas announced luncheon was served in the dining room. Giles and Theo joined them, and the conversation turned to other matters. Giles asked how the garden transformation was progressing. Grace described the work they had done the, her enjoyment in being part of it, obvious.

Theo studied Grace while she talked, wondering why she had been so quiet in the carriage, trying to work out what it was about her that fascinated him so. Yes, she was breathtakingly beautiful. Her height gave her an almost regal bearing, and her extraordinary colouring would turn the head of many a man. Theo had seen many attractive women, and none of them came close to stirring him the way Grace did.

There was something more to this woman, an indefinable quality which set her apart. Theo didn't know whether it was because of what she had suffered, or whether she had always possessed it, but it tantalised him.

He forced his mind back to the conversation, which had evolved into a vigorous debate about the merits of sheep over goats, and whether piglets were really such a good idea, bearing in mind they tended to turn green meadow into churned mud.

It was the most ludicrous discussion. Billie and Grace were laughing helplessly at the bizarre stories of misadventures in animal husbandry, Giles and Theo were coming up with, designed to deter Grace from buying any livestock at all. When Billie was able to catch her breath, she informed them they were shameless, and if Grace desired any kind of creature it was up to her.

The two men took pity on Grace, conceding it wasn't any of their business and, should she choose to fill her meadow with half the baby animals of Hampshire, they would gladly share their knowledge.

Giles pointed out Evans had a cousin who farmed somewhere over near Nether Stanton, who, he was certain, would be pleased to offer extra advice if necessary. Theo remembered his conversation with the butler and realised this could be the perfect opportunity to organise a visit.

As their conversation wound down, Theo asked Giles whether they might adjourn to the study because he had one or two things he still needed to discuss. Giles nodded, stating all this sitting around and gossiping wasn't getting his work done and, before his wife could stutter her indignation, the two men had gone.

"Well, did you ever hear such cheek?" Billie giggled when the door swung closed. "Gossiping indeed. I'll sort him out later."

Grace grinned and, before long, both women had forgotten their exasperation, absorbed in organising lessons for the school. By and by, satisfied they had done all they could, Billie noticed the rain had eased and the sun was trying to break through. She suggested a walk through her herb garden, something Grace was happy to fall in with.

Collecting their cloaks, Billie told Thomas where they would be, should Giles want her, before leading the way across the courtyard to the walled garden beyond. It was too wet to tend to any of the plants, but it was refreshing to wander around. To breathe in the soothing bouquets of the different herbs and the rich loam of the earth, discussing which plants proved efficacious for what ailment.

The afternoon sped by, and it didn't seem as though they had been in the garden long at all when Thomas came to ask whether they would like tea or coffee, adding his Lordship and Dr Elliott would join them in the library.

Upon entering the charming room, Grace noticed a tray of heavenly-looking little cakes, and was moved to murmur to her hostess, "If I keep enjoying afternoon tea, I will need to exercise more.

Billie giggled and, handing out hot drinks, replied in undertones. "Surely all that gardening yesterday means you are permitted to treat yourself to a cake or two today."

Despite it being August, the rain made it unseasonably cold and the two women had been standing for some time in the damp air. Grace could not get warm and, while they chatted, unconsciously edged closer to the fire, unable to prevent the odd shiver from running down her body, feeling a trifle achy.

Yesterday's efforts must be catching up with her. She wished she hadn't doffed on her cloak, fighting an absurd longing to go home and curl up in her warm bed.

Theo, sensitive to any change in Grace's demeanour, noticed she seemed overly quiet, and raked his doctor's eye over her features. Her mouth was slightly pinched, and he thought he saw a tremor or two ripple through her slender frame.

He frowned, but made no comment, deciding she would not thank him for drawing attention to whatever was going on.

Glancing at the ormolu clock on the mantle, Grace saw it was after four and, although had no desire to take Theo away from his friends, neither did she wish to outstay her welcome.

Making a decision, she placed her cup carefully on the tray and stood, thanking her hosts, trusting his Lordship would let her know when next he would be able to visit the stud farm.

Billie was surprised, but one look at her friend's face was enough for her not to comment. She rang for Thomas, who came in so quickly, Grace wondered whether he had second sight.

"Thank you for your invitation, it was such a generous gesture and a most enjoyable way to spend a rainy day. Billie, you have been kindness itself and I hope soon to return the favour. No..." when Theo moved to come with her, "...please, Dr Elliott, I assume you are expected here for dinner, and you have already given up one evening with your friends to escort me home. The rain has stopped, and a brisk walk will do me good."

Theo didn't know how to respond to this. He wanted to take her home, more to ensure she wasn't coming down with a chill than for any other reason, although another half an hour in her company would not come amiss. He could not force her, so inclined his head, saying he looked forward to seeing her anon.

Grace dropped a deep curtsy and left the room with Thomas. Billie turned to her husband and Theo, spreading her palms indicating she too was at a loss, before following the other two. She caught up with Grace as the latter was being helped into her cloak, which although damp, was at least heavy, making her feel warmer immediately.

"Grace, wait. What's going on?" Billie's elfin-like face was wreathed in concern. "Are you quite well?"

"I am fine, Billie. Do not fret. I think 'tis all that gardening yesterday. I had forgotten how tiring it can be. Thank you again, please do not stand here getting cold. Giles will not be pleased."

Billie acknowledged the sense of Grace's words and, although aware it was more than tiredness plagued her friend, did not want to pry. Nodding, she gave Grace a quick hug and told her not to dawdle, waving over her shoulder as she hurried back to the warmth of the library.

"Well!" Billie exclaimed when she burst through the door. "What was all that about?"

Neither man could tell her, although Theo commented Grace seemed more than just tired.

"Maybe I should go after her," he said, "It is not a short walk back to Oak Stanton and, if she is feeling less than well, it will seem even longer."

Giles stared at his long-time friend, realising so much more was going on here.

Theo smiled sheepishly. "I noticed she was trying to stifle shivers while we were drinking coffee and am concerned, she may have been in the damp air for too long."

"She wore her thick cloak, Theo." Billie said, piqued the doctor might presume they had spent the afternoon outside without wearing proper attire.

"It's not so much that, Billie. I know you are sensible when it comes to wrapping up warmly, but Grace has spent the better part of a year rarely leaving her home, prior to which she was gravely ill. It is likely her natural defences, borne of a healthy appetite, and plenty of fresh air, not to mention a modicum of exercise — none of which I believe she has bothered with lately — are lower than they should be."

That Billie did not question his words, made Theo realise

Giles had told her about Grace. He raised a surprised eyebrow at Giles who had the decency to blush.

"You know Billie would have wormed it out of the woman sooner or later, Elliott. I felt it was easier if I just told her and have done with it."

"How could you keep it from me, Theo?" Billie cried. "That poor girl. I believe she will tell me herself in good time, and I don't want to push her, but oh dear, my heart aches for her." Her face reflected her sadness.

"I have heard from Jemima Withers, you know. Apparently, she met Grace at a museum or art gallery, or some such place and they have become close friends. Grace eventually confided in her, but Jemima wonders whether there is anything Lucas can do to bring this man to justice.

"She, Jemima I mean, has asked Lucas to make discreet enquiries into the man's… err… activities. Knowing Grace was coming here to live, she wanted us to keep an eye on her. Not that I would ignore the creature anyway!" She finished, slightly affronted by the notion.

Her husband chuckled, knowing how desperately his wife wanted Grace to trust her. He leant over to pat her on the knee. "Give her time, my love. She'll come around. Remember, she has had little reason to trust anyone of late."

Billie nodded, curling her slender fingers around the much larger hand of her husband.

The two of them were starting to forget Theo was in the room and he cleared his throat. Billie went pink and apologised, while Giles grinned.

The sky was lowering again and, glancing out of the window, Theo decided, regardless of Miss Fitzgerald's sensibilities, she did not need a good soaking.

"I believe I shall go after her," he stated. "Do not worry about dinner. Martha will be able to rustle up something for me," referring to his long-suffering cook who never knew from one minute to the next where her employer might be and whether he would want feeding.

Billie gave the doctor an arch smile, which Theo ignored.

"I shall defer the trip to the stables until the next fine day," was all Giles said in response. "Let the roads dry up rather than drag the carriage through the quagmire which will have resulted from all this rain."

Theo agreed and, nodding at Giles, excused himself, giving Billie a quick hug.

After he had gone, Billie went over to where Giles was standing near the hearth and snuggled against him. He wrapped his arms around her and kissed the top of her head.

"I think Theo might have fallen for my Miss Fitzgerald," murmured Billie, luxuriating in his embrace.

"I think you might be right, my Willow," replied Giles, "but right now I don't care." He bent his head to kiss her soundly and for long moments, they were heedless to everything around them.

CHAPTER 11

Grace was trudging home, huddled in her cloak. The shivers she tried to suppress in the library had not abated and her head felt muzzy. Determined she wasn't succumbing to a cold; Grace straightened her shoulders and forced her legs to keep moving.

Under normal circumstances, the walk from Whiteoaks to The Gables might take around half an hour to forty minutes, but today it seemed never ending. In actual fact, she had only been walking for about ten minutes; it just felt longer. It was getting darker too. That couldn't be right. It was only late afternoon; the nights weren't drawing in until much later than this.

Fighting the urge to sit down and weep — she was five and twenty, and young women of that age didn't cry like babies — Grace pushed on. She was marching along the road, well passed the huge wrought iron gates at the bottom of the driveway, when she heard the sound of a carriage behind her.

Turning, she recognised Adam. *Had Theo come after her?* The relief when the coach drew up was almost too much.

Adam jumped down and helped her into the carriage, where Theo held a huge rug in which he enveloped her.

"Why didn't you tell us you were so cold, Grace?" he chided gently. She had cut such a lonely figure walking along the road. It was all he could do not to follow the rug with his arms.

Grace snuggled into the rug. It was lovely and cosy, and she was finding it hard to keep her eyes open. *Goodness, how would she have made it home if she'd fallen asleep?* Her thoughts were becoming jumbled, and she made a concerted effort to reply to Theo's question.

"I am perfectly fine, Dr Elliott," she muttered, trying not to let her teeth chatter. "I just need to get warm. I can't seem to g..." whatever she was going to say was lost because, without warning, she fell fast asleep.

Theo, uncaring it was less than appropriate, pulled her against him, arguing to himself, it was far more sensible than have her sliding off the seat onto the floor of the carriage.

While he made sure Grace was as comfortable as possible, she sighed and nestled against him, her head resting on his shoulder and, although she continued to shiver, her breathing evened out. That was more than could be said for Theo's, which quickened at her proximity.

It did not seem very long at all before the carriage halted outside The Gables. Theo tried to wake Grace, but she was too deeply asleep. Adam opened the door and Theo lifted Grace out, still wrapped in the rug, asking his groom to fetch Evans.

For so a tall woman, Grace weighed next to nothing, another reason for Theo's misgivings about the state of her health. Evans rushed down the path and between them they carried her up the stairs and into her bedchamber.

Polly and Becca appeared, hustling the two men out saying they would inform them when Grace was settled in bed. Several minutes later, Polly came to get the doctor, who explained what had happened and he wanted to be sure she hadn't caught a chill.

Grace hadn't stirred, but her temperature seemed normal, her cheeks didn't show any indication of fever, and her breathing was steady. A quick check confirmed she had warmed up, and Theo surmised it was nothing more insidious than being over tired as a result of the previous day's exertions.

Evans brought some hot coffee for Theo, and he sat by the bedside drinking it, chatting quietly with Polly while occasionally running his eye over Grace. With no sign of her waking, the doctor left the maid with a set of instructions, asking Evans to call him if they were at all worried.

Much as he would have liked to, Theo had no valid reason to stay. He climbed up next to Adam and the two trundled home, where he was heartened to find Martha had a large slice of game pie with hot vegetables ready for him, followed by a bowl of steaming sponge pudding.

When Grace awoke, it took her several moments to work out where she was. The last thing she remembered was walking back from Whiteoaks. She sat up and looked around, relieved to see she was in her own bed at The Gables. Chewing on her lip — a childish habit she seemed unable to break — trying to recall how she got here, an image of Theo helping her into his carriage swam across her vision.

A hot flare swept up her face. *Gracious, what had happened?* Surely, she hadn't done anything so ridiculous as faint? She did recall feeling shivery and achy, neither of which seem to have lasted. She stretched. Her body was no longer sore, and she was warm and comfortable.

Someone, presumably Polly or Becca, had undressed her and got her into bed, so they would doubtless be able to tell her.

She had slept like the dead. No dreams, she wasn't even sure she turned over, the bed covers usually in a disordered heap, looked almost pristine. Goodness, she must have been tired; it was an age since she had slept so well.

She grinned to herself, she ought to devote long days to gardening more often. Pushing back the bedclothes, she went into the adjoining room to wash and dress. She had no definite plans for the day but, after the rain of yesterday, wanted to get back to clearing the garden.

Glancing out of the window, Grace smiled at the splendour of the morning. The dressing room had a view of the back garden, to the meadow beyond, and it was as though the rain had rinsed everything clean.

The green of the leaves seemed to sparkle in the sunlight and, even though the garden was still untidy, here and there pockets of brilliantly coloured flowers, glowed like gemstones.

Grace flung the window open wide, and rested her elbows on the sill, breathing in the scent of the damp earth mingled with that of the fading honeysuckle blossoms clinging on tenaciously, despite the onslaught of the rain.

An unfamiliar joy of being swept over Grace, while she took all this in. This was hers, all of it, and the contentment she first registered two nights previously, when she watched the stars, stole in again to warm her heart.

A quiet knock brought Polly into the room to help her mistress dress. So she didn't have to change once breakfast was over — which was time-consuming and somewhat senseless, bearing in mind there were no guests to entertain

— Grace suggested she start the day in one of her older morning gowns. Polly frowned, but once Grace explained her reasoning, was less discomfited.

"Thank you, Polly. Pay no mind to my whims. I cannot see any point in dressing up when there is only me." Polly grinned, and turned to brushing Grace's hair. "This might seem an odd question, but how did I get home last afternoon?"

Polly laid down the brush and began twisting the burnished locks into a thick plait before pinning it up into a neat bun. "Dr Elliott brought you home in his carriage, miss. You were fast asleep. I think he was worried you had caught a chill, but once Becca and I got you into bed you soon warmed up."

Grace felt her cheeks redden. "Errr… and… how did I get upstairs?"

Polly patted her mistress on the shoulder in a motherly fashion, amusing Grace who was several years older than her maid.

"The doctor and Mr Evans carried you, they did. None of us could wake you. 'Twas all that gardening they reckoned. Tired you out it did." Polly noticed Grace's hot face and chuckled. "'Tis of no matter, miss. You were tucked up in a blanket and doctors are doubtless used to such things."

Grace returned Polly's smile, self-consciously, accepting she was right. There was not a whole lot she could do about it anyway. Thanking Polly for her help, Grace took herself down to the kitchen where Agnes was preparing another mouth-watering offering.

"Thank you, Agnes. That smells divine."

The cook flapped her hands and shooed her mistress off to the dining room where said breakfast appeared shortly thereafter. Porridge followed by eggs and an abundance of toast, which Grace fell upon. She was famished, forgetting she hadn't eaten anything of any substance since luncheon yesterday.

Once her plate was cleared, Grace picked up her cup of tea and went along to the Snug, opening the doors onto the terrace. It was just after nine and, although the air was cool, the cloudless blue of the sky promised a warm day.

Aware she would get muddy pulling out the weeds, Grace was looking forward to it. Moving one of the chairs closer to the doors, she snuggled into it and enjoyed the hot drink, contemplating her plans for the day.

She doubted the other men would come after so much rain, it was too wet, anticipating their return once the ground started to dry out. Grace wasn't overly concerned. She was used to working alone and the quiet never bothered her.

Taking her cup to the kitchen, she informed those of her employees who were present of her intentions and took the time to thank Evans for his assistance the previous afternoon.

Evans smiled, and said it was nothing, he was just glad she was no worse for wear. Grace chuckled, and resting her hand lightly on his arm, declared how blessed she was to have such caring staff.

Leaving them to their various tasks, Grace slipped her feet into sturdy boots, tied a straw bonnet under her chin. Pulling on her faithful gardening gloves, she walked purposefully out into the garden.

Hands on hips, she stood for several minutes assessing what they had achieved, working out the best plan of action while on her own. She didn't want to tackle anything which might require tools, because the men had taken theirs with them, so it was weeds or nothing.

Starting where she had finished the other day, Grace worked methodically along what appeared to be the original garden beds, quickly losing track of time. Evans appeared at some point mentioning it was time for luncheon. She ate, sitting on the bench, registering the food was tasty but for the life of her could not have told anyone what it was.

Towards the end of the afternoon, she was on her knees, resting on her heels, trying to stretch out her tightening back muscles, when she heard a familiar voice. Evans poked his head around the back door to inform her Dr Elliott had called to see how she fared.

"Please show him through, Evans. I haven't time to make myself look presentable."

Evans nodded and disappeared, reappearing almost immediately, followed by Theo. Grace was standing up and attempting to brush the mud from her dress.

Her hat had fallen back, only held on by the barely tied bow under her chin. For once, her hair had weathered better — or Polly had stuck so many pins in it, a hurricane would fail to blow it loose — because it was still relatively tidy. Only one long strand falling over her brow.

Theo took all this in, pleased to see her cheeks were a healthy pink, and she showed no ill-effects from whatever ailed her the previous day.

"Good afternoon, Dr Elliott," she called, gaily, determined to maintain a friendly rapport.

"Good afternoon, Miss Fitzgerald. I am glad to see you are looking well. You gave me a bit of a scare yesterday."

"I beg your pardon, Doctor. I do not know what came over me. Please accept my sincere apologies for apparently dropping asleep at your feet. Highly improper of me."

"Well, better at my feet than in the middle of the road. I am relieved I decided to follow you home, because I am uncertain you would have managed the walk. You fell asleep the minute you got into the carriage, half-way through a sentence actually." His deep voice was laced with amusement and she eyed him suspiciously.

"Are you laughing at me, sir?" she demanded.

"No, of course not..."

She raised an eyebrow.

"...perhaps a little. Only because you show no evidence of the cold, I worried you had caught," he confessed. Grace grinned and walked over to where he loitered at the edge of the terrace. "You have achieved a lot today. I am impressed."

She turned and surveyed the garden. "Goodness, I've cleared more than I expected. No wonder I am sore."

Theo looked at her sharply.

She shook her head. "'Tis only from spending too long in an awkward position, a hot bath will help, and maybe a touch of arnica."

"You know of arnica?" Theo asked in surprise.

"I know of several herbal remedies. I spent considerable time reading about traditional treatments for minor ailments while I was..." she stopped. She had been about to tell Theo that which she wanted to keep private.

Hoping he hadn't picked up on her slip, she hurried on, "...never mind. I believe the countess and I share this interest. Her herb garden is splendid. I love gardening and know a lot about cultivating regular plants but am only a novice regarding those herbs typically used as curatives. I hope I may learn more now I am here."

Exuberance coloured her tones and her eyes were sparkling as she went on to explain her ideas for the garden, which began to percolate during the day.

"So, I am thinking that, this side," waving her hand out towards the wall at the left side of the plot, "should be suitable for herbs. It faces south so will get the warmth of the sun for longer and the wall will protect the plants from the wind. In the winter, I may have to come up with a way of sheltering them, possibly a kind of wooden lean-to.

"Anyway, I have enough time to work it out, maybe I will start them next year. I think I might keep this section closest to the terrace as grass, and then fill that middle area with all different flowers, each section edged with rosemary or lavender — which is what was probably planted there before it got all out of control."

She pointed to the far end of the garden. "For the back wall there, some pyracantha, which is very pleasing when grown along walls. Its dark green leaves, white flowers and red berries will offer colour all year. I believe it to be a relatively new species.

"My old footman has a brother, Joe, who works in the gardens at Kew Park, and he generously gave me a small cutting. I used to visit the Park occasionally, a most agreeable change of scenery and Joe, knowing my love of plants was very informative. It is growing well. At least it was up until a couple of weeks ago. I must admit, I am not sure from where else to purchase stock, so may have to contemplate a trip to the city." She suppressed a shudder at the thought.

"I believe 'tis a hardy variety and should do well here. I haven't made up my mind what to do with this section yet," nodding in the direction of the wall at the right-hand side. For now, I shall just turn the soil and leave it fallow. I'm sure something will pop into my head."

Theo listened to Grace's eager chatter, her love for all manner of growing things obvious. Evans brought out with a tray of cool drinks and biscuits, which they drank and ate absently, engrossed in their discussion.

Theo interposed with questions, registering how knowledgeable Grace was and, if this impulsive scheme to add chickens and lambs to the mix came to fruition, she would ensure they were properly nurtured.

He became distracted by the recalcitrant strand of hair, which insisted on falling over her eyes. His fingers itched to tuck it into her bun, because all Grace did was blow it out of the way. In the end he couldn't help himself and, leaning forward, gently pushed the errant lock back into place.

Grace froze, the gesture so intimate. As always when Theo was close to her, she had no feelings of panic, but she wasn't sure what to do. Such gentle touches were alien to her, and despite her blossoming feelings for the doctor, instinct warned her not to trust them.

CHAPTER 12

Theo dropped his hand, watching confusion flit across the young woman's face. He knew he had to take this slowly. The slightest misstep could end in disaster for both of them. He took a pave back.

"Thank you for sharing your ideas, Miss Fitzgerald, I think they sound perfect and I hope to see them come to fruition." His tones were formal.

Grace floundered. *What just happened? He tweaked her hair, now he was leaving? What was she supposed to do with that?* Giving up any attempt to speak in the riddles so loved of the elite, Grace demanded point blank. "*Now* what have I done?" Her vexation clear.

Theo gaped at her.

"Well, what am I supposed to think? One minute we are chatting happily, then you fiddle with my hair and in an instant, you become overly polite and stilted. I do not understand, Dr Elliott. What is going on here? Was the other night an aberration? Did I imagine it?"

Bewildered, Grace wrung her hands together, and Theo grasped them in his.

"No, Grace, you did not imagine it, but you are a woman alone and, although I do not wish to disregard the rules, I find myself at your mercy, with no clue how to handle it."

Grace stared at him for a long time, then without warning, giggled.

Theo looked perplexed. *Here was he baring his soul, and she found it amusing?*

"Forgive me," she spluttered, "I have been battling similar emotions and am as clueless as you. You always seem in control, and I feel as though I'm going to gabble like a gibbering idiot not a relatively well-educated woman of five and twenty."

Her laughter broke the tension beginning to bubble between them, and Theo found himself grinning along with her.

"Mayhap we should do this properly," he chuckled. "Miss Fitzgerald, while we have known each other but a short time, I enjoy spending time with you. If you are agreeable, I would very much like to call on you."

"Dr Elliott, I do believe that would be acceptable, and please, call me Grace." Grace replied.

Theo took her hand and bowed over it, his lips brushing the back of her fingers. Lifting his head, he smiled the same slow, sweet smile which never failed to send trickles of warmth through her body.

"Only if you agree to call me Theo," he held her gaze, waiting. After a long moment, Grace inclined her head in tacit assent. "Until our next encounter, Miss Fitzgerald... Grace. I bid you good afternoon," and he was gone.

Grace remained where she was, trying and failing to come to her senses. What was she thinking? This could never end the way she hoped it might. As soon as he knew of her past — as there was no way she would let this, whatever 'this' was, go too far before apprising Theo of who she really was — he would have to stop calling on her.

Even if he cared for her, she could not allow his name to be dragged through the mud, as doubtless it would be. Despite these eminently sensible arguments against their courtship, Grace relished his words and his obvious sincerity; they warmed her, and the ripples his touch sent along her body really were quite divine.

Maybe she could enjoy it for a little longer.

The following day Ralph returned, along with Duncan and the others, who all resumed their efforts, declaring themselves astonished with the amount of work Grace had achieved on her own.

Their praise was a bolster to her confidence, and she continued to assist wherever she could, even if all that entailed was moving mounds of dead bushes or piles of weeds.

Harry and Owen built two huge bonfires, and late on the following Saturday afternoon, five days after the rain, they were lit. Once the walled garden was cleared, they took it upon themselves to wrestle with the neglected front garden, tidying up that area for her too.

The shelter was finished, and Grace felt as though she had made several more, if not good friends then definitely close acquaintances.

Acknowledging men and women rarely shared friendships beyond their youth, Grace believed Ralph and she — and to a certain extent Duncan — as a result of numerous summers spent together during their childhood, shared a bond, which remained strong.

She was cheered by the cordiality which had sprung up

between her and the other three men, who were astounded at Grace's willingness to throw herself into what to them was unladylike and back-breaking labour.

The two bonfires were crackling merrily, when Evans appeared bearing trays laden with hot pies and cold beers. The men fell on the food gratefully, munching through the crispy crust into the gravy-soaked meat inside, before washing the lot down with the beer. Grace made a little speech, determined to thank them, formally, for their efforts.

She had spoken at length with Ralph regarding payment and that was already settled. The difference they had made, not only to her garden, but also to her self-esteem was, to Grace, invaluable. She chuckled when she saw her praise made them blush but knew her words were appreciated.

The afternoon waned, and each started to make their way home, saying if ever she needed them for anything, to ask, and so on. Ralph and Duncan were the last to leave, and while Duncan carried one of the trays into the kitchen, Ralph caught his cousin's hand.

"I am glad our paths have crossed again, Grace. I had forgotten how much of a tomboy you used to be…"

Grace smiled ruefully.

"…but I must ask, and please this comes from a cousin's concern, whatever happened to crush your spirit? You used to be light-hearted and vivacious, nothing could keep you down. Now you seem a shadow of the girl I remember. These last few days have cheered you, and there are hints of who you once were. Whatever it is, Grace please let me help."

Grace stared at her cousin, seeing in her mind's eye the gangly youth who included her in everything they did. He hadn't changed much.

He was taller now, quieter maybe, probably somewhat less spontaneous; but his unruly dark brown hair still flopped across his forehead, and his eyes still twinkled with mischief, despite his being close to thirty years old.

"I wish I could, Ralph, but I am not ready. I am surprised you do not know. How is it you have avoided the family grapevine? Aunt Bea knew. Are you sure she didn't tell you?"

Ralph looked mystified, and Grace was assured he had no knowledge about what had occurred.

"Aunt Bea and I talked all the time, and she told me nothing of your life, save she was bequeathing you The Gables — for which I am eternally grateful," he added in an aside. "I have my own home and did not need another. If you are not comfortable telling me I understand, but I am always here for you, Grace, never forget that."

Grace hugged her cousin impulsively, something she would have balked at doing scant weeks ago. "I will when I am able," she promised, grasping his hand in hers. "It is difficult for me, it is too raw, and I like that here no-one seems to know. It has afforded me the chance to breathe again."

Ralph searched her face seeing a darkness lurking beneath the surface and knew better than to push her. He returned the squeeze and released her fingers. "Thank you, Cousin. It means a lot to me," was all he said, and Grace grinned at him.

They both turned as Duncan trudged back from the kitchen, shoulders drooping with fatigue.

"Duncan get you home, sir. You look exhausted," Grace chuckled, "and take this lummox with you, he's about asleep on his feet."

She walked with them through the house. Evans opened the door to let them out, and Theo was there, his hand raised to knock. Caught unawares, Grace smiled without reserve.

Ralph noticed how it lit her whole face. *Ahhh, so that's the way the wind blows is it?* he thought to himself. *Well she could do worse.* He nodded to Theo. "Elliott. Nice to see you."

"Montgomery. I hear you finished up today. Just saw Nate, they mentioned something about going along to the Cross Keys."

"Not for me, Doc, I have a wife who awaits me. Far more important than a beer in that alehouse."

Theo grinned as Ralph strode off down the road. Duncan waved his goodbyes as he headed in the opposite direction to meet Nate and Owen, and then it was just the two of them.

"Good evening, Dr Elliott," breathed Grace, inordinately glad to see him.

"Good evening, Miss Fitzgerald. As I said, I understand it's all done."

"Would you like to see?" she asked demurely. Theo nodded and she led him through to the back garden. Theo's jaw dropped. The change was astonishing. Except for a few small bushes of rosemary and lavender, which had survived the defoliation, the garden was completely stripped.

The little pathways running between the garden beds were cleared and ready for new flagstones or maybe gravel, Grace hadn't decided yet. She pointed out this and that, and Theo realised how sizeable an area it actually was.

Unbidden, he pictured children dashing along the paths shouting and laughing as they jumped the low hedges. Grace trying to tell them to be careful but unable to do so for her own laughter. *Was he with them? Were they his children?*

The thought of Grace married to anyone other than him was unconscionable, and he could only hope she might come to feel the same way. Pushing the idyll aside, he dragged his attention back to Grace who was chattering away, unaware her companion's mind was distracted.

Satisfied she had told Theo enough about the garden inside the wall, Grace tugged on his arm, drawing him to the gate, in order to show him the shelter in the meadow beyond. He was even more astounded with this structure than the garden, for it looked enormous. That Ralph and Duncan had built it in so short a time was extraordinary.

Grace was pleased with the doctor's reactions; it was gratifying to have someone be genuinely happy for her.

"Before I forget," Theo said as they walked out of the shelter, "Giles sent word he hopes to travel to visit the horse stud the day after tomorrow. Weather permitting."

"How exciting! I cannot wait to have my own horses. What a thrill!" They were strolling back through the garden, Grace making sure she latched the gate in the wall. Glancing at the sky, she surmised it must be nearly seven and, hesitantly, asked the doctor whether he might like to join her for dinner.

It wouldn't be much, she clarified, but he would be most welcome. Theo smiled and accepted graciously. Grace reciprocated in kind, little realising how luminous her skin appeared in the light of the evening sun.

"You must allow me a few moments to change. I cannot enjoy a meal looking as though I have been wallowing in a mud bath."

Theo chuckled and said to take all the time she needed. He settled himself on the bench and lit a cigar, while Grace flew into the house and along to the kitchen to inform Agnes, they had a guest for dinner, but not to worry about anything fancy.

Then she fled upstairs to try and clean herself up. To her undying gratitude, Polly had drawn a bath in which Grace allowed herself a brief soak and it went a long way to soothing her aching muscles.

As she relaxed in the warm water, Polly attempted to untangle her mistress' hair and to remove the pieces of grass and leaves which seemed irresistibly attracted to it.

A little under half an hour later, and a trifle on edge, she found Theo lounging on the bench, enjoying his cigar. He stood when she came out of the Snug through the French doors.

"You look exquisite, Miss Fitzgerald," he murmured, and smiled at her gently.

Grace smoothed her dress self-consciously, brushing off a non-existent piece of fluff, and thanked him. He waited for her to sit before he joined her and, after a moment of awkwardness, they relaxed, resuming their easy conversation.

The light was fading by the time Evans announced dinner was served, and the two made their way to the dining room. Grace's eyes nearly popped out of her head when she saw the room and she looked over her shoulder at Evans who smiled mysteriously at her.

It had, obviously, always been an attractive room — despite the furnishings being a little tired — but her staff had made it look splendid.

Candelabra, polished until you could see your face in them, were dotted around the room. Someone, Evans or Gibbs she presumed, must have checked the chimney was unblocked, before lighting the fire; the warmth from the dancing flames adding a welcoming glow.

The table was laid with fine, white china, delicately patterned around the rims, placed between gleaming silver-ware. The setting was completed by crystal glasses whose facets scattered flickering rainbows across the snowy white napkins.

Grace had no idea her aunt owned anything so beautiful. She hadn't bothered to check in the drawers and sideboard.

Evans pulled out a chair at one end of the table for Grace, while Theo seated himself opposite. It seemed a bit ridiculous being so far apart, but it was plain her staff wanted to do this properly, and Grace wasn't about to upset them.

Laying a hand on Evans' arm, she said, "Thank you very much, Evans. This is perfect. I had no idea this room could look so charming."

Evans grinned and bowed, saying nothing and moving to serve the first course. The food was delicious, and far more than Grace could eat, but she gave it her best effort.

A light soup to start with, followed by roast chicken, hot buttered potatoes and some seasonal vegetables, complemented by a light red wine, before finishing up with a lemon syllabub — so much for nothing fancy.

Grace was certain she wouldn't need to eat again for a week. Thankfully, engaged in lively conversation, they remained at the table long after the food was cleared away, enjoying a glass of tawny port as a digestif. Grace asked Theo whether he would like to retire to the Snug. It was more comfortable there and, as the evening was still mild, they could leave the doors onto the terrace open.

Excusing herself for a moment, Grace popped along to the kitchen, to thank Agnes and the two girls for their hard work. "I cannot thank you enough. The dining room looked splendid and the food was superb. That lemon syllabub was heavenly, Agnes. I am in awe."

Agnes beamed, and Becca and Polly grinned in delight. While Grace was engrossed in the garden, her two maids were going through the rooms one at a time, slowly bringing each one back to its former glory.

Aunt Beatrice closed all those she no longer used, and they had lain neglected for a considerable period of time. They had several left to tackle, but Becca and Polly were relishing the challenge of making the weary-looking rooms sparkle and shine again, and were, understandably, proud of their achievements.

"You have made this evening extra special." Grace smiled her appreciation, and hurried back to where Theo was waiting, leaning on the mantle, port in hand, chatting with Evans. The butler bowed when she entered and slipped out of the room.

Grace glanced at Theo who, although wearing grey trousers, a simple white shirt, charcoal grey waistcoat and matching cravat — probably his normal everyday business attire — looked devastatingly handsome.

For no reason she could come up with right then, she felt shy, and didn't know how to regain their relaxed camaraderie. She sipped her port, scouring her mind for a topic of conversation which wouldn't sound forced. To no avail.

Grabbing her shawl, which she had dumped unceremoniously over the back of one of the chairs the day before, Grace muttered something about fresh air and slipped out through the doors.

Theo, keenly aware of her discomfiture, chuckled to himself and followed her outside. The sun had set. The gossamer blanket of stars glimmered in the inky blue sky over their heads, yet on the horizon a translucent pink streak could still be seen, heralding a dry day on the morrow.

Grace had wandered a little way from the house and Theo almost lost sight of her in the shadows. Her quiet voice gave him a hint as to where she stood, and he walked towards her.

"I could stare at the stars for ever," Grace sighed, gazing upwards. "The immeasurable vastness of the sky makes me realise how utterly insignificant we actually are." She turned to Theo, who was now less than two paces away watching her, an unreadable expression on his face.

It reminded her of the night he kissed her. Well almost kissed her. Well, all right, it was barely even a brushing of lips, but the same magical feeling began to tease at her senses, and her heart did that weird hiccup again.

He took a step closer. Grace tried to speak but couldn't. Her brain and her mouth appeared to have disengaged so she just waited. One more step and Theo was at her side. He reached for her hand and entwined his fingers with hers. His hand was cool, and the pressure of his fingers sent pleasurable little tremors up her arm.

She felt herself leaning towards him, and this time did put her hand out, more to prevent herself from falling against him than anything else, although she didn't touch him.

The night closed around them and all was peaceful.

"Theo."

"Grace."

Whispered names, they sounded like endearments and, for several seconds, neither moved.

Theo curved his free hand around the back of her neck, tilting her head so her face was illuminated in the ethereal glow from the stars, and briefly pressed his lips to hers. So light, it was like the brush of a butterfly's wing.

Grace did place her hand against Theo's chest then, feeling the erratic beat of his heart, secretly gladdened he seemed as affected as she. Tall as she was, Grace only came up to Theo's shoulder and, unable to help herself, rested her head in the hollow of his neck, hearing his breathing catch.

He squeezed her fingers and rubbed his thumb over her palm, his other hand stroking down her back, and she could feel his cheek on her hair.

For Grace, who would normally take fright at such proximity, this was a pivotal moment. For Theo, aware how hard this might be for her, rejoiced that she hadn't pulled away. Curiously, Grace felt as though she had been waiting her whole lifetime for this moment and didn't want it to end.

The two stood together for what seemed like an age,

although was probably scant minutes. Grace felt Theo kiss the top of her head and she lifted her face so she could look at him. Just when she was sure he was going to kiss her again, a sound from the house disturbed the quiet.

Theo broke away and the moment was lost.

CHAPTER 13

The sound was Evans on his way to ask them what hot drinks they would like. Not where he expected them to be, he came out onto the terrace and spotted them in the garden, repeating his question, which gave Grace a moment to recover her composure. Both chose hot chocolate, and Grace asked her butler to pour Theo a whisky.

They ambled back into the Snug, where several candles had been lit creating a cosy ambience; the open French windows allowing the soft evening air to filter through the room.

Evans brought in the drinks, placing them on the small table. Grace sat, pulling her shawl from her shoulders and fiddling with the fine wool of the material, confusion ruffling her mind. She recalled what he said about wanting to call on her. Yes, they enjoyed each other's company, but maybe he was just making sure she was settling in, being friendly — the way he was with Billie.

Theo stood near the mantel until Evan left the room, then took the chair next to hers and made himself comfortable. Reaching across the gap, he grasped her slender fingers, untwisting them from the soft wool and entwining them, once again, in his large ones.

"Grace, I…"

Grace interrupted. She couldn't bear him to say it. To tell her he didn't mean it. To spoil the magic. "Please Theo, don't say any more. I would prefer to assume it was a whim, induced by wine and starlight. You have no need to apologise…" her voice dropped "…I don't think I could endure it." So quietly, Theo wasn't sure she'd even uttered the words.

"I have no intention of apologising, Grace. I have wanted to kiss you, really kiss you, from the moment I first saw you."

Her head snapped up and she gaped at him. "W-what? B-but…why?" Shock laced her tones.

"Because I think you are the most enchanting woman I have ever seen, and you have bewitched me!"

Grace didn't think her jaw could drop any further but was pretty certain it had.

"If you had let me finish. I was about to say, I know I have overstepped the bounds of propriety… hmm, twice now," his eyes twinkled wickedly, "but what I said the other day holds. When I mentioned I enjoy spending time with you it wasn't in friendship, although that is part of it, and I apologise if my intent was unclear. I hoped you understood I was asking whether you might not be averse to my courting you."

Grace looked down at his hands still holding hers, his long, tapered fingers curled around her slender ones. Even his hands made her heart thrum, and she wondered what it would be like to have them caress her.

Shaking her head to dismiss brazen thoughts, she looked back into his face, searching for and finding the truth in his eyes.

She would give anything to have this man in her life, to get to know him, to discover what they had in common, the differences which made life interesting, but it wasn't fair. She had to stop this before they were in too deep, although she surmised it might be far too late.

In the brief time they had known each other he had cracked the shell; the shell she thought was unbreakable, somehow reaching through to touch her heart.

"I… that is, maybe… what I mean is…" Grace gathered herself. "Dr Elliott," he raised an eyebrow. "Theo," she blushed a little, "while I believe your sentiments to be true, I am very much afraid I cannot allow this to go any further. I am… there are… if you…" she faltered, and to her horror felt hot tears pricking behind her eyes.

She would not cry. Never again would she cry.

Her voice became flat, unyielding. "If you knew me, you would not wish to stand next to me, never mind court me. I think it would be better for you if you took your leave, and then forgot about me." Grace clenched her jaw to stop it from trembling and tried to disentangle her fingers from Theo's.

Theo was having none of it. He had already decided that if they had any chance of coming together, he needed to be honest. He held onto her hand and turning it through his, rested both against his heart.

"Grace Aldeburgh," her eyes flew to his. He held her gaze and inclined his head. "Grace Aldeburgh, I already know much about you and while I wish you had not suffered such trauma, it in no way changes my feelings towards you. Since I'm declaring my hand, I first saw you a little over two years ago at the Duke and Duchess of Richmond's Christmas ball, and I have wanted to kiss you since then."

Grace didn't know whether to feel betrayed or relieved. Neither did she know where to look. This man held her darkest secret, which did not bode well. Right at this moment, surprisingly, relief was the overriding emotion.

It was arduous concentrating on every word she said in

case she let something slip. She could feel his heart beat strong and steady against the back of her hand. *Was there any hope this could work?* His expression was open, he believed what he said, but she felt it unlikely he knew it all.

She stared at him, silently arguing with herself. "Theo, if there is any chance for us at all, which I doubt highly, you must be prepared to hear the unvarnished account from me. My great aunt may only know what my family felt she should, filtered information and abridged so as not to offend.

It is not an easy tale and will take too long to relate now, for it is late. If you truly wish to hear it, perhaps you might call on me tomorrow? Maybe we could take a walk along the lanes, or find a little privacy in the meadow, and I shall tell you everything. I imagine you will understand why I believe it would be better for all concerned, that you no longer seek my company."

"You may try to push me away all you like but I know you feel something for me. I can see it in your eyes. Grace, I am no feckless rake, hungry for my next conquest. All I want is for you to have a little faith in me."

She stared at him, blinking away those treacherous tears, threatening to spill over, hardly daring to breathe. Slowly she nodded; it was all she was capable of. Until she told him, she would not presume anything. It was already going to be painful enough. Despite his assurances, she knew how this would end.

Theo drew her up and brushed his lips over the back of her hand yet did not relinquish his grasp. "I must go. It is, as you say, late and I am keeping you from your rest. I will return around ten, if that meets with your approval?" He held her gaze, her eyes shimmered like liquid amber in the candlelight, and he could have stared into them forever.

Grace, her hand still clasped in Theo's, felt the same warmth as earlier gliding up her body, and she didn't want him to let go. Unbidden, she recalled the next day was Sunday. "I forgot, 'tis Sunday tomorrow, are you… should you… do they expect you at church?" She broached diffidently.

"My time is my own and, as I am often called upon at the oddest moments, no one questions my absence. Further, it is my choice."

"In that case, tomorrow would be agreeable," she replied, her voice husky.

Theo dipped his head, and pressed a kiss to her hair, squeezing her fingers just a little tighter, then he let go and, saying he would see himself out, left.

Grace wanted to rush after him, to stand at the door and watch as he walked away, but remained where she was, her legs refusing to move. She heard him say goodbye to Evans, who latched the front door before coming to check whether she required anything else.

Collecting wayward thoughts, Grace thanked him, and affirmed she was retiring for the night. Her affable butler closed and locked the French doors, before dousing the candles, and ensuring the rest of the house was secure.

Requesting she be woken at eight and, after such a long day, Grace slept solidly, waking to a room filled with sunshine, and the sound of Polly singing softly to herself as she drew back the curtains and opened the window.

Although anxious about her upcoming conversation with Theo, the cheerful chirping of the birds as they welcomed the morning, made her smile, while she prepared herself for the day.

A refreshing wash, after which she massaged in some lightly perfumed cream and slipped into her underthings,

Grace dressed in a morning gown of pale green lawn, ably assisted by Polly, who set about brushing her mistress's hair.

Grace suggested a tidy plait would suffice, but Polly was having none of it. She gathered the vivid locks into a neat, yet loose bun, which Grace had to agree, did suit her.

Making her way down to the kitchen she greeted Agnes who was bustling about preparing breakfast, asking whether it would be easier for her to eat it there. Her cook, chuckling at Grace's lack of propriety, hustled her out saying the kitchen was no place for a lady, and breakfast would be served in the dining room as was proper.

Grace took herself off smiling and wondered what they would think if they knew she had spent the last two years eating breakfast in a kitchen much like this.

She tucked into another scrumptious repast, then apprised Evans of her plans for the morning and Dr Elliott would be calling around ten. Evans told Agnes, who produced a picnic for the two of them and, when Theo arrived as the church clock struck the last chime of ten, a basket materialised by the front door.

"Agnes wanted me to tell you, this was just in case," Evans said by way of explanation.

"Please thank her for me," smiled Grace, appreciation clear in her tones. Evans nodded and opened the door to admit Theo, who looked dashing in cream trousers, a white shirt, brocade waistcoat and dark green tailcoat.

He greeted Grace with a bow, remarking as he thought a drive might be just the thing on such a glorious day, a picnic would come in handy. The doctor picked up the basket, while Grace, bowing to convention — and the sun — tied the ribbons of a wide brimmed, straw bonnet under her chin and draped her shawl over her shoulders.

Farewelling Evans, she followed Theo down the path. Theo had chosen his gig for their outing, which he was driving himself. He assisted Grace onto the bench seat, stowed the basket securely, and hopped up beside her.

~

The gig rolled out of the village and along the road. Theo mentioned a ruined Cistercian abbey not far from Oak Stanton and, as visitors did not frequent it, a pleasant place to spend an hour or so. It would give them somewhere to talk where they would not be overheard.

Grace was glad of his sensitivity, her stomach beginning to tie itself in knots. She had never told anyone the full extent of what happened to her, not even Jemima. Scant few people knew any of it, others thought they knew everything but really didn't.

It would be difficult, and she was very much afraid Theo's solicitude would turn to, if not outright revulsion, certainly distaste by the time she finished. *Too late, Grace*, she admonished herself. *You gave your word you would tell him, now you'll have to deal with the consequences.*

It was one of those perfect late summer days. Not too warm, a gentle breeze keeping the worst of the heat at bay, the sun rising slowly to its zenith in a sky of cloudless blue. Birds zipped about, their trilling song uplifting the senses, as they chased down all manner of bugs made sluggish by long hot days.

In some of the fields, huge bales of hay signalled the approach of autumn. The freshly mown smell reminded Grace of her childhood, when she and her cousins climbed them, more often than not rolling off and ending up covered in dried stalks.

Even her nerves could not stop her sighing with pleasure as she made herself comfortable on the seat and enjoyed the ride.

· · ·

It didn't take long to arrive at the abbey. Theo found a shady spot near a full water trough and tied his horse to a post suited to the purpose. Tucking a rug under his arm and hooking his hand through the handle of the basket, he offered his other arm to Grace, the pair setting off towards the ruin. Leaving the basket in a secure corner, they took some time to explore.

Not a large complex, the abbey followed the traditional layout typical of all Cistercian monasteries and, as with so many others, it had fallen into ruin after Henry VIII ordered their dissolution. Only a skeleton of the original building remained, yet it retained a simple beauty.

Grace was captivated by the architecture, especially the soaring Romanesque arches of the church, and the remains of the vaulted ceilings in what would have been the under-croft. It was peaceful too, nothing but the distant baa-ing of lambs and the faint hum of bees.

Strolling back to where they had left the basket, Theo shrugged out of his coat, laying it over a handy section of wall, before unfolding the rug onto the soft grass and unpacking the picnic.

Agnes had supplied a tasty selection — small pies, bread buns and slices of fruitcake. Grace removed her bonnet, placing it next to Theo's coat and, leaning against the stone wall, nibbled at the food, her anxiety over the upcoming conversation deadening her appetite.

Theo realised what was going on and, after pouring two cups of lemonade — from a well-stoppered flagon — to quench their thirst, re-packed the basket, covering up anything the flies might take a shine to.

Grace fiddled with her empty cup, the gesture betraying her nerves.

"Would you like to get it over with, Miss Aldeburgh?" Theo asked quietly, deliberately using her real title in an attempt to give her some sense of distance.

Grace nodded, trying to gather tumultuous thoughts. "Are you still sure you want to hear it?" she replied just as quietly. "I must beg you not to leave me here to find my own way home when your…" pausing trying to find a less stark way of phrasing it, "…disposition toward me changes."

Her entreaty wrenched something inside Theo. Aggrieved she believed him callous enough to abandon her here, miles from her home, indignantly, he began to respond.

She interrupted him. "Theo, please. I know what I'm about to say, and it will not be easy to hear. I believe you to be an honourable man, but this may be too much even for you."

Theo realised she was offering him an excuse to break their blossoming relationship or whatever this was becoming, and unable to help himself, moved to sit next to her on the rug.

Leaning on the same stone wall, he took her fingers in his. He heard her draw a tremulous breath, but did not look at her, simply rested his head back, and asked her to tell him everything.

Grace began to speak, she was hesitant at first, but the more she talked the more confident she became, and for Grace herself it was a catharsis. For the first time since the scandal, she opened her heart.

CHAPTER 14

"It started about three years ago. We were at our country estate. We used to spend the majority of the summer there, because it was far more congenial than London.

When I was younger, I would come here, to Oak Stanton, but father had decided I needed to start behaving like the lady he wanted me to become. I had already suffered one season. It wasn't a total disaster, but I did *not* enjoy it, too many gossips. I spent most every ball I attended with the other wall-flowers or hiding behind the potted plants."

A cynical smile curved her lips as she recalled those uncomfortable evenings.

An image of a young and somewhat gamine girl, trying to act decorously made Theo chuckle. Grace glanced at him and squeezed his hand lightly.

"Then we went to Europe, stopping in Paris and Rome, and I hoped we might stay. Father refused to consider Paris, what with the war and all, but I found Rome more impressive anyway. The antiquities there are astonishing. I could wax lyrically about them all day. Moreover, being minor English nobility, I was able to participate in the dances and galas without it seeming as though I was on the hunt for wealthy European princeling.

"I have no idea why Father decided to come home, but I remember being disgruntled, and asked whether he might let me remain in Italy. He refused. Even with chaperone, it was unacceptable for a young, single woman to live alone. I understood, but I don't think I was particularly gracious about it."

Theo could well imagine how the young Grace might balk against such restrictions, but he had to agree with her father, it would have been impossible.

"We came home, and my parents wanted me to have another season. One ended up being two and I abhorred them even more than the first one. We had been away for so long, the few friends I had were either married or affianced, so I was mixing with all the young incomparables. It was ghastly.

"Three years ago, we went out to Hawkesworth Manor for the summer. I loved it there. I could ride, wander the gardens, mess about with my plants — nobody bothered — I could just be me.

"We had been there maybe three weeks when guests started arriving. Mother liked to entertain; it made her feel more important than she really was. I think in her way she loved, or certainly was fond, of my father but she always felt she had married beneath her. These grand house parties were a way of increasing her standing, and all manner of people would be invited.

"One afternoon, I was walking back to the house when a guest, a man I recognised vaguely from society balls, caught up with me. He introduced himself as Jonathon Huntington — the Duke of Aldwych, no less — and chattered away, telling me about his journey to the estate. He is several years older than me, and I imagine I was flattered. I am under no illusion I am a catch. I am not particularly pretty, deemed too tall to be feminine, and I suppose he's attractive, in a brash sort of way.

"We talked all the way back to the house, before going our separate ways. Over the next few days, he sought me out more than occasionally, and in the beginning, I thought he was just being polite — you know, talking to the daughter of his hosts — but he continued, and I began to believe he was serious. How naive could I have been?"

Grace stopped and bent her head, memories crowding in, the horror of what she was about to divulge threatening to overwhelm her.

"If you would prefer not to con—"

"No, I can do this. I have to do this. I just need a minute."

Theo moved a little closer, so their legs, stretched out in front of them, just touched. Grace felt the warmth from his body seep through the fine lawn of her dress and took strength from it.

"There was a garden party, at least I think that's what you would call it. Lots of games for children to play, people wandering around the grounds with glasses of wine or champagne. Men in small groups chatting about whatever men talk about. Women sitting on rugs, gossiping about their children whether they be youngsters or adults.

"It was wonderfully convivial. I was sitting on a bench near the house, content in my own company when he came and asked to sit beside me. I was flattered, so when he asked whether we might take a stroll, I thought nothing of it.

"I lost track of where we were walking and somehow, we ended up near the orchard. It was cool and quiet and away from everyone else, away from prying eyes and wagging tongues.

"I should have realised, but I had never been courted before, I had no idea how it worked. Without any warning and the instant, we entered the seclusion of the trees, he grabbed me, pushing me to the floor and his hands…" she swallowed, and closed her eyes briefly, "…oh, those awful hands, were all over me. I struggled to escape but could not get him off me.

"When I look back on it now, I see he was practised at this, everything was too easy for him." Grace's voice hardened. "He wrenched up my skirts and forced himself onto me right there under the apple trees. I tried to scream, but he was ready for that too, and clapped one hand over my mouth, holding both of my hands with the other.

"It seemed to go on forever, the pain was unbearable, and I thought I might suffocate from his hand. When he was finally satisfied, he spilled himself into the grass. I should be grateful for small mercies.

He wiped himself on my dress — *on my dress, dear heaven* — stood up, straightened his clothes, warned me if I uttered a word of what happened to anyone, he would see my family ruined, and calmly walked away.

"My clothing was in tatters and I was covered in blood. I just lay there, too sore to move, thinking I would likely die, for no one could lose that amount of blood and survive. I forced myself to stand and reached my room unseen. I washed him off me, so thoroughly I abraded my skin, but I didn't care. Later, when no one was around, I burned my dress on the bonfire in the kitchen garden.

"He knew I could not say anything. Who would believe me? My parents would not want any hint of a scandal with all those guests and, because I had three seasons without an offer, they would think I orchestrated the whole thing to coerce him into marriage.

"For the remainder of the house party, he sought me out

every chance he got. The riskier the place, the better he liked it. He even tried coming into my bedroom, but I locked my door. I lost count of how many times I cried for help, when I knew I should be heard but no one came to save me and, in the end, I stopped trying.

"I hoped when we returned to London, he would grow bored, and find someone else to torture, but he was not finished with me. It went on for about a year, and the longer it continued the more violent he became.

"He never spoke except to intimidate, saying because I was ugly, and fat, and ungainly, I would never land a husband so I should consider myself lucky he wanted to f…" Grace couldn't say it. "…take me. There was always that underlying threat to my family.

"I have no idea what hold he had over them, but after so many occasions when my bruises were ignored or blamed on clumsiness, I started to believe they knew what he was doing. Whether I was traded for something, whether they were powerless to stop him, or simply didn't care, I will never know because now they are both dead."

The strain was clear in her voice, and it was all Theo could do not to cradle her to him. He knew she would push him away. Any sympathy right now would likely be the undoing of her. She continued, still in those hard and emotionless tones.

"After a while I gave up fighting. It only egged him on anyway and usually ended up the worse for me, so I let him have his way. There was nothing I could do, and I was already tainted. Even if a man offered for me, the first time he tried to consummate the marriage he would know and then I'd be ruined all over again.

"I stopped going out, stopped mixing with anyone. I only attended those dances I could not get out of, and the last time he found me was at the engagement ball for the Marquis of Stroud.

"This time we were discovered, on the terrace I might add…" a humourless laugh escaped her lips at the recollection. "…I begged for help, but he persuaded them I had thrown myself at him.

"They ignored my bruised face and torn clothes. I think I fainted, and recall waking in his carriage. He grunted something about paying the price for my foolish tongue, and the next thing I remember was waking up at home, days later."

Grace took a deep breath, and Theo started to speak, appalled at the heinous treatment of this trusting young woman. She shook her head.

"I haven't finished. I've said this much, please let me finish."

He could see it was taking all her self-discipline not to break down, so he just nodded and let her continue.

"They knew. The whole household knew what he did and hadn't been able to stop him. He dumped me on the doorstep and fled like the cur he is. My parents and brother came home, apparently horror-struck at the scandal, and took themselves off to the country leaving instructions forbidding me to follow.

"Not long after, I was unwell for a week or so and when the doctor examined me, he informed me I was expecting a child. The one time he spent himself inside of me, how ironic." Tears began to roll down her cheeks, but Grace scrubbed them away angrily, she would not cry.

"I had no one to help, only the few staff left by my family. I believe one of them wrote to my mother but still no one came. I carried that babe for nine months. I felt it move and began to hope something good might come from the whole debacle — and no, I definitely was not going to apprise *him* of my condition. He had not been back since the night we were discovered, and I never want to see him again.

"I have little recollection of the birth, except it was difficult. The babe died. I did not find out until weeks later because I succumbed to infection and fever. When they thought I was well enough to be told, the doctor explained the birth was so traumatic, it was unlikely I would ever carry another child. It was strange to hear, and I knew I ought to feel sad, but my overriding emotion was one of relief."

Unaware of how tightly she was gripping Theo's hand, Grace fought for control, her distress almost tangible.

"I presume my brother paid for the upkeep of the house, more because he did not want to lose a city residence than in any concern for me. I realised I might need to find my own way in the world and had been mulling over whether there was any hope of me attracting a benefactor. Someone who might be prepared, if he could ignore the scandal, to keep me as his mistress. In such circumstances I presumed there would be no questions over my innocence.

"My other option was a brothel, but perhaps I'm already too old to be a courtesan. Even then I'm uncertain I could allow a man to..." Grace paused. The self-disgust, which always enveloped her when she recalled what Huntington had done, making her nauseous. Forcing it aside she continued, "...do that again. Although if there are others like him, they probably prefer an unwilling whore."

She bowed her head, humiliation flooding through her. Theo didn't react, he waited, aware she wasn't done. After a moment she lifted her head raising her eyes to his.

"I was so shocked when I was granted this boon, this home away from the city, where no one knows me, and where I hoped to begin my life anew. It was surreal, but in a good way. Then, once here, I met you and for a brief moment pretended I was like every other woman, unsullied by her past, and able to love without fear of rejection.

"It was a false hope, for now you know the truth you must see you cannot risk having your name connected with mine. But your kindness for the short time I have enjoyed it, and that almost kiss will be enough to last me a lifetime. You will never know how much it means to me."

CHAPTER 15

Theo began to extricate his hand from hers. To Grace, even though it was what she expected, his action was akin to a blow and she felt herself recoil.

She was surprised when, instead of getting up and walking away, he turned her to face him, cupping his hands around her cheeks. She couldn't look at him, fearful of what she would see in his face, of what he was about to say.

His voice with its rich deep tones, wrapped itself around her, and his words compassionate but not patronising or judgemental.

"My beautiful Grace, I cannot begin to imagine the heartache you have suffered with no one to love or support you. No one to end the pain you were subjected to, or to believe in you. You have intrigued me since first I saw you across a crowded ballroom, clinging to the shadows. I thought to approach you, to beg just one dance, but you would vanish, and for a time I wondered whether you were an illusion.

"After that night, even when you had disappeared completely, the rumours kept circling and I knew any attempt to call upon you would be rebuffed. Your family, you, did not know me and I presumed they were trying to protect you from the gossipmongers. I wish I had known the truth.

"The story your aunt told me was much the same as the one you have just shared. She was desperately worried for you but was informed you had gone abroad. She believed you were being cared for."

Grace jerked her head up at this, her mouth forming a bewildered 'O', the tears she was determined would never fall, brimming onto dark lashes.

His heart clenched.

"Th-th-they told h-her I w-was abroad?" she stammered. Her voice rose in shock as her shoulders slumped. *No wonder no one came. They must have thought she had been sent to Europe to escape the gossip.* "I-I c-c-can't believe they d-d-did this to me. I was a-all alone."

All at once, it was too much, and she could fight her distress no longer. The tears spilled over and her whole body was racked with sobs. She made a half-hearted attempt to move away. Theo took no notice and pulled her to him, curving one arm around her back and tucking her head into his neck.

Giving up, she let go and rested against him, discovering, now she had started to cry she couldn't stop. Two long years of loneliness and despair, abandoned by those she presumed loved her, and ostracised by everyone else.

Theo let her cry it out, doing nothing other than hold her, while stroking her hair. When she showed no signs of stopping, he became concerned she would make herself ill if she couldn't control her sobs.

"Come on, sweetheart, you need to try to gather yourself or you will become unwell. Take a deep breath…" waiting while Grace tried to do as instructed, aware hysteria tickled the edge of her senses, "…that's it, and another."

Her shuddering breaths tore at his soul. She sounded utterly wretched. In an attempt to divert her, Theo began to speak, reminding her she had a home here, with people who wanted to tend to her needs, and friends who cared for her well-being. His words soothed her and slowly, she began to regain her composure.

Theo still held her, and Grace revelled in the comfort his embrace brought her, amazed she could cope with such close contact and not panic.

When she felt able to speak without stuttering, she lifted her head from his shoulder. "Thank you, Theo, for your generous words and your gentle touch. It is long since I enjoyed or was comfortable with either."

Theo smiled his slow sweet smile, the dark mahogany of his eyes mesmerising, and she was unable to tear her gaze away.

"You have more than my words and my touch Grace, you have me. You will always have me."

He cupped his hand around the back of her head and brushed his lips over hers. Her heart fluttered and although she wanted more, much more, fear of how she would react held her back.

"You scarcely know me," she murmured.

"I know your face never leaves my thoughts. You have surmounted odds, which would bring a lesser person to their knees. You are kind and considerate of others." He began unpinning her hair.

A shiver vibrated down her spine, and she realised it was not borne of dread.

"Your eyes are like burnished amber, and I desire greatly to run my fingers through your hair while I kiss you until you forget everything except how much you mean to me."

Whilst Theo had given up trying to persuade himself, he wasn't in love with Grace, he didn't want to scare her with so important a revelation — not until she believed his intentions were true.

Her lustrous hair fell loose, and his breath caught. He wove his fingers through its silky length and drew her face back to his. "Oh Grace," it sounded like a prayer. Theo kissed her and this time it wasn't a brush, or a hint of a promise, this was a sensual caress.

Tentatively Grace moved her mouth under his, having no experience of how to respond. Familiar tendrils of heat circled around her body. Just as she was growing accustomed to this sensation, Theo broke away and stared at her.

"Grace…?"

She stared back.

"Grace would this be your first proper kiss?"

She bit her lip, a delicate pink staining her cheeks, and she nodded wordlessly.

"He never…"

She shook her head, still unable to speak and feeling totally unsophisticated. Here was she a woman of five and twenty and never been kissed. Honestly, he would think her pathetic.

A note of wonder underlined his question. "I am the first?"

Grace shifted uncomfortably under his gaze. *What did he want from her, a written declaration?* She found her voice. "No, Theo, I've never been kissed," her tones stilted. "He wasn't interested in the finer points of lovemaking and to be honest I'm…" she never finished her sentence.

With a groan, Theo re-captured her lips. His kiss, gentle as the breeze, reignited the warmth which had begun to fade.

Grace stopped trying to figure out how this kissing business worked and, letting instinct take over, relaxed into

Theo's arms. Following his lead, she allowed the kiss to deepen, her body reacting in a way she could never have imagined. Delectable quivers rippled through her and unable to help herself she whimpered.

Abruptly, Theo drew back, searching her face. "Am I going too fast? I do not wish to frighten you. You must tell me to stop if I do."

Grace shook her head, incapable of speech, bringing his face back down to hers. This time he wasn't quite so gentle and as their kiss intensified, Grace felt a wondrous emotion building, the whole of her body was tingling. This was so very different from how the duke made her feel.

Her hands went through Theo's hair as her arms went around his neck holding him to her and, seemingly of its own volition, her body arched towards him.

She wanted to feel him, all of him, against her and, bearing in mind her past experiences, the practical half of her tried to fathom how on earth this could be happening while the other half didn't actually care.

They ended up full length on the rug, still kissing and, to Grace, it was almost dreamlike. Theo's lips were weaving some kind of spell over her. Her behaviour might be seen as wanton, but she was powerless to stop it and wasn't sure she wanted to.

Their passion escalated as Theo's fingers stroked along her jaw, down her throat and fluttered across her neck. Tenderly, his lips followed his fingers and the feather-light touch on her warm skin made her shiver in response.

This need to touch him, to feel him, warred with Grace's innate shyness, and her extreme aversion to any form of physical contact. Need won and, keeping one hand cupped around the back of Theo's head her fingers entangled in his thick hair, Grace hesitantly slid her other hand over his shoulder and along his arm, slowly tracing the muscles under his snowy white shirt, his skin, through the fine material, warm against her cool fingers.

She felt his heart rate skyrocket and heard his breathing hitch. Smiling, she stroked her fingers back up his arm and over his chest, loosening his cravat and just brushing the skin at his neckline before trailing down towards his stomach.

Then, more than anything, she wanted his lips back on her mouth, so when he lifted his head from his delectable exploration of her neck, she kissed him with an ardour she thought would never be hers.

Theo, his body thrumming with desire for the woman in his arms, fought to regain some kind of control. Grace was such a contradiction. Her behaviour was that of an innocent, for although she had suffered carnal abuse at the hands of her tormentor, she had no knowledge of the process of making love.

He feared she might panic if he didn't take this steadily. More than this, he wanted to court her properly, to prove to her not all men were scoundrels, simply taking what they wanted without redress. Hard as this was going to be for him, it would be worth it.

Reluctantly, he broke their kiss, lifting himself up on one elbow and twisting a bright strand of her hair through his fingers.

"Much as I desire to ignore all reason, and seduce you here in this picturesque setting, I prefer to take this slowly and enjoy a proper courtship, which is what I was, apparently rather clumsily, alluding to the other night. Do you think that is something you might consider?" He held her eyes, damp from her tears, willing her to believe in him.

Grace stretched up her hand, resting it against his cheek.

"Theo, in less than two weeks you have turned my world upside down. You have reached the part of me I thought buried so deep it was lost forever. Much as I long to be with you, to get to know you, to…" she blushed again "…to feel your lips on mine and be wrapped in your arms, do you not realise, if you step out with me, you open yourself up to scandal? Would it not be easier if I were to become your mistress? That way, when you meet a woman who would be a much more suitable wife, you are free to marry."

Theo frowned, caught off guard. Not the response he expected and about to chide her for suggesting such a thing, he paused. This was Grace. She had already been shunned and, having borne the brunt of vicious tongues, knew how hurtful they could be. She was giving him the choice. Her concern for his good name, more important than her own happiness.

"Grace, I do not want you to be my mistress. If this feeling, this connection, I believe is growing between us is real, I want it all and I refuse to allow you to belittle yourself. I would be proud to have you walk alongside me, your arm through mine. I cannot think of anything I would like more…" smiling down at her, "…well actually yes I can, but that is another matter entirely."

Grace felt hot colour rush up her face.

Theo leant close to brush her lips with his. "You have done nothing of which you ought to be ashamed. The shame is how you have been treated not just by him, but by the rest of society and most especially your family.

"All I ask is the chance to prove I am here for you. I will not abandon you or treat you with anything less than the respect you deserve." His gentle smile softened the formality of his words. "Oh, and if you are agreeable, I would very much like to be able to kiss you any time I like."

He stroked his large hand along her flushed cheeks, grazing her bottom lip with his thumb. An innocent gesture, yet she could feel herself thawing.

Her defences were crumbling.

Was it worth the risk?

Dare she take this chance?

She lifted herself up, so they were face to face, and their eyes locked, dark chocolate on molten amber.

"Are you sure you are prepared for what I know will come? There will be whispers and rumours. I would be devastated if you lost your good name because of me."

"Are you prepared to step out with a lowly country doctor? You are the daughter of a baron."

"And while you may be a country doctor, Theo Elliott, you are certainly not lowly and also the second son of a marquis. What of your mother and brother? They may not be so understanding."

Theo smiled, his lips curving in a way which made her heart thud. "I believe you will discover my family are not easily swayed by scandal-mongers and those who seek to malign others with…"

"Yes, but in my case, the gossips only speak the truth, Theo. He *did* ruin me. Thankfully they do not know how many times and it will be years, if ever, before I am free of the stigma." Grace interrupted, her voice dropping, the dream beginning to dissolve.

"It was a beautiful dream, but the reality is closer to a nightmare. How can I expose you and your family to such a thing?"

"Grace, love, you need to trust me. I do not make promises lightly and I promise you, we have a future. I already knew much of what you endured, and it only served to make me want to know you better. Quite frankly, I'm not sure I can ever let you go."

His last sentence did it. When he uttered those simple yet heartfelt words, everything else fell away.

Grace blinked, those pesky tears were gathering again,

sucked in a convulsive breath and decided to take a leap of faith.

"While I think your argument impossibly naive, I also find it persuasive. If you care so much, you are prepared to risk everything to be with me, it would be churlish of me not to let you." She smiled then and to Theo it was like the sun breaking through a storm.

"So, Miss Grace Aldeburgh, I believe we have an accord," he grinned.

"Dr Theo Elliott, I believe we do." Grace replied and reached her hand out to his "Shake."

Theo shook his head.

"I have a better way to seal the deal," he muttered and kissed her.

CHAPTER 16

Several heart stopping moments later, they came up for air. Theo, grinning like an idiot, suggested maybe they should at least try to eat the food Agnes had so kindly provided.

Grace was startled to realise she was hungry, having had little appetite earlier. Theo opened the basket and handed out all manner of treats in a very random fashion making Grace giggle, diffusing the tension lingering in the air.

"There's nowhere to put all this, Theo. Do be sensible and put the cake back for now. How on earth do you expect me to hold so much food in my hands?"

Theo lifted his head from the depths of the basket and handed her two plates saying if they weren't enough, to make good use of the napkins. "I'm not re-packing it, we'll have to eat it all and that's that. Right, where are those cups? Some more of this nectar will wash the food down nicely."

Refilling their two cups which had ended up on the wall, although neither remembered putting them there, Theo handed one to Grace. She had placed most of the goodies on two of the napkins, so was able to take the glass without spilling everything. They were quiet for a while, enjoying the food, finishing up with the rich fruitcake.

Replete, Grace lay back against the wall, her mind swirling with their conversation, and how much she had revealed. A burden of which she was hardly aware, had lifted, and she was conscious of a discernible lightening of spirit. While this was all running through her head and for no apparent reason, she remembered Jemima, a thought occurring to her.

"Theo." He glanced over. "Theo, my friend in London, Jemima, says she knows Billie and her husband — Jemima's not Billie's — was something to do with whatever happened last year with Lord Ashbourne." Raising her eyebrows in an unspoken question.

"Jemima Withers?" Theo asked. Grace nodded "Yes, Lucas Withers, her husband was the man who proved Billie could not have set fire to her family home. He was also with us in London when we foiled Billie's cousin's plot to steal confidential documents."

Grace grimaced.

"Why?"

"She is the only other person who knows something of my past, well except *him*. So now I have shared it with two and I am not convinced telling you was the best idea, although I must admit to some relief.

"It is exhausting constantly watching what I say in case I inadvertently mention something which leads others to question who I am. Please remember I am Fitzgerald here in Oak Stanton, not Aldeburgh. 'Tis name with too many bad memories."

Theo smiled gently in understanding, his eyes crinkling, making her insides melt.

Trying not to get distracted she continued. "Anyway, I believe she, Jemima that is, will write to Billie."

"Would that be such a bad thing?" Theo asked, compassionately.

"Of course, it would. I have only just met her and she's so charming and kindness itself, but once people know they change. Not everyone is as empathetic as you, Theo. Neither do I want my history bandying about the village. I came here to start afresh. The less anyone knows, the happier I will be.

"My cousin has no idea what happened, although how he could possibly have avoided hearing about it is beyond me. He did ask me, but I cannot tell him yet. I may never tell him, but I think he is worried about me."

Grace became anxious again, the thought of more people knowing upskittling her.

Theo remembered his conversation with Giles and Billie the previous Saturday afternoon. He debated whether to admit the earl and his wife knew, and Billie had already received a letter from Jemima.

Taking her hand, Theo confessed, "You have to stop panicking, and I need to be honest with you. I mentioned a little of what I knew to Giles before your arrival. In the last few days, Billie has since coaxed it out of him. I know also she has received a letter from Jemima. Billie scolded me roundly for not telling her, she was terribly upset for you."

Grace stared at him in consternation, and began to speak, but he put his finger against her lips, effectively hushing her.

"Grace, I did not know what else to do. At that stage we had yet to meet, and your great aunt had died, leaving you a sizeable house with no one to run it. I realised you might require help and support as you settled in.

"Giles runs a large home, a huge estate, and manages a multitude of people. He understands what is needed. I have a small home and, while I am able to organise many things, staff and horses are not usually part of my purview."

He took a deep breath. "I gave him the barest outline. I have known Giles all of my life. I trust him and he trusts me. In that regard, I also trust Billie. She is the soul of discretion and, unless you decide to take her into your confidence, she will continue to behave towards you the same way she has begun. Billie hasn't a hurtful bone in her body and knows a little of what it is like to be gossiped about.

"The scandalmongers would have had her up for murder last year, declaring she set the fire so she could run away with her lover. At the same time, they were maligning her name, she was injured and ill with fever, with no memory of who she was and how she came to be near Whiteoaks. She was lucky Giles found her when he did, for I doubt she would have survived another night in the cold."

Holding her hand against his chest in much the same was as he had done the previous day, Theo concluded. "We all respect your desire for privacy but, at some point, you are going to have to have faith not everyone wishes you harm."

Grace searched his face for any sign of deception but could find none. Theo was right. She had to learn to trust again, but it was so hard. It had taken long enough with Jemima, and here she hoped it would never come up, that her life could begin again. Well perhaps it could, but she had to start by being honest with herself.

"Will you help me, Theo?" she whispered. "I think somewhere along the line, I lost myself and, although I accept, I have to begin to live again, I'm not sure I know how, or even have the strength to do it on my own."

Theo pulled her close, encircling her within his embrace. Kissing the top of her head, he murmured, "Why, Grace Fitzgerald, there is nothing I would like more."

She smiled at his words and brushed his cheek with her

lips. He turned at the last second and captured her mouth. With a sigh which seemed to come from her very core, she gave in and sank into his kiss. Theo kissed her until she was breathless and wanting more.

Wise to her history, he did not want to push it. There had been too many revelations, too much emotion lurked near the surface, and he wanted Grace to remember this day with fondness not with grief.

Breaking the kiss, he settled them both back against the wall. Curving one arm around her shoulder, he gathered her against him, reaching across with his other hand to interweave his fingers with those of the slender woman beside him.

Grace twisted slightly to look at him. She didn't want to let him out of her sight. He had become vitally important to her. Her whole body warmed when she looked at him, and when he smiled at her it was as though she was the only woman in the world.

Was such a thing even possible after, what was it, ten days? Grace didn't know, and she wasn't naive enough to assume all was rosy, but it was a wondrous start.

The afternoon was hot, but they were in the shade of the abbey. It was peaceful. Everything was still, not even a breeze rustled through the trees. Grace gazed out over the countryside.

The heat created a haze, the landscape slightly indistinct, as though a web of fine gossamer had been flung over it. In the field beyond where they were sitting, she could see golden ears of wheat or barley, standing tall, ready for late harvesting. She could stare at this view forever.

"What are you thinking about?" asked Theo, watching her eloquent face.

"I'm thinking I cannot believe how blessed I am. And, much as I could sit here with you and admire this view until the end of my days, I think we should probably think about setting off for home. Do you even know what time it is?"

To her surprise, Theo withdrew a watch-fob from his waistcoat pocket. Grace had only seen one or two. They were somewhat of a luxury item, although of late were becoming more popular.

"It was a gift from my father when I became a doctor," he explained modestly, when he saw her expression. "It helps when I am checking a heart rate."

"Not to mention it tells you the time," she grinned. "It is splendid, Theo. Please may I take a look?" Grace studied the miniature timepiece, turning it in her hand to admire the delicate pattern etched on the reverse and the simple yet elegant clock face.

"A most thoughtful gift," she said returning it to its owner, who dropped it back into his pocket. "Would it be presumptuous to ask, maybe one day you might tell me of your father?"

Theo pressed a light kiss on her forehead. "I should be glad to. I will save it for our next sojourn, for you are correct, the day is nearly over, and tomorrow you will be very busy."

Grace had forgotten she was accompanying Giles and Billie to the stud and a thrill ran through her at the thought of buying horses.

"Oh, it had flown out of my mind that I have call on my time on the morrow. I blame you." She chuckled at Theo's affronted face. "Well, if you hadn't distracted me by suggesting a picnic in this picturesque setting in order to hear my sorry tale uninterrupted, you..."

Her words were cut short because Theo captured her mouth, the touch of his lips making her tremble. Her arms went around his neck and he drew her tightly against him.

She could feel how much he wanted her, but he did no more than kiss her. Mind you, he did that until she was reeling, and was very pleased they were still sitting on the rug… her legs felt more than a little wobbly.

"By all that's sacred, Grace, you enthral me," his breathing was ragged. "I think it would be sensible if we were to leave before my baser instincts get the better of me." The deep brown of his eyes had darkened almost to black and Grace could feel the rapid tattoo of his heart, matched no doubt by her own.

He took a steadying breath, and released his hold, stroking one finger along her cheek as he did, making her own breath catch. After a long moment they collected themselves, packing everything into the basket and folding the rug neatly.

Grace pinned her hair into some semblance of order and put on the despised bonnet, tying the ribbons loosely, before slinging her shawl over her shoulders, while Theo shrugged back into his tailcoat. The pair making sure they looked the picture of respectability.

Theo's horse standing patiently in the shade nickered on their approach. Theo stroked the mare's nose, crooning to her.

"There we are my beauty. I'm sorry we made you wait for so long." Palming an apple he plucked from the basket, he let the horse munch through its crisp juiciness.

Sliding the rug and basket under the bench seat, he helped Grace into the gig, then climbed up beside her, chancing a quick squeeze of her knee when he took the reins.

The return ride did not take long and they didn't talk, content to enjoy the quiet of the waning afternoon. Too soon, they reached The Gables. Grace was loath to say goodbye to Theo, unsure after spending all day with her, he would want to stay for dinner.

Theo held her hand while she stepped down. They stood facing each other, his warm fingers caressing hers, and it seemed to Grace he was reluctant to leave.

"Thank you, Doctor Elliott. The patience and solicitude you have shown me today has been a balm to my aching soul, and I am very much looking forward to our next encounter." *Altogether formal and polite, good effort, Grace,* she thought.

"Likewise, Miss Fitzgerald," Theo replied. Smiling that sweet smile, his eyes twinkling.

Throwing good intentions to the winds she bent a little closer and whispered, "I would invite you to return for dinner if I didn't think it should make me seem too bold."

"I would accept if it didn't make me look too eager," came the murmured reply.

She stepped back and gazed at him. He inclined his head ever-so slightly, and her heart thudded.

"Would you?"

"I should be overjoyed."

"I'll see you soon then, shall we say seven?"

"Sounds perfect." As casually as possible, Theo hopped back up onto the seat and clicked the horse. Trotting off towards his house he glanced back once to see Grace watching him leave.

He raised a hand and she dipped her head, a smile pulling at the corner of her mouth. She was so beautiful, the joy he felt in her company was inexplicable. *Honestly, Theo,* he admonished himself, *act your age. You're supposed to be a respectable country doctor, not a lovesick boy.*

CHAPTER 17

Grace floated into the house, the smile teasing her lips. Then, not wanting to upset Agnes, hurried along to the kitchens to advise her cook, Dr Elliott would be returning for dinner and at the same time, asking Polly and Becca to draw her a bath.

A relaxing hour later, she was downstairs having enjoyed a long hot soak, dressed in a gown the colour of which could only be described as warm cinnamon. The unusual shade complimented her hair, now neatly curled and twisted into a fashionable style under the nimble fingers of Polly.

Grace had butterflies in her stomach and realised she was looking forward to the evening for, while she accepted much was to do with her burgeoning affection for the doctor, she knew it was also because she actually relished his company. He was intelligent, funny and interested in hearing her opinion on any number of matters.

In the two years before her arrival in Oak Stanton and, except for rare afternoons with Jemima, Grace could count on the fingers of one hand how often she engaged in lively conversation.

For the last ten days she had done nothing but. Starting with the evening of the funeral, when she chatted with Billie, Giles and Theo as though they had known each other for a lifetime.

She checked the dining room. It looked very welcoming, the candelabra were ready to be lit, the table laid for two. In fact, much as it had been the previous night, although this time the settings were somewhat closer. Grace smiled to herself when she noticed this subtle change.

Satisfied everything was in order, she went along to the Snug and, uncaring it was not in any way ladylike, curled up in one of the large comfortable chairs with a book.

The soft warm air wafting through the French doors was perfumed with honeysuckle, its relaxing fragrance, along with a day in the fresh air caught up with her, and within minutes she had fallen asleep.

Theo knocked on the front door of The Gables promptly at seven. He was admitted by Evans, who explained in decorous tones, Miss Fitzgerald was currently indisposed and if the doctor wouldn't mind waiting a moment, he would advise her of the arrival of her guest.

Theo chuckled and asked whether Miss Fitzgerald was, in fact, asleep.

Evans and the doctor were well acquainted, so the former had no qualms about confirming this was the case. Theo patted the butler on the shoulder, saying he would do the honours, sauntering through to the Snug, whistling under his breath.

He entered the room, spying Grace curled up in the chair. Her dress tucked up under her feet, her head pillowed on her hand, and the book open on her lap. She looked like a child.

How so tall a woman could make herself so small was beyond him.

The sight of her never failed to take his breath away, and he shook his head at the thought of anyone telling her she was ugly or ungainly or that her hair was anything other than glorious. His opinion might well have been ever-so slightly coloured by his feelings, but there was no denying, Grace was an attractive woman.

He settled himself in the chair next to hers and watched her sleep. Running an experienced eye over her features, Theo surmised her face was much less pale than it was when she first arrived.

Surreptitiously, Agnes had apprised the doctor, Grace's appetite — undoubtedly owing in the main to days spent working in the garden — had improved which, combined with the clean country air was giving her skin a healthy glow.

After several minutes of scrutiny, Theo decided he ought to wake her, and rested his hand lightly on her knee. Grace came awake immediately, shrinking back in the chair, until she realised who was in the room with her.

"Oh, Dr El … Theo. Please forgive me, how unpardonable to fall asleep when I am expecting a guest!" Slightly disconcerted from her reaction, Grace stood and brushed her skirts out, patting her hair to make sure it was still relatively tidy.

"Grace, please sit. It is I who should apologise. I did not mean to give you a fright." Theo stood when she did, and now took her hand in his.

Her fingers were trembling, and though she showed no other outward sign of fear, he knew its cause. "I am not he, Grace. He does not know where you are. You are safe here. I will not let any harm come to you."

"I… it's just… after…" she took a breath. "'Tis irrational,

but I expect him to appear out of nowhere, like he used to. Coming to claim what he believes is his."

Theo, uncaring it was simply not done, pulled her close, wrapping his strong arms around her, cradling her to him.

"You are nobody's property, Grace but if you allow him to dominate your thoughts, your life this way, he has won. I hope you are free of him, but much as I would like to, I cannot say you will never again cross paths. Now, you have me, and Billie and Giles, and Jemima and Lucas, and Ralph and Duncan…"

Theo carried on, naming all who had been helping her, along with the whole of her staff. "Do you, for one minute, think *any* of us will permit some craven coward to spoil your life?"

"But he's a duke."

"So what? His title does not give him the right to abuse young women and get away with it." Blithely ignoring the fact, many men of the elite often did precisely that, although not usually to the extent Huntington had done. "Come, let us enjoy our meal without worrying about anything other than which horses you are going to buy tomorrow."

Her face lit up at the prospect. Theo was relieved to see her love of horses diverted Grace for the time being, although he did notice the odd shadow cross her face throughout the evening. *Damn Aldwych.*

Mentally making a note to write to Lucas Withers, and to plan his visit to Evan's cousin, Theo kept the conversation light, and by the end of the meal Grace was back to her usual self.

Dinner over, they retired to the Snug. Without asking what they preferred, Evans brought in a tumbler of whisky for

Theo and a small glass of port for Grace along with two hot chocolates.

"It seems already we are predictable," giggled Grace when the butler left the room. Theo chuckled and commented if it meant her staff was comfortable with his presence, predictable was fine by him.

She gazed at him. The doctor was standing by the candelabra on the mantelpiece, trying to light a cigar, giving Grace a chance to study him unobserved

Probably too tall and thin — what was the new term people had started to use, lanky, a word which made her want to laugh, it sounded so odd — to be considered handsome in the conventional sense, Grace thought his angular features, softened in the gentle glow of the candlelight, arresting.

She wanted to trace her fingers along his jaw and smooth her hand over his cheek. She wanted to watch his eyes darken and she really, really wanted him to kiss her again. Lost in reverie and not realising he had moved from the hearth, she jumped, nearly spilling her port, when she became aware Theo was sitting next to her and asking her a question.

"Oh, so sorry, I was… errm…" she blushed, and shyness threatened to overtake her. Theo smiled and said it was of no consequence. Leaning back in the chair, he sipped his whisky.

Grace continued watching him from under her lashes. It was as though she needed to imprint his face into her mind, not that she could ever forget what he looked like. They sat in companionable silence for a while, the peace of the room soothing Grace's tumbling senses.

For want of anything better to say she asked, "Are you still accompanying us tomorrow, to the stud?"

"I am," Theo replied, grinning. "Mother still needs a horse."

"Oh, yes silly of me. I don't really know why I asked." Grace fumbled her words and found she couldn't look at Theo, painfully aware of him sitting so close, yet he may as well have been a mile away, suddenly the distance seemed huge.

"Grace?" he quizzed.

"'Tis nothing, pay me no mind..." she trailed off, and without warning shot out through the doors into the garden, needing the darkness to hide her hot cheeks.

She was hopeless. How did this courting thing work? Was she allowed to touch him first, or did she have to wait for him? How was it that she desperately wanted him to kiss her, yet seemed unable to enunciate it, without sounding like a simpleton, or worse a strumpet? Oh, it was the very devil.

Theo, somewhat bemused, placed his glass on the little side table, and followed her outside.

"Grace, is something amiss?"

"I don't know, this is all so new. I don't know what is expected or how to behave. I don't know whether the things I want to say or do are acceptable, and I dare not ask for seeming addled."

Her hands were fluttering with nerves. "I'm sorry Theo, I never used to be such a pathetic excuse for a woman. I was confident and impetuous. I laughed all the time, and always knew what to say. I want to be that person again, but I fear she is buried too deeply ever to be found."

"I beg your pardon but I'm at a loss here. What is it you want to say or do which bothers you so?"

Taking a deep breath, Grace answered. "If we are indeed courting, how does it work? I know there are rules, but I do not remember what they are, and when you are near, the oddest notions disturb me. For so long I have believed this," she waved her hand between them, "was never something I needed to concern myself with, and I do not wish to overstep the bounds of propriety."

Annoyed with herself for sounding feebleminded, Grace began to stride along the gloomy pathways.

Theo watched her for a moment, trying to get his thoughts in order, anger at those who allowed this woman to be so badly neglected, once more gnawing at him.

"Grace…"

She continued to march.

"Grace!" He spoke a little louder. She came to a halt and stared at him, her face pale in the moonlight. "Grace, please come here."

There was a moment's hesitation, before she walked over to where he stood on the terrace.

"Tell me what it is you really want."

She muttered something, but he didn't catch it.

"What did you say?" He heard her draw a huge sigh.

"I want to hold your hand, and stroke your cheek, and trace your jawline, and I would very much like to kiss you. But I'm almost sure none of it is perm…"

The rest of her words were lost when Theo's lips stole hers and his arms enclosed her. Unable to help herself, she moaned and opened herself to him, heat spiralling through her.

With one arm Theo held her close, while his other hand began to trail along her body, gently exploring and caressing, but tentatively, so as not to frighten her.

Grace, convinced she was melting, gave herself over to the irresistible sensations Theo was inducing. His lips, so cool and firm, moved from her mouth down her neck and across her shoulder, scattering feather light kisses over her warm skin.

A tremor ran through her as her arms — which so far had

hung limply at her sides — lifted, seemingly of their own accord, to wrap around his back.

Theo's head was spinning. This wasn't how he wanted to handle it. He was determined to take it cautiously, steadily, but when Grace was close, his good intentions were turned upside down.

He could feel their passion building. He had to stop this madness, but her perfume was so alluring, and her body felt sublime, fitting against his frame perfectly. It was as though he'd been waiting for her, for this moment, his whole life.

Reluctantly, he broke their kiss.

"Nooooo," he heard Grace whimper.

"I must, sweetheart," he murmured, his breathing erratic. "Although I would dearly like this to continue, I do not wish to rush you. Let us take our time and enjoy the journey. I think the destination will be very much worth it."

Grace raised her head to look at him, pleased to note, even in the dim light, she could see how dark his eyes had become and feel how fast his heart was beating.

"It's just, I really like kissing you," she muttered. "You make my body tingle all the way from my head to my toes." Silence, then, "Oh, that was a tad audacious of me."

Theo chuckled, and rested his head on hers.

Standing like this, with his arms around her, she felt safe.

"I am very pleased, my love because you have the same effect on me."

Grace's head snapped up and she locked eyes with him, her own wide with shock.

"What? Now what did I do?"

"D-d-did you just say what I think you said?" she stammered, a thread of hope beginning to glimmer.

"I believe I did. Do you mind?" He smiled his irresistible smile, and her heart thudded in response.

"Mind? It is the most wonderful thing I have ever heard. Might I be so bold as to ask you to say it again?"

"With pleasure, my love."

Completely ignoring what he had just said about taking it slowly, Grace pulled his head back down to hers and kissed him.

CHAPTER 18

The next morning Grace woke, as had become her habit, with the dawn chorus and, despite the early hour, felt as though she slept more soundly than she had for years and had no desire to go back to sleep.

She snuggled under the covers, listening to the beautiful avian melodies, letting her mind wander back over the remainder of last evening.

After Theo's astonishing declaration, they stood wrapped together for a long time, holding each other, savouring the closeness. Grace couldn't believe he had said it and even though it was far too soon for so momentous an admission, and much as she wanted to, she could not say it back to him.

It wasn't that she didn't reciprocate his feelings. In truth she acknowledged she was head over heels in love with Theo, but everything was happening moderately quickly — all right, with extraordinary rapidity.

Moreover, much as the promise of living happily ever

after appealed, that only happened in fairy tales. Her life was anything but a fairy tale. Then again, recalling the stories she had read as a child, some were very dark — hers would be one of those.

Shaking her head to rid it of such flightiness, Grace pondered the day ahead. Choosing horses aside, it was another whole day in Theo's company, only this time Billie and Giles would be there also. *Would Theo show his hand? Did he really mean he would be honoured to have her by his side?*

She deemed him sincere, but their relationship was new, and he may not wish anyone else to know yet. She would have to wait and see. Years of burying her feelings had made her adept at maintaining a dispassionate façade. Until recently showing any emotion at all was a rare phenomenon.

Pushing back the covers, she grabbed her dressing gown and slid her feet into soft house slippers. Padding down to the kitchen, she found Agnes preparing for the day, and Evans polishing his shoes.

"Good morning, Agnes, Evans," she smiled. "I wondered whether there might be enough hot water for a cup of tea?"

Agnes smiled back and, after bidding her mistress a good morning in return, affirmed Evans would bring one to her in a jiffy. Grace thanked them and said she would be in her usual spot. Walking along to the Snug, she opened the French doors, before turning one of the chairs to face the garden and curling up in its leather comfort.

A hot tea and a thorough wash later, Grace was dressed ready for the day. With absolutely no intention of purchasing a horse she hadn't trialled, she wore a riding habit rather than a travelling gown, hoping the others understood her choice of outfit.

Munching through a suitably filling breakfast, Grace gave herself a stern talking to about behaving with poise in front of the earl and countess. An exhortation wasted the instant she saw Theo, when he arrived on the stroke of nine, and smiled at her. Her legs trembled like one of Agnes' jellies, and her heart tripped.

Seriously, Grace, she chided internally, *you are like a debutante having her first tendre.* Saying she would join him momentarily, Grace hurried to the kitchen to say goodbye to her staff. Having already apprised them of her plans, they were startled when she burst through kitchen door.

"Please take today as an extra day off. The weather is beautiful, and I would prefer you got the benefit of some free time than be stuck indoors. Evans, would you be so kind as to apprise Matt and Gibbs? Soon it will be too inclement for such things. Do not bother about the evening meal either, Agnes. If I am hungry when I get home, I will be able to fix myself something. Now promise me you will?"

She held their eyes as she entreated them, and they nodded. Becca and Polly grinned from ear to ear.

"Thank you, Miss, 'tis me brother's birthday so 'tis, and he'll be that excited to see me. Means Polly can come too." Becca curtseyed, and Grace smiled at the two cousins.

"I'm so glad, Becca and you too Polly. I trust you will all have a lovely day and I shall see you later, hopefully with horses." Then she flew back to where Theo was waiting patiently at the front door, picking up her riding cloak and another detested bonnet — both of which were laid ready — as she passed. He raised an eyebrow on her approach.

"Giving my staff the day off," she grinned. "You would think it was Christmas."

Theo chuckled. When she reached his side, he took her hand, and drew her to him, kissing her lightly on the lips. She gazed into his eyes, breathing a little erratically.

"I wanted to say good morning properly," he said in answer to her unasked question.

"In that case…" she raised herself on her toes to kiss him

back. She felt his heart rate increase and smiled against his mouth. "…good morning to you too."

Theo hugged her and, offering her his arm, they strolled down to his carriage. Adam was driving, and he called a hello to Grace, as Theo helped her up.

~

The drive to Whiteoaks was over in the blink of an eye, or so it seemed to Grace who wanted more time with Theo. Nevertheless, her delight at the prospect of a day with Billie, and horses was enough to counteract her brief disappointment.

"How do we…? Is there…? Should we…" For the life of her, Grace could not get her mouth to form the words she wanted to say.

Theo seemed easily able to interpret her vague utterances. "You are worried about what, if anything, to say to Billie?" he asked. Grace nodded, blushing. Theo squeezed her hand and the warmth of his fingers through her gloves steadied her nerves. "How about we see how things unfold? If they realise something has changed between us, we tell them."

Grace bit her lip and nodded again.

As they drove through the huge gates onto Whiteoaks driveway, Theo risked another quick kiss. Grace batted at him. He grinned and whispered, "It's all right, love. No one's looking."

It was no use; she was defenceless against him. She gave up, relaxed, and smiled, turning her head to admire the house when it first came into view, as they swung around the long curve up to the courtyard.

The carriage rattled across the flags and, at the sound, Will and Jake came out of the stables, shouting a greeting to

Adam, who jumped down to drop the step. Theo climbed down, then held out his hand for Grace.

She gripped his hand more tightly than necessary, needing to gather strength from him. He rubbed his thumb lightly against her palm, immediately soothing her, and then relinquished his grasp, at the same moment as Billie flew through the door to catch Grace in a great hug.

"Grace! It seems like an age since we last spoke. Why I believe it is a week, an utter travesty and cannot be allowed to happen again. Come, Giles is concluding something with one of his stewards, and then we shall set out."

Dragging Grace along with her, Billie whirled along to the library, where hot coffee awaited them. The rich aroma was heavenly and the three sipped the brew with relish. Several minutes later Giles strode in, his eyes searching out his wife at whom he smiled before greeting the other two.

Grace had noticed this of the earl. Billie was his first thought whenever they had been apart even if only for a few minutes. This depth affection was unusual amongst those of the *ton* whom she knew.

Those who professed to care for their spouse were rarely seen together unless attending a social function. Even then, the men tended to congregate around the tables while the women gossiped with their friends. Grace liked the relaxed intimacy Billie and Giles shared. It was obvious they truly enjoyed each other's company.

The conversation swirled around her and Grace conceded not only did she want, nay yearn, for that same affinity, but also wished, quite desperately, for it to be with Theo.

She wanted to be his first thought every morning when he awoke, and his last thought at night before slumber claimed him. She wanted him to hurry to her when his work was completed, and not be embarrassed if, on a whim, she sought him out during the day simply because she wanted to speak with him or touch him or yes even kiss him. She knew many men kept mistresses, but the thought of him with another woman would be the finish of her.

She did not want a conventional relationship — or dare she hope, marriage — she wanted it to be ridiculously, irrationally, passionately and hopelessly, unconventional.

She raised her eyes, to see Theo watching her. Her heart hiccuped, and she felt warm colour bloom up her cheeks. He raised an eyebrow, and she shook her head imperceptibly, she might tell him later, if she felt brave enough.

Grace felt a smile tug at her lips, and when Giles declared it was time they left, Theo stretched out his hand. Without thinking she took it. The doctor drew her up from the chair, his own smile suggesting he knew exactly what she was thinking.

This little interaction did not go unnoticed by their hosts, who wisely kept their counsel, although Giles expected Billie to drag the tale from either or both of their friends before the end of the day.

It was a long time since Giles had seen his friend so happy, but he was worried the wounds, both physical and emotional, Grace had suffered might prevent them from finding contentment together. He hoped they could but only time would tell. That was for another day. Today was for horses.

Thomas appeared with a wrap for Billie, which he laid over her shoulders, before helping Giles shrug into his coat. Giles corralled them out to the courtyard where Will had the Winchester carriage waiting. Jake helped the ladies inside, before climbing up onto the driver's seat.

At the flick of the reins the two huge horses, Castor and

Pollux, clip-clopped down the driveway towards the main road. Billie and Grace began to talk about the day ahead, Grace asking all manner of questions about horse studs, never having been to one before.

Billie wasn't particularly knowledgeable, but Giles and Theo interjected here and there, and the journey passed almost without notice.

~

They entered the horse stud through an imposing gateway which looked to be straight out of a Roman fort, coming to a halt in a vast square, surrounded by stables. To Grace's inexperienced eye there looked to be hundreds, and was surprised when Giles informed her this was only the carriage horses.

The racehorses were stabled at the far side of the track, and the hunters were in a block a little further around the property. Giles strode over towards one of the doorways, and Grace found her attention being drawn to said track, visible through a gap in the buildings, where horses were being trained or trialled. The sound of hooves, although muted at this distance still echoed around the square.

The odour of warm animals mixed with hay and sawdust was so familiar to Grace, she fairly itched to get a proper look. Theo grinned at her expression, explaining Giles had gone to make their party known, and he expected a groom would appear momentarily to show them the available horses.

While they waited, Grace and Billie strolled over to the stalls. The animals looked huge but were actually no bigger than Castor and Pollux. Grace walked along the stables, observing each animal, they looked docile, a trait she assumed was preferred in carriage horses.

Selecting two would be difficult and, in truth, as long as Giles and Theo felt them suitable, any two would suffice. It was the thoroughbreds she wanted to see. Patience was something she had learned the hard way, and she tried to look interested. She had to admit, they were splendid creatures, and the grooms employed by this breeder obviously took great care of their charges.

Giles returned with two stable hands, who pointed out those horses currently for sale. There were so many and, to Grace all were admirable, making it too hard to choose She felt a little overwhelmed, and stood back to let the men negotiate the deal.

Nothing was finalised at this point, because they knew Grace wanted a horse for riding. It wasn't too far to the next stable block and, after sitting in the carriage, Grace was glad of the walk. They were all wearing sensible footwear and the pathways were properly flagged.

They rounded the building and got a better view of the track. Grace halted, spellbound by the magnificent creatures hurtling along it. Unable to help herself, she walked over the grass to the fence at the edge of the track and leant on it. The thunder of hooves was deafening here, and she was almost enveloped in the clouds of dust trailed behind the animals as they sped by.

She was entranced. This was what she had missed. The sight of these noble creatures at full gallop never failed to lift her heart, and she smiled in unaffected happiness. Theo, watching her from the pathway was enamoured by her animated countenance. *This* was the Grace they needed to bring back.

"Be careful, Theo," Giles cautioned his friend. "This could be a long haul."

Theo glanced at Giles, touched by his concern. "Do not worry, Giles. I am not an idiot. I have no intention of rushing anything. I know what I'm in for, and it will take as long as it takes."

"And if it takes a lifetime?"

"Then it will be worth the wait." Theo smiled at Giles and walked towards Grace. He called her name. She turned and beamed at him, their mirrored expressions making Giles catch his breath. He felt a small hand slip into his.

"Methinks it is too late to stop them, Giles," Billie smiled up at her tall husband. "Do not fret, I believe this is as it should be. You should trust Theo. He is a clever man you know." Giles stared down at Billie her green eyes sparkling in the sunlight. "Do you not wish him the same happiness we have?"

"I do, but I worry Grace has suffered too much to have faith he will not hurt her, that she won't let him get close, and ultimately break his heart." A conversation he never thought he'd be having, but this was his wife, and this was no longer an unusual topic.

"I think you might be surprised. Jemima said Grace is not frigid. Oh yes," seeing Giles was about to interrupt, "I imagine the thought of a man, well anyone for that matter, touching her is something with which she will take a long time to be comfortable. Jemima said it took almost a year for Grace to feel at ease enough to allow even the briefest of hugs — the girl has been thoroughly neglected. No, I believe 'tis more that she's lost inside herself, and mayhap Theo is the one to draw her back out."

Giles bent to kiss the woman, who less than a year ago turned his neatly ordered world upside down. He struggled with the upheaval she wrought, and they clashed several times before eventually landing on the same page. Who was to say it would be any different for Theo?

"I love you, my Willow."

She grinned at him and kissed him back, rather passionately to say they were in a large open space.

"I love you too, my Giles, and don't you think they," she waved her hand over to where Grace and Theo were walking along the fence line, "deserve the same? Let us just see how things unfold." Unknowingly echoing Theo's thoughts the night he lost his heart.

CHAPTER 19

Grace and Theo were chatting about the horses racing along beside them, Theo asking Grace what she wanted in her mount.

Not too spirited, but definitely not a quiet ride was Grace's answer. A good horsewoman, who could handle most horses expertly, she didn't want to fight with her mount every time they rode out.

Before either of them realised, they had walked to the end of the track, turning in time to see a huge thoroughbred gallop towards them. The rider turned the stallion at the last minute, and then thundered up the other side, kicking dust everywhere.

They meandered back, catching up with Giles and Billie who did not even appear to have noticed their absence. The four walked around to the stables where the thoroughbreds and Arabians were housed, and here Grace came into her own.

Her family owned several, usually kept at their country estate and, despite it being two years since she had ridden, she still knew how to recognise a good horse.

They walked along slowly, Grace stopping occasionally for a more detailed discussion with the grooms regarding a particular specimen. Grace peered into the last stable in the second row which, at first glance, appeared to be empty.

As her eyes adjusted, she noticed a horse of medium height, standing at the far side of the loose box. A mare, facing away from the door, head down, sporting a coat not nearly as shiny as those of the other animals Grace had inspected.

"What is the story behind this horse?" Grace quizzed the groom.

"She'm one we got a week or so ago. Came in with three others we bought from an estate over yonder," which could mean anywhere within a thirty mile radius. "Owner said this one was useless and was going to shoot it. Only fit for t'glue factory he reckoned.

Boss gave her the once over and said she looked as though she had potential. He figures she's mebbe been put to the whip once too often and needs a gentle hand. Sometimes, I think his love for horses overrides his business sense but who am I to question him? He seems to know what he's doing."

The groom shrugged his shoulders, perplexed at the actions of his boss, but Grace understood the man's motives completely.

Grace stared at the horse wishing she would turn around. There was something about this creature. The four were following the groom to the next block when Grace spun on her heel and retraced her steps.

Leaning against the stable door, she began to talk to the animal. The mare's ears flickered while Grace described the shelter, and the meadow, and the wide-open space. She wanted to see whether they had a connection.

Whether this was because she discerned a kindred spirit

or whether her soft heart couldn't bear the thought this horse might be presumed unsellable, Grace had no doubt this was the one for her.

The mare was dapple grey. She looked to be about fifteen hands, maybe a hand or so taller than her former horse at her family's estate. Grace was taller now and the extra hand would give her a better seat.

"Can she be saddled?" Grace questioned the groom who had come back to see what she was doing.

"I'm not sure, Miss. Let me ask Bert over there, he was t'un brought her in." The groom trudged over to an older man who was swilling out an empty stable. They overheard a muttered conversation and Grace smiled when she saw the groom shake his head.

Obviously confused as to why, when this party had chosen two exceptional carriage horses, a crummy old mare warranted their attention. Bert walked across and addressed Giles, presuming him to be the decision-maker of the group.

"Reggie says you're interested in this 'un. What d'you want'a try 'er for? She's nobbut a nag."

Giles looked at Grace, who strode forward, the light of battle gleaming in her eyes.

"I believe, sir that this horse is merely in need of some care. I would guess she is about three years old and, although on the thin side, appears healthy enough. Her coat, despite needing a proper wash and brush is in relatively good condition. Her stubborn behaviour is likely a result of mishandling."

At this juncture, Grace delivered a spirited speech regarding behavioural issues with horses along with an explanation of methods, proven to be successful, making it clear she knew what she was talking about.

"Now, I do not expect you or your grooms to waste your time trying to get to the bottom of her problem, but I *do* have time and patience, and I would like to try her out. I ask again, will she take a saddle?"

By this time, her hands were on her hips, her colour higher than normal. It was all the other three could do not to laugh at the expressions on the faces of both Bert and Reggie.

Bert capitulated and walked over to the tack room, grumbling about women who thought they knew what they were talking about. Grace turned to the others; her hands pressed to her hot cheeks.

"Lord Winchester, Giles, forgive my rudeness. I quite took over, but this horse, this beautiful horse, needs someone to love her. I can tell by her stance, she only expects rough handling. It will take time for her to trust I will not abuse her, but I believe it will be worth it. I have some expe..." She stopped abruptly, aware she had almost said too much.

At that moment, Bert returned with a saddle and bridle, distracting them. Her slip had been noticed, and they knew her entreaty about the horse was far more than simple concern for a neglected animal.

Theo glanced at Giles who raised a brow, but neither spoke. Billie watched Grace, as she straightened her shoulders, wishing the young woman would open up to her.

Pushing this aside for the moment, the four walked back to the stable door. Bert entered, but the mare was unsettled, tossing her head and whinnying.

"Bert, please hang the saddle over the door and let me try," Grace pleaded in an undertone. Bert tutted but did as he was asked and stepped out of the stable. Immediately the mare quieted. Grace walked into the loose box, talking all the while in a sort of singsong voice.

She moved slowly towards the mare, one hand outstretched, her palm up. Halfway across the space she stopped and waited, still talking. The mare lifted her head, her eyes rolling, and she snorted through flared nostrils.

Grace kept talking or rather crooning; it was like listening to a lullaby.

The five outside the stable held their breath as the mare began to change her stance. She turned and looked at Grace, head still tossing, but now instead of snorting, she was nickering. After what felt like hours, but was less than fifteen minutes, the horse walked over to where Grace waited, and sniffed her hand, blowing softly over her palm.

Grace stroked the mare's nose, then up her jaw and down over her neck. Several more minutes ticked by while Grace did nothing more than stroke the creature who moved slightly, meaning Grace was standing against her flank. Taking advantage of this, she reached out for the lead rein, slipping it over the mare's head.

So far, so good. Still crooning, Grace began to lead the horse towards the stable door, quietly asking the others to move away, so the mare didn't feel crowded. At the door, Grace hefted the saddle and, despite it having some weight, slid it over the creature's back.

She didn't try to buckle it up or mount the horse, allowing her to become used to the weight. Patiently, she continued to stroke the mare, and unlatching the door, led her out into the yard.

The horse tossed her head at the unfamiliar space. Grace didn't react. Seeming to perceive this human wasn't going to harm her, the mare became calm. Another few moments, and Grace felt she was ready to be taken out to one of the empty paddocks behind the stables.

The track was risky, too alien an environment. Bert led the way around to the paddock and, at the gate, Grace, one hand never leaving the flesh of the horse, buckled the saddle securely in place. The mare didn't even flinch.

Breathing a sigh of relief, Grace used a set of wooden steps, built for the purpose, to mount the horse and once in the saddle sat, until sure the mare would not try to throw her. Clicking the reins, they moved into the field.

Billie, Giles, Theo, and the two grooms, watched as Grace took the mare through her paces.

It was evident the horse had potential. Her gait was efficient and her stride steady. Using her knees to guide the horse, Grace lifted the mare into a trot before allowing the horse her head, and they cantered around the paddock at a fine speed.

Bert was stunned. He could not equate this proud creature with the forlorn misery who had been sulking in the stables for the past week. Giles, knowing there was no talking Grace out of this purchase, asked Bert to take him to the steward to negotiate terms.

Since the horse was deemed worthless, he believed he could barter for a good price. Theo accompanied him, while Billie waited for Grace.

Horse and rider enjoyed a few more circuits around the paddock, before Grace, reluctantly, returned to the stables. She slid down when she reached the gate and, grasping the reins, led the mare to her loose box.

Billie walked alongside, admiring the horse and, once in the stable, spent a few moments stroking the mare while Grace started to rub down the animal.

The young groom came in with brushes, and politely requested Grace permit him to take over, saying it wasn't right for her to be sorting out the horse. Grace grinned, and did as she was bid, asking Billie where Giles and Theo had gone.

"Over to the steward's office, I think. They are agreeing terms for the three horses. I am pleased for you. They are superb."

Grace smiled. "Aren't they! This creature especially, she needed someone to save her." She spun to study the horse, who was panting from her exertions, but seemed less down-trodden than she had earlier.

Something in her tone caused Billie to glance at Grace, noticing a shadow flitting across her friend's face. *Not yet* thought Billie, *not quite yet, but she will tell me soon.*

Making no comment, Billie took Grace's arm, and pulled her friend over to the track, where several horses were being trained, asking Bert to tell Giles and Theo where they were.

The two men concluded their business. Giles extracted a promise the three horses for Grace would be delivered with dispatch. Theo also finalised a deal on a carriage horse for his mother, arranging for the animal to be transported to London the following week. Theo opened the door to leave, and a man strode through, almost shoving both men out of the way in his haste.

"Oh, beg pardon," the newcomer tossed out casually, clearly intent on speaking to the steward and presuming anyone else would get out of his way. Theo and Giles nodded, but when the man glanced at them, Theo drew a sharp breath.

"Your Grace," Theo inclined his head. "You are a long way from home."

The man looked Theo full in the face and then did the same to Giles, recognising who he had so rudely barged into. "Winchester! Elliott! Well met. What the deuce are you two doing here?"

Loath to give this man anything more than the briefest of information, Theo said he had been negotiating to buy a horse for his mother, not mentioning Grace at all. Giles frowned slightly, but followed Theo's lead, stating he had come along as an advisor. Nodding, the man turned to speak to the steward.

Giles and Theo left the office.

"Theo?" Giles questioned. "What was that about? Do I know him?"

"It's Jonathon Huntington, Duke of Aldwych," replied Theo, desperately scanning the yard. "We cannot let him see Grace."

Giles stared at his friend in bewilderment. "Why on earth not?"

"Because he's the one who hurt her," hissed Theo.

"The devil you say?" Giles' jaw dropped.

The scandal had been big news in the city amongst the *ton* when it happened, but Giles had taken no notice, too busy trying to get his head around running the estate. Occurring not long after the death of his father, Giles and the rest of his family spent much of that year at Whiteoaks, away from tawdry tittle-tattle.

Nor was the uproar surrounding Grace the only controversy of the season. As usual, there had been several other — for want of a better word — incidents, involving impressionable debutantes and unscrupulous rakes, typically prompted by desperate mothers hoping to trick a rich peer into marriage.

Moreover, the same names repeated themselves on a regular basis and, in general, as long as their own families were not caught up in it, the men of the elite closed their ears.

The world fell apart for Grace, but once the hue and cry died down, those on the periphery soon forgot it ever happened — except when indulging in malicious gossip. Another scandal would happen along soon enough, to push the last one out of their minds.

Unfortunately, the relatively large circle Grace had moved within, neither forgot nor forgave, shunning the young woman completely, fear of being tainted solely because of their association with her. It was a harsh world.

~

"We have completed our business. The steward will arrange for the horses to be transported. We need to leave now, before he comes back out." Theo started towards Billie and Grace, who were turning to walk back from the track.

A loud bang distracted them as the office door was flung open. To Theo's disquiet, the duke waved, crunching across the gravel to where they stood. He followed the direction of Theo's gaze, and noticed the two women. Something about the regal bearing of the taller one pulled at the duke's memory, but he could not hold on to it.

"Do you know them?" he asked, nodding in the general direction of Grace and Billie. Neither man answered immediately, and he continued, "seems odd, don't you know, two women out here. A couple of chits from the local tavern perhaps or maybe there's a brothel nearby." Roguishly spoken.

"One of those 'chits' as you so eloquently put it, is my wife, Aldwych." Giles pointed out in a remarkably calm voice. "The other lady," emphasising the word 'lady', "is her friend, a widow from Northumbria. The last I looked, neither were barmaids or whores."

Lord Aldwych had the sense to blush and to give him his due — if they *really* had to — he apologised for his vulgarity. "The tall one, what is her name? I'm sure I know her."

Theo sent a pleading look to Giles, who said. "Her name is Penelope Barrington." He used the first name that came into his head. It belonged to Duncan's mother, but Giles knew she wouldn't mind, given the circumstances.

The duke ruminated for a moment. "Hmm, no the name is unfamiliar to me. I must be mistaken. Ah well, mayhap it will come to me when I see her close up." He shrugged offhandedly.

Theo was in a ferment. He could not in all conscience walk away from the duke; the man was, after all, his social superior. Neither did he want Grace to come upon them unawares.

He need not have worried, because as they began to make their way back towards the stables, Grace spotted the third man talking with Giles and Theo. At the same moment the duke thought he recognised her, she definitely recognised him.

"Billie!" Grace gripped Billie's sleeve. "Billie, please help me. I cannot rejoin Theo and Giles while *he* is with them."

The venom in Grace's voice, floored Billie, but one glance at her friend's face told her she was serious. She was sheet white and her jaw was clenched.

"What do I do?"

They dithered, then inspiration hit, and Billie said.

"How about this? We start walking towards them. After we have taken a few steps, I want you to bend over sharply, as though in pain. Maybe do that twice. We keep walking, and then you hurry over behind the stables. I shall tell them you suspect an upset stomach. Men hate women being ill, they can't handle it. Theo can come and help you,"

Grace started to protest.

"Grace, he's a doctor what better excuse. He can assist you to the carriage, while I meet up with Giles. We make small talk with this person until we can politely take our leave saying we must get you home."

Grace stared at Billie, running the idea through her head. It might just work. She nodded. "Let's do it."

Billie grinned, and squeezed her hand. "Now, 'tis important you make it believable, just a few small twinges, then bend over as though you are in real agony. That will scare him off for certain.

"Thank you, Billie, I am in your debt."

Billie looked at Grace, her green eyes dark with sympathy and replied quietly. "As long as you promise to share your burden with me, there is no debt."

Grace studied Billie for a moment and then offered a tremulous smile. "After what you are doing for me today, I believe 'tis a fair request. I promise."

"Come on then, act away."

The men were watching the women head their way, when they spotted one of them hunch her shoulders, and put her hand out to her diminutive companion.

Giles folded his arms, a smile twitching at the corner of his mouth, realising what was going on, knowing without a doubt, it was his minx of a wife who came up with the plan.

The two were nearly upon them, when they heard a low cry, and the taller woman bent double, arms clutching her stomach. Her friend said something and pointed beyond the stables.

As the tall lady staggered in that direction, her accomplice flew over to the three men, two of whom were gaping at the tableau.

"Theo! Please, Theo! Can you see to her? She thinks she is going to be dreadfully sick. Cannot think what brought it on. She was fine one minute, then the next she went all green and said her stomach fairly griped. Dear me, I hope she will be all right for the journey home."

Theo shot off after Grace, while Billie turned to the man standing alongside her husband.

"I'm sure Miss Barrington will be fine my dear. These northerners are known for their strong constitutions," interjected Giles, smoothly, before Billie could say another word. His wife accepted Grace's new name with aplomb and nodded vigorously.

"I hope so and now Theo is with her all will be well. Giles, my dear, please introduce me to this dashing gentleman."

The duke glowed at this description and bowed over her hand. "Jonathan Huntington, Duke of Aldwych at your service, my Lady. It is an honour to meet the lady who thwarted spies."

She was surprised he knew of this chapter of her life but made no other comment because she was concentrating on not yanking her hand out of his grasp. His fingers gripped hers too tightly, and his breath would slay a boar at five paces.

Billie was nothing if not polite and dropped a deep curtsy. "The honour is all mine, your Grace."

The three exchanged pleasantries, after which Billie turned to Giles. "Giles, I think we ought to get Penelope home. I will go and find them, if you would like to summon Jake."

Giles nodded and Billie excused herself. Bobbing another curtsy, repeating her delight at meeting the duke, who preened under her words, Billie hurried to where she hoped Theo and Grace were waiting. Giles signalled Jake, who went to ready the carriage which was in the shade of a stand of trees keeping the horses cool and therefore somewhat out of view.

Giles chatted a moment longer with the duke, discussing the possibility of meeting up at White's the next time they were both in London. Saying his goodbyes, he strode casually over to his coach.

Jake opened the door and as Giles climbed in, he saw the other three were already seated. Grace was pale, and she was trembling like a leaf. There were about to set off, when a noise startled them and the duke appeared alongside, riding a huge stallion.

Grace nearly did cast up her accounts at that point, ducking her head before he saw her, the hated bonnet hiding her distinctive hair.

"Sorry, Winchester. Wanted to invite you all to Blackheath Hall, Saturday week. Mother's having a garden party or some such flummery. A few fresh faces would be agreeable. Anytime from three. You know where it is?"

The duke's horse was prancing under his tight rein and, from under her bonnet, the sight of those cruel fingers almost undid Grace. Spots began to appear before her eyes, and unbeknownst to her she moaned.

Lord Aldwych, who truly believed she was going to be violently sick, jerked his horse away.

Her head was spinning, images flooding her mind, images she had fought so hard to bury. Instructing herself not to faint, Grace bit the inside of her cheek and pinched her leg in an attempt to prevent it. Nothing worked, and as Giles accepted the invitation, she crumpled ignominiously into oblivion.

The duke rode away, completely unaware it was his proximity which had caused such a reaction. Billie fell on her knees to the carriage floor, lifting Grace's head and cradling her. Long tremors rippled through the older woman's body, and again she moaned.

Theo grimaced, so much for preventing any upset. Giles pinned back the curtains, letting the fresh air filter through and, although the carriage was rocking, it was a soothing motion.

Grace showed no signs of waking. Theo, rather than leave her on the floor, lifted her into his arms and resumed his seat, settling her against him. Billie and Giles gaped at him, but he shook his head.

"Do not lecture me. I know what I said to you last year. This is different."

Giles started to speak.

Theo interrupted, "All right it isn't so very different, but she cannot lie on the floor and how else are we to make sure she does not slip off the seat again?"

"I could sit with her, Theo," Billie pointed out, reasonably.

"Yes, but she is much taller than you, and you shouldn't be heaving people about at the moment."

Billie stared at him in consternation, then at Giles who was equally dumbfounded.

"I am a doctor, my Lady. Do you think I cannot recognise the signs? What I fail to understand is why you are taking so long to tell me?"

Billie's mouth had formed a perfect 'O' and her eyes were like saucers. "I… we… it's… well… Giles…" she looked at her husband for input. Giles grinned. Billie glared at him to no discernible effect and spluttered incoherently.

Theo, concentrating on Grace, chuckled softly. Giles took pity on his wife and pulled her close, kissing her cheek.

"We wanted to be certain before we shared the news," he said, quietly. "We have an appointment with a specialist in Harley Street next month."

"Name?" demanded Theo. Giles named a doctor who was arguably the best in his field, and Theo nodded in satisfaction.

"He's a good man, we studied together. Tell him you are a friend of mine, and if he doesn't treat Billie like a princess, I shall tell all his colleagues about the curious incident with the bovine dissection."

Giles raised an eyebrow.

"No, I'm not going to tell you. 'Tis a useless threat if people already know. Now, let me rouse Grace. In my opinion, she has been unconscious too long."

Theo turned his attention to Grace.

Giles hugged his wife. Some weeks ago, Billie believed she was increasing, but wanted to keep it between her husband and herself for as long as possible, relishing their secret. Once everyone knew it would be all baby talk. People would start offering advice and assistance, and all manner of interference would happen — well-meant or otherwise.

Billie did not do well when she felt she was being organised. Typical Theo, she might have known he would guess.

"I'm sorry, Theo," she said. "'Tis not that we did not want to tell you. I liked we were the only two who knew. You know what will happen once people hear about it."

Theo smiled sympathetically. "I do know, Billie but now you have finally admitted it, may I say how pleased I am for you both. Congratulations. Mind you look after her, Winchester."

Giles was now the one spluttering, making Billie giggle,

and lightening the moment, which was threatening to become emotional.

While the earl and his countess focused on each other, Theo observed Grace. She hadn't stirred but her features appeared less pinched and, despite her higher than normal heart rate, her breathing had stabilised. The tremors continued, but the doctor fancied they were abating.

He had seen similar reactions many times before, usually in soldiers returning from the wars. Loud noises, akin to gunfire, would be enough to send them into a total panic. He knew, having spoken with them, they would see the battle-field and the blood and the mutilated bodies instead of whatever was actually in front of them.

He contemplated the possibility Grace was experiencing a similar phenomenon. It would not be unexpected given the period of time she suffered the abuse.

Grace shifted in his arms, and he sensed she was coming around. Holding her close but not too tightly, he spoke in low tones, hoping the sound of his voice would allay any alarm she might feel when she awoke. They had travelled a few more miles before Grace opened her eyes, and they immediately locked with Theo's.

Terror clouded her gaze, but she did not yell or try to pull away, recognising the doctor immediately. She stared at him for an age, her fingers fisting around his waistcoat then, without warning, burst into tears.

Recalling in whose company she was, Grace was morti-fied, yet despite this she couldn't seem to stop crying. Theo did nothing other than draw her closer against him, nestling her head on his shoulder, completely ignoring Billie and Giles sitting opposite.

Good grief, Grace thought, in dismay. *Theo will think all you do is cry.* She struggled to regain her composure, but the shock had been acute, and it took until they were almost home before she felt anything like normal.

Billie stretched across to press her knee. "I think you should stay with us tonight, Grace. Jake will pop over to The Gables to collect anything you might need and inform Evans. You should be surrounded by those who love you and, while I realise your staff care deeply for you, it is not the same thing."

Billie's tender tones soothed Grace who smiled back wearily, thanking her friend in a quaking voice. She swallowed her, admittedly, half-hearted objection, aware Billie would win in the end. In truth, she was not looking forward to an evening alone with her thoughts.

By now Grace was sitting upright and had disentangled herself from the warmth of Theo's embrace. He refused to let go of her hand, a gesture she found comforting.

Shortly thereafter, they came to a halt in the courtyard of Whiteoaks, and Thomas appeared to usher them indoors. Billie gave Jake a set of instructions. He rode off to The Gables to pass them on, returning a short while later with a small valise for Grace.

Having updated their own staff on the extra numbers suddenly added to their household, Billie and Giles joined Grace and Theo in the library for hot coffee, a glass of brandy — for those who felt the need, medicinal or otherwise — and a very luscious slice of cake.

Several miles away at Blackheath Hall, a reprehensible specimen of humanity was sitting in his own library, smoking a very pungent pipe and slurping his third whisky. He was ruminating on his afternoon, when the memory which had been gnawing at him, finally surfaced, coalescing into a coherent picture.

His lips curled into what could possibly, if you were feeling really generous, be described as a smile.

"Ah, so that is where you have been hiding, my pretty. Methinks it is time for us to become reacquainted."

CHAPTER 21

Thankfully, none of the four sitting around the fire in the library at Whiteoaks were aware of this revelation, for although he was part of their thoughts, it was under very different circumstances.

Once they had all munched through the cake and were settled with a drink, Grace asked Billie whether now might be an appropriate time to share her story. The day's events had precipitated things to a certain extent, and Grace just wanted it over with.

"I agreed to speak of my past and, since you will tell Giles anyway, if he wishes to stay, I do not mind. I believe you to be a compassionate man, my Lord." She regarded the earl, steadily.

Giles, who was lounging against the mantelpiece, inclined his head, his expression kind.

"This way it is done. I wish Ralph was here for I know he is worried about me. I will find another time to tell him and Tessa. Then, I am done. 'Tis not a tale I wish everyone to know and, after I tell it, you will understand why."

Grace inhaled a wavering breath and, while the other

three watched, she straightened her body. It was as though she was hardening herself. That the shell they had so very nearly broken through was reforming before their eyes.

She began to speak. As when she told Theo — was it only the previous day? It seemed so long ago — her tones were emotionless. Her calm voice was at odds with the dramatic nature of her story, and her listeners were held immobile by her words.

Theo had taken the chair next to Grace and, even though she did not look at him, occasionally her hand crept towards his, needing his touch to steady her nerves. The slightest brush of his fingers enough to soothe her.

At the end, her voice petered out. Nobody spoke, each lost in thought, and all unwilling to shatter the silence which had descended across the room while the heinous tale unfolded. Grace was exhausted.

A long day, the shock of seeing Huntington and now this — she understood why creatures hibernated. All she wanted to do was go to bed, and sleep until someone promised he would never find her.

Grace knew it would not take long for him to work out where she was, and her haven would be no more. She recollected something Theo had said; if she let *him* overshadow her life, he had won. She was not the same innocent girl anymore. She had survived his molestations and, although not unscathed, believed she was stronger now.

She raised her head and looked at the trio surrounding her, holding the gaze of each one, waiting. Billie was the first to respond. She crossed the rug to where Grace was sitting and drew the older woman into a warm hug.

"Grace, my dear. My heart goes out to you and, while I am unable to take away the nightmare, remember you have friends here who care a great deal for you. Now we all know who is responsible, hopefully steps can be taken to ensure he cannot do such a thing again."

Grace smiled at her friend, "Thank you, Billie. You have no idea how much it means to hear you say that. I know I do not trust easily, but since my arrival, the support and kindness I have encountered has restored my faith somewhat. Now I must learn how to deal with him. I am bound to run into him, look at today, and I cannot keep hiding."

Giles added his own sympathy, commenting he would do everything in his power to see no other woman would ever again be on the receiving end of Huntington's venal predilections.

"I appreciate your gesture, your Lordship… Giles, but he is cunning, and his status affords him more protection than most. I cannot believe I am the only woman he has treated this way. His approach is planned, his method skilful. He knows what to do and how to do it. It was pure chance we were caught and, while eternally grateful he no longer pursued me, I am not sure I was any better off."

The other three gaped at her.

"Grace! You cannot think it was better to have him treat you that way than be free of him?" Billie stammered, perturbed.

"I'm sorry, no, you misunderstand. I didn't mean I wanted him to continue, but I have spent the last two years on my own. I might as well have been on a deserted island. Except for Jemima and, very occasionally, Anthony, I haven't spoken to a single other person from the set with whom I used to socialise.

"Four people, *four*, those of our staff whom my family deemed suitable to tend to my needs, are the only ones who cared, and they became like family. My own parents, now dead, refused to have anything to do with me and, to be honest, I have no idea why my brother bothered. He could have sent instructions through the bank or our solicitors. His visits were painful in the extreme.

"That *man*," Grace almost spat the word, "shattered the whole of my life. Every aspect of it was destroyed, and I could not see any way out. I expected to spend the rest of my days within those four walls, only stepping out to visit with Jemima or tend to my garden, and you ask why I imagine myself no better off? I was ruined either way.

"Then came Aunt Bea's legacy. It was like a gift from God. I have no words to describe the joy I felt when given the news. Even though the idea of removing to somewhere I remembered only vaguely and having to run a household alone, worried me, the freedom it offered was marvellous. Now he has found me again..."

all three started to speak at once,

"...I know you think we fooled him, but he will work it out. This is part of his game. The hunt, the chase, this is what he lives for. He will find me, eventually."

She sucked in a quavering breath. "I need to learn how to deal with him. How to prevent him from ever touching me again, to stop having ridiculous anxiety attacks whenever I see him. Granted, today was the first time since..." Grace shuddered, "...that night, but when he came over to the coach, it was as though I had gone back in time. His hands, the way he gripped the reins, it was..." she could not continue, images reared up, distorting her vision.

Theo squeezed her hand, an idea percolating at the back of his mind. Not one he intended to broach yet, but it might be an answer to her concerns, and it would please him more than anyone could imagine. He set that aside, there was something else he had to share.

"Grace, I need to tell you something,"

Grace, glad of the diversion, looked at him expectantly.

"I took the liberty of mentioning to the men on your staff

they needed to be observant. In case a stranger to these parts started asking questions about the new owner of The Gables."

Grace fidgeted and tried to pull her hand away. Theo kept hold, his thumb rubbing along her palm, a reassuring gesture.

"Evans told me his cousin's wife used to be in service, and the lady she was maid to, took her own life after being preyed on by Aldwych. I have written to Lucas Withers apprising him of this, asking him to make discreet enquiries. Evans said it would be acceptable to visit with Hetty, that's his cousin's wife, to talk to her about the lady for whom she worked.

"If someone has died, even if by their own hand, as a direct result of his actions, we must find a way to stop him. Not everyone is as strong as you, Grace."

Grace studied Theo, her jaw working. "You think me strong?" She was flabbergasted.

"Indubitably. You are here aren't you? After everything you have endured, you are still here and, from where I'm sitting, managing very nicely."

She couldn't say those words, not yet, but she felt them. They flooded through her every time she was near this tall, gentle man in whose gaze she could happily drown. A subtle cough brought her back to reality, and she blushed. "I beg your pardon. Err... well... it's just..." at a loss for words, Grace shut up.

Billie chuckled, remarking dinner was about to be served, and did Grace wish to freshen up first? Gratefully, Grace nodded and untangled her hand from Theo's. He smiled at her, and she was pleased to note, even after the fright of seeing the duke, she was not troubled at the thought of Theo touching her.

She *did* feel stronger; at least she had until this afternoon.

She enjoyed her life in Oak Stanton. She relished the small amount of independence it offered, and she loved her new home.

A strange sensation flooded through her, as though some inner power had been unleashed. She had friends who knew all there was to know and had not abandoned her. She had Theo who obviously cared for her. She had staff who made her life so much easier, and she had herself.

What Theo said was true; she *was* still here — against all the odds.

The others watched her draw herself up. Her stance almost defiant; head back, chin up and shoulders squared.

"You are correct, Theo. I am not the same person he so easily cornered. I am wise to the way his mind works. I will not let him take my life from me again. I have faced the worst Society can throw at me, and somehow, I *am* still standing, and I have met you.

"You, all of you, welcomed me without reserve, yet I was wary of sharing my story, for fear of seeing the shutters fall over your eyes, and feel the chill of your withdrawal. But you listened, believed and accepted. Your generosity of spirit knows no bounds and I thank you from the bottom of my heart."

The trio responded with gracious friendliness. Billie grasped Grace's hand. "Come, before you reduce me to tears, I will show you to your room where you can refresh yourself. We will talk no more of dark matters. I for one, do not wish that man to take up any more of our thoughts tonight."

With this Billie hustled Grace out of the room and up the stairs to one of the many guest rooms at Whiteoaks.

～

Giles and Theo remained in the library. Neither man spoke. What was there to say? Any other topic of conversation would seem banal after such revelations, but to discuss the matter further would be fruitless until they had more information.

"There is no way I am taking Billie to Blackheath." Giles growled, "I do not want her within ten miles of that blackguard."

Theo agreed. "She is expecting. I'm sure there's a possibility she might become indisposed, and you shall be forced to send your regrets," he offered, his brown eyes twinkling with mischief.

"By Jove you're right." Giles slapped his friend on the back, his genial smile, missing since they departed the horse stud, returning. The doctor's comment broke the tension, and the two men began to chat about mundane estate matters until the ladies rejoined them.

Grace looked much happier and she grinned at Giles and Theo when she entered the library. Before she could say anything, Thomas announced dinner was served, and the four made their way into the dining room.

During the meal, Billie steered the conversation towards upcoming events in the village. The harvest festival and the autumn fair, a much larger version of the market Theo had escorted Grace around on her first Saturday in Oak Stanton. That young woman quickly realised there might be some baby animals she could purchase.

The evening was spent in a hilarious debate about chicken coops and pigpens, the smell of the animals and the amount of muck they produced. None of which seemed to deter Grace, who said such things would be most beneficial to her garden beds.

They retired to the library, where Thomas had lit the fire and now was carrying in a tray of hot coffees. He placed these on a side table, and poured two whiskies, asking Billie and Grace whether they preferred Madeira or port. Billie plumped for Madeira and Grace opted for port, and while they were waiting, Theo and Giles both lit up a cigar.

A tranquillity settled over the room while they sipped their drinks, the only sounds were the hiss and pop of the wood on the fire. The distinctive aromas of tobacco and coffee hung in the air, their familiarity helping Grace relax. She glanced around and recognised, with these people, she was safe.

CHAPTER 22

The next day, following a good night's sleep and a breakfast fit for kings, Theo escorted Grace home to The Gables.

None had revisited the topic of the duke, and Billie extracted a promise from Grace she would return in the afternoon, two days hence, to observe the lessons in the little schoolroom — with a view to taking some on herself — and stay for dinner.

Grace accepted gratefully and, thanking everyone for their generous hospitality, departed.

Grace and Theo were quiet on the way back to the village, but it was a comfortable silence and Theo seized the opportunity to hold Grace's hand the entire way. She stared at their conjoined fingers, still amazed she liked, nay loved the feel of his hand around hers.

"Will you be all right, my dear?" Theo asked gently as they approached The Gables.

Grace smiled shyly. "I am sure I will, thank you. Oddly enough, I do feel much better after last evening. It is as though he has ceased to have any power over me. I do not think that is the last I will see of him and, while I do not relish the thought of a further encounter, I am no longer scared. That is mainly because of you." She watched his face as she spoke, her fingers squeezing his.

Theo leant close and brushed his lips gently over hers. A frisson ran through her, and without thinking she caressed his cheek with her free hand, feeling the pulse along his jaw line jump at her touch.

He moved his head to kiss her palm, at the same time instructing himself not to drag her against him and continue the kiss he had just started. They were outside her house and, despite everything, it would not do for her to be caught in so compromising a situation.

"Thank you for saying so, but I believe it was your own inherent courage which recognised he no longer holds sway over your life. That said I will happily take the credit." He grinned, "I just wish I could take away the pain he caused you."

"I think perhaps you have started to or at least it has begun to diminish. Fading to a place where it no longer haunts me." Grace smiled, her eyes holding his, both forgetting the carriage had rolled to a stop. Adam's face appeared at the door, as he opened it and dropped the step.

Theo got out and held out his hand so Grace could step down. They stood gazing at each other, unwilling to say goodbye, yet knowing they had to. Theo had house calls to make and Grace needed to check what was happening in her own home.

"May I call on you later?" he asked, relinquishing her hand.

"I should like that of all things," she replied. Bestowing on him a beam which could easily light the darkest of rooms, she picked up the small valise containing her overnight essentials and hurried up the path, turning once to wave before disappearing through the door.

Theo remained where he was, lost in thought until a cough from Adam brought him back to reality. "Sorry Adam, I was wool-gathering." He hopped back into the carriage, "Let's go, work to do and all that."

Adam chuckled and, clicking the horse, they trundled the short distance to Theo's house.

Grace was welcomed home like a long-lost daughter, her staff appearing from all directions, asking whether she was all right. Their concern took her breath away and she assured them, everything was fine. Before applying her mind to the rest of her day, she asked Evans to call everyone together in the parlour. There was something she needed to share.

The previous night snuggled under layers of luxuriously comfortable covers in one of the palatial guest bedchambers at Whiteoaks, Grace had mulled over her circumstances.

Pleased, she now felt able to cope with anything the duke might decide to throw at her, she was also shrewd enough to know he might try to undermine her through others in her household. Peggy had informed Grace that, before the scandal broke, there was many a time he called at the London residence trying to gain access to her.

For the most part, the loyal staff had persuaded him that Miss Aldeburgh was not at home, but there were several occasions when her mother intervened, forcing Grace to endure the duke's company, often without a chaperone. Giving Grace one more reason to believe her family knew what was going on.

. . .

While Evans gathered the staff, Grace went up to her bedchamber and sat for a few minutes collecting her thoughts. She did not intend to tell them what Lord Aldwych had done, but they deserved to have some awareness of her circumstances, especially if she wanted them to continue to work for her.

She did not expect any to abandon her and, truth be told, her private life was none of their business. In this instance, if she wanted to retain their respect and their loyalty, she needed them to know they were trusted. Billie had told her the people chosen to work at The Gables were handpicked because of their discretion. She hoped her friend's instincts were right.

When she entered the parlour, everyone was waiting and looking a trifle confused. After thanking them for their time and apologising for upsetting the morning routine, Grace explained why she requested this meeting.

"You may know Miss Beatrice Montgomery bequeathed The Gables to me on her death. What you probably don't know is why." She forced her voice to remain steady.

"Two years ago, I was caught up in an incident which resulted in my being ostracised by Society. My family shunned me and, until my removal here a little over two weeks ago, I lived on my own in our London house. I will not bore you with the sordid details. Suffice it to say it was not an easy time. Once everything was out in the open, the person responsible no longer bothered me and, until yesterday, I had not seen him since the night the scandal broke.

"Regrettably, he turned up at the horse stud and, despite the best efforts of the countess to shield me, I believe he will have worked it out. I am telling you this for two reasons. The first is that I understand completely if, now you know something of what happened, you prefer not to remain in my household.

"Secondly, should you decide to stay, and truly, I hope you do because you have become important to me in the short time we have known each other, you need to be aware he may try to gain entry to this house by fair means or foul.

"I shall tell you who it is and give you a description, so you are prepared. I do not imagine he would intentionally harm any of you, I am the one he seeks, but he is skilful in obtaining what he believes to be his and is utterly unscrupulous." Grace took a calming breath, determined to get this over with.

"Once I have provided his name, I will leave you to talk amongst yourselves, so you can come to a decision without feeling pressured by my presence. If any of you decide to leave, I promise you will take with you a glowing reference."

Grace wound up by furnishing them with the duke's name and his description, and left the parlour, going along into the Snug while they discussed the matter.

The staff was silent for several minutes, stunned by Grace's revelations. Evans reported what Dr Elliott had said to him, Gibbs and Matt on the day they had arrived at The Gables.

Telling them the little he knew about the young lady who had taken her own life, presumably as a result of the duke's debauchery. They listened and, although appalled, the older ones especially were not wholly surprised.

The bizarre tendencies of the nobility were not unheard of, but most had not been this close to someone to whom it had actually happened.

Agnes spoke first, saying, as far as she was concerned, Miss Fitzgerald was a pleasure to work for and she for one was staying put. The rest followed suit, without exception. They all liked and respected their employer and did not want to see her hurt, declaring it courageous of her to share this chapter of her personal life, risking further condemnation.

Agnes and Evans went to find Grace who was reading in the Snug. It must be admitted the words were not making any sense, her mind anywhere but the book on her lap.

She glanced up when Evans knocked and stood, awaiting their verdict.

"Miss Fitzgerald," said Agnes coming forward wringing her hands together and vainly trying to contain her discomfiture. She gave up and throwing propriety to the winds, pulled the tall woman into a motherly embrace.

"You poor love. Why would you think we'd leave you to fend for yourself? I never heard such nonsense. You're stuck with us, my lamb and that's all there is to it."

Grace looked over Agnes' shoulder at Evans who shrugged and grinned his agreement with the cook. She felt the threat of tears and blinked furiously to stop them brimming over.

Agnes released her, and in a voice, which wavered just a touch, Grace thanked them, saying how much she appreciated their devotion to a person they hardly knew.

She returned to the parlour where the others were waiting and thanked them all over again. Her grateful smile was enough for them to know they had made the right choice.

Without further comment they all went about their duties and, for a while, the discussion was pushed into the background, all but forgotten.

The rest of the day was filled with domestic duties and preparations for the arrival of the horses. Grace involved herself in every aspect of her home and was not above helping when she could.

An inordinately large amount of food and bedding had been delivered and was distributed between the carriage house and the shelter. The floor of each of the stalls now sported a thick layer of straw, and fresh hay filled the racks.

The tack, including saddles, bridles, reins and harnesses would arrive with the horses. Giles had arranged for the stud to provide them as part of the deal. Gibbs had obtained the equipment necessary for grooming. The troughs were scrubbed clean and filled with water.

Grace, checking everything for the umpteenth time took a moment to stop, and breathe in the warm aroma of straw and hay permeating both shelter and carriage house, before congratulating everyone on their hard work.

It was approaching six in the evening when Theo called. He had spent a busy day dealing with a bout of sickness affecting several households within their small community.

After questioning some of the afflicted, he believed the likely cause was food related not an infection. Confirmed when one of the husbands mentioned they had all eaten some chicken, which tasted 'reet peerculeea,' at a recent family gathering.

Dressed in a gown the colour of ripe wheat, after enjoying a proper bath, Grace was in her favourite chair in the Snug, her legs tucked underneath her, once again trying to immerse herself in the book she thought to read earlier in the day. Now she couldn't concentrate owing to her anticipation at seeing Theo again.

She had mentioned to Agnes that Doctor Elliott might be

calling and, if so, she would invite him to stay for dinner. Agnes never batted an eyelid, telling Grace not to fret, there'd always be enough for an extra mouth.

Mind wandering, she was staring out of the window and didn't hear the doctor's quiet knock or the several minutes of muted conversation between him and Evans, as the butler brought Theo up to date on Grace's revelations.

In fact, she didn't even hear Theo's footsteps in the hallway as he came along to the Snug, where he paused for a moment to study her while she gazed sightlessly at the newly turned garden.

"Good evening, Miss Fitzgerald," he greeted in undertones, so as not to alarm her or break the tranquil mood. Grace turned to face him; her eyes distant. He watched their amber depths focus on him, warming in recognition.

"Dr Elliott, please forgive my rudeness. I was lost in my thoughts. How was your day?"

Theo grinned and recounted the tale of the 'peerculeea' chicken in so amusing a manner, she was giggling helplessly by the time it was told.

"I apologise for laughing for I am sure they feel sorry for themselves, but dear me that is very funny."

"I am relieved it was food not infection, but I do wish people would listen to me. If the skin of the chicken is green it should not be eaten, no matter how long it has been cooked." He sat in the chair next to hers. "I hear you told your staff today. That was brave."

"I felt it only proper. They need to know. What if he turns up here asking to call on me? They would be none the wiser and then he has gained entry to my home. I am not about to let that happen again." Needing to touch him, she reached out and then thought better of it, her hand dropping back on her lap.

Theo stretched over and, as had become his habit, wove

his fingers through hers, resting both of their hands on the arm of the chair, the feel of his skin on hers sending the most sublime quivers snaking up her arm.

"Will you stay for dinner?" her voice ensnared him, and he could not have refused even if he thought it prudent to do so.

"I have been hoping you might ask and, yes, I would like to."

Grace smiled, desperately wanting to kiss him, or for him to kiss her. He seemed much better at it than she. "Perhaps a turn around the garden before we eat?" she invited and, at his nod they both stood, hands still clasped and moved towards the terrace.

The evening was mild and there was a slight breeze. They drifted slowly down the central pathway and into the shadows. Her stomach fluttering, Grace tried to steady her breathing. This courting thing was tricky. One had to be decorous, yet when she was close to Theo, all she wanted him to do was hold her close and kiss her, cradling her against his body.

Shaking her head in an attempt to dismiss such thoughts she became aware Theo was rubbing his thumb along hers. She didn't know whether he even realised he did it, it seemed an absent-minded gesture, but it was making her tingle all over.

Admiring the was the evening sun glinted on the red highlights in her hair, Theo was, had Grace but known it, battling similar desires. Her lissom body swayed slightly when she walked, her dress flowed around her like liquid gold. He began to think of anything to curb his ardour — jagged wounds, trepanning, blood, guts and gore — nothing worked.

They reached the end of the path and Grace halted, looking down to make sure she didn't trip.

She raised her head, their eyes met, and he could deny it no longer. Lifting their joined hands, bringing them both to his chest, he cupped the back of her neck with his free hand, tilting her head so she had to look at him.

"Grace," he whispered.

She stared at him willing him to do what she dreamed he would do. Her body simmered.

"Theo," she murmured and, without thinking, grazed her hand along his cheek to weave her slender fingers into his unruly hair.

"Please may I kiss you?" he asked, his voice hoarse.

"I shall be most upset if you don't," came her reply, and he needed no further invitation. Bending his head, he brushed her lips lightly with his and then drew back, watching. She moved closer, lifting up onto her tiptoes to kiss him back.

He felt a tremor ripple through her and, with a groan, captured her lips again, heat snaking through him when Grace responded.

She leant into him, letting her intuition guide her, still uncertain about exactly what to do. Extricating her hand, she used both of hers to cup his head, while Theo tucked her against him with one arm, the other sweeping over her delectable frame.

He was very gentle, stroking his hand slowly down her spine and then back up to the hollow of her neck, his fingers barely caressing her skin. Grace was losing herself in his kiss, heat coiling around her stomach banishing those annoying flutters and making her whole body feel as though she was molten.

Their kiss deepened and passion flared. If not for Theo's arm, Grace believed it likely she would have puddled at his feet. In fact, she was positive she had no bones left. She heard a moan — *was that her? Goodness Grace, you'll have Evans out here checking up on you. Evans!* The thought of her butler coming upon them like this panicked her and, abruptly, she pulled away.

"Grace, what's wrong? I'm sorry, did I scare you?" Theo's concerned tones caught her heart.

"You didn't scare me. I just remembered Evans."

"Oh, errr… well, there's a sentence I never expected to hear with regard to my kisses." Slightly perplexed.

Grace giggled. "No, he will probably be coming to call us for dinner, and I didn't want you to be caught kissing me."

"I really don't mind Grace. 'Tis yourself, you should be worried about, not me."

"Yes, but I thought, it's just now they know… what if…" coherence long gone, Grace wasn't sure how to phrase what was bothering her, except she didn't want to place her staff in an awkward position. Theo, becoming used to this young woman's thought processes, believed he understood her anxiety.

"Grace, I think, by now, Evans knows how I feel about you, and he also knows neither you nor I would do anything untoward. You need to trust them, and me. Evans is discretion itself and, to be honest, I think he approves." He bent his head to kiss her again, "…but if you prefer I stop…" he let his sentence hang, and as he studied her face in the mellow light, several emotions flitted across her delicate features.

Grace gazed back, the practical, sensible, very wary part of her warning this was dangerous, while her romantic side told her to stop being so damn careful and savour the moment. Her romantic side won. Sighing, she leant against the doctor, revelling in the feel of his body on hers, wishing this moment would last forever.

Theo felt her relax and pressed his lips to her forehead. She lifted her face and touched her lips to his, aware of the drum of his heart as he held her close, hoping her actions conveyed what she struggled to articulate.

Evans announced dinner and the rest of the evening passed comfortably. After another fine meal, the pair indulged in a digestif each and, ensconced in the Snug, continued their easy conversation, which revolved around the arrival of the horses the following day.

It was clear to Theo how thrilled Grace was and he could have listened to her lively chatter all night. However, he had call on his time the next morning and, although neither wanted the evening to end, common sense dictated they must say goodnight. Their enjoyment of each other's company meant Theo wished he never had to leave, and Grace wished he could stay.

Propped against the doorframe, Grace watched Theo — who was whistling to himself — stroll down the path and through the gate, turning once to tip his head in her direction.

The tiny spark of hope fluttered into life.

CHAPTER 23

Awoken by the morning chorus, Grace was up, washed and dressed before Polly had the chance to help her. Grinning at her mistress' enthusiasm, the young maid persuaded Grace into letting her do her hair. As Polly was always able to make it look less like a bird's nest, Grace acquiesced, although struggled to sit still, excitement making her fidget.

Grace inhaled breakfast with little regard to what was on her plate. Thanking Agnes, as was her habit, she flew around to the stables, greeting Gibbs and Matt with a merry smile.

"Good morning, Miss Fitzgerald. We believe the horses will arrive around ten o'clock," said Gibbs in reply to her unspoken question. "Apparently the steward advised his Lordship they would depart the horse stud early."

Unable to help herself Grace clapped her hands in glee. "That's good, it will give us all day to settle them. I wonder whether they already have names. I suppose I should have asked. I never thought about it."

"Usually they do, Miss Fitzgerald, but I'm sure you can change them if they are not to your liking." Matt replied, chuckling at her expression, which reminded him of his younger sister when she was about to get her favourite treat.

The three discussed the horses, distracting Grace, and it did not seem too long before they heard the thud of hooves. Grace led the way through to the front of the house where she found Evans speaking to three lads. She recognised one of them. It was Reggie, the groom with whom she had spoken at the horse stud.

"Hello, Reggie. How lovely to see you again," she strode forward, a cheerful smile lighting her face.

Reggie turned at her approach and, remembering Grace, grinned back. "Good day, miss. Well, 'ere we are, your'n three 'orses. I 'ope this mare dunnt let you down." Nodding at the dapple-grey horse and shaking his head. Baffled as to why this well-to-do lady would be daft enough to buy an old nag.

Evans and the two other grooms looked shocked at such familiarity, but Grace winked at her butler and, imperceptibly, shook her head.

"Well, we shall see, shan't we? Please would you and…"

"Walt and Toby," Reggie supplied, indicating who was who.

"…Walt and Toby," she smiled at the two youngsters who grinned back shyly, "…assist Gibbs and Matt with the stallions, while I take the mare" was all she said. She waited until the five guided the two enormous carriage horses to their new abode before turning to the dapple-grey who was standing quietly at the gate, head down.

Speaking to the horse in the same singsong tones she had used two days previously, Grace walked slowly over to the mare who, hearing a familiar voice, lifted her head, and whinnied softly.

Reaching the animal, Grace calmly took the lead rein, and steered the horse along the path at the side of the house to the field beyond, never breaking her flow of words. The mare followed trustingly.

Latching the gate securely behind them, Grace unclipped the rein and, patting the animal's warm flank, encouraged her into the wide green space.

Nothing happened. The mare didn't move. She sniffed the air, blowing through her nose and occasionally stamping one of her front legs. Grace stroked the horse's neck, allowing her creature to adjust to her new surroundings.

Suddenly, the mare tossed her head and neighed, trotting forward into the open expanse of land. The trot became a canter as the mare let loose, and explored her new home, stopping now and again to sniff the grass or nibble on what might prove to be a juicy leaf.

Grace smiled to herself, knowing at least one of the three horses was happy to be here. Walking over to the shelter, the young woman opened the doors, so the creature could come and go as she pleased, and left her to it, heading back to check on her other acquisitions.

Gibbs and Matt had settled the carriage horses into their loose boxes, and the two animals were busy munching on fresh hay. Evans had escorted Reggie, Walt and Toby to the kitchen, where Grace found them enjoying a hot drink, a plate of sandwiches, and several slices of ginger cake.

"Thank you, for your assistance today, young sirs. I'll have my men water and feed your mounts before you set off, and please have as much cake as you can eat. Oh, and Reggie, I meant to ask. Are any of these creatures already named?"

"Not that we know of, miss. They wasn't bred at the stud, and you know how we came to have yon grey. Naming rights is all your'n." Reggie replied. The three thanked her, grinning cheekily, relaxing for a little longer under the watchful eye of Evans, revelling in the attention of Polly and Becca, who plied them with eager questions.

Grace chuckled quietly at the three youngsters and asked them not to leave without seeing her. She returned to the field, where the mare was standing under a tree, chewing contentedly at a bale of hay, slung over a branch by either Matt or Gibbs. Appreciating the thoughtful gesture, Grace walked over to the horse and stroked her nose.

"So, my sweet girl what name shall we choose for you?" Studying the animal, Grace noticed the way the light flickered over her dappled markings, like shadows in moonlight, and it came to her. "Luna," she breathed, rolling the word around in her head.

The mare blew in her ear, which Grace took to be a sign she wasn't displeased.

"Luna, hmmm, a more suitable name I cannot imagine." Pleased with her choice, Grace rushed to the stables, determined to strike while the iron was hot and name her two carriage horses as well.

"Gibbs! Matt!" she called when she entered the carriage house. Her driver and groom appeared from the far end of the building.

"Yes, Miss Fitzgerald?" replied Gibbs, "How may we help you?"

"I have been assured these two have not been named, so we can decide. I would like strong names, but nothing too long or fancy." She observed the handsome stallion in the first loose box, admiring his reddish-brown coat and the black of his mane and legs.

Tall as she was, he towered over her, but for all his size he was a gentle creature, and stepped closer to have his nose stroked, nickering softly when Grace obliged.

After several minutes, she went to the adjacent stable where the other horse, also a bay, was stamping impatiently. Grace crooned to him, asking whether he was jealous, to the amusement of Gibbs and Matt.

"Not sure as they understand jealousy, Miss Fitzgerald." Matt chuckled.

"Of course, they do, don't you my beauty," Grace faced the horse. "Now, what shall we call you? You need names with stature and gravitas." Both men looked perplexed at this. "Dignity," she clarified. "They should have noble names." She pondered this for a while.

Each offered several suggestions, none of which seemed to fit such majestic creatures.

"I cannot stand about all day deciding," Grace said, eventually, "I will think on it and come back later. Please could you keep an eye on the mare? Her name is Luna. That's one out of three."

She grinned at the two men and took her leave, letting them get on with the rest of their day. Glad to have the horses under their care finally, Gibbs and Matt were soon busy with their chores.

In the kitchen, Grace noted the three lads were finishing their last slice of cake. She pressed some coin into their hands, repeating her thanks for transporting her horses with such good care.

"Oh, Miss, we cannot take this," said Reggie, blushing to the roots of his scruffy hair and trying to return the money. "'Tis our job, so 'tis and we get a fair wage."

Grace refused to take it back. "This is a gift from me. Please accept it. I expect it is nice to spend the day delivering horses, but 'tis a fair distance from the horse farm, and this is a token of my gratitude." By their red faces, Grace could see her gesture embarrassed them, but she wasn't about to change her mind.

Grinning unrepentantly, she reiterated the sentiment and

assured them their horses were ready whenever they were. The three young men bowed and, shoving their caps hard down on their heads, bolted to where their horses were waiting at the front gate.

~

Grace waved them off and then headed indoors, realising she had missed luncheon when her stomach growled. After devouring a light meal, Grace spent the rest of the day helping Polly and Becca, make lists of things required in the rooms they were freshening up; bed linens, window furnishings and so on.

A fairly mindless task, Grace mulled over several possible names while, apparently, focused on what colour coverlets would suit which bedroom.

The afternoon was drawing to a close when, unexpectedly and to the mild consternation of her two maids, Grace whooped, dropped her pile of notes, and shot off to the carriage house.

Gibbs and Matt were bringing the two stallions inside as she fell rather than walked through the door.

"I think I've got it, them," she announced importantly. Gibbs glanced at Matt who shrugged uncomprehendingly and they both looked at Grace. "The names. I think I've come up with perfect names." Understanding dawned and the two men waited expectantly.

"Titus and Nero," she said with a flourish, beaming at the two men, who grinned back, repeating the names to themselves, nodding slowly as they registered how well they suited the two stallions.

"Titus and Nero. Weren't they emperors or some such thing, back in Roman times?" questioned Matt, surprising Grace with his knowledge.

"Yes, yes they were. I had no idea you knew anything of classical history, Matt."

Matt chuckled. "I was taught by his Lordship's father, up at Whiteoaks. He loved Roman history and encouraged us to memorise an inordinately long list of emperors. At one time I could manage about twenty, but I've forgotten most of them now. Nero, I remember because of something about Rome burning, and Titus stuck in my head because of the Sack of Jerusalem."

It was about the longest speech Matt had made in her presence, and Grace gaped at him. It was one thing to know the names of these rulers, but to recall something of their notoriety astounded her.

"If every you want to read more about them, I have several books about their lives and the crazy antics they got up to and would be happy to lend them to you. Now, what do you think? Are Titus and Nero worthy names for this magnificent creatures?"

Gibbs and Matt confirmed, in their humble opinion, they were perfect and that was that. Grace spoke to both horses apprising them of their new names, certain they approved. She was leaving the stables, when she heard the gate click and, coming around the corner of the house spotted Theo striding up to her front door.

"Doctor Elliott!" she called. He turned at the sound of her voice and smiled. Grace felt her heart thud and hundreds of butterflies fluttered in her stomach. *Seriously Grace,* she chided herself, *you must get a grip. Rubbish you are, absolutely rubbish, so much for poise and elegance.*

The doctor walked over and Grace, attempting to master her emotions, asked whether he would like to see the horses in their new abode. Theo nodded and offered Grace his arm, listening as she described her day, the arrival of her horses and how well they had settled, finishing up by telling him their names.

The couple stood near the gate in the wall, watching Matt walk Luna into her stable for the night, and Theo declared her choices to be excellent.

This earned him a smile which made his toes curl, and an invite to stay for dinner, which he accepted with alacrity. The remainder of the evening passing in a flurry of food, laughter, conversation, and at least one very passionate kiss.

CHAPTER 24

September dawned and, when most of the harvest had been gathered in around Oak Stanton, lessons in the little school at Whiteoaks resumed in earnest.

Billie and Grace were well prepared and Grace, to her own great surprise, proved to be a natural teacher. She was more at ease with the younger children, but was not daunted when, on the odd occasion, she took a class with those older children still able to attend the small school.

When she wasn't teaching, Grace became accustomed to helping Billie in her herb garden. The pair devoted hours to discussions on the benefits, or otherwise, of particular plants, relishing the pleasure gained from sharing their knowledge.

For Grace, this regular contact with lots of people took some getting used to. For two years, her world had been restricted to her home, her skeleton staff and infrequent visits with Jemima, and she had forgotten how to socialise.

Now, in addition to the six members of her own household, it was not unusual for her to talk with dozens. Theo, Billie, Giles, the children who attended class, their parents, the staff at Whiteoaks, the list went on.

At first, she was reticent. New to the area, she was concerned people might think she had wormed her way into the lives of the Winchesters. When it became clear no one thought any such thing, her confidence blossomed.

A few weeks after she started at the school, Grace acknowledged how much she enjoyed the diverse conversations she had with these people who were now her friends and neighbours.

If the weather was decent, she rode on Luna to Whiteoaks, and the locals soon recognised her, waving or hailing a greeting when she passed. The feeling she had been accepted into this small community was a gift Grace never expected, and one she cherished.

During this time, several things occurred which, on their own, seemed inconsequential but were part of a chain of events which would have fatal consequences.

The first was when Giles, with apparent regret, declined the duke's generous invitation to Blackheath Manor, citing sickness in the family.

Without going into detail, he declared it was discourteous in the extreme to carry illness into so genteel a gathering, where they may infect the duke's other guests.

The earl received a polite reply. Reading between the lines, Giles was of the opinion, Aldwych suspected prevarication, and their failure to attend would be neither forgotten nor forgiven.

. . .

Grace decided her cousin was owed at least the same, if not more, consideration she had shown her staff and explained, briefly, her recent circumstances to Ralph and Tessa. Ralph had been so solicitous, he deserved nothing less.

With no other family in London, her cousin and his wife had heard nothing of the scandal and, as with Aunt Beatrice, were given to understand Grace had spent the previous two years mixing with the elite of Europe.

Both were aghast when the truth was revealed, perceiving far more from what Grace didn't say than what she did. For Ralph it was sufficient his cousin trusted him enough to share her ordeal, and was determined to protect her, should the duke ever dare to put in an appearance in Oak Stanton.

Theo and Evans arranged to visit with Evans' cousin Bill and his wife Hetty, to glean what they could regarding the death of the young lady for whose family Hetty used to work. The story surrounding the poor girl echoed what had happened to Grace, the only difference being that Grace was still alive.

Hetty informed Theo that the whole household knew what was going on and, whenever possible, the domestic staff attempted to keep the duke away from the daughter, Lavinia. Despite their best efforts, the family seemed to approve of his presence.

Hetty did allude to the family's finances being strained, and whether Lord Aldwych had some kind of agreement with them over debts due, or whether they believed their daughter might marry him to the saving of them, Hetty couldn't say. Whatever their reasoning, one afternoon the two were caught in so compromising a situation, there was no room for manoeuvre, and the disgrace took its toll.

Aldwych claimed Lavinia forced her attentions on him, and somehow came out of it without blame. Lavinia shut herself away and, sadly, a few weeks afterwards, was found, unresponsive, by her maid. The family doctor had been unable to revive her, and it was put about her death was the result of an infection.

Her personal maid swore the empty bottle of laudanum found next to Lavinia's bed had not been there the previous night. The tragedy was hushed up — as these things often are — and the duke was allowed to get away with his actions.

Appalling though this tale was, it was not particularly noteworthy, although most girls did not take their own lives. The nobility had more than its fair share of cads and rakes.

Notorious for their reckless behaviour, such men were more interested in taking their pleasure than worrying whether their actions might ruin a young girl's reputation. Sometimes — if caught — to save face and, indifferent to the feelings of the two involved, a couple would be expected to marry.

A large dowry along with a wife who could be persuaded to ignore her husband's excesses for the sake of her good name, usually sweetened the deal, and the *gentlemen* in question rarely curbed their decadent ways.

What *was* uncommon, was how often Aldwych seemed to be at the centre of such scandals, yet nary a hint of disgrace blemished his name. Listening to Hetty's account, Theo was even more resolute the duke could not continue to behave in so heinous a manner and sent Withers an update.

Throughout these weeks, Theo called upon Grace as often as his duties allowed and their courtship progressed unhurriedly. Theo, his hand declared, and his heart stolen, knew what he wanted from their relationship. Determined not to push Grace into anything she wasn't ready for, he was content for it to develop slowly, letting Grace take the lead.

Grace was not unsympathetic to his feelings, for even though she had not the courage to tell him, she loved Theo, and her ardour mirrored his. The issue was that she dreaded her reactions should their blossoming passion lead to more intimate encounters, and the last thing Grace could countenance was hurting Theo.

Understanding something of her anxieties, Theo talked to Grace about her ordeal. He was part of a small group of doctors who had helped returning soldiers cope with the horror they faced on the battlefield.

They had discovered, by encouraging these men to talk with others who had been through similar experiences, their ability to readjust to a world where most could never understand what they had suffered, became a little less challenging.

Often, being aware they were not the only ones who still struggled to adapt, was enough to initiate the slow healing process.

In the beginning, Grace was reluctant, given she had already told Theo everything. When he explained her reaction to seeing the duke's hands was not wholly dissimilar to how soldiers reacted to certain situations, she conceded it could do no harm. They were making headway. It would take time, but both felt it worth the effort.

They continued in this vein, savouring their time together, partaking of afternoon constitutionals, weekend carriage drives and, whenever they could, long horse rides.

Grace treasured these hours, away from prying eyes and gossiping lips, as even though, for the most part, none in the village gave them a second glance, there were always those for whom juicy chitchat was more sustaining than food.

Theo dined with Grace more than at his own home and if, after their meal, they spent more time kissing than talking, neither was complaining. Both relished their stimulating conversations and occasional heated debates.

Grace was an intelligent woman, and Theo took great satisfaction in challenging her on all manner of subjects from local issues to government politics, from medicine to herbal remedies, what was happening in the little school, ways to help him administer his growing practice and, frequently in Grace's case, whether pigs or sheep would be preferable in the back paddock as she had not forgotten her fancy for more animals.

One day, while enjoying a ride across the fields, the couple was startled by the rapport of more than one gun. Living adjacent to a vast estate such things were not unusual, as periodically, especially at this time of year, the farmers would shoot game.

Theo's mount, used to loud noises did not flinch, not so Luna who panicked, almost tossing Grace. Thankfully, that young woman was not so easily unseated and hung on while Luna fled at full gallop over the fields, clearing several hedges and a stream before coming to a panting halt not far from The Gables. Rolling her eyes and snorting, Luna, who was thoroughly spooked, took some soothing.

Grace had patience in abundance and, remembering Bert's comments about the mare being maltreated, wondered whether her anxiety was related to loud noises in general or guns in particular. Wanting to test her theory, Grace called for Matt and asked him to crack the whip within the confines of the stable while she and Luna stayed in the meadow.

The enclosed area made the sound of the whip far louder than when cracked outside, and Luna's reaction mimicked her earlier one. Calming the mare and, with a care for her staff, Grace explained to Gibbs and Matt her theory Luna had been traumatised at some point, and to be aware loud bangs were a trigger.

The incident confirmed Theo's opinion that Grace recognised in Luna an echo of her own terror. Grace spent hours coaching the mare, in an attempt to reduce her anxiety with some success, but she worried it was already ingrained. This made no difference to how she felt about the creature. Luna was now a beloved member of Grace's family, and nothing would ever change that.

~

Between teaching, helping Billie, being courted by Theo, and training Luna, Grace found time to help Polly and Becca spruce up those rooms at The Gables which had become sadly neglected. It was an activity Grace truly enjoyed, and by now the three had a number of lists, with Grace acknowledging a trip to London was probably a necessity.

She preferred to choose materials and linens herself than relegate the task to someone she didn't know — although she acknowledged Jemima would likely be pleased to offer her services. A visit to the capital might also afford her an opportunity to visit Kew and maybe persuade Joe Gregson to part with a small selection of cuttings for her garden, in particular the pyracantha.

She was discussing this with Billie one afternoon after classes had finished. The two were relaxing with a cup of coffee in the library at Whiteoaks.

Billie, who had kept her news a secret, mentioned Giles and she would be going to London the following week to attend her brother's wedding, and perhaps they could travel together. Grace could trial her new carriage horses on a proper journey and two coaches would provide plenty of room for any purchases.

Engrossed in their discussion, neither heard Giles and Theo enter the library. Arrested by the enthusiasm on the faces of Billie and Grace, husband and suitor respectively, simply observed for a few moments, unwilling to interrupt such uninhibited pleasure.

Their presence was soon detected, and the two men were drawn, somewhat reluctantly it must be admitted, into a conversation about drapery, materials and linens, which they not a single clue about.

Still, it was an amusing diversion, and kept them occupied until dinner was announced. By the time the meal was over, plans had been made for the four to spend a week in the capital. Each would have their own appointments, but they could chance to meet frequently.

"Once it is known we are going up, I imagine, in addition to Stephen's nuptials, there will be one or two events where Giles and I shall be expected to put in an appearance. It is no longer the Season, but there always seems to be some soiree or ball to which we just *have* to go," Billie grumbled, making her husband and Theo laugh, aware of how much she disliked such social events and only attended them under sufferance.

While the others chatted about parties and how to avoid them, Grace remained silent, a cold finger of dread slinking down her spine. She would not be invited to, or accepted at, any function organised by the *ton*.

This did not bother her, but she realised it might bring her courtship with Theo into question. *What would his mother think? Had he even told her?* No doubt she would prefer him to find a bride to whom scandal didn't cling.

Yes, Theo cared for her, but Grace understood the machinations of society. Love — if indeed he did love her — however enduring, often had to be set aside for the reputation of the family, and Grace did not think she could endure hearing Theo had danced more than twice with another, far more suitable lady. She became aware Billie was asking her a question and all three were looking at her in puzzlement.

"I do beg your pardon, Billie, my mind was elsewhere. Perhaps it might be better if you did not associate with me while we are in the city," she said in her quiet way. Three pairs of eyes pinned her to the chair, making her cheeks flush.

Spreading her palms, she clarified. "You know of the disgrace attached to my name. It seems unfair for any of you to risk being tarnished by association. My staying at Hawkesworth House means there will be no need to meet. I could never forgive myself if you, Billie and you, my Lord had your reputations besmirched..." she drew a steadying breath "...and you, Theo," holding his gaze. "What of your family? Your brother is a marquis. He will not thank you for attracting unwanted attention, and I am certain your mother would agree with him."

Theo stared back, seeing the pain Grace fought so hard to bury, lurking in her extraordinary eyes, which shimmered with sudden tears. His heart lurched and it was only that he did not wish to embarrass her in front of their hosts, which prevented him from whisking her into his arms and kissing her distress away.

"When are you going to get it into your head, you are my friend, and I do not give a fig about the *ton* and their small-minded ways?" Billie expostulated.

"Grace, please, you must not assume everyone is cold and

unforgiving. Theo's mother welcomed me with open arms when I stayed with her prior to my marriage, and I had been accused of murder. Giles' family was equally congenial. This man who harmed you, who ruined your name, is in the past, and should not be allowed to define your future."

Grasping Grace's hand in her earnestness, Billie entreated her friend to believe what she was saying.

"My wife is correct, Grace," affirmed Giles. "Whether you attend any balls while in London is your choice, but I cannot in all conscience agree to ignoring you for the duration. What kind of man do you think that makes me? Moreover, how you expect to do all that shopping without Billie's assistance is beyond me, neither would she have intention of letting you."

The earl winked conspiratorially, and Grace, studying his expression, saw it to be open and untroubled. He spoke truthfully.

Theo was the last to respond. His family would be aware of the whispers surrounding Grace, but his mother was not one to accept, at face value, anything spread by the rumour-mongers.

Further, he believed once his mother met Grace, she would understand exactly why her son wanted to spend the rest of his life with her. Taking her hand, he looked deep into her eyes when he spoke, wanting her to see the words were from his heart.

"Grace, I want you to trust I will never place you in a situation, which might cause you upset. That said, I know how cruel society can be. She is a fickle mistress but…"

Grace flinched and tried to withdraw her hand.

"…but…" he continued, refusing to let go, "…she is also one who recognises courage and strength of character. You do not have to prove yourself to anyone. You are a survivor. You were dealt a terrible blow, but you have risen above it, and I think it's about time the rest of the world appreciated that.

"Thank you for your concern about my family's good name but, whether you like it or not, I am not going anywhere. I know you think you are shielding us but now it is time for us to protect you. The words I spoke the afternoon you laid bare to me your soul, hold true. I will never leave you or let you face anything alone."

Leaning closer he murmured so softly she wasn't entirely sure she heard him properly, "I love you, Grace, and will do so until the stars no longer shine."

Grace stared at Theo, several things tumbling through her head at once. He *had* alluded to the strength of his affections, and then there was the evening when he called her 'his love' — but he hadn't repeated it... well, except once when they were in the coach and that didn't count.

As those who lack confidence are wont to do, she had persuaded herself it was imagination. Although she desperately wanted to believe his feelings had become more than just attraction, he had never overtly declared them to her in quite so undeniable a way.

She was stunned. Opening her mouth to reply, it appeared her voice had forsaken her, for nothing came out. She tried again; this time she managed a croak. She swallowed and gave it one last go

"Theo... d-did... was I... I-I nev..." her brain and her mouth frustratingly refused to coordinate and all she could come up with was, "truly?"

He smiled his sweet smile and nodded. Grace went fiery red and squeezed his fingers, still intertwined with hers.

A not so subtle cough from Billie reminded the pair where they were. Grace spluttered an apology, which was waived aside by both Billie and Giles, who were grinning like idiots at the little tableau unfolding in front of them. Billie clapped her hands in joy.

"Think nothing of it, my dear Grace. I am just happy he has finally told you with us as witnesses no less. Yes, Theo," when the doctor, presuming only Grace had caught his admission, gaped at Billie, "I know that was for Grace, but I watched your lips form the words, so do not even think of denying it." Sounding in no way contrite.

"Giles and I have known how you felt for ages. Now we've all said our piece, I assume there will be no more arguments about who shall see whom during our time in London. Grace, you and I will accompany each other to all the places we need to visit, while our men discuss whatever it is men discuss when in the city. If we absolutely have to attend some insufferable ball, I for one think we shall be the ones who have all the fun."

Billie pulled the most grotesque face, when she said this, leaving no one in any doubt how she felt about such occasions, and the others could not help but laugh. The mood lightened and, shortly thereafter, Theo and Grace took their leave.

Grace was quiet on the drive home, leaning against Theo's shoulder, their hands clasped and resting on Theo's thigh. Grace could feel the warmth of his skin through his pants and, unbidden, her head filled with images of said leg without any material between it and her hand.

She heard herself groan softly causing Theo to ask whether she was feeling unwell. Grace blushed scarlet, glad of the darkness, which would surely hide the hot flare.

"'Tis nothing, just a picture appeared in my head," she

stuttered, mortified at being caught out having such amorous thoughts.

Theo chuckled and gripped her hand. "Care to elaborate?" he queried, smiling gently and kissing her forehead, just because he could.

"Err… hmmm… no, you will think me shameless," she muttered.

Theo tilted her head and kissed her full on the lips, sending frissons of heat tripping down her spine. He let it deepen, until Grace thought the carriage had disappeared and in its place a chorus of angels serenaded them, and then leisurely withdrew.

"Don't stop," she whispered, "please don't stop."

He chuckled. "Tell me about the picture in your head first."

"That's unfair," she grumbled. "You're blackmailing me."

"Blackmail is such an ugly word." He grinned, unrepentantly. "I prefer to think of it more as an equitable exchange."

Grace grimaced and stared at him. "Promise you won't laugh."

Theo promised, so Grace told him, keeping her head bent so he could not see how red her face was. When she mentioned touching his skin, his breathing hitched, and his heartbeat went haywire.

"Oh, Grace. I cannot think of anything I would enjoy more. Well actually I can, but that would do for starters."

Her head snapped up and she fell into his rich brown eyes as he bent his lips back to hers and kissed her until she was certain she was about to burst into flames.

The sudden quiet of the coach coming to a halt at her gate jolted them back to reality. Adam opened the door and dropped the step, while Theo offered Grace his hand to help her down.

The doctor's driver hopped back up to his seat, leaving

the two to say goodnight with a modicum of privacy. Drawing every ounce of courage around herself like a cloak, Grace leant close to Theo, gripping his fingers, while reaching up to cup her free hand around his cheek.

She murmured quietly, yet clearly.

"I love you too."

CHAPTER 25

For Theo it was as though the world had stopped. He had shared with Grace what was in his heart, more because he believed it important for her to understand his support and concern went far beyond his encouraging her back into society the way he had, than in the expectation she would respond in kind.

The doctor presumed she had some idea how he felt, but he recalled how it had been with Billie and Giles, and that sometimes, when profound emotion was involved, the slightest hint of ambiguity could have unfortunate repercussions.

He knew she was physically attracted to him — her reactions when they kissed were unmistakable — but he also knew she feared the next step.

He could feel her trembling and appreciated the effort it took her to admit her feelings. He pulled her close, wrapping her to him, stroking his hand along her back. "Grace my love, you have just made me the happiest man on earth."

She blinked at his declaration, smiling a little hesitantly.

"Now I am very much afraid I must kiss you again."

"Why, Doctor Elliott, I do believe I should be quite cheered if you did."

Requiring no second invitation, he suited his words to actions, kissing her passionately, and leaving them both breathless. Hearts aflame they might well have thrown propriety to the four winds had not Theo recollected where they were.

"Allow me to walk you to your door, Miss Fitzgerald," he said, politely.

Grace took his arm, and the pair strolled decorously up the path for all the world as though they were mere acquaintances, Evans opening the door before Theo had the chance to knock.

"I will see you tomorrow, my love." He whispered for her ears only. She smiled and nodded, incapable of much else and drifted into the house as though on a cloud.

Trying and failing to come back down to earth, Grace thanked Evans and went upstairs, allowing Polly to unbutton her gown, brush her hair and help her into her nightdress, the smile never leaving her face.

The next day, Grace informed her staff about her impending trip to London and asked, should the household require anything, to please let her know. Then spent the day consolidating the other, numerous lists her maids and she had already compiled, into something more comprehensive. The whole time she appeared to be concentrating on the task at hand, she was thinking about Theo.

Logic and rational thought were discarded as though they never existed and, even though a tiny corner of her brain insisted this could never lead to happily ever after, the rest of her mind ignored it, believing, for once, she might just deserve a fairy tale ending.

Guessing Theo would come around after his working day was over, Grace mentioned to Agnes the doctor would probably stay for dinner. Since this was now a regular thing, Agnes had begun to assume, unless advised otherwise, Theo would dine with her mistress every night.

By the end of the afternoon, hot and sticky from sorting out rooms, Grace relaxed in a proper bath, luxuriating in the scented water and taking the time to wash her hair. Dressed in a gown the colour of warm rust, Grace allowed Polly to rub her hair dry and twist it into a tidy bun.

Grace was sitting in the Snug with a hot sweet drink and a book open but unread on her lap, when she heard the knock at the door. Heart fluttering, she made herself wait for Theo to come to her, not wanting to seem too eager. His eyes found hers when he entered the room and he smiled that endearing smile.

She stood to greet him, trying to maintain a semblance of formality. Totally wasted when Theo walked over and took one of her hands in his, gathering her close and kissing her until she forgot everything except the man holding her.

"Good evening, Doctor Elliott," she murmured, breathlessly, when he finally lifted his head.

"Good evening, Miss Fitzgerald," His eyes were dark, his breathing as ragged as hers.

"I hope you had a good day," she strove for normality, difficult to achieve while Theo's fingers were trailing along her spine.

"'Twas much as expected. The weather is changing, which always seems to cause infections of the throat and chest, but nothing too serious." Inhaling the light floral perfume, which seemed inherently Grace, he hesitated and then stood back, still holding her hand.

"Grace, there is something I should like to speak to you about. I have been wanting to ask you for a while and I imagine there is never a good time or a perfect moment, and I do not think it can wait any longer," he said soberly.

Theo looked so solemn, Grace was gripped by trepidation. What could he possibly need to talk to her about that warranted such seriousness? Her new-found confidence faltered. Her free hand fluttered towards him, dropping back to her side as her other hand let go of his. She moved away, needing to put distance between them.

"Theo, I... what is it? Your gravity concerns me. If 'tis bad news, please tell me forthwith, do not try to sweeten it. Is it about him? Have you heard something?" She paced in front of the fire.

Theo noticed she had gone pale. "No, oh God no, Grace, my apologies. 'Tis nothing like that. I did not mean to upset you. It is just... well I'm not sure... you might..." fumbling his words, he broke off.

Grace realised Theo, always so sure of himself was at a loss. After all they had shared, and the declarations they had made, nothing between them should be this difficult.

She walked over to the fire, where he stood shifting from foot to foot, dragging at his cravat as though it constricted him. Curving a cool hand around his cheek, her fingers stroked his jaw, even so light a caress enough to make his heart pound.

"Theo, whatever it is, please tell me. What causes you such disquiet?"

Theo gazed at his love wondering whether he dared, and knowing he really had no choice. He could not think of anything else to say which might sound credible now, so he took a deep breath and opened his heart.

"Grace, I love you. When I look back, I think my heart has been yours since first I saw you, even though it took my mind a little longer to catch up." His eyes crinkling when he smiled gently. "Would you do me the very great honour of becoming my wife?"

Grace started to speak, but Theo shook his head, worried she would decline his offer before he could allay her misgivings.

"No, please let me finish. I cherish every minute we are together and find the hours we are apart interminable. I cannot wait to see you every day and when it comes to saying goodnight I am consumed by a strange melancholy.

"I know you are worried about how you might cope with the deeper intimacy which comes with marriage, but I promise I will not push you into or expect from you anything for which you are not ready.

"Grace, until I met you I did not believe in fate but I cannot imagine my life without you in it, so maybe we are destined to be together and, if this is indeed true, then everything else will surely fall into place in its own time."

Grace looked at him. This man who had turned her life upside down, who had broken down her barriers and touched the deepest part of her soul. She knew, whatever happened, she could face it as long as he was by her side.

Theo's posture was of someone steeling themselves for disappointment. His hair was sticking out at odd angles for he had been running his fingers through it, and his eyes were wary.

Her chest constricted — he feared she might reject him. Grace smoothed a hand over his waistcoat, recalling her thoughts all those weeks ago, at Whiteoaks, just before they set off for the horse farm.

"Theo, I have loved you for some time, but for so long my heart has refused to believe I would be lucky enough to find someone who could look beyond what happened and offer the same in return. Before I answer your question, may I beg your indulgence a moment longer?"

Slightly bewildered, Theo nodded.

"One thing I have noticed about the Winchesters is, whenever they have been apart, even though it may only have been a matter of minutes, Giles always looks for Billie; she is his first thought. One day, after witnessing this, I knew I wanted the same and, moreover, I wished, fervently, for you to be the one doing the looking."

Theo's expression relaxed, just a fraction.

"I want to be your first thought every morning when you wake and your last thought at night before you sleep. I want you to hurry home to me when your day is through for no other reason than you long to be with me.

"I don't want it to be a problem should I decide, on a whim, to seek you out at random, simply because I have a hankering to be near you, to talk with you or, yes, even to kiss you. I know many men of the nobility keep a mistress, but I am afraid I could never share you with another woman; it would be the death of me.

"Further, I will not stand in the shadows, or wait on the sidelines. I refuse to be seen and not heard. I have spent two years doing that and shall no more."

She held his gaze, her incredible amber eyes glowing the light from the crackling fire.

"If, truly, you wish to marry me, you must understand, I cannot countenance a conventional marriage. I want it to be ridiculously, irrationally, passionately and hopelessly unconventional and, in this, I will not be swayed, selfish though my demands may seem.

"I want to laugh with you, and cry with you, and dance with you. I want to be your right hand, your partner, and your best friend, even your mistress. If you are agreeable to these things, then yes, I would be overjoyed to be your wife."

It was a long speech, and Grace wasn't entirely certain she had been clear enough but couldn't say anymore. *In her attempt to retain a modicum of independence, had she placed too many conditions on Theo?* Perhaps he wanted a traditional marriage with a traditionally biddable wife.

She thought she understood him better than that and, physical attraction aside, marriage was far more than courtship. It was sharing someone's life, for better and for worse and, before she took the next step, Grace needed to know they were in accord.

Theo watched Grace, reading the emotions and uncertainties in her eloquent eyes, as she tried to articulate what she craved, hoping she hadn't scared him off.

"Grace, my darling girl, what on earth makes you think I would want it any other way?"

His simple sincerity did more to convince her than any flowery speech and she gulped, feeling the prick of pesky tears under her lids. Determined not to cry, she blinked fiercely, and tried to respond, but couldn't, her words caught in her throat.

As always Theo seemed to grasp the problem and, uncaring Evans was likely to call them for dinner, drew her to him, kissing her with an exquisite gentleness, which threatened to undo her completely.

Several blissful moments passed. He lifted his head and cupped her face. "So, Miss Grace Fitzgerald, you are my betrothed. I admit to a great partiality in being able to say that. I will probably say it a lot."

Grace took one of his hands and entwined it in hers, loving the way he rubbed his thumb against her palm. "I admit to a great partiality in hearing it, Doctor Theodore Elliott," bestowing on him a bright smile which sent warmth tumbling through him, all the way to his toes, "and, much as I do not wish to end this moment, I do believe dinner is served."

Nodding towards the doorway in which Evans was waiting, unobtrusively, to announce the meal, a knowing grin lighting up his usually sombre face.

~

During dinner they began to plan their wedding. Neither wanted a large affair, just an intimate gathering with their closest friends, and as soon as possible.

While they were talking, trying to decide when and where, Theo surprised Grace by producing a special licence, something he had organised when he realised marriage to Grace was his greatest wish.

Grace was stunned. Such licences were costly and not easily procured. A trifle self-consciously, Theo explained his reasoning and, if possible, she fell more deeply in love with him.

That he was prepared to marry her not knowing whether she loved him, but in a bid to protect her, revealed much about his strength of character. She was both touched and humbled. The licence also meant they were free to marry the next day should they so decide, and in a place of their choosing.

Theo wanted to marry before they went to London, something to which Grace was not opposed and by the end of the evening they had settled on the coming Friday. Three days hence.

It left little time to organise everything, but neither was overly concerned. Before Theo left, the couple spoke to the household, sharing their news, but entreating them to keep it quiet until they were able to tell the Winchesters.

Everyone declared themselves elated for the pair. Witness to their blossoming romance, all had been taking guesses as to how soon the doctor would ask for their mistress' hand, hoping she would accept.

Theo affirmed would call at nine the next morning, before saying goodnight in *the most* sublime fashion. Grace watched him walk down the path and along the darkened street, her head whirling with the events of the evening.

Dubious as to how she would react to the physical side of the marriage, she knew without a shadow of a doubt, the only man in the world who would be able to help her overcome her aversion was Theo. More than this, she wanted him, her body cried out for him, and she trusted this was a sign she was ready.

When Grace finally floated into her bedchamber, she found Polly waiting for her. The young maid helped her undress and brushed out her hair, the long soothing strokes, soporific, and Grace was asleep almost before the bedclothes were drawn up.

CHAPTER 26

Theo arrived on the stroke of nine and escorted Grace to his carriage. Adam was driving and, when he dropped the step, he tipped his cap, congratulating Grace on her betrothal, making her blush as she thanked him, prettily.

The short journey seemed to be over in the blink of an eye, and Grace was aware of the flutter of nerves when they drew up outside Whiteoaks. Gripping Theo's hand as Thomas showed them through to the library, she fought to remain calm and in control, but by the time Billie appeared Grace was trembling.

"Good morning, to what do I owe this pleasure? I am not complaining, but Thomas said you needed to see *both* Giles and me. I trust nothing is amiss?" Billie grinned engagingly at the couple.

It took one look at their expressions for her astute mind to guess why they were there. Joy flooded through her. "Giles will be here momentarily, and Thomas is bringing…oh, here he comes," as the faithful butler came in carrying a tray of hot coffee and sweet buns.

"Sit, please sit, we do not stand on ceremony here, you are like family to us." Directing them towards the wing backed chairs which circled the blazing fire.

An oddly awkward silence fell, one no one seemed willing to break. They remained thus until Giles strode through the door several moments later, his face lighting up when he saw Billie. Grace glanced at Theo whose lips twitched in quick understanding.

"Good morning you two. Thomas said you needed us... ahhh," as Billie waved her hand at her husband who sat on the arm of his wife's chair and looked expectantly at Grace and Theo.

"So, what is so important, I am summoned from a meeting with my stewards. No matter," when Grace started to apologise, "it was a most boring meeting regarding the price of wheat. I am not wholly upset. How may we help?"

Grace looked at Theo, and the doctor surmised she was unsure about what to say. Walking over to the mantel, he stood, clasping his hands behind his back, and rocking just a little on the balls of his feet.

"Grace and I hope you two might stand as witnesses for us on Friday."

Giles looked somewhat confused, as Billie stifled an exuberant squeal. "Witnesses? What the devil have you done, Elliott?" he queried, looking askance at Billie who was now stuffing her hand in her mouth to stop herself laughing. "What? What am I missing?"

"We are to be wed, Winchester," clarified Theo, twinkling at Grace whose cheeks were glowing, and not from the warmth of the fire.

"Oh," was the less than encouraging response they received.

Billie stared at her husband in consternation. Theo frowned, and Grace felt her stomach plummet.

Despite his comments the evening they talked about their London trip, Grace was aware Giles had reservations about whether she could make Theo happy, for she could read him better than he realised. Taking hold of her courage, she went to Theo's side and linking her fingers with his, turned to face Giles.

"My Lord."

Giles' brow creased at this formality.

Grace ignored it, stubbornly putting a verbal distance between them. "I know you are concerned, after my past experiences, I cannot be the wife you feel Theo deserves. I am unable to offer you any argument to the contrary except to say I love Theo with every fibre of my being and would never do anything to hurt him.

"For two long years, I lost myself, lost my heart and my soul in a dark place and I thought they were lost forever. After what happened, never did I imagine anyone might care enough to bring me back to life.

"Then I met Theo, who saw beyond the rumour and the scandal, and took the time to get to know me. He found me. He found my heart, and revived my soul with his gentle kindness, his patience and his love.

"I realise this may seem sudden, but you must trust it is not a decision I took lightly or without serious reflection, and whether you believe me or not, Theo is my whole world. Without him in it, I will be empty as a husk of that wheat you were so bored discussing."

Theo could feel Grace trembling as she said this prompting him to press her hand, gently. Her tone was lightly chiding, but she smiled while she spoke taking the sting out her censure.

Giles studied her, his expression unreadable and, Grace felt a flicker of indignation. After everything Giles had said during the time she had known him, his reaction seemed out of character.

Did he consider her only suitable as Theo's friend or maybe even his companion, but not as his wife? Did he deem her unworthy? Straightening her shoulders and looking the earl dead in the eye, she continued in a voice much less accommodating.

"My Lord, I know, after Billie, Theo is your closest friend, and I know you hold his best interests at heart. It is one of the things I admire about you, your staunch support for those of whom you care.

"I could not bear it if Theo, if any of you, was placed in an untenable position because of your association with me, but we have talked about this before. I thought you understood? I thought you had accepted me?"

She glared at Giles, having to tilt her head to hold his gaze for he was taller even than Theo.

"Grace..." Giles started to speak, but Grace was having none of it and, with scant regard for civility or for that matter etiquette, interrupted him.

"Perhaps I am only welcome when you are able to classify me as merely an acquaintance. To ensure a genteel distance between us is maintained. Someone who is good enough to help your wife teach in the school, and maybe to assist in her herb garden, and quite entertaining as a dinner guest, but no closer.

"I am who I am, your Lordship. I cannot undo my past and I have nothing left to say which might convince you of my devotion. Now, I have said my piece and been unconscionably rude in front of your lovely wife. I do beg your pardon, your Ladyship. I think I should excuse myself. I will see you later, Theo."

Theo made a reflexive movement when Grace released his hand. She dropped what could only be described as a cursory curtsy, and marched towards the door, anger bristling off her.

"Grace, a moment of your time?"

She spun on her heel and, folding her arms, regarded Giles, her expression unyielding. "Is there any point?" she questioned.

"Please, I think I deserve the right to respond," he stated reasonably. An earl did not make such overtures. Grace hesitated, conceding it was only fair. Theo's face was thunderous, and he glared at his friend, fighting the urge to punch him.

Giles raised a placating hand. "I am sorry, Theo. I had no mind to upset either of you. It was surprise. I had not expected you to ask for her hand yet and it caught me off guard."

Theo was still scowling.

"Trust me, my friend."

Theo nodded slowly.

Giles turned back to Grace who was hovering near the door. "Grace, please accept my sincere apologies. The last thing I think is that you are wrong or bad for Theo. Firstly, it really is none of my business…"

Grace raised a sceptical eyebrow,

"…yes, I admit to being uneasy when you began spending more than a little time together. To clarify, Theo and I have been friends since childhood, and together we have been through much. I owe him my life and because of this, perhaps I am overprotective. If I am honest, the little I knew of your circumstances gave me cause to worry.

"When we visited the horse stud, I saw the way you looked at each other. It was obvious, even if neither of you realised, you had fallen in love. Then you shared your story, and although you had my deepest sympathy, my unease grew.

"After suffering such trauma, I wondered whether

anything more than a gentle friendship would cause you to retreat and so, yes, I worried for Theo."

Giles held the eyes of the woman before him, willing her to understand he wanted this to work as much as she did.

She searched his face. "Your Lordship. I realise our announcement seems precipitous but, other than the obvious, I think Theo wishes to be married before we leave for London, so I have his protection.

"Regardless, whether we wed now or at some future date, it will make no difference to the depth of my love for him. So why delay? My Lord, I know I am tainted. My reputation is likely ground into dust, but do you not think I... we... deserve this chance at happiness?

"I believe the love Theo and I share comes only once in a lifetime, a step in either direction, and we would have missed each other. Would you be the one to deny us the possibility?"

Her words struck a chord in Giles. He had fallen in love with Billie at first sight, despite knowing nothing about her. Even when scandal whispered around her, it was too late, his feelings were irrevocable.

"Grace, please trust me when I say, I wish you and Theo the same bliss I enjoy with Billie. I never intended to hurt you or make you think I believe you are somehow unworthy of Theo because of what you were subjected to. My wife..." he smiled at Billie, who beamed at him, "...often takes me to task for I am wont to forget how my words or actions might be interpreted.

"I was neither angry nor upset with your announcement, and I surely do not want to deny you one iota of the felicity I know you deserve. I apologise unreservedly for making what should have been a joyful morning into one of sadness. 'Twas just your news was the last thing I expected to hear and, yes, because it came out of the blue, my response was ill-considered, and in no way reflective of my true feelings."

He paused and took both of her hands in his. "Grace, I do not think it too soon, and even if I did, that is my issue not yours. I wish you all the happiness in the world and would be proud to stand as a witness on Friday. More than this, if you permit, I should like to offer Whiteoaks for the ceremony. You may invite whomsoever you please and afterwards we shall have a feast befitting the occasion."

Candour shone from his eyes, and Grace heard veracity in his words.

"Thank you, my Lord..." he arched an eyebrow, "...Giles," she offered a hesitant smile.

Giles saw several emotions flicker across her mobile face and, ignoring propriety, pulled her into his arms for a brotherly hug. "You will be as a sister to me once you are wed to Theo. I believe a hug is allowed."

This did more to persuade Grace than any words might have done. Such familiarity was only acceptable between family members and went a long way to restoring her equilibrium.

Theo's face relaxed while he watched this interaction, knowing Giles was sincere. "Thank you, Winchester. I did not relish the thought of calling you out." Waggling his eyebrows in a most comical fashion and making them all laugh at the image his suggestion evoked.

The atmosphere in the room lightened and, as Thomas came in with more coffee and a plate of freshly baked Eccles cakes, the four began to organise a wedding.

The next two days vanished in a whirlwind of preparations. Between trying on gowns, planning and re-planning the wedding breakfast, Grace penned the few invitations and hand delivered them.

Agnes joined Sarah at Whiteoaks, the two women coming up with all manner of delicacies with which to tempt the palates of the wedding guests.

Grace worried about what to wear, presuming all her fashionable gowns remained in London, until Polly reminded her of the sage silk.

It was Grace's favourite, and one of three stunning gowns Peggy had placed in the trunks, ignoring her mistress' assurance she would never require such finery. Grace was touched Peggy cared enough to include this dress, agreeing it was absolutely perfect.

In the midst of all this activity, Grace began to feel as though everything was spiralling out of control and was thankful, as were the rest of her staff, when Theo appeared every evening as usual. His presence keeping her, more or less, calm.

Friday morning dawned cool but clear. After luxuriating in a long hot bath, Grace submitted to Polly's ministrations. Her favourite light floral fragrance was dabbed on her wrists and behind her ears before her rich auburn hair, washed the night before so it was properly dry was pulled and twisted into a most ornate style.

Next came the dress, beneath which were several layers of exquisite undergarments — a gift from Billie — although from where she acquired them at such short notice, was anybody's guess.

Polly helped Grace into the beautiful gown, fastening the multitude of tiny buttons. A pair of soft leather slippers with satin ribbons, in the same shade of green as the dress, completed the ensemble.

Grace stood for a moment, gathering herself, amazed by her reflection in the mirror.

"Polly, you are a miracle worker. I look almost elegant," smiling at her maid who blushed prettily.

"You are always elegant, Miss, all I did was enhance what already was there."

Grace squeezed Polly's fingers. "Thank you, my dear. I am very grateful to have you in my life. Now get on with you, the coach taking you to Whiteoaks will be waiting." Polly hesitated. "I will be fine, go," hustling the maid out.

All her staff had been invited, as had those who helped with the garden, Ralph and Tessa, as well as Theo's household. Theo himself would be moving into The Gables. Grace was unwilling to leave the home, which had become her haven, and Theo didn't care as long as he was with Grace; his meagre staff already slotting seamlessly into their new abode.

He would retain his old home and continue to use it as a surgery. It might also prove advantageous as a guesthouse, should they ever be called upon to entertain large numbers.

Aware married couples often had separate bedrooms and, unsure whether Theo might prefer to sleep alone, Grace helped Polly and Becca prepare a bedchamber for her new husband.

Despite her unease about the physical intimacy that came with marriage, she hoped they would share a bed. It seemed pointless having two chambers, but it was a subject she was not comfortable broaching, and certainly not this day.

~

Giles who had offered to stand in her father's stead was waiting in the Snug. The earl cut a fine dash in a snowy white shirt, wine coloured cravat and waistcoat, under charcoal grey tailcoat and pants. He bowed when Grace walked into the room, and crooked his arm.

"You look beautiful, Miss Fitzgerald. Shall we?" He escorted her to the carriage, chatting about their upcoming visit to London during the short journey to Whiteoaks, more to settle Grace's obvious nerves than for any other reason.

Will was there to drop the step when the carriage halted, to Grace's surprise, at the front of the house.

"Well, you surely did not think we would allow the bride to arrive at her wedding through the back door, did you?" Giles grinned at her expression. "You need to sweep in."

He winked and tucked her hand under his elbow. "Come, your husband-to-be awaits with great impatience," his words drawing a chuckle from Grace.

They climbed the steps and, before they entered the house, Grace stopped.

Turning to Giles, she whispered, "Thank you, my Lord… Giles. Your generosity humbles me. This is beyond my wildest expectations."

He smiled and patted her hand, leading her through into the ballroom, where their guests were already seated. Theo stood at the other end of the room, alongside a gentleman in black vestments, whom Grace knew to be the vicar.

Her breathing caught when she studied the man who would, in a matter of moments, become her husband. He was also wearing a crisp white shirt, dark charcoal pants and tailcoat but, his waistcoat and cravat matched the colour of her dress.

Grace was astonished at the lengths to which people had gone to make this day perfect in every way.

CHAPTER 27

Clutching Giles' arm, Grace walked slowly up the improvised aisle, smiling at her friends, savouring the moment. A moment she thought would never be hers. Theo grinned when she reached him, and took her hand. Grace reiterated her thanks to Giles and smiled at Billie, who moved to stand next to her husband.

The liturgy was brief but moving. The age-old words resonated with Grace, and she made her vows in a voice, she was pleased to hear, sounded steady. Theo slid a cool gold band onto her fourth finger, holding it there while he pledged his life to hers.

The ceremony concluded, and they were pronounced husband and wife. The newlyweds stood for long moments gazing at each other. Their love shining clear as the sun over a lake.

"Come on you two, plenty of time for that later," Billie interposed beaming happily, as she and Giles congratulated the couple. A sign for their other guests to follow suit, and the celebrations began in earnest.

~

At some point in the afternoon, Theo and Grace, after expressing their sincere gratitude to their hosts and guests, slipped away. The occasional brush of fingers, the odd secret smile and the hint of a kiss not enough to quench their desire. The last three days had been joyous, but utterly chaotic, and they longed to be alone just the two of them, away from, well, everyone.

Theo knew Grace would be nervous, and consummation of their vows might take a little longer than for most couples. That said, he believed they could reach a level of intimacy, which ought to obliterate the horror inflicted upon her by her tormentor, and she would see true lovemaking was a most wonderful pastime.

Grace was quiet on the ride home, her slender fingers nestled in Theo's larger ones, her head resting against his shoulder. Adam drew up outside The Gables, and the couple walked down the path into what was now their home.

"Our home. I do like the sound of that, Theo," Grace murmured when Adam opened the door. "Thank you, Adam. Please rejoin the party, I know it will go on for a while yet."

The young man hesitated, unwilling to leave them unattended.

"Truly Adam, we will be fine," affirmed Theo. Persuaded, Adam rushed off, the carriage rattling along the road at great speed. Theo chuckled. "Bless the lad, I just hope he's careful along that track, last thing I need is a call out to an injury today of all days."

Grace blushed and Theo dropped a light kiss on her forehead.

Upon entering the Snug, they saw Evans had, thought-fully, left a decanter of wine, from which Theo poured two glasses. Relaxing in the chairs, the couple let the quiet envelop.

Grace found she could not sit still. She gulped her wine with unladylike haste and wandered about the room, lining up books which were already aligned, twitching the curtains into place, fiddling with the candelabra.

Trying to stifle a chuckle, Theo — amusement lacing his tones — asked, "What has you so fidgety, my love?"

"I'm nervous. I've wanted to be with you, really be with you, for so long, but I don't know what to do. Yes, I know *how* it is supposed to happen, but this…" waving her hand between them, "…this is different. This is us, and I am afraid I will let you down."

Chewing on her lower lip, she stared across the room at the man who was now her husband, wringing her hands together, uncertainty radiating off her.

Theo walked over to his wife — oh, how he loved that she was his wife — entwining her hand in one of his and, with the other, cupped the back of her head, threading his fingers through her hair. He grazed his lips against hers, the barest hint of a promise.

Grace felt her heartbeat increase. Involuntarily, she moved closer, needing to touch him with more than her hands. An image of them naked in front of this very fire popped into her head and her breathing hitched.

"Do you trust me, Grace?" Theo murmured against her cheek. She nodded, words failing her right at that moment. "Then let us see where our adventure takes us." He recaptured her lips, only this time there was no hint. This time he possessed them, eliciting a soft mewl from Grace.

Theo drew her against him, moulding her to him, one hand stroking along her spine. She wrapped her arms around him revelling in the sweet intoxication, letting him take the lead, knowing, at this point, she would follow him to the ends of the earth.

Theo let his fingers skim over her throat and down her neck, his thumb tracing the hollows there, his lips never leaving hers.

"Show me what to do." Grace muttered, "Show me what you like."

"Follow your instincts, love," Theo replied in a gruff voice. "I have absolutely no objections to making love to you in front of this cosy fire, I think I know a far more comfortable place. I would prefer to be away from any unexpected visitors."

Grace giggled at the thought of someone coming upon them in such a manner as Theo led her up the stairs into what was now their bedchamber.

Theo closed the door and took Grace into his arms, kissing her until she thought the room was spinning, her own ardour increasing to match his.

She let her hands meander over him, feeling the erratic beat of his heart against her breast as they held each other. Just when she thought she might actually faint from desire, Theo broke their kiss.

"Grace," he murmured against her mouth.

"Mmmmm," she replied, dreamily, needing his lips back on hers.

"I do not wish to rush you into anything, but perhaps there are too many layers between us."

Leaning away so she could look at him, Grace read the hunger in the dark brown depths of his eyes and felt her body sizzle in response. "I agree," she whispered, smiling shyly. "I'm just… only… how does…"

Theo chuckled at her incoherence, thoroughly used to it by now, and hushed her gently. "Let us see whether we can work this out together, shall we?" He resumed his heart-stopping kiss, much to her gratification, and his hands began to roam up her back, his fingers finding the tiny buttons on her dress.

Slowly, oh so slowly, he undid them, allowing the material to fall away bit-by-bit, exposing a little more of her creamy skin over which he trailed his lips, causing Grace to quiver in expectation.

Unable to stop herself, her fingers pushed against the pristine white of his shirt, tracing the muscles up his arms, savouring the warmth of his skin under hers.

Theo reached the last button and the green silk slithered to the floor.

Feeling more than a little wanton, Grace fumbled with Theo's waistcoat and cravat, somehow divesting him of both, her hands tugging at his shirt, desperate for their bodies to touch.

Theo, without breaking their kiss was making light work of the layers of her gossamer fine underthings, their passion escalating in direct proportion to the amount of clothes piling up on the floor. Suddenly Grace was naked, and despite being cocooned in Theo's embrace, she felt vulnerable and tried to wrap her arms around her body.

"My love, you have no need to hide yourself from me. You are the most beautiful woman I have ever seen with or without clothes." His words were reverent, and she smiled, apprehensively. This was a huge step for her, the next few moments would be telling.

"Theo, I hope we can…but if I panic, I'm sorry."

Theo hushed her, by dint of kissing her soundly. "Trust me, Grace." His fingers wound through her hair, unpinning the intricate style, the auburn glossiness tumbling over her shoulders.

Grace sighed and stopped trying to over think it. His hands began a magical dance over her skin, and she was aware of the delicious slow burn coiling through her body.

Being an obedient wife, she did as Theo suggested and let instinct guide her, her hands casting their own spell across her husband's torso. She heard his breathing catch as her cool fingers lit the spark deep within his soul, her caress never failed to ignite.

"Theo, remember what I said about touching your leg?" she murmured. He nodded. "Well I cannot do so if your pants remain on." Growling in frustration as she made a futile attempt to rid her husband of the remainder of his garments.

She felt his chest rumble with laughter, and he divested himself of this last barrier.

They faced each other, no longer anything between them and the world seemed to hold its breath. In the silence, Grace let her eyes wander over this tall man who had stolen her heart, drinking in his lithe physique.

His chest, sprinkled with a few dark hairs, tapered to a trim waist, and as her gaze dropped, she saw how much he wanted her, aware of an answering throb deep within her core.

"Err… Grace?" Theo muttered, reaching for her.

"What is your hurry, husband of mine? I am trying to decide whether to keep you."

Emboldened, she trailed one finger from his jaw along his throat, down his breastbone, briefly pausing over his heart, smiling when she felt the irregular thud. On over his stomach and still further down, grazing against the muscle pulsing under her palm.

Theo groaned, the spark threatening to burst into flame. "Have you seen enough, wife?" he choked out.

"I believe you will prove eminently suitable," she answered primly. Resting her hands on his chest, she threaded her fingers through the smattering of hairs.

"My turn," was all Theo could gasp, whisking Grace back into his arms, he slanted his mouth over hers in a searing kiss. He carried her over to the bed, and joining her there, took his time to discover the whole of her body with both his lips and his hands.

He explored every inch of her willowy form. Gliding his hands over her fevered skin, teasing her contours. His skilful fingers making her cry out his name.

Slowly, tracing his thumb over the pulse fluttering in her throat, his fingers tracking an addictively tortuous path down the column of her neck, to the rise of her breasts.

His ceaseless caresses caused a multitude of vibrations to skitter through Grace who arched into him, her body demanding more.

For her own part, Grace could not get enough of Theo. Her hands had a will of their own, stroking over his warm flesh, scorching a path from his chest, across his back, until she curved her fingers around to his inner thigh, recreating the image from the day in the carriage, loving the feel of the soft skin against her hand.

While her fingers were driving her husband to distraction, she kissed him everywhere her lips could reach, and Theo knew he could not hold out for much longer.

"Grace," he muttered against her cheek.

"Theo," she was threading her fingers through his hair, and squirming against him, wanting all of him to be touching all of her. Her sinuous gyrations tipping him over the edge.

"Grace, how far would you like me to take this?" His voice was hoarse with suppressed need.

Grace stilled and held his head in her hands; her fathomless amber eyes dark with longing, her tousled hair splayed over the pillow like liquid bronze, and her breath coming in short bursts.

"Just don't stop, Theo. Please don't stop." She lifted her head to catch his lips drawing from him a guttural sound. His control slipping almost beyond his grasp.

"Are you sure? I have no wish to frighten you or make you recall…" he did not want to shatter this moment, but it was not fair to take her so close only to find it terrified her.

Grace took one of his hands and deliberately placed it over her heart, holding it there. "Theo, every touch, every kiss, every caress is banishing the ghosts of my past. Your tenderness weaves life into me, your passion brands me as yours. You just need to let your body claim mine."

Theo stared at his wife; her face flushed with the intensity of her emotions. Her expression of absolute faith would have brought him to his knees had he been standing, making him exceedingly glad they were lying on a comfortable bed.

Needing no further encouragement, he recaptured her lips. His hands skimming over her downy skin, he allowed the sensations to build, heat coursing through them until Grace thought they would melt into one another.

Impatient to give Theo the same rapture he was giving her, Grace tentatively curled her fingers around him. She felt the muscle quiver when she gently squeezed, teasing her fingers around the rigid flesh, forcing a primal moan from Theo's lips.

Virtually undone yet determined to make this as pleasurable as possible for his wife, Theo smoothed his hands along her body and down over her stomach his fingers seeking out her most sensitive part. He increased his gentle pressure until frissons of ecstasy tumbled through her and the smouldering flame, blazed into incandescence.

Working his magic until he was certain her desire for him far outweighed any residual fear, Theo slowly slid into her, holding back as long as he could, allowing the heat of her arousal to swallow him.

Grace suspected all reason had abandoned her. Without rational thought, she wrapped her legs around Theo, pulling him in deeper, matching his rhythm until they were in perfect harmony.

Just when she thought it couldn't get any more wondrous, a new sensation began building. It started at her toes, surging through her and for a split second she pondered whether she was going to burst into flames, as Theo took her beyond the stars.

She would not have been in the slightest surprised, to discover a whole galaxy of them had exploded in their room as wave after wave of euphoria erupted through her.

It seemed an age before everything came back into focus. Grace expected the room to be in uproar and was astonished to see it was only their bed which looked as though a whirlwind had passed through recently.

Hearts aflame, they lay entangled, Theo whispering words of love to his wife while she nestled against him.

When her breathing resumed something resembling a normal rhythm, Grace lifted herself up on one elbow, her hair falling around her and spilling across Theo's body. He twisted a lock around his fingers, while Grace drew lazy circles over his chest.

"Thank you, my love. You have saved me."

Theo shifted so he could look at her properly. "I am more than happy to take the credit, my dear but I think you probably saved yourself," was his thoughtful reply.

Grace shook her head. "No, you reached inside me to the

place where I had hidden everything away and unlocked my heart. Never could I have imagined that having someone love me, truly love me, could be so freeing. I wish my aunt were alive so I could thank her for her legacy. Without it, we would not have met, and I think I might have withered away."

She stretched over him, brushing his lips with hers. "And I believe I am going to want to do this as often as possible." Trailing her hand down his chest, a wicked grin playing around her mouth.

"Oh, you do, do you?" Amusement threaded through Theo's voice. "Well, I suppose if I must, although I do not recall promising to obey..." he let the sentence dangle, knowing exactly how Grace would react, gratified by her outraged expression.

"Ooooof..." he grunted when she pummelled him, "...hey, no need for violence, we've only just wed," catching her hands and pulling her against him,

"You asked for it," she huffed. Theo ignored that, kissing her into sublime submission. Taking his time, he made love to his wife, leisurely and tenderly, yet no less passionately, taking her to heights undreamed of until, satiated, they fell asleep wrapped in each other's arms, surrounded by an aura of utter bliss.

Theo and Grace would have liked nothing better than to spend the weekend in their bedchamber, but they had a trip to London for which to prepare and there was the not inconsequential matter of organising Theo's belongings.

All of his medical equipment remained at his old home, but the rest had been packed carefully by Martha and Ellie,

Theo's cook and housemaid respectively, and delivered early the previous morning.

Uncertain whether her husband would expect them to have separate bedchambers, Grace decided she ought to broach the subject while they surveyed the several trunks, currently cluttering up one of the guest rooms.

"Will you require your own bedchamber, Theo?" she queried, not sure she wanted to hear the answer.

Theo meditated on her question. "A separate dressing room might be useful, my love. I imagine it will be easier if our clothes are not all crushed into your two armoires." He heard an odd sigh, immediately stifled. Turning, he caught a pensive expression flit across his wife's face. "What is it Grace?"

"Nothing," she forced a bright note into her voice. "There is a room prepared. I trust you will find it satisfactory. If not, please let Polly know which you would rather have."

None of the married couples she used to know shared a bed regularly. Many of her former friends had made it clear they preferred it. She wanted it to be different for them, but there was no way she was going to demand it.

"I shall make start on the dressing room." Her words were overly formal, but for the life of her she could not tell him what bothered her. *Honestly, Grace,* she thought, *scant hours ago you were naked in his arms, and now you can't discuss with him the most basic things. You are hopeless.*

"Grace, wait." Theo grasped her hand before she could leave the room. "Grace, I do not wish to sleep alone. I want your face to be the last thing I see before I go to sleep and the first thing I see when I wake."

She flushed. He could read her like a book.

"Come," he chided gently, "when something troubles you, please do not let it fester, just ask me. One of the things I love about us is how we are able to talk about most everything, and I have no desire to lose that.

"Our lives are intertwined, everything we do affects the other and we cannot start married life with confusions and misunderstandings. We must always be true and open with each other, for that is how we shall stay strong."

"I'm sorry, Theo. 'Tis just we have not t-talked about it and I know what I wanted b-but you hadn't said anything… and m-most couples… I-I was not…"

Stuttering, and feeling pesky tears building for no reason she could think of, Grace clamped her mouth shut determined not to cry on the second day of married life.

"Hush love, I know. It's a mite overwhelming isn't it?" Theo drew her into his arms, kissing her gently as she nodded into his chest."

"I d-don't know w-why I'm crying, I never cry," she muttered helplessly. Blithely ignoring the fact, Theo had been treated to at least one or two tearful outbursts.

"I imagine because the last few days have been emotional and," he paused tilting her chin so he could look into her glistening eyes, "you might be a little tired," he smiled, mischievously.

She giggled then, blinking her tears away. Theo kissed her until they were both breathless — which had the added benefit of making her feel so much better — before saying they really must get on, or he would not be responsible for his actions.

This made Grace laugh all the more, and the two turned their attention to the tasks of the day.

CHAPTER 28

After the house was almost set to rights, and nearly all the clothes were in their proper place, the newly-weds took a walk around the village. Many of the locals knew they had just married and wished the couple every happiness.

For Grace it was another sign she was now wholly part of this little community and, while they wandered along the market stalls, the couple chatted amiably with the villagers, answering excited questions about the previous day's celebrations.

Their sudden wedding would keep the gossips happy for weeks.

Reaching the end of the main street, they came upon the field where the animals were kept. Today there were only a few cows, and a small collection of baby goats. They paused by the gate, Grace ruminating over the possibility of purchasing a goat or two. They would keep the grass down in the field, and she did not think Luna would mind.

While Theo and she were discussing this, a gentleman she did not recognise came over, and tried to engage the couple in conversation. Presuming he was an acquaintance of Theo's, and uncomfortable with such familiarity from a person she did not know, Grace excused herself, and went to talk with the owner of the animals.

Theo had no clue who the man was either, but ever the polite doctor, passed the time of day with the newcomer. He was puzzled to note the man was trying, in a circuitous manner, to elicit information about Grace. On guard now, Theo allowed the conversation to continue until it reached a point where, without seeming rude, he could extricate himself. Doing so, he joined his wife.

Grace turned when he reached her, beaming at him, her animated countenance lifting his heart. She took his hand and drew him closer. "These three would be perfect, Theo, they could live comfortably in the field. There is enough room in the stables if the weather is bad, they could share one of those stalls. Do let's take them. They are such little dears."

Even without her eyes beseeching him, Theo was unable to deny his wife anything ever, and capitulated with little argument. Grace bartered over the price, more because she enjoyed the banter than because she felt the cost too high.

Once an amount was agreed, she extracted a promise the kids would be delivered on the morrow. Clapping her hands in triumph at her purchase, Grace spun around; her eyes sparkling, her face a picture of child-like exhilaration.

Theo smothered a laugh at her high spirits and, catching her hand, the pair turned back towards The Gables, Grace talking nineteen to the dozen about the goats.

As they reached the gate, something prompted Theo to glance behind, not unduly surprised to see the stranger standing watching them from a short distance away.

"Keep walking, Grace," he adjured.

Grace looked at him, his serious expression enough to

compel her to obey. "What's wrong, Theo?" she asked, concerned.

"I'm not sure. I just want to test a theory."

Shrugging, she was happy enough to keep walking. The afternoon was mild, and the village basked in the golden light of the late summer sunshine. It was very pleasant. She was with Theo and she had just bought goats. Grace was supremely content.

Theo led her towards his old home, along the narrow lane, and in through the rear door to his surgery. As soon as they were indoors, he asked her to stay there and retraced his steps, locking the door when he left.

Bewildered Grace wondered what was going on. It was several minutes before her husband returned, by which time she felt unnerved.

"What is wrong, Theo?" she begged when he came in and sat down.

"I think the man who spoke to us in the field has been following us," he replied.

Grace gawked. "Why would he want to…?" she stopped speaking as the obvious answer came to her. She stared at Theo who inclined his head.

"Yes, unfortunately I do not think it was pure chance he met us today."

"How would he know we would be at the market? How would he know what we would do?"

"I expect it involves several hours watching The Gables, or this house, in the hope of gleaning whatever information he has been asked to glean. We need to be extra vigilant, Grace," he cautioned, "especially in London."

"Will I ever be rid of him? Now he has tried to spoil our special weekend. Do you think his timing was deliberate?"

she mused. "No, he could not have known we were to be married. Has this person been asking questions in the village?"

Theo could not answer. "I do not know, love, but rest assured neither he, nor the man we saw today, will be able to approach you. I will advise our staff and tomorrow we shall tell Giles. I think Ralph and Duncan also ought to be apprised. They know enough people in the village to put the word around that anyone trying to garner information about you should be avoided and then reported."

"Maybe I should confront him once and for all. Get it all out in the open. Even if his reasons are vile and unscrupulous, at least I'll know. I do not want to spend my life looking over my shoulder." She shivered, images rearing up in her mind. Deliberately she focused on the previous night and Theo's touch, blotting out the duke and his cruelty for a moment.

"Let us just bide our time. While we are in the city, I intend to meet Lucas and see what he has been able to uncover. If he has found something, we may have leverage."

Grace moved to Theo, needing his arms around her, needing to feel safe. Attuned to his wife's moods, Theo drew her close, holding her against him, resting his chin on her head as she snuggled into his chest.

"I could stand like this forever," she whispered. "Who would have believed, I who less than three months ago still found it distressing to be touched, yearn to have you hold me."

"I consider myself extraordinarily lucky to be the one for whom you yearn," he smiled, pressing a kiss on her forehead. Grace looked up at her husband. His eyes had darkened almost to black. Her breathing quickened and her heart rate doubled as they drowned in each other's gaze, amber on obsidian.

"Theo," her voice was hushed as she stroked her hand along his jaw feeling the muscle pulse under her fingertips. Theo caressed her, and she thrilled under his touch, the turbulent heat of passion, so easily ignited, flowed around them. "Can we… is there anyone… I… urrghhhh…" when Theo's fingers slipped under her dress and found her centre.

Her head fell back and she would have fallen if not for her husband's embrace.

"Oh God, Theo!" Grace cared not that they chanced discovery, or that they were still clothed, or that they were in the middle of his surgery. All she cared about was the exquisite torture he was inflicting and that she wanted him to take her now. Risks be damned.

She reached for the fall of his buckskins, desperate to undo the buttons. "Please."

Theo shuddered at her plea. Kissing his wife, he brought her to the peak, at the same moment as she freed him. Moving to a conveniently placed wooden bench Theo pushed the soft material of her gown out of the way and lifted her onto him.

Trembling with a hunger she had never experienced, Grace surrendered to Theo's expert ministrations and let him take her to the heavens.

Unbeknownst to them, a solitary figure had noticed Theo slip along the path to his surgery. Nodding to himself, he returned to where he left his horse, tied to a post at the edge of the village.

Using the fence to mount, he rode off and a little over an hour later, trotted into a large stable yard. Dismounting, he handed the reins to a groom and made his way through the large house to a study in the east wing.

"Well?" a sibilant voice welcomed him.

"It is true, they are wed. 'Twas yesterday I believe. Seems they are leaving for London the day after tomorrow and should be there at least week."

"Nicely done, Trotter. Let us make our plans. I will be pleased to reconcile with Miss Aldeburgh, or is she now Lady Elliott? I care not for, by the time I have finished with her she will be lucky if she can be called Madam." Chuckling at his own wit, Jonathon Huntington, Duke of Aldwych hauled himself out of the vast chair and summoned his staff.

Back in Oak Stanton, it was a thoroughly blissful while before Grace and Theo returned home. Theo advised the household what had transpired with the stranger.

He warned them to be on their guard should they be approached and asked apparently innocuous questions about Grace, or anyone else for that matter.

The three goats duly arrived and, if the way they skipped around the field was anything to go by, were partial to their new surroundings. Grace spent much of the afternoon with the kids, as did Matt who pronounced himself keen to undertake their care.

The horses, enjoying a day in the meadow, came over to check out the new arrivals, but found them wholly uninteresting, and soon wandered back to the hay bale strung up around one of the trees.

By the end of the day, all had settled, and Grace returned her attention to the considerable matter of the luggage Theo and she required. Polly and Becca had been busy packing, and everything was in order. It would be an early departure for they hoped to arrive in the city two days hence.

Satisfied all arrangements were in place, Theo and Grace spent the evening relaxing, before retiring to bed maybe a little earlier than usual, their afternoon activities in no way assuaging their ardour.

The journey to London was uneventful. The Montgomery carriage — as Grace insisted on calling it, much to Theo's amusement — proved to be comfortable, and Titus and Nero behaved impeccably. Grace was proud of her two stallions, and Gibbs affirmed they were easy to handle, unfazed by other carriages or the alien sounds of the approaching city.

The closer they got to the capital, the more anxious Grace became. The prospect of meeting Theo's mother for the first time, as her son's bride no less, tied her stomach into knots.

She did not share Theo's confidence his mother would view their marriage favourably. By the time they drew up outside the imposing residence in Portman Square, she was a bundle of nerves. When Theo helped her down from the carriage, he could feel the tremors running though her body.

"Do not fret so, Grace. All will be well, you'll see," Theo soothed, squeezing her fingers, and brushing her lips with his. Leading her up the few steps to the front door, he rapped lightly with his cane. The door opened with a flourish and a smartly dressed butler ushered them inside, calling for the footmen to bring in the luggage.

Grace gripped Theo's hand so tightly she thought he might complain, but he made no comment and rubbed his thumb along hers, the gesture, as always, going some way to calming her.

"Good afternoon, my Lord, my Lady, welcome," intoned the butler.

"Thank you, John, it is good to see you. Is mother home?" queried Theo.

"Lady Beaumont is in the parlour. She said to go straight in." John made as though to announce their arrival. Theo, shrugging out of his greatcoat, shook his head.

"You do not need to stand on ceremony, John, 'tis just me."

John looked mildly affronted but, used to Theo, merely nodded, disappearing upstairs, no doubt to check on the footmen. Theo tucked Grace's arm under his, their fingers still entwined, and they entered the parlour.

The room, while the epitome of refinement, decorated in shades of cream with a hint of burgundy here and there to alleviate the simplicity, retained a welcoming aspect. Having spent all day travelling, Grace was loath to do anything other than stand in the middle without touching any of the delicate furniture for fear she would muddy it.

A lady, nearly as tall as Theo, stood to greet them. "Theo, my dear boy. It has been too long."

Theo swept his mother into a hug and kissed her cheek.

"This must be Grace. Hello dear, I am so glad to meet you, finally. My son writes of nothing else in the markedly few letters he sends his poor mother," she shot a chiding glance Theo's way, her mischievous smile removing the sting. Theo grinned, self-consciously, while Grace dipped a deep curtsey.

"I am very pleased to meet you, Lady Beaumont."

"Come closer dear, let me see you properly."

Grace edged into the circle of light cast by the candles, her cheeks colouring soft pink, uncomfortable with such scrutiny, as Lady Alicia Beaumont studied her new daughter-in-law.

"My goodness, you are beautiful. What striking hair and your eyes … why you must be the envy of all your friends."

"I doubt I have anything of which people should be envious, except perhaps Theo," she smiled at her husband who twinkled at her.

"Well, I beg to differ, and am glad Theo won your hand. He was certain you would turn him down."

Grace giggled at Theo's mortified expression.

"*Mother*," Theo expostulated. "My letters to you were not written so you could share their contents."

"Fiddlesticks," was her considered opinion. "Grace is your wife. I would not have mentioned it otherwise. I think it admirable you sought my advice.

"Mother, please, I'm begging you," he pleaded, desperately.

"Oh yes, dear, by all means. I know you have had a long day, but tonight we are going to the theatre, I have a box. The Winchesters will be joining us, as will Giles' mother and sister. We have been invited to supper at their home afterwards. It will be quite the convivial evening."

Grace was not convinced but could see no way to excuse herself. Something she discussed with Theo a little later as they were changing for the evening. "Might I claim a headache, Theo?" she asked hopefully.

Theo chuckled. "And hurt my mother's feelings? No, my love, you must be stoic. Mother loves these evenings and she wants to show off her new daughter-in-law."

"That's what I'm afraid of," she muttered.

Spinning her to face him, Theo kissed her gently. "I will be with you, Grace, do not worry."

She leant against him wishing they could stay at home, at the same time acknowledging there was no option but to face Society. "It's just... I hoped... it's been so long..." she faltered.

"Grace, stop panicking. As you say, it has been so long, I doubt anyone can recall why you have not been seen lately. Perhaps they believe you went abroad."

This was indeed a possibility. Moreover, there would likely have been many other scandals since she was ostracised. Was it too much to hope they might have forgotten? "We shall see," was all she would say, but grinned and kissed him back until Theo was moved to comment, maybe her headache idea was not so bad after all.

Laughing now, Grace batted at him to release her so she could finish dressing, grateful when one of Lady Beaumont's maids appeared, to lace up Grace's gown and style her hair.

To Grace's surprise the evening passed pleasantly. Those to whom they spoke at the theatre seemed wholly unaware of who Grace was, and the meal at the Winchester's was a most relaxed affair, full of light-hearted banter and much laughter.

It was clear Giles' family were curious about this young woman who had married Theo, but far too polite to press her for details. By the time they eventually returned to Beaumont House and retired to bed, even Grace was prepared to grant that the evening had been a success.

The subsequent days were so busy Grace barely had time to take a breath. Lady Beaumont coaxed her new daughter-in-law into visiting Madam Thibault, her modiste, where they ordered more clothes than Grace would ever need. Theo's mother was in her element, and Grace did not have the heart to refuse.

Billie and Grace spent a pleasant few hours wandering the bazaars on Bond Street, the Pantechnicon and Harding Howell's to fulfil the list of necessary bed linens and curtains, as well as persuading each other into the occasional, not quite so necessary, luxury.

There was the inevitable round of calls, unavoidable but which, for the most part, were not as disagreeable as Grace anticipated. No one made sly comments or whispered behind gloves. Grace began to think Society might have forgiven her, or — at the very least — forgotten.

Sending word to Joe Gregson, her old butler's brother, that she was in London, Grace orchestrated an invitation to Kew Park with a view to acquiring some plants.

She cajoled Theo into accompanying her; not that he took much persuading. Joe met and escorted them through the park, pointing out any new additions to the already vast collection.

Despite an autumnal crispness to the air it was a beautiful day. For Grace, it was an escape from all the hustle and bustle, a chance for Theo and her to spend time alone together.

To her unending delight, Joe had organised a selection of plants for her, including the pyracantha, which would be delivered the next day, in gratitude for which, Grace left a generous donation.

They arrived back at Portman Square in the late afternoon and spent the remainder of the evening with Lady Beaumont. When they were preparing for bed, Theo mentioned his brother had sent word he would be calling the next morning.

"Will it be just him, or will his wife attend also?" Grace asked, sleepily, turning for Theo to unbutton her gown. She had dismissed the maid, assuring the girl she was capable of undressing.

"I believe it is just him. I think Sophia prefers to remain in the country at this time of the year. Also, if I recall correctly, she is expecting their second child around Christmas. I imagine she finds travelling too arduous." He made quick work of the silk covered fastenings.

"I had not realised your brother had a child, Theo. You never talk about him. Are you not close?" Theo shook his head, freeing the last button and pushing the gown off her shoulders.

"Sadly not. Giles is more a brother to me than Benedict. Mayhap it is because Benedict is almost ten years older than I. Maybe it was because he knew he was the heir to the marquisate; he took that knowledge seriously. We never spent much time together as children and, owing to our age difference, were not at school at the same time. Then there was the war..."

Theo trailed off, distracted by Grace's creamy skin. "Do we have to talk about him now? Time enough tomorrow..." his lips tracing a path across the back of her neck.

"Hmmm... why, my love, is there something you would rather be doing?" grinning wickedly at her husband, Grace twisted in his arms to slide her hands under his shirt, running her slender fingers over his taut frame.

Theo gasped when her cool touch sent shivers all the way to his toes.

"There is..." he grunted, pulling her close and demonstrating exactly what he'd rather be doing and, suddenly, Grace didn't feel sleepy at all.

The next morning, after a later than normal breakfast, Grace excused herself, retiring to their bedchamber claiming there were one or two letters which required her attention.

She had received some documents from Mr Handley, nothing of any great urgency, but wanted to respond before they left London, in case a meeting with her solicitor proved necessary.

Theo proposed they go for a walk after she completed her business, so it was with a light step she tripped down the stairs an hour later, her cloak, much preferred to her pelisse, already around her shoulders. She was placing her letters on the platter, when John appeared at her elbow to inform her the family was in the parlour.

With a bright smile, she thanked the butler, and made her way along the hall, hesitating when she overheard raised voices. A little confused, for she didn't recognise the speaker, Grace moved towards the door which stood slightly ajar, to be halted in her tracks by his next words.

"I cannot believe you did this without prior referral to

me, to our mother. What in Hades were you thinking, Theo? She is little more than one of those ghastly Covent Garden strumpets. What of mother? What of my wife? If you are so enamoured of her, why on God's good earth did you not simply install her as your mistress? That way she can never sully our family name." The deep voice thrummed with revulsion

"Benedict!" Grace heard Lady Beaumont exclaim in horror. "Please! This is not about some wretched prostitute. Grace is the daughter of a baron and my daughter-in-law. How dare you be so vulgar in my home."

"I will not apologise, Mother. If my beloved brother had thought for one second what his actions would do, he might have realised how ridiculous this is. You are the second son of a marquis, Theo. You have responsibilities and none of them involve taking pity on some idiotic chit who could not control herself. How can I possibly face my colleagues in parliament now, let alone at White's and, if I lose my Almack's voucher…"

Obviously the enormity of this proved beyond utterance because there was a long pause.

"You have no alternative but to divorce her. Since she is already disgraced, I imagine the courts will be sympathetic, especially if we tell them you did not know and were tricked into marrying her."

Grace felt her cheeks burning. This was not good, poor Theo. Listening to the man railing on, decrying her as though he knew all about her, her own ire increased. Enough! She had taken more than any gentlewoman should have to take and no more. She was sick and tired of justifying her very existence.

Straightening her shoulders, Grace removed her cloak, draping it over a conveniently placed chair. She smoothed her skirts and patted her hair, believing she looked presentable. Without waiting to knock, she pushed open the door and stepped into the room.

Theo, propped against a window frame, his face dark with anger, saw his wife's expression and his heart constricted. She had heard too much.

Sitting near the fire, Lady Beaumont looked pale and shocked, one hand resting on her throat. The third man in the room, whom Grace presumed to be Theo's brother, was in a steaming temper.

Executing a flawless curtsey, she regarded him steadily. "Good morning, Lord Beaumont. I had hoped our introduction would follow different lines, but I imagine there is little likelihood of that now."

She cocked her head on one side, studying his enraged countenance.

"So, you think me no better than a strumpet?" she asked quietly. "Never having met me, or bothered to discover anything about me, you are prepared to believe any old rumour spread by malicious gossips?

"I wonder, do you do the same on your parliamentary committees? Take everything at face value, never bothering to check facts and figures, or do you investigate properly, determining whether the information you are receiving is to be trusted? I, for one, would be most concerned if our country is being run by men who do not care for the truth."

Theo bit down on a bark of laughter, proud of her calm and dignified demeanour. He moved towards her, but imperceptibly she shook her head a small smile, albeit humourless, curving her lips. He watched her draw herself up to her full height.

A tall woman, Grace did not feel intimidated by the imposing man in front of her. Benedict was broad, his powerful physique dominating the genteel room with its fine furniture. He was so huge, she surmised he would snap any chair he might decide to sit in.

"Do you know anything of your brother?" Her voice was empty of inflection.

Theo heard the deadness of her tones, and unease began to gnaw at him.

"Theo is the kindest, most remarkable man — no, person — I have had the good fortune to meet. Before we were introduced, he knew much about my past, the torment inflicted on me, and never once judged me. He became my friend, helping me to adjust to a life I never expected to be granted and gradually he stole my heart.

"There is nothing about me he does not know and, despite my misgivings and apprehension over how a courtship with me might appear, he assured me his family were understanding, and would not condemn before the facts were disclosed.

"I tried to persuade him we had no future, that because Society had ostracised me, any association with me would taint him. He refused to let the ignorance of a few small-minded people influence his decision."

She cast a fleeting look at Theo who was like a stone, his eyes locked on her, and she could see the apprehension in their mahogany depths.

"I am no grasping female desperate for a title and money. I have my own home, staff, a carriage, horses, and an annual stipend, which will keep me comfortable for the rest of my life.

"You know nothing about me. You do not care that a man of status persecuted me, that he still hunts me like a hawk hunts a mouse. That he stole my innocence, not once but as often as he could, without recourse and so, yes, while those rumours you are quick to take for granted are not completely inaccurate, they are not the whole story.

"It wasn't some hurried tumble under luxurious coverlets in the hope of finding a rich husband…"

She could hear the anger in her voice and made a concerted effort to retain some form of control.

"…he *abused* me! He violated me for more than a year and then, when he was finally caught in the act, he blamed me. Everybody shunned me. My family abandoned me, and I never spoke to my parents again. Now they are dead, and I do not know the cause of their demise. Moreover, while we are sharing so *courteously* here, not long after he was discovered, I found I was with child."

Lady Beaumont gasped, her classical features contorting. Grace did not know whether it was with sorrow or disgust.

"I lost the child and following the birth — for which, by the way, I had no assistance — I nearly died. I remained alone for over two years until my aunt bequeathed me The Gables.

"Finally, I had something that was mine. I did not seek, nor did I expect to find, anyone who cared enough to see me for who I am, as opposed to the pariah Society painted me."

Distress warred with her anger, gaining the upper hand. She took a different tack.

"Do you know your brother applied for a special licence?"

Benedict shook his head, his eyes on stalks.

"He applied for it, weeks ago, not knowing whether I returned his feelings, and a considerable time before either of us spoke to the other of our affection. That he has known for so long, yet allowed our courtship to unfold gradually, tells me more of Theo than anyone else could.

"We live a good distance from London, in a small village where we are simply Theo and Grace, and apart from a handful of people, no one there knows who I am."

Grace bent her head, trembling from the effort of sharing this part of her life without screaming with rage or collapsing in tears. Bowing to the inevitable, she drew herself up one last time.

"That said, I cannot change your opinion of me, and I cannot change my past. I love your brother and he loves me but I refuse to be the one who causes a rift within a family. I have seen the devastating result of such discord."

She walked over to Lady Beaumont. "Thank you for welcoming me into your home. Your kindness was a balm to my soul. I am truly sorry my presence has created such dissent."

With a brief glance at Theo, she faced Benedict again.

"My Lord, I know how Society works. I know you have to maintain your good standing, and the last thing I wanted was to threaten that. I just believed… never mind what I believed. 'Tis my own fault. I should not have allowed myself to trust I could be so lucky. I will never be free of it. I knew this was too good to be true. Now," she infused practicality into her tones, "I have taken up too much of your valuable time.

"Please excuse me. Theo, I am going to visit my old home. No," when he made to join her, "I think it more important you talk with your brother, I will be back soon. I love you."

The last murmured so quietly, Theo wasn't sure she'd said it. With another curtsy, she slipped away, closing the door behind her with a click, which sounded ominously final.

For what seemed an age, the room was silent save for the ticking of the clock over the fireplace, and the crackle of the wood in the hearth as the flames consumed it.

"What did she mean 'I knew this was too good to be

true'?" Lady Beaumont asked, breaking the quiet, reeling from the revelations of the last hour or so.

"She assumes I will be persuaded to divorce her for the good of the family," replied Theo bleakly.

"Well you cannot do that. The poor girl needs you and she obviously loves you very much," his mother protested incredulously.

Theo looked over at his brother who was leaning on the mantel. "There is nothing I would like more, but she would prefer that, than be responsible for tearing our family apart. So, Benedict, this is on your head. Grace means more to me than anyone else in this world and without her my life is really not worth much at all.

"Are you prepared to rise above snide gossips and be an honourable man or are you going to allow society to dictate your next step? I will leave you to ponder this while, whether she wants me to or not, I shall spend the rest of the day with my beloved wife."

He kissed his mother on the cheek. "We will be home for dinner, Mother. Try to talk some sense into him." He nodded at his brother.

His mother patted his hand. "Leave him to me, dear."

Smiling up at Theo, she waved her hands at her youngest son shooing him out as though he was still a child, not a well-respected doctor of nearly twenty and nine years. Theo grinned and went upstairs to find Grace. She was not in their bedchamber, so he rang for John, who informed him Lady Elliott had left, but had not requested their carriage.

Theo thanked him and, grabbing his great coat, hurried out into the cool and dull early afternoon, standing for a moment trying to work out which direction she might have taken. John popped his head out of the door to say Lady Elliott turned right at the far corner of the square, pointing as he spoke.

Theo thought to walk, only to decide the carriage might be a better idea and ran back inside, calling for their groom. Thus, it was some time before Theo followed Grace, his gnawing unease becoming outright alarm.

～

Grace arrived at Hawkesworth House. It was not far from the Beaumont residence and the brisk walk helped clear her head. Despite the gloomy day, the fresh air was conducive, and her temper began to evaporate.

Reaching the familiar town house, she hesitated for a moment. Admiring the elegant façade, Grace recognised she bore no emotional connection to the place, which had been home for most of her life. Smiling grimly, she climbed the steps and rapped the knocker.

The door was flung open, and Wilfred stood on the threshold.

"Good afternoon, Wilfred. May I come in?"

Wilfred's jaw all but hit the floor, so surprised was he at the sight of his erstwhile mistress. He pulled himself together, his inherent professionalism taking over. "Miss Aldeburgh, Miss Aldeburgh. Come in, do come in. You should not have knocked. This is your home."

"Not really, Wilfred but thank you for saying so," she smiled, removing her gloves. "I am visiting London and thought to say a quick hello to you all if it wouldn't be too much of an imposition."

"Imposition, well I never heard the like. Jane will be so pleased to see you. She's been right worried about you being on your own." He hustled Grace through to the kitchens where she was welcomed like a long-lost sister.

They were all there, and Peggy burst into tears when she saw her mistress. Grace sat in the warm room for a little while telling them everything she could, regarding her new home and her very new husband, skirting right passed the current drama. Everyone declared themselves happy for her, and as Grace wound up, Peggy mentioned the baron was in town.

"I do not imagine he will care to see me, Peggy. In fact, I think I shall take my leave before he returns, that way he has no call to pretend I do not exist." She said this with a grin, but none in the kitchen was fooled.

Wisely refraining from commenting, they said their goodbyes, and Peggy accompanied her through the house. As the maid opened the front door, a large figure loomed up in their vision. It was Anthony, Lord Hawkesworth. He saw his sister and, startled, stumbled a little.

"Do take heed, my Lord. I should be most distressed if my appearance caused you to trip." Grace stepped passed him to go on her way, but he caught her arm. Clenching her teeth at this unexpected roughness, Grace yanked her arm out of her brother's grip, and glared at him.

"Grace, what are you doing here?" he demanded.

"Worry not, Anthony, I was just visiting my… your staff. I am in London with my husband and wished to spend a few moments with those who looked after me so well."

"Your husband? What the deuce are you wittering about?"

"I was married a little under a week ago. You probably know the family. My husband's name is Theo Elliot and he is the younger brother of the Marquis of Beaumont."

Anthony spluttered in shock. "Why was I not informed? It is your duty to advise me of any change in your status."

"My *duty*? Since when are you so concerned about duty? You showed little interest in my well-being over the last two years, so I fail to see why you are surprised. I reached my majority long ago and am a woman of independent means. Please do not pretend you care what happens to me."

Her tones took on a dangerous edge, which had Theo, Billie or Giles heard, might have prompted them to warn the Baron, his sister was about to explode.

"Grace, lower you voice. I will not have our dirty laundry aired on the front step."

Grace folded her arms and studied her brother. He looked pasty and was not as lean as once he had been, likely the result of too many hours cooped up inside.

He was no taller than she, his hair more sandy than auburn, and his eyes pale green rather than hazel. In fact, they were not particularly similar at all. He was quite good looking, she supposed and, when younger, they had shared an amiable relationship.

Grace believed him weak, and easily swayed; getting involved in affairs from which he struggled to extricate himself. She discerned, with a certain sadness, she had no feelings at all for him.

Any vestiges of sisterly love had been well and truly quashed partly because of his woeful indifference and, partly owing to his rare yet tedious visits.

"I beg your pardon, your Lordship. Please excuse me, I have an appointment I must not neglect."

Anthony gawked at her, trying to equate this self-possessed young lady with the pale, sedate and somewhat reticent sister whom he last encountered less than six months previously. "Grace, as your older brother I have certain rights with which you should accord me." His manner more bombastic than usual.

Swallowing her outrage, Grace marched back into the house, tapping her foot on the spotless tiles while she waited for Anthony to follow her inside.

"*Rights*? You relinquished any rights you had over me when you allowed that *villain* to ruin me," she hissed. "Have you *any* idea what I've been through? Have you ever, for one single moment of your pompous, selfish and thoroughly spoilt life, stopped to ask yourself what happened to me? How a man such as he did what he did? Wondered how I was doing? Whether I might need anything? Or had any kind of concern for me whatsoever? No, you haven't. Do you know what he did to me?"

Grace, fairly shrieking now — uncaring the whole household, and likely half the street would hear — informed her brother in no uncertain terms exactly what she had been subjected to, and that she knew their parents allowed it to happen.

"You, all of you, sacrificed me for the sake of this family and to what end? Where did any of it get you? Now I have my own home and a husband who has more love for me in his little finger than you have in your whole body. If I ever hear from you again it will be too soon! Good day to you, my Lord."

She fled down the steps and hailed a passing hackney, directing it to the Withers' address.

By the time the cab pulled up outside Jemima's house Grace had herself back under control. Thanking the driver as she paid him, she walked up the path admiring the last of the Indian Cress blooming in the window boxes, colourful flowers bobbing in the breeze.

Jemima was looking out for her and, after taking her cloak, drew her friend into the parlour where she had tea and cakes already waiting.

"Grace, I am so glad to see you. It has been an age. I do miss our afternoons."

Grace smiled at Jemima's enthusiasm and agreed, it had

indeed been too long. The two women fell to gossiping and time flew by.

Jemima, ever astute, perceived something was troubling Grace. She said nothing, hoping Grace would tell her in her own good time. Grace shared the news about her marriage. It was clear to Jemima, her friend was deeply in love with her new husband and he with her, but she sensed all was not as it should be.

Eventually, she gave up being polite. "Grace, what is wrong? You are obviously upset. How can this be less than a week into your marriage?" Jemima implored, taking Grace's hands in hers.

Grace shrugged her shoulders. "'Tis naught save what I should expect."

Jemima crinkled her nose in confusion. "What do you mean, my dear?"

Capitulating, Grace explained what had happened at Beaumont House adding she had also just given her own brother a telling off.

"I love Theo, Jemima. I love him more than my own life, but if I become a bone of contention between him and his brother, I could not forgive myself. In time, Theo will resent me.

"I suspect Benedict will have his way, and mayhap a divorce now will be less heartbreaking. Benedict believes they can concoct a tale about me tricking Theo into marriage, to obtain an annulment."

Shaking herself, Grace tried to smile. "I do not wish to spoil our afternoon with tales of woe. Tell me what you have been doing since I left."

Accepting Grace would discuss the situation no more, Jemima did a creditable job of diverting her friend with several amusing anecdotes. Shortly thereafter, Grace excused herself and, declining Jemima's offer of their driver, began the long walk home.

Worried about her friend, Jemima was watching Grace trudge along the pavement, when she saw a coach pull alongside her. Intrigued and, presuming it was Theo, Jemima was smiling as she imagined their reunion, when Grace jerked away, trying to put distance between herself, and whoever was talking to her.

The wife of an investigator, Jemima ran to the front door, near pulling it off its hinges in her hurry to get outside. Grace was looking up and down the street, frantically, but before Jemima had the chance to do anything, her friend was hauled into the coach.

Panicking, Jemima flew up the road, screaming for help at the top of her voice. Typically, no one took any notice. The black, unmarked carriage rolled away, leaving Jemima trying to see which way it went.

Trembling with shock, and unsure what to do, Jemima went home. Contemplating whether to send a message to Beaumont House and maybe another to her husband, she was disturbed less than five minutes later by a loud knocking.

Half expecting it to be Grace, although after what she just witnessed that seemed implausible, she opened the door with a ready smile to see Theo Elliott on her doorstep.

"D-Doctor Elliott. What are you… no… what? Where is Grace?" Perturbed now, Jemima's smile vanished.

"Isn't she here?"

"No, didn't you just… was it not you in the carriage?"

"What carriage? Our coach is here," thumbing over his shoulder. "Where is my wife?"

"Theo, oh no please no, it cannot be."

"Jemima, what on earth has happened? Please, where is Grace?"

Jemima drew him indoors and told him what she had just seen.

Theo, following Grace to her old home, had come upon Lord Hawkesworth who was still seething from his sister's verbal clip around the ear. The baron had no qualms about informing Theo he needed to control his wife.

An acrimonious exchange ensued with Lord Hawkesworth denying any knowledge of Grace's whereabouts. Theo was about to leave, when Peggy rushed up to inform him, Grace had mentioned an appointment, and Theo remembered Jemima.

"If only I had not engaged Hawkesworth in wasted argument, I might have prevented this," he groaned. "I think it might be Huntington, Lord Aldwych, or at least one of his lackeys."

Horrified at the idea of the duke getting his hands on Grace again, Jemima thought quickly. Snatching her cloak, she pushed Theo out through the door.

"We have to find her, Doctor Elliott."

He nodded.

"Come, if you are willing. Let us go to Lucas. He will know the most expeditious way to locate the duke with as little fuss as possible."

Theo thought this eminently practical and helped Jemima into the waiting coach. "I do not care if the fuss I raise is the size of the Houses of Parliament. If he harms one hair on my wife's head, I will kill him," he growled.

Jemima patted his knee. "Well let's hope it doesn't come to that, Theo. A lot of use you'll be to Grace locked up in Newgate."

Theo chuckled weakly as the carriage rattled through the busy streets. It did not take long to reach the building in which Lucas worked, and Jemima ran in calling for her husband.

Startled to see his wife in the middle of the afternoon, Lucas Withers appeared at the door of his office, getting an even bigger surprise when he saw Theo.

"Elliott," he grinned. "Well met. What brings you to London?"

Theo shook the proffered hand, and told Lucas what had happened, his agitation clear in his abrupt sentences.

"Calm down, Theo," Lucas placated. "We'll get her back in one piece. I have men watching Aldwych, as soon as any of them see Grace, I will know."

Grace found herself sitting opposite two men. One she recognised as the stranger who had followed Theo and her at Oak Stanton, the other she had never seen before.

"Would you like to explain what the dickens you think you are doing? Seizing me off the streets in broad daylight. I suppose this is all at Huntington's orders? I do hope you are prepared for the consequences." Grace was pleased to note she sounded cross and not at all scared.

The two men stared at her unspeaking.

"Come now, you think your behaviour acceptable?" She asked, conversationally. "I cannot imagine *what* will happen when my husband, or the Earl of Winchester, or the several soldiers whom I know, get their hands on you. Are either of you proficient with a flintlock?"

She studied her gloved hands with deliberate disinterest, aware the two men were looking at each other. "You cannot possibly believe you will get away with this. My husband knows of the duke's intentions, and the Bow Street Runners have been warned he might attempt something like this. I daresay they'll be following us already." Praying this was true.

There was a protracted silence. The only sound, the rumble of the carriage over the dry clay and grit.

The man she did not recognise spoke. "'S'cuse me, Miss… are you telling me you are married… to one o' gentry?"

"Yes, my good man. Did your associate here omit some of the details? I am married to Lord Elliott and imagine there is the distinct likelihood I carry his child." Calmly ignoring the fact this was highly improbable. It was merely a ruse in the hope they would take pity on her. "I do not suppose you wish to come to the attention of the authorities."

Squirming uncomfortably on the bench, the man frowned at his partner. "Oi, this weren't part o' the bargain. There weren't nuffin said about her bein' wed, 'Erb. I aint gonna be responsible for fetchin' 'im some lady married into the haristocracy. 'E said she was a blummin light-skirt, keen an' willing.

"It's all right 'im wantin' a bit o' fun, but she'm dunnt look that willing to me. Wot's 'e tek me for, a blasted kidnapper? My missus'll kill me if she hears o' this. No, no, I don't want nuffin' to do wi' this. I don't need them bleedin' Runners after me. We 'ave to let 'er go."

The other man, referred to as 'Erb, shook his head, a mulish expression on his face.

"Don't be daft, Jimmy, she's talking rubbish. Bow Street Runners indeed. Nah, 'is nibs said to bring her, and bring 'er is what we shall be doing. That's all's to be said."

Jimmy growled sullenly, refusing to agree.

The two men began to argue, neither prepared to listen to the other, paying no attention to Grace, who noticed the carriage was slowing down. Shuffling over to the window, she glanced out to see a snarl up of traffic ahead. Two carriages trying to pass and neither giving the other room.

Waiting until she was certain her captors were not concentrating on her, she slid her hand cautiously along to the handle and in a flash she was out.

Jumping down from the coach, she landed awkwardly, twisting her right ankle, but did not stop. Heedless of the fact she was supposed to be a lady, Grace hoisted her skirts, and fled across the busy road and between the two carriages causing the hold up.

She ran until the noise was far behind her, only slowing, to work out where she was. The street she was on looked familiar, and it was with huge relief she recognised Madam Thibault's, whom she had visited with Lady Beaumont, was just ahead.

She flew along the path, and into the dressmakers, dropping onto a chaise, panting for breath.

The modiste gasped at the intrusion and, about to upbraid this woman for barging into her shop, recognised Grace. "Why, my Lady, you look a trifle discomposed."

Grace nearly laughed at the woman's restraint.

"Are you quite well?" Madam Thibault feared her client might well have been taken by some form of mania.

"I do beg your pardon, Madame, but I have just escaped a singularly distasteful situation. Please, may I rest here momentarily? When I catch my breath, I will be on my way."

Madam Thibault regarded Grace, observing the pale cast to her face, despite her headlong dash. Reading the panic in her eyes, she realised there was more to this than met the eye.

Ushering the exhausted woman through to one of the back rooms, away from the windows, the modiste called for one of her assistants to bring a cup of tea.

"Where is Lady Beaumont or your husband? Surely you were not alone?"

"Unfortunately, yes I was alone. 'Tis a long and very

tawdry tale, Madame, and one with which I do not wish to bore you. Suffice it to say, I was… errr… collected when I left a friend's home and was able to slip away when my… hmm… escorts were otherwise distracted."

Grace rested her head against the back of the chair, her heartrate beginning to steady. "Do you perhaps have a messenger? Maybe I could send a note to my husband. He might be somewhat perturbed by my prolonged absence."

Madam Thibault guessed 'somewhat perturbed' would be an understatement. Assuring Grace, they would get word to Theo, the modiste left her to gather herself, while she dispatched a lad to Beaumont House with instructions to hand the note, she gave him to Doctor Elliott and no one else.

Grace, who had dozed off in the warm room, was a roused by someone cupping her cheek. Terror roiled through her and unable to prevent a moan of fright she pushed herself away, preparing to flee, certain the duke's men had run her to ground. A gentle hand forestalled her.

"Grace, hush, 'tis me."

That beloved voice. She forced herself to focus, and Theo's face swam into her vision.

"T-Theo?"

"Yes, my love. I'm here, you are safe." Forgetting she was in a boutique full of women who would no doubt pounce on this juicy piece of gossip, Grace flung herself into Theo's embrace and held on as though she would never let go.

Theo wrapped his arms around his wife, stroking up and down her back, talking to her about anything and nothing, his velvet voice soothing her.

"What happened? Jemima saw you being dragged into a coach."

"You saw Jemima?"

"I followed you to Hawkesworth House, where your brother and I had words. Peggy mentioned an appointment, and I recalled you wanted to visit with Jemima. I arrived there about five minutes after you were… errr… picked up."

He explained their visit to Withers, who had informed them the duke was under surveillance. When the carriage arrived at the Huntington residence, the only people who alighted were 'Erb and Jimmy.

Flummoxed, a couple of Withers' men had intercepted the two would-be kidnappers but, before they began to question them or threaten them with gaol, Jimmy had fallen over himself in his haste to divulge what happened.

They returned to where Jimmy reckoned Grace had jumped from the carriage at the same time Theo who, at Withers' suggestion had gone home in case Grace turned up, received the note from Madam Thibault.

"And here I am. I think Lucas would like to speak with you, but if you would rather wait until tomorrow he will understand."

"No, no. I prefer to get this over with while it is fresh in my mind. I am unharmed, although my right ankle is sore. I refuse to let this afternoon's… errrm… escapade spoil our time in London."

"That's my girl."

The light of battle in Grace's eyes encouraged Theo.

"Now, let me check your ankle," he ran his hand along her leg.

Grace nudged at him, giggling. "Not here, I have given the gossips enough fodder this afternoon. I will be fine until we are home. Wait… you and my brother had words? Theo?"

Her husband gave her a brief run-down of his encounter

with Anthony. Grace grinned at the image of her tall and distinguished husband haranguing Anthony.

"Poor Anthony, a tirade from both of us in under an hour, he will rue the day I was born," her tone indicating little sympathy. "Where is Major Withers? I shall tell him everything, then I should be very pleased to go home."

Theo smiled and escorted his wife to a waiting carriage, Grace thanking Madam Thibault profusely as they left. Lucas was in the coach, as, to Grace's surprise, was Jemima.

"Jemima, my dear, I apologise for causing such a fuss. It was not my intent to have our afternoon end in so deplorable a fashion."

"Grace, it was not your fault. The blame for this lies with the duke and no one else. Lucas had men watching his townhouse. Had you not fled, his attempt would have been thwarted when you arrived there."

Grace pulled her friend into a quick hug. "Thank you," was all she said, but it was enough. Jemima smiled and sat back while her husband took over.

Succinctly, Grace told Lucas everything, adding that Jimmy appeared to have been hoodwinked into believing she, Grace, was a prostitute with whom Lord Aldwych frequently had liaisons. Theo ground his teeth on hearing this, but Grace was so involved in her tale she didn't notice.

"Please go easy on Jimmy," she begged Lucas. "I truly believe he was appalled at what he was expected to do. He was more worried about his missus, than any repercussions from duke should they fail to carry out his orders."

Lucas nodded but forbore to comment further because Grace continued, "It puzzles me why Huntington is going to such lengths to force me into his presence. I cannot understand what motivates his actions. You would expect, after evading censure two years ago, he would prefer to avoid me at all costs. Why is he preying on me again?" she mused.

None could throw any light on the matter, so she pushed it aside, returning to the immediate problem.

"What will happen now?" she asked when they concluded their discussion.

"We will maintain our surveillance. He is becoming reckless. Our hope is he will trip himself up and we can catch him in the act."

"He is a duke," Grace whispered. "No one can stop him. He will never face a court, he has too much power and influence."

"Maybe not, but if we are able to obtain proof of his depravity, I believe he could be persuaded a change of scenery might be more beneficial than having his family dragged through the dirt. I've heard the Americas are agreeable." He winked at Grace, easing the tension.

Satisfied he had all he needed, Lucas thanked Grace and, taking Jemima's hand helped his wife down from the carriage, waiving aside Theo's offer to transport them home.

"Thank you, Elliott. One of my men has a coach. Take your wife home. She looks all in."

Theo glanced at Grace who just wanted to sleep.

"I'm fine, Theo, I'm just tired. 'Tis many years since I have run so far." She chuckled wearily and snuggled against her husband who draped his arm around her anchoring her to his side as the carriage trundled back to Beaumont House.

Grace stayed awake until she reached their bedchamber but, before the maid had a chance to help her mistress undress, Grace was fast asleep. She slept the clock around, never stirring until well after luncheon the next day.

Theo enlightened his family and the staff about the alarming event, indicating he needed to be informed of any callers, unknown to the household.

$\sim$

Grace put in an appearance in the early afternoon, feeling groggy and out of sorts. There were a few things Theo wanted to discuss with his wife, but one look at her face convinced him now was not the opportune time. Instead, after she had eaten, he took her into the orangery, at the rear of the house, where a large collection of plants awaited her attention.

This did the trick, and she clapped her hands with glee when she saw how many Joe had included. Dropping to her knees, she ran her fingers over the leaves, and checked to make sure the pots had enough moisture.

Calling Theo over to help her, the two spent a happy couple of hours cataloguing the plants, with Grace noting where in her garden each would be best suited.

It must be admitted, proceedings were interrupted frequently by Theo, who was unable to resist the sight of his wife with smudges of soil on her cheeks.

His argument being that kissing her was the only way to rid her of said smears, reducing Grace to helpless laughter, and brightening her mood.

This was where Billie and Giles found them when they called at Beaumont House following Billie's appointment at Harley Street. Theo had not broken his word and, although Grace had an inkling the Winchester's trip to London wasn't all about socialising, she had no idea her friend had been to see a specialist or for what reason.

John, who added that afternoon tea would be served shortly, showed the earl and his countess into the orangery.

Grace took one look at Billie who was grinning from ear-to-ear and wondered, since they had already celebrated Stephen's wedding, what could cause her jubilation. She made no comment, other than to suggest the parlour might be more comfortable, the orangery cooling quickly as the afternoon waned.

Billie, having spied the plants, begged to be shown them before they sought the warmth of the main house, desirous to see what Grace had procured, leaving the two men to talk over their heads. It wasn't long before the thought of tea and cakes enticed and soon the four were settled around the fire.

"We heard what happened, Grace. I hope you were not injured," was Billie's first comment after they had reduced the plate of cakes to mere crumbs.

"I am unharmed, thank you, Billie. I did land heavily on my right ankle, which aches, but Theo says it was jarred not sprained. Other than that, I am perfectly fine. It was unnerving, but I am safe now, and Major Withers assures me he has men watching the duke. Let us put it out of our minds and enjoy the few days we have left in London. What have you two been doing since last we met?"

Billie looked at Giles who bestowed a loving smile on his wife. Grace could not help but glance at Theo, receiving an almost identical smile in return.

"We have something we wish to share," Billie floundered. She was bubbling with exhilaration but knew it improbable Grace would ever experience the same happiness and had no wish to remind her friend of what might never be.

She opened her mouth and then closed it again reaching for Giles' hand, her eyes beseeching him.

"We are very pleased to announce we are expecting our first child," interjected Giles, taking pity on her. "I believe my wife is too elated to speak with any coherence right at this moment," grinning at Billie who blushed becomingly.

Grace whooped in an undignified fashion, drawing Billie up out of her chair and into a warm embrace, congratulating them both as she beamed in joyful surprise.

"Billie this is the most blessed news. I cannot express how delighted I am for you both. How far along are you? Have you seen a specialist? Do make sure you get enough rest.

Giles, I hope you will ensure she does not continue to throw herself at life."

Giles chuckled, promising he had been doing his best to persuade Billie to take things easy, but she wasn't always inclined to follow his advice. Billie pooh-poohed the suggestion, saying she would rest when she was tired and not to pester her.

Theo watched all this, adding his own felicitations, but keeping an eye on Grace, for the same reason Billie had been anxious. His wife showed no signs of distress, Billie and she beginning an animated conversation about babies and the like.

Giles and Theo moved out of hearing range, while Theo updated Giles on the Aldwych situation.

"I confess I prefer to return to Oak Stanton as soon as possible. I was thinking of departing two days hence. There are too many places in London where Grace is vulnerable. I do not wish to tie her to this house or curb her freedom, but I worry when she is out of my sight.

"Even the thought of a brisk ride along Rotten Row or a drive through Hyde Park has lost its lustre. If he thinks nothing of sending his henchmen to pluck her off the streets in the middle of the afternoon, a couple out riding is not much of an obstacle."

Giles mulled over his friend's words. "I have no objection to returning home sooner than planned. We can make the excuse we wish to be back at Whiteoaks before the autumn rains set in. I have plenty awaiting my attention anyhow.

"Do not feel it necessary to accompany us, Giles. I know you intended staying longer. I have no mind to take you from your family."

"You would be doing me a favour, Theo," Giles chuckled.

"You know I prefer the country. We spent long enough in the city during the season for Helena's sake, who, I am given to understand has several beaus, all of whom she is determined to keep at arm's length.

"I am of the opinion she is interested in one particular gentleman but has yet to admit it. If his suit is serious, I daresay I will hear in due course. Mother and she are busy with their own interests, I do not imagine we will be much missed."

Theo accepted his friend's argument, knowing it to be the truth. When the two men proposed an early return to Hampshire to their wives, both agreed gladly. Plans were made, after which the Winchesters took their leave, Giles indicating it was high time they shared their news with their own families.

Later that evening, Theo and Grace had a lengthy chat about his brother, and his comments of the previous day.

It transpired, Lady Beaumont had given Benedict short shrift, calmly pointing out, if he shunned Grace, he was tacitly approving the duke's behaviour and how did he think that would sit with Sophia? By the same token, bearing in mind the duke did not honour the bonds of marriage, how would he feel had Sophia been the object of his proclivities?

Furthermore, and probably the clincher, Benedict's wife was patroness to at least one charity whose sole purpose was to provide a safe environment for women who had escaped an abusive situation. A place where they could learn a craft or trade, giving them the wherewithal to start afresh.

For him to suggest to Sophia, his own sister-in-law was undeserving of the same would be akin to him informing her, the work she did was worthless. For all his bluster,

Benedict loved his wife and his family; he just needed the error of his ways elucidating in words of one syllable.

In all fairness, Benedict was horrified when he heard what happened to Grace and had begged an audience with his brother the evening before while Grace slept. By the time the two came out of the study, they were more in accord than they had been for as long as Theo could recall.

Lady Beaumont made no comment, other than to tell her sons how proud she was of both. Benedict left a letter for Grace, apologising for his crass behaviour, affirming he no longer expected Theo to divorce her, and in time hoped their relationship might take on a more cordial tone.

Grace appreciated his effort, knowing how hard it would be for Benedict to ask for her forgiveness.

"So, my love…" said Theo, after much discussion, tucking an errant strand of auburn hair behind his wife's ear, while kissing her gently. "…will you *please* put any thought of divorce or annulment out of your adorable head? I do not think you understand how much I love you. You are my world. You are my sun, my moon and my stars. Without you I would be in darkness for, poetic as it sounds, you are my light."

He held her eyes with his. Polished bronze on burnished copper.

Grace felt her heart melt. Captivated by his darkening gaze, several things ran through her mind. The most important being her fears had dissolved, replaced by that same inner power she had felt all those weeks ago.

As surely as blue sky follows the rain, Theo and she were meant to be. Their coming together was fated, and no one, especially a loathsome duke, would ever put their love asunder. With her husband by her side, Grace knew she could face anything.

Theo watched, and it seemed to him that Grace glowed. He recognised the strength he knew she possessed surge through her.

"My darling husband, I love you. I love you more than I ever believed I could love anyone. You are my day and my night. You are the reason I get up every morning and my last thought as slumber takes me. You have saved me more times than I care to count, and you have made me whole. Theo Elliott, you are my heart."

Grace kissed him slowly and tenderly, letting her body tell him what she could never truly articulate. She moved her hands over him, exploring, teasing, her fingers tantalising until Theo could take no more.

Lifting Grace onto the bed, he spent the next little while weaving his own brand of magic. The clock had long stuck midnight before they finally fell asleep, wrapped together. Their lives as entwined as their bodies.

$\mathscr{A}$ carriage rumbled to a halt on a quiet street. Titus and Nero stamped impatiently, hungry for fodder, as Gibbs hopped down to drop the step.

Two weary travellers stepped onto the pathway and beheld a welcome sight. Sparkling windows reflecting the evening light, nestling within warm red brick walls, smoke curling up lazily from the chimneys, white against soft purple.

Through the front door flung open for their return, the glimmer from a multitude of candles flickered a salutation.

They were home.

Theo smiled at Grace who squeezed his fingers, a bubble of happiness fizzling through her. From the carriage house, Matt appeared to assist Gibbs with the luggage and the horses, while Evans and Polly swept the couple into the house each talking over the other in eager greeting.

After saying hello to all of their staff, Theo and Grace were ushered into the dining room, where a hot meal awaited them, lovingly prepared by Agnes.

"I know 'tis earlier than you would normally dine,"

explained Evans, diffidently, "but I… that is we, thought you would likely be fatigued from your journey so best to eat now and then, if you need to retire, you have enjoyed a proper meal."

Grace thanked him for his foresight, agreeing she was indeed tired. In fact, it wasn't long at all before both Theo and she were fast asleep.

~

That night, the dream came again. It was some time since Grace had been troubled by nightmares. Bearing in mind the accumulation of regrettable events including fleeing two would-be kidnappers, it wasn't wholly unexpected. Tonight, there was a subtle difference, and it felt like a warning. It was, as always, dark; tendrils of mist rising from the ground like ghostly claws.

Aldwych stalked her through the maze, and she cried out for Theo. She made it to the exit and saw him waiting for her. His hand outstretched to pull her to safety. She almost grasped it, but as their fingers touched, she was caught and dragged back into the fog.

Her screams were drowned in the maniacal laughter of the duke, and she desperately tried to fight him off. No, he was not going to have her, she was done with him, he had no power over her.

~

"Grace, sweetheart, wake up. 'Tis just a dream."

Through her terror she heard his voice, calling her back to him, but the nightmare held her in its thrall.

"Come on love, I'm here. You're safe."

She whimpered and tried to respond but her mouth refused to follow instructions.

"Grace." A gentle hand cupped her face, stroking her cheek. A madman would not be so courteous. Willing herself to wake up, Grace forced her eyes open. Blinking, she saw it was early morning, not long after dawn, the pale iridescence giving the room an unearthly quality.

"T-Theo?"

"I'm here, love."

She was tangled up in bed covers; her hair was tousled and damp, her breath coming in tormented gasps. "It was the dream. You were there. You tried to pull me free, but he caught me. He always catches me."

To her utter mortification, Grace burst into tears, sobbing brokenly against Theo's chest. Her husband held her close, and let her cry, knowing she needed the release. She had just endured a fairly emotional week. Slowly Grace gathered herself, scrubbing dry her eyes and regaining a modicum of control.

"Oh, Theo. I do apologise. I am spending far too much time crying on your shoulder at the moment," she hiccupped.

"Think nothing of it, my love. I am surprised it has taken you this long. I thought to see tears after the aborted kidnap attempt, but you were more angry than upset. If I cannot be a shoulder for your woes, I am not much use to you, am I?" He kissed the tip of her nose.

She burrowed into his arms revelling in the security of his embrace, pressing her lips to the hollow at his throat and feeling his heart rate increase.

"Banish my nightmares, Theo?" she entreated huskily, sliding against him, inflaming his passion.

Theo readily obliged.

~

Life in Oak Stanton settled back into a blessed routine. Grace taught at the little school, helping Billie with her herb garden and, at the countess' invitation, became involved with the estate's winter preparations.

Theo did what doctors do. The typical round of maladies associated with the changing weather keeping him busy, along with the occasional injury due to carelessness — not unexpected on a busy country estate.

The Harvest Festival and Autumn Fair came and went, both proclaimed highly successful. Grace was overjoyed to be able to buy several chickens at the Fair, begging Ralph and Duncan to build a coop for them — which, naturally, they did — hoping her new hens might produce plentiful clutches of eggs.

The goats were thriving; their voracious appetites ensuring the grass in the field remained scrupulously trimmed. A prodigious variety of plants, conscientiously tended by Grace, now filled the beds in the walled garden.

It would likely be spring before she knew whether they had taken root, but so far, they looked healthy enough. The pyracantha was already sprinkled with red berries, a cheery spot during the darkening days.

By mid-November, the last of the gaudy autumnal colour had faded, the trees were bare and the air, redolent with wood-smoke from copious bonfires, was chill.

It was late afternoon, and after riding home from Whiteoaks, Grace was rubbing down Luna, enjoying the quiet of the stable. Matt normally took care of grooming, but Grace found the repetitive brushing cathartic and it was a good way to maintain the bond between her and the mare.

Patting Luna on her flank to encourage her into the loose

box, Grace latched the half door and went to fill the rack with hay. Dropping the last bundle into the feeder, she heard a heavy footfall and, expecting to see Theo turned, a ready smile on her face.

To her everlasting shock it was Jonathon Huntington, Duke of Aldwych. She gawked at him. How on earth had he got here? Into her garden, into her stable?

He smiled, a singularly malevolent smile.

"May I help you, your Grace?" she questioned, sounding anything but hospitable. He closed the gap between them.

"Oh, I am sure you may, Miss Penelope Barrington," his tones were silky.

Grace frowned, uncomprehending. Giles had never apprised of their subterfuge at the horse stud and she thought perhaps the Duke was unbalanced. "I beg your pardon, your Grace. I have no idea who you are talking about."

"No, but I'm sure Winchester could enlighten you. His attempt to divert my attention, even going as far as to decline my invitation to Blackheath. It almost worked, but you make a lasting impression, Miss Aldeburgh."

Grace studied him in the fading light. "I sincerely doubt it, your Grace. Now, as you have not been invited onto my property, and I have no desire to converse with you, I suggest you leave."

"I intend to, my dear, but before I go, I thought you might be interested to know why I asked my assistants to escort you to my home."

"*Escort me*! An interesting turn of phrase. And no, I stopped caring about what makes you behave the way you do long since." Hands on hips, she let her anger burn.

Aldwych was not finished. "You think it was chance,

brought me to you? That my presence at your parents' estate three years ago was coincidence?"

Grace stilled, wary now.

"I have long wanted you, Grace Aldeburgh, and know more about you than you could possibly imagine."

"Why? What is it about me?" Curiously and against her better judgement, Grace leant on the door of Luna's stable and tilted her head. To her own surprise, she was not afraid, and it was time this sordid tale was done with.

"Your heritage, my dear. *That* is what draws me to you. You are a debt I am owed, and I shall never relinquish it."

"A debt? How am I a debt? I am a person not a bank note." She was genuinely puzzled now.

Huntington fingered his riding crop and took a moment, as though deliberating over his answer.

"Many years ago, a little more than twenty and six to be exact, a young woman was enjoying her first season. She was stunningly beautiful and had many admirers. She only had eyes for one, the son of a duke and heir to the title. Neither family approved of their courtship because they were both young and she, being the daughter of a lowly viscount, was not of equal status.

"Parental disapproval had little effect, and the couple was determined to be together, taking every opportunity to meet — at balls, picnics, garden parties, carriage rides and the like. The more their families tried to keep them apart, the closer the two became."

He waited to see whether his listener had put the pieces together yet.

Apparently not, for all she said, in a calm voice was, "Go on."

"Despairing that they would ever be allowed to marry, they eloped to Gretna Green. Unfortunately, during the journey their carriage rolled, and they were trapped in the wreckage, lying undiscovered for some time, although no one knew exactly how long. When they were found, the young man was beyond help. He must have been in extreme agony for near every bone was shattered, and he died shortly thereafter.

"The young woman, who sustained injuries also, disappeared. That seemed to be that. A year later, a baron and his wife came to town. They had a son perhaps seven years old and a young daughter, who was a babe in arms.

"Everyone knew of the boy, but the babe was unexpected. Rumours circulated, for the baroness had been seen in London frequently over the previous months and no one mentioned she was increasing. It was a conundrum."

Grace felt the beginnings of a headache and her stomach tightened. Something was niggling at the edge of her conscious but refused to be pinned down.

"Time went by, and the little baby grew into a most unusual child. Tall with auburn hair and amber eyes, quite dissimilar to her parents and older brother.

"She didn't come to the city very often. Her parents preferred she either stay on their country estate or visited with a maiden aunt who lived in a tiny village in Hampshire."

Nausea roiled through Grace and she desperately wished Theo were there. "Presumably, I am the child to whom you are referring?" Glad she sounded annoyed not upset.

He nodded, taking a step closer. "Yes, my dear, you are that child. The young man who was killed because some silly chit would not see reason was my brother, and the silly chit was…"

"…my Aunt Beatrice." Grace finished quietly. She slumped to the ground uncaring that she was in a stable and her skirts were now covered in straw and mud.

Everything made sense.

The reason she was bequeathed The Gables. The reason she was kept away from London. The reason they spent so long in Europe. The reason her parents abandoned her — they weren't her parents, after all.

Did they ever care about her? If her mother — Anthony's mother — had not wanted her, why did she agree to take her in?

Grace had no answers, maybe she would never have any answers. She dragged her attention back to the man towering over her. The enmity with which the duke eyed her was almost tangible, and he bent closer, his riding crop tracing a path along her jaw. The threat clear.

"I am the debt you will not relinquish because I was given life while your brother's was taken?" Consternation laced her tones, seeing Aldwych's lips curl.

Another thought occurred to Grace, and although — if at all possible — it made her feel more unwell, she needed to voice it. "B-but you are my uncle. What made you think r…" she still could not say the word, "…taking your pleasure with me would atone for what you consider to be my aunt's… my mother's…" this was taking some getting used to, "…fault? You cannot hold her responsible for your brother's death. It was an accident."

"Had your witless mother not been so hell bent on marrying my brother, they would not have been in such a tearing hurry to get to the border. She must have been a good tumble for I cannot see how else she persuaded him to marry her."

His voice rose in anger and he waved his crop in emphasis, causing Grace to flinch when it whizzed dangerously close to her ear.

"What makes you think it was she who persuaded him? Might it not have been your brother who talked her into fleeing to Scotland?" Grace, back on her feet, lost her temper at his ludicrous logic and yelled this last sentence.

Luna, sensitive to the heightened tension, stomped restlessly, tossing her head and snorting.

Aldwych shook his head. "No. My brother would never bring shame on the family name. It was *she*, and because of her, you are mine. You will always be mine. You are my prize, my recompense." He roared the words.

"I became duke at ten years of age. **Ten**! My brother was killed, and within a year my father died. My childhood was ruined, and for two decades I have had to listen to my mother droning on and on and on about her wonderful son. The son who could do no wrong, the son who was born to be a duke.

"It did not matter how hard I tried. I was never good enough. I was not George. I have had to play the role, which should have been his. He was twenty. He had been prepared to assume the responsibilities the title brings and, if not for your selfish trollop of a mother..."

There was a loud crack.

Grace slapped his face with every ounce of strength she possessed.

Aldwych's face flared so red, Grace wondered, distractedly, whether he was about to be stricken with apoplexy, conceding it would be most convenient.

"You would hit me?" he bawled, stupefied she had been bold enough to raise her hand to him. Unnoticed by either, the riding crop fell from his hand.

"How dare you? How dare you! You think stealing my innocence, and abusing me, your niece, is somehow justifiable because you had to step up and take over a duty you did not expect to assume? You are deranged.

"You know nothing of my aunt … mother, yet you decided to play judge and jury with no clear understanding of the facts. You were not privy to their courtship. You were what, *eight*? *A child*.

"If it was anybody's fault it was your… their… families who tried to prevent them from being together. They were in love. They should have been encouraged, not deterred. Do you have *any* idea how lucky a person is to have someone love them? Imagine your life had your parents approved the match. Think on *that*."

Grace was incandescent with rage. Another thought struck her. "And if I was the one you sought, what of Lavinia?"

"Who the hell is Lavinia?" Aldwych was momentarily confused.

"You mean you do not recall others whom you have victimised? Oh, your Grace," she expostulated, her voice full of contempt, "you are *the* most objectionable excuse for a human being. Lavinia killed herself, because of what you did to her. She could not live with the shame. What possible reason could you have for treating her thus? Why?" She challenged, her eyes flashing with fury.

"Practice!"

Her jaw dropped and for a moment they just glared at each other.

"You bloody bastard!" Her words fell into the sudden silence and, unable to stop herself she slapped him again.

Goaded beyond reason, Aldwych snarled something utterly incomprehensible, and launched himself at her as the last remnants of sanity slipped from his grasp.

"Shrew!"

"Delinquent!"

"Harlot!"

"Snake!"

The insults flew as Aldwych grabbed Grace by the hair, dragging her to the floor. She was screaming now, realising his intentions. Beating her hands against him, she made a valiant attempt to fight him off, but he was a huge man, and had far greater strength than she.

Aldwych tore at her clothes, while Grace kicked at him, gouging her nails down his face making him bellow in pain. He struck out with his fist catching her on the side of the jaw, her head swirled, and she saw spots, but continued to struggle.

Luna, neighing in terror, echoed her screams. The cacophony unnerved the creature and she was rearing, her hoofs drumming against the wood of her stall.

Theo and Ralph were ambling along the road, chatting about nothing in particular when Theo spotted a lone horse tied to a post, just along the street.

A horse neither of them recognised. Its presence niggled at him, and he stood for a moment ruminating on where he had seen the creature before. Abruptly, it came to him, the horse stud. It was the Duke of Aldwych's stallion.

"The devil, Montgomery. If that creature is the one, I think it is, we have to find Grace." Fear lent urgency to Theo's tones and Ralph needed no further bidding. The two men ran the last few steps to The Gables.

"Evans! Where is Lady Elliott? Where is Grace?" Theo demanded as he burst through the door.

Evans appeared along the hallway, totally unruffled. "I believe she's rubbing down Luna, Doctor Elliott. Is there a problem?"

"Yes, I think the duke is here."

Evans' demeanour changed in an instant. "Quick my Lord, that way," pointing to the kitchen, "it is shorter. I'll get Gibbs and Matt." Evans shot off towards the carriage house, while Theo and Ralph hurtled along the hall, out through the back door, and along the path which led to the meadow.

When they reached the gate in the wall, they could hear the distressed horse, and voices bawling at each other. Theo almost wrenched the gate off its hinges in his haste, and the two men rounded the stable with alacrity.

~

Grace recognised this was how her nightmare ended. She was tiring. He would win. He always won.

Aldwych was on top of her, one hand around her throat, the other unbuttoning the fall of his riding breeches.

Pummelling him Grace squirmed, determined to escape but he merely tightened his grip around her neck.

"Let me go," she croaked.

He ignored her.

Grace focused the remnants of her energy on heaving her body, trying to throw him off.

He barely moved.

Luna was beside herself and Grace was worried she would break through the wooden panels. As the last of her stamina drained away, Grace remembered the mare's reaction to gunfire, and a minuscule spark of hope kindled.

Stretching, she banged on the wood, but it made little noise, certainly not loud enough to bother Luna. Thinking there might be a stray piece of wood lying alongside the stall, she scrabbled around in the dust, her fingers finding and curling around the discarded riding crop.

Thanking her lucky stars, Grace sent a tacit apology to her beloved mare, and slapped the crop hard again the wood several times, to great effect.

The sound reverberated around the space spooking poor Luna, who, in her desperation to escape the clamour, kicked out at the wood splintering it. Shards exploded in all directions.

Aldwych, registering Grace's ploy, grabbed her hand. He tossed the crop into the corner and shoved her so she could not reach the stall.

She screamed again, but her voice was hoarse with effort.

The duke laughed, a mirthless sound and angled his body closer. Before he had a chance to speak, his rancid breath finished what his tale began, and Grace vomited all over him.

"You slattern," he hissed, and smashed her head on the dirt floor.

Everything was coming from a great distance, and Grace realised she could no longer breathe. Clawing at the duke's arms, she tried to make him loosen his hold, to no avail.

A grey mist coloured the edge of her vision.

Detachedly, she accepted it for what it was, wishing she could have said goodbye to Theo, saddened she would never see him again.

The last thing Grace saw before darkness claimed her, appeared to be a confusion of horses and men, all tumbling over one another and she thought she heard her name. *Was it Theo?*

She could not concentrate — and then nothing.

CHAPTER 32

Theo and Ralph fell into the stable to see Aldwych on top of Grace, intent on satisfying his bestial urges.

The next few moments unfolded in slow motion.

"Grace!" hollered both Theo and Ralph. Theo saw Grace's hands fall to her sides, her head lolling at a strange angle.

Distracted by the intrusion, the duke's head, shot up, at the precise moment Luna — who had had enough — kicked out. The wooden stall could take no more, collapsing under the onslaught.

The mare reared over the pair on the floor, her right front hoof catching the duke, splitting his head like a knife through butter. She kicked again, her powerful forelegs flinging Aldwych off Grace and, as the horse fled, her back legs landed on his chest, crushing him.

Blood spurted everywhere; arcing from the head wound splattering the four in the shattered stable. Grace hadn't moved, and Theo could see no sign of life. Dropping to his knees next to her, he grabbed her wrist, feeling for a pulse.

Seconds, which seemed like hours, ticked by before he

was rewarded with a faint flutter. Running his eyes over her, he saw bruising on her jaw and a pool of blood under her head. Her throat was turning purple, the marks from cruel fingers livid against her pale skin.

He could not tell whether she had any other injuries, and knew he needed to get her to bed where he could examine her properly but was loath to carry her without some kind of support.

Ralph stooped over Lord Aldwych, seeing wounds resembling those more typical of the battlefield. Despite the duke's actions and, even though Ralph was certain no one could survive such injuries, they could not leave him unattended.

"Elliott, I know your priority is Grace, but we cannot leave Aldwych in this state. If there is a chance of life, we must try everything. I will sit with Grace."

Unwilling to leave his wife's side and uncaring whether the duke lived or died, Theo knew he had check Aldwych for, if nothing else, Grace would never forgive him if he didn't.

It was clear after a quick examination, the tortured soul of Jonathon Huntington, Duke of Aldwych had forsaken him. His body was too badly broken, and his skull mangled beyond recognition.

Pondering how to get Grace into the house, Theo glanced around, spying a large section of the damaged wooden stall, swinging haphazardly on one nail. Yanking it off, he laid it on the floor, and carefully slid his wife onto it. Theo covered her as best he could, her clothes torn beyond any hope of repair.

Grace was ashen, her lips bloodless. For a split second he hesitated, the thought of his life without her as grey as her skin. Ralph rested a hand on the doctor's shoulder offering to help ferry Grace, and his calm words broke through Theo's anxiety.

Gathering himself, Theo took one end of the makeshift stretcher, Ralph the other.

It was dusk when they exited the stable, but light enough to see Matt with Luna. The young groom had calmed the horse, a lead rein securely around her neck. Gibbs came to offer his assistance, and the three men carried Grace into the house. Evans was waiting, as were Agnes, Martha and the three maids.

The five women stood together, twisting their hands in shock. Their eyes and mouths formed perfect 'O's, and looked so alike, at any other time, Theo would have burst out laughing. As it was, all he did was request a bowl of warm water and plenty of cloths, a glass of brandy and a jar of honey.

He instructed Evans to send Matt or Adam over to Whiteoaks. Giles, as magistrate, would need to be informed, and Theo asked that Billie accompany Giles back to The Gables. He might need her help.

It was one of the longest nights of Theo's life. Despite being undressed — or, in actuality, having her clothes cut away — examined thoroughly, her head wound cleaned and bandaged, and her bruises treated with arnica, Grace did not regain consciousness.

Not even the pungent aroma of the ointment caused a flicker. Her breathing and heartbeat steadied and strengthened, but she remained unresponsive.

Billie and Giles arrived, assessing the situation immediately. Ralph took Giles out to the stable, and the two men made arrangements to transport the Duke's body to Blackheath Manor. That his death could be judged accidental would be a blessing to his family as the alternative would cause them undue suffering.

Aldwych was dead. No longer could he harm anyone. His actions had been unspeakable, but to humiliate the rest of his family would make those in a position to accuse, no better than the duke.

The past should be laid to rest.

Billie stayed with Theo throughout the night, more to keep the doctor company, than to help Grace. She did talk to her friend though, chattering away about all manner of things.

The preparations for the Christmas Ball, the different lessons they might try — such as history and geography — how both of their gardens would look in the spring and, of course, the baby. Billie posited that the baby was expected to arrive sometime after Christmas, but she wasn't entirely sure.

Worried as he was, Theo chuckled while she talked about this, her expression one of excitement mixed with trepidation.

"I will need your help, Grace. Giles and Theo are quite useful, but you know men. Not always good when it comes to practical matters." Serenely indifferent to Theo's spluttered repost pointing out both Giles and he were far more practical than Billie, and for that matter Grace, could ever hope to be.

"Hush, Theo. Don't interrupt, there's a dear. Grace and I are talking," She winked at the doctor.

Grateful for her irrepressible good humour and unflappability, Theo smiled at Billie and sat back, letting her gentle voice wash over him. Unable to do any more than he already had, he held his wife's hand, rubbing his thumb along hers, willing her to wake.

None of the household slept. When Giles and Ralph returned, it was the early hours of the morning. Evans was there to greet them and take their greatcoats, ushering them into the Snug for a hot coffee and a whisky. Agnes came in with a platter of hot food, and gave them an update, such as it was, on Grace's condition.

Theo appeared at some point, Billie having sent him to get something to eat, or at the very least a drink. It was hours since his last meal, but he had no appetite.

"Come, Theo. You must try a little," Giles encouraged him. "Agnes has gone to a lot of trouble to tempt you with tasty fare and, if you do not eat, you will be of no use to Grace."

His words did the trick and Theo forced down a few mouthfuls. He did swallow a large measure of whisky, and gulp a hot coffee and, with that, his friends had to be satisfied.

"Thank you for everything." Theo said, the three now cosily ensconced around the blazing fire. "I-I…" he stopped.

No one in the room was given to demonstrative outbursts, but Theo wanted them to understand how much he appreciated everything they had done. "I am indebted to you both," he said, his tones heartfelt.

Ralph grinned. "No debt is owed, Elliott. Fret not. I think you will find my cousin is more resilient than we give her credit for. I remember…" Ralph described several incidents from his childhood, demonstrating just how resilient, reducing the others to gales of laughter, and effectively distracting Theo for a time.

The hours ticked by, Giles and Ralph refused to leave,

commenting the chairs were more than comfortable, and why leave a roaring fire and good whisky for a cold walk home?

Much earlier, while waiting for Giles to arrive, Ralph popped home to tell Tessa what had occurred. His wife assured him it was more important to be there for Grace this night, hustling him back through the door, affirming she would come over on the morrow to offer her help.

In the early hours, Theo took over from Billie, talking himself hoarse. Infusing calm reason into his voice, he suggested it was time she woke up, informing her she no longer need fear Aldwych and, Luna had saved her life.

He mentioned her loyal mare kicked the duke off her, as he and Ralph arrived on scene. Also, did Grace realise it was near daybreak, and there was much to do? Who would tend her plants? Who would feed the goats? Who would exercise Luna? She ought not to be lying abed like this.

Anything to provoke a response, anything that might persuade her to come back to him.

He continued in this vein until the light in the room began to change. A perceptible lessening of the darkness, foreshadowing the dawn. Theo stood, stretching his body, his back aching from leaning over the bed for so long, and went to gaze out of the window.

He rarely attended church but, despite being a man of science, Theo clung to his childhood faith, for without it he felt there was little hope for humanity.

Resting his head against the window frame, watching the colours of the sky morph from dark blue-grey through purple and pink to an almost golden hue, Theo prayed.

. . .

The house was quiet, the street was quiet — far too early for anyone else to be abroad — and it seemed to Theo that the whole world was quiet. A breath held and a heartbeat stayed. Time paused, suspended, waiting for the signal that the new day had triumphed over the dominion of the night.

The sun glimmered on the horizon, sending rays of light though the pearly sky, a flock of birds rose from the nearby trees, welcoming the morning with their melodic chorus, and life resumed its rhythm. The utter perfection of this scene held Theo enthralled, and he could have admired it forever.

One last look and he went back to the chair by their bed, his heart faltering as he saw Grace hadn't stirred. She *must* have felt that shift when the world revolved? He took her hand, entwining it through his, and holding both to his chest, hoping she could feel his heart.

"Come back to me, Grace," he murmured. "I love you, and we have not had enough time together. I absolutely forbid you to leave me."

Exhaustion creeping up on him, Theo angled his body in the chair, so he did not have to relinquish his wife's hand. He lay his head on the covers thinking to snatch a few minutes sleep.

"You forbid me, do you?" Barely a whisper, so faint he thought it was his imagination.

His head snapped up, and his gaze met most beautiful pair of amber eyes studying him in mild indignation.

Theo shrugged with apparent nonchalance. "I thought it might annoy you enough to wake up… turns out I was right," he was unrepentant.

A slight smile tugged at her lips as she pulled him closer. "What happened?"

"I think you might have to tell us that, my love. It was all over by the time Ralph and I found you."

"Maybe later, I am so tired. It hurts to talk, and it hurts to think," her voice was little more than a rasp.

"Then don't, but here, before you go back to sleep, drink some of this."

She eyed him suspiciously. "Is this one of your concoctions or Billie's?"

"Joint effort, but it has honey in it which is soothing. Please try it just for me." His eyes held hers, and she reached up with her free hand to cup his face.

"There is little I wouldn't do for you, Theo." She swallowed a decent dose of the mixture, the cool liquid slid over her throat relieving the ache. "Please lie with me, I need you to hold me," her voice was fading, and as Theo settled himself alongside her, she murmured, "don't let me go…" and was asleep.

Theo tucked her against him and, dropping a light kiss on her hair, answered just as quietly.

"Never."

CHAPTER 33

The weak winter sun high overhead, Theo awoke, disorientated for a moment, wondering why he was fully clothed on his own bed. Memory flooded back, and he glanced down to see Grace sleeping peacefully in his arms, their fingers interlaced and resting on his stomach.

Relief spiralled through him. She would recover. Her responses from earlier did not indicate any form of damage resulting from lack of air to her brain. Sending up a quick prayer of thanks, Theo began to get up, thinking to let her sleep more comfortably but, as he moved, her hand tightened around his.

"Where do you think you are going, husband of mine?" Her voice had improved from a rasp to a croak.

"I thought to wash and dress, to check on our household, and our guests."

"Not yet." She drew him closer, nestling into him. A brief silence. "Was it a dream?" She questioned tentatively.

"No, my love, I am afraid it was not, but you are free of him now. He can never hurt you again."

Grace shook her head. The gesture made her wince, and

she ran her hand over her hair feeling the bandages. She raised her eyes to Theo's. "It's all muddled. Luna! Is Luna all right? She was agitated, and I made it worse, banging the crop on the wood so she might get someone's attention. Did anyone hear her?"

Theo realised Grace could not remember what happened from the seconds before he and Ralph arrived on the scene.

"Yes, we heard her. She saved your life, and she is fine. Matt calmed her down and within an hour she was happily munching hay in the stables with Titus and Nero. The stable in the paddock will need a bit of repairing." He sought to soothe her concerns.

"I'm sorry, I cannot seem to hold anything in my head. There are lots of images flickering, but they insist on skittering off. Everything aches, Theo."

"I know, my love. Would you like a little of that draft? It helped last evening."

Grace nodded, and Theo helped her sip a suitable amount.

"Do you wish to rest some more, or would you prefer to go down to the Snug?" he asked as he replaced the cup on the bedside table.

"I would like to stay here, I think. I feel weak and somewhat pathetic. I know you likely have call on your time, but might you stay a little longer?" She entreated, wistfully.

Theo drew up the covers, and propped himself against the pillows, cradling his wife to him. Stretching, Grace kissed him on his jaw, it was all she could reach, and smiled, her eyes already drooping. The draft worked its magic, and within seconds she had drifted back to sleep.

Theo waited until he was sure Grace was settled and then, without disturbing her, eased his long frame off the bed. He freshened up with a thorough wash, and a clean set of clothes, which made him feel much better.

When he got downstairs, he found what appeared to be a large crowd of people in the kitchen, eating a hot meal. In fact, on top of the usual staff, there were only three extra. Everyone turned expectantly as he entered and he nodded, smiling.

"Grace has woken, twice. Once shortly after dawn and again just now. She is lucid and I do not believe there will be any lasting damage, although she has difficulty talking and her memories of last night are unclear."

This news was received with beaming smiles and no little amount of relief, all clamouring for more information.

Laughing, Theo held up his hands in mock surrender. "That is all I can tell you. Hopefully the next time she wakes her recollection has improved. We will have to be patient." He paused. "Thank you for being here for Grace. I know she will be most appreciative."

"'Tis not only Grace for whom we are here, Theo," chided Billie gently. "Our care is for you also."

Theo felt his cheeks redden and he grinned sheepishly. "I too am grateful." He acknowledged and before the moment became too emotional, turned their conversation to more practical matters.

Ralph advised he would call on Duncan to ask whether he would have some free time to help repair the stable. Giles intended to send a report to Withers, because that gentleman ought to be apprised of the Duke of Aldwych's demise, as well as the formal registration of same.

Billie declared she was not going anywhere until she had spoken with Grace and, since Theo likely could use a proper rest, she would sit with her friend. The staff said they would continue as normal. Agnes remarking that she and Martha would make sure there was enough food for any and all visitors.

Theo gave the jolly cook a warm hug.

She batted him away, telling him to stop such nonsense, but was secretly delighted.

It was almost the end of the day before Grace roused. The room was bathed in candlelight, and this time it was Billie who was sitting with her, reading from a heavy tome. The words sounded familiar, but Grace could not place the tale.

"Hello Billie," she whispered. "How lovely to see you."

Billie placed the book aside, taking a cool slender hand in her small one and squeezing it gently. "I am glad to see you have woken, my dear. You have had us in a bit of a flap. Here, Theo tells me you managed a sip or two of this earlier, please try a bit more. It will help your poor throat."

Grace drank enough to satisfy Billie before sinking back against the pillows. "It seems to be my lot in life to cause worry," she sighed, huskily. "Where's Theo? Has he had a rest? He looked so tired."

Billie could see every word was an effort and she patted her friend's hand.

"Theo had a good few hours of sleep. He has just gone around to his office in case there was anything to which he should attend. He will be home shortly, and do not ever think you are a worry, Grace. 'Twas not your fault a mad duke decided he just had to try to throttle you." Billie grinned as Grace touched her throat.

"I can't remember," she muttered. "The last thing I recall is arguing with him. He told me why he wanted me, why he stalked me. Oh, Billie, 'tis a pitiable tale and one I will gladly share, but not yet. I am too tired to concentrate properly. Maybe in day or so..."

Billie could see Grace was losing focus, confirmed seconds later when she said in wonderment,

"...well, goodness me, I do believe I'm floating, how odd," and slumber re-claimed her.

Billie chuckled and, knowing Grace would sleep for a good while, took this opportunity to pop into the kitchen to see how the staff fared. All was as it should be, and Billie updated them on Grace's progress. Polly said she would go and sit with her mistress while Billie took a break.

"Dinner'll be served in about an hour, my Lady," Agnes informed her. "Now you shouldn't be in here, it isn't right. Go on with you, I think his Lordship is in the Snug. Evans has just taken him a coffee. I'll send one along for you in a jiffy," she hustled Billie out.

That young lady did as she was told, where she found her husband and the two were chatting about something to do with the estate when Theo joined them shortly thereafter. He had peeked in on his wife, but Polly told him she was fine, and to go and have a proper meal.

"It seems I am surplus to requirements, even when it comes to looking after my own wife," he grumbled.

Billie giggled at his disgruntled expression. "Stop being a grouch, Theo. Polly is correct. How many times do I have to remind you, you will be useless to Grace, if exhausted and faint from hunger?"

Giles stifled a bark of laughter at this, and Theo conceded Billie's point. The three resumed their easy conversation until dinner was announced. Giles informed him Ralph, Duncan and Nate had worked all afternoon on the stable and they reckoned the repairs would be completed the following day. Thankfully there was enough spare wood from the initial delivery to fix up the damaged panels.

Luna seemed content to share the carriage house for the time being, and the goats could sleep there also. Theo checked on his wife several times during the evening and, even though she did not stir, her vital signs were normal.

The next two days followed a similar pattern and, on the third day after the attack, Grace woke early. She could hear the birds calling lustily to each other making her smile; they sounded so earnest. Her head no longer thumped, and her throat no longer felt as though it was clogged with rose thorns.

Shifting slightly, she saw Theo asleep in the chair next to the bed, his hand holding hers. Tutting, she tightened her grip and he came awake immediately, momentarily confused, his mind befuddled from sleep.

"Grace, what is it?"

"'Tis you, Theo. You cannot sleep comfortably there. Come." She drew him towards her.

"I do not wish to jar you, love. You took a nasty bang to your head."

"I wish for my husband to get into bed with me and, being the invalid here, I imagine you have to do as I ask."

She heard laughter rumble through his chest. "Yes, my Lady." He made as though to slide under the comforter as he was. Grace informed him, not only did she expect him to undress, she also expected him to get between the sheets.

"I will not break, and you are not going to do me any harm by sleeping next to me."

"That's what you think," he muttered almost inaudibly. She heard him and could not prevent a giggle.

"I do believe being kissed is an essential part of the healing process," she pointed out artlessly. Theo chuckled and, dropping the last of his clothes on the chair, got into bed.

Grace sighed with pleasure, moulding herself against him, her nightdress in no way disguising her willowy form. Her fingers ran over Theo's warm body, their coolness sending ripples right down to his toes, and desire flared. She brushed her lips over his chest and upwards to his throat, catching the hollow there and making him groan.

He sucked in a sharp breath. "Grace, 'tis no more than three days since we carried you here unconscious. You still have a sizeable lump on the back of your head and a throat, which must feel as though you have swallowed razors. I refuse to let you inveigle me like this."

Grace smiled a wicked smile and ignored him. "My throat is much better, my love, and my head no longer feels as though it is being used for hammer practice. Now shut up."

Effectively shutting him up, Grace continued to seduce her husband with her lips and her fingers, until he caught her hands in his and captured her mouth with a passion which sent thrills up and down her spine.

"Is this not the perfect way to start the day?" she murmured against his lips in a voice which was less than steady when he finally lifted his head.

Theo was breathing heavily, and he fought to retain some semblance of control. Resting on one elbow, he smoothed her fiery hair off her face, tucking it under the bandage and stroked her cheek with one finger.

"See how much better we both feel," she grinned, a cheeky smile catching her lips.

Theo could not restrain his mirth. "You are a minx, Grace Elliott," he chuckled. Sobering suddenly, he cupped her face in his hands. "I nearly lost you. When I saw you lying on the floor in the stable, so white and still, I thought I was too late." His voice was gruff. Grace realised he was close to tears.

"Oh, Theo," she kissed him, gently. "I am sorry I caused you such distress, but I didn't die, and we are here, and we are safe. Moreover, I know why he did what he did, and my story has yet another bizarre twist."

Theo raised an eyebrow and gathered her close. Cradled in her husband's arms, Grace explained Aldwych's reasoning. It took some telling for Theo had plenty of questions and, despite the fact Grace struggled to recall the last minute or so before Luna kicked the duke, eventually it was told.

She hesitated when it came to confessing she was a by-blow. While it clarified so much of her life, it was hard to come to terms with being illegitimate, and also that her great aunt was her mother. Chewing on her lip when she shared this with him, Grace tried to read her husband's face, old fears plaguing her.

Theo, wise to his wife's convoluted reasoning, gave her no time to say what he knew she would say. "Grace, if you dare to suggest this is grounds for us to not be together, I will put you over my knee and spank you."

Grace doubled over with laughter, warning him if he tried, he'd be sorry. Her amusement subsiding, she said, "It's confusing, Theo, and will take some adjustment. I wish I had known before Aunt Beatrice died. I would have liked to hear her side."

Theo realised this was the moment to give Grace the letter Beatrice had entrusted to him. "Grace, before your aunt... mother, died she gave me a letter asking that I give it to you when the time was right. I was unsure how I would know when this was, but I believe it is now. Do you feel up to it?"

Grace nodded, pushing herself up on the pillows. Theo vanished from the room, with a sealed document. He handed it to his wife, before getting back into bed and tucking her against him.

Nervously, she turned the smooth paper in her hands, recognising the neat script used by her au... mother. Breaking the seal, she opened the letter and unfolding it carefully, began to read it aloud.

My darling Grace,

I am sorry I did not get the chance to tell you what happened. Had I any inkling as to what Jonathon might do, I surely would have tried to protect you.

Many years ago, during my first season, I met a wonderful man. He was three years older than I, handsome, clever and the most amusing companion. He was the son of a duke and heir to the title, while I was the daughter of a mere viscount. Our families did not approve and tried to keep us apart.

We were young and in love and did everything we could to see each other as often as possible. Sadly, it became clear, George — that was his name — would be expected to put me aside for the sake of duty.

Neither of us could countenance a life without the other, and the more we talked about it, the more we knew it was worth risking everything to be together. We made a plan to travel to Gretna Green. It was our only chance.

We arranged everything with much thought. My parents believed I was going to stay with a friend in the country. George's family presumed he was travelling to Blackheath, their estate. No one would miss us for a few days and, by the time they did, we hoped to be wed.

We made it. It was a long journey. I was terrified the whole way we would be followed, and forced to go back, but we made it, and we were married.

Grace paused here, raising shocked eyes to Theo.

"T-they married? I am not a by-blow? I am the granddaughter of a duke?" This was more baffling than ever. Trembling a little she went back to the letter.

We stayed in a coaching inn near the border for three days. They were among the happiest days of my life, but we had to return home to face our families, and deal with their wrath. On the journey back we drove into a storm, and the road became churned with mud.

The carriage overturned, flinging us both out and as the horses tried to flee, they dragged the damaged coach over both of us. George, who tried to cover me, bore the brunt.

I held him, talking to him, trying to keep him alive long enough for someone to come upon us, but his injuries grievous. By the time they found us, it was too late. I had slipped into a stupor and when I awoke, he was long buried.

Soon after, I realised I was increasing and, although we were legally wed, I could not bring myself to tell his family of the child. That child, that darling child, was you, Grace.

I wanted to keep you. You were all I had left of him. My parents would not hear of it. I had already brought shame on them by daring to elope with the son of a duke, and a month after your birth, they took you from me.

My cousin offered to raise you as hers, agreeing to keep the name I had chosen. She had long wanted another child but had been unable to conceive. For everyone, except me, it was the perfect answer, but I loved you before ever I saw you, and losing you broke my heart all over again.

I persuaded my parents to allow some contact, and you became my great niece. Your visits were the highlight of my life, and there were hundreds of times when I nearly broke my word and told you everything. In the blink of an eye, you were grown, such a beautiful young woman. I pictured you going to balls or being courted with carriage rides and long walks.

Whispers of a scandal reached me, and you vanished. I eventually discovered something of what happened and tried to convince your mother to let you come home to me. They refused. All I got was a brief missive, telling me, since your behaviour had humiliated the family, you had been sent on an extended tour of Europe until the furore died down.

My darling daughter, I never imagined my actions of so many years ago would come back to haunt you, resulting in such dire consequences.

I discovered I was unwell, and, despite my very clever doctor's best efforts, I knew it was simply my time. In truth I am ready to go. I believe George waits for me and I have missed him these long years.

The Gables is my legacy to you. I wanted you to have something of me. Something to remind you that you were conceived with love, and this is all I have. I hope it offers you sanctuary.

In a postscript of sorts, I wish to add, should a certain Doctor Theodore Elliott, yes, the same very clever doctor, find the courage, I hope you will be sympathetic to his approach.

Theo, as we all call him, already knows of you and, if the tone of his voice is anything to go by, is already halfway in love with you. I do believe you will make a most devoted couple.

My greatest regret is we were not granted the chance to know each other better, but maybe this is how it is supposed to be.

I wish you a life full of joy, my beloved child, my daughter, my saving Grace.

Beatrice (Mama)

Grace was silent for a long time when she finished. The effort of speaking had exhausted her, and the emotional upheaval took its toll. Understanding all this was too much. Theo hugged her close, stroking his hand over her shoulder and pressing a kiss on her bandaged head.

"Had she shown... she thought you... did you? I-I..." Grace felt muddled, and couldn't think of anything to say so, quite sensibly she thought, burst into tears.

Theo continued to hold her, allowing the storm to abate before commenting that, no, he had no idea about what was in the letter and, yes, Beatrice was correct — he was already smitten, long before they actually met, and her aunt was obviously a perceptive lady for he also believed they made a most devoted couple.

His placid demeanour in the face of her turmoil effectively calmed Grace. Once she had gathered herself together, the two discussed the significance of the letter, concluding they would reveal its contents only to those whom they trusted. Then it would be put aside, relegated to history.

It was well into the morning, and they could hear the sounds of people moving through the house.

"Do you wish to get up today, love?" queried Theo. Grace nodded, saying she really must get on with all the jobs she had neglected, such as her plants, the goats, and Luna, giving Theo pause to wonder whether she heard his entreaty the night she was injured.

Grace grinned impishly, and he had no chance to query her words as a quiet knock on the door interrupted them. Wrapping a banyan around his shoulders, Theo admitted Polly who declared herself thrilled Grace was awake and seemingly much better.

Their day began.

$\sim$

Later that afternoon, Theo entered their bedroom to find Grace staring out of the window, absently fingering the letter.

"Grace?"

She turned, coming back to the present, her eyes focusing on her husband. "Theo," was all she said her voice still husky, as she folded the paper and slipped it into the drawer of the bedside table. Glancing at her face, Theo noticed his wife was wearing the most mischievous expression.

"Out with it, Grace, I know that look. It never bodes well."

She chuckled and kissed him before saying pertly. "We…ll," drawing out the word, "I was pondering. This whole thing is quite the facer. How on earth will your poor brother cope?"

Theo barked with laughter. "I think discovering you are the daughter of a duke will place you on his list of most esteemed friends, and likely promote you to his inner circle. His biggest problem now is that, since you have married beneath your station, he will expect *you* to divorce *me*!"

Theo winked and the two chortled, their mirth as they pictured Benedict's reaction carrying away the last vestiges of sadness.

The past was consigned to memory.

*L*ife in Oak Stanton quickly and quietly resumed its leisurely pace after the events of that fateful November evening. Anybody visiting The Gables shortly afterwards would have no idea of the catastrophe which had occurred there.

The stable was repaired within two days, allowing Luna and the three goats to return to more familiar sleeping quarters and, once Grace told the rest of her story to the people who mattered most, nobody mentioned the duke again.

To all intents and purposes, it was as though he had never existed and, for those whose lives he affected, this was as they preferred. Even Grace, who was beset by the occasional nightmare, rarely thought of Aldwych, for which Theo was most grateful.

On another and most agreeable note, especially for Grace, Lord Hawkesworth — she found it peculiar to refer to the baron as her brother now — had been coxed into parting with Peggy. That young lady had arrived just before Christmas. Her exuberance, and obvious love for Grace, saw her settling into the household with aplomb.

~

It was late March, and the long hard winter was over. There was a definite promise of spring in the air; the light was beginning to change. The harsh shades of winter softening into the warmer hues of spring and the air smelt clean, as though freshly washed.

The dawn had only just broken when Grace stirred and, lifting herself up on one elbow, glanced out of the window. It was going to be another fine day.

Wide awake, despite not getting home until midnight, Grace moved to get up, rousing Theo as she fidgeted about. He pulled her against him, muttering it was far too early, easily convincing her to stay under the warm covers for a little longer.

Her husband once again deep in slumber, Grace eased out of bed and stood for several moments admiring the bright morning. She hugged herself, a secret smile playing about her lips, hurrying to wash and dress before going down to the kitchen to consult with Agnes and Martha.

Grace took a cup of tea outside and, wrapped in a warm shawl, sat on the bench revelling in the peace and quiet. The previous day had been full of celebration.

The christening of a certain Maximilian Theodore Edgar Trevallier — named for his father, his godfather and his maternal grandfather — the one month old, first born son of the Earl and Countess of Winchester. A most auspicious occasion.

Theo and Grace, along with Ralph and Tessa, and Lucas and Jemima, had been asked to stand as godparents. Billie and Giles eschewed the ridiculously long list, which was the current trend, commenting, as their child already had uncles and aunts aplenty, twenty godparents was just plain greedy.

After the church service, the large gathering of family and friends were invited to a celebratory feast at Whiteoaks. The day passed in a flurry of good cheer, the festivities continuing well into the evening. Hence the reason for retiring at such a late hour.

Theo appeared, later than usual, but dashing as ever. While they were partaking of a wholesome breakfast, Grace enquired whether he might spare some time to take a drive with her. Content to fall in with her suggestion as long as no one required his medical expertise, Theo asked where she would like to go?

"This is my surprise, and I have asked Agnes to make up a picnic."

Intrigued, Theo departed for the clinic at his old home and, after dealing with a couple of labourers who had cut their hands on some farm equipment, returned to The Gables a little before eleven.

Matt would be driving the coach, and Grace whispered something to him as he dropped the step. Matt nodded and then they were off. Although the sun was shining, the day was chilly, and Grace was glad of her winter cloak. She snuggled up to Theo, and they chatted about this and that, nothing of any great import, inconsequential things of those whose lives are bound.

Theo realised where they were headed when they turned off the main road about five miles outside of the village.

"We're going to the Abbey?" he queried.

His wife nodded. "I accept it might be a bit muddy, but I had a fancy to walk the grounds again and admire the architecture. For me 'tis a special place."

Theo's heart did its odd hiccup and he smiled, taking her hand and pressing his lips to her gloved fingers. Grace squeezed his fingers. Had the carriage not been jolting so alarmingly on the rutted track, she might well have risked a kiss, but it was unlikely their lips would have aligned, despite desirous intent.

Soon they arrived, and it was a great relief not to be bounced around anymore. Grace commented it was fortunate they had decided not to bring milk, because by now it would probably be butter.

"Matt," she turned to the young groom, "we shall be here for a while. If you prefer to return home and come back in, say, three hours, I have no objections."

"I might just do that, my lady," he said, with a nod, "There's a bit of work to do in the stables."

"Thank you, Matt," Grace smiled. Lifting down a rug, a blanket and the picnic, Matt hopped back up into the driver's seat and the carriage trundled away.

Grace picked up the rug and the blanket while Theo did the honours with the picnic basket. In tacit consent they strolled over to the same wall they had leant against so many months ago.

Leaving everything tucked neatly against the lichen covered stones, the couple strolled through the ruined abbey. Here and there signs of spring could be seen. One or two hardy daffodils reaching for the sun and a few crocuses bobbing their heads in the breeze. New leaves, vivid green against the soft blue of the sky, were sprouting on the trees.

Grace stood for a moment and breathed in deeply. The air was cool, but the sun had taken the edge off the earlier chill. The scent of slightly damp grass and loamy earth, with just a hint of blossom, was a welcome fragrance.

They walked around the whole of the abbey but, despite being the one to have orchestrated this outing and for no reason Theo could think of, Grace seemed flustered. Trying not to let it bother him, Theo distracted her with what he believed to be brilliant and insightful conversation but received little more than yes or no answers in response.

In the end he gave up, and enjoyed the architecture and the scenery, and before long they were back at the wall. Checking the ground was not too damp, Theo laid out the rug and, placing the blanket over the top, started to unpack the picnic. He hadn't even lifted the lid, when his wife's voice stayed his hand.

"Theo, before we eat, there is something I must tell you. I cannot keep it to myself any longer."

Inexplicably, Theo felt dread trail down his spine, and he knew he had gone pale. "Grace, please what is it? 'Tis clear something bothers you. You have been out of sorts since we arrived. Have you received some bad news?"

"No, Theo, no it is not bad news. Well I don't think so… oh I'm not sure… 'tis just I don't know whether…" completely inarticulate now, Grace was wringing her hands together, obviously in a ferment.

"Just tell me, love."

She stared at him, her lips trembling and her astonishing eyes anxious. She had not been this distraught since… he let that thought hang, not wanting to let bad memories intrude.

"Grace?"

She took a deep breath. "I think I'm increasing. No, that is not true, I know I'm increasing, 'tis early, but I recognise the signs. I…" She said it almost apologetically, and her eyes, glistening like burnished copper in the sunlight, held his. Theo gaped at her, his brain refusing to connect with his mouth. The minutes ticked by. "Theo, talk to me."

Theo could feel elation bubbling through him, but he

knew his wife's fears. He knew what her doctor had told her, and he didn't want to get excited until he knew how she felt. "How do you feel about this, love?" cautiously asked, his voice relatively calm.

"As we have not done anything to prevent me from conceiving, I assumed having a baby was not going to be part of our marriage. I admit to desiring a child quite desperately. A child who is part of you and me, but after what the doctor told me when…" she could not complete her sentence. Theo knew to what she alluded, "…I did not dare to hope. Then I noticed certain changes…"

"Which you have kept well hidden, wife of mine," interjected Theo.

Grace chuckled, "…and I wondered. If I have calculated correctly, I believe I am maybe four months along. This child was conceived at around the same time…"

"…you read your mother's letter," Theo deemed this a much more auspicious reference point than the one Grace was about to use. His wife mulled that over and smiled at him. A smile so full of joy and happiness, he would not have been at all surprised had rainbows popped into existence over their heads and a carpet of flowers sprung up in front of them, complete with a herd of unicorn.

"We will need to go to London. You should see the same specialist, Billie saw. He is a friend of mine, so I know we can get an appointment. You will have the best of care," he paused, "I ask again, my love. How do you feel?"

Her expression gave him the answer he hoped for, long before she whispered it was the third happiest day of her life so far.

"And what were the first two?" He grinned, roguishly.

"The evening you told me you loved me, and the day we married," she admitted, shyly.

At some point soon, they would have to deal with the

risks this pregnancy brought. For now, they rejoiced.

Theo tilted Grace's head and looked deep into her eyes. He could feel his heart beating erratically and his breathing was anything but steady. Running his hands through her hair, mussing up the neat style, he cupped her head. Bringing her face to his, he kissed her gently, teasing her bottom lip with his teeth, tasting the sweet softness of her mouth.

Desire, as always, flickered into life, and heat licked through their veins. Her arms went around him, and she fitted herself to his body, her hands moving over him, his clothes hampering her attempts to touch his skin.

Uncaring that they were in the middle of a ruined abbey and that anyone might come upon them, Theo and Grace lost themselves in each other. Their passion overriding any fear of discovery. So early in the season, they believed they would remain undisturbed, it being unlikely anyone else would be fool enough to venture forth on so cool a day.

There on the warm rug under the ancient Romanesque arches, with an audience of several sparrows — who were actually more interested in what was in the picnic basket — Theo made slow, sensual yet exquisitely tender love to his wife. Their bodies in perfect harmony, their souls as one.

It was as though here in this place, where Grace had stepped out from her past, every kiss, every touch and every heartbeat, defined their future. A future full of promise, like the bright dawning of spring after the bleak darkness of winter.

When they descended from the heavens, ardour in no way cooled and hearts thrumming, Grace murmured that in some ways they should be grateful to the duke.

"Really! You need to spoil this moment by dragging his

name into it?" Theo was nonplussed.

Grace giggled, enlightening her exasperated husband. "Of course, my love. If not for him, we might never have met and my heart, my soul would remain buried beyond recall."

"That's all you know," he smiled, entangling his fingers through her tousled hair. "I had a plan and was simply awaiting the right moment to unlock your heart."

He drew her into his embrace, kissing her into delicious ecstasy while the world around them dissolved, and they were swept away on a cloud of euphoria.

~

FIVE YEARS LATER

It was a warm afternoon in early summer and Theo Elliott, tired after a long day treating patients, had just arrived home. He walked through the house, looking forward to a relaxing evening. A hope immediately doused when he reached the terrace.

In the garden, two children appeared to be running amok and, in the middle of it all, his wife, wearing the most ridiculous hat — its brim large enough for a carriage to shelter under — was calmly planting lavender.

A boy of about five years old was taking great delight in hurling clods of mud high in the air and trying to catch them when they showered back to earth. His faithful acolyte, a girl maybe a year younger, ran behind him, picking up the lumps and handing them to him. Both were covered, head to toe, in mud.

Staying within the shade of the house, and leaning against the wall, Theo enjoyed the rare privilege of being able to watch their interactions unobserved.

"Max," Grace called as she patted down the soil around

the last seedling and poured some water over it from the small bucket next to her. "Sweetheart, please would you leave some of the soil for the plants, they need it to grow…"

Max stopped in mid-throw, so abruptly, the little girl bumped into him and tumbled over,

"…and do watch where you're going Bea. Honestly, it will take me a week to get all that dirt off the two of you."

Bea stood up, beaming at her mother while brushing her hands over her little dress, grimy fingers adding to the growing layers of muck.

"Here, Aunt Grace."

Theo chuckled, as Max presented Grace with a veritable mound of soil. She thanked him, and the boy grinned, throwing his arms around her, wiping soil over her face and neck.

Bea followed suit by which time Grace was almost as dirty as the two children. She didn't seem unduly perturbed, kissing their smudged cheeks and, laughingly, shooed them off on their next adventure.

Theo was reminded of the picture, which had floated into his head all those years ago — Grace laughing at children who were jumping around the garden. He smiled to himself, endlessly glad it had come true.

On a rug at one side of the garden, shaded by a huge parasol stood a cradle. Theo detected a hint of movement, the indication of a waking child. A sound made him turn, and Billie came out through the glass doors carrying a tray of drinks and biscuits, a little girl clinging to her skirts.

She squeaked in surprise when she saw Theo in the shadows. "Theo Elliott! I nearly dropped the tray. What on *earth* are you doing skulking over there?"

"Just watching the chaos unfold," Theo stepped forward

to help her. He took the tray and placed it on a convenient table, while Billie sorted out the little girl.

"It is uproarious isn't it?" Billie smiled, impishly. "This charming child decided the compost heap was the perfect place in which to romp around and got upset when I refused to let her continue playing while smelling like rotting plants."

Billie handed the small girl a biscuit, suggesting she sit down to eat it. Her daughter had no such intentions and raced off after the other two.

"Vivienne has quite the independent streak, hasn't she?" smiled Theo watching her catch up to Max and Bea, the trio tippling headlong into another wild frolic.

"She certainly has," Billie gurgled. "Poor Giles is already panicking about her first season, despite my assurances, by then she'll be a perfect lady."

That set them both off for, if Vivienne was anything like her mother, a perfect lady she would never be. They were still laughing when Grace joined them, having rinsed some of the mud from her hands.

"What is so funny?" she queried, stretching her back, and feeling the warm afternoon sun on her face. Theo explained and Grace guffawed, the three adults watched their offspring playing happily around the paths, chattering nineteen to the dozen in childish babble.

A disgruntled muttering caught their attention. Grace walked over to the cradle, lifting a tiny baby from its sheltered depths.

"There, there, my poppet, are you hungry again?" she cooed, as the little face scrunched up, heralding a loud squall.

"I'll be back soon. Theo, please watch Bea. We have discovered, while Max is very good at thinking up mischief, your daughter is usually the one to carry it out," grinning at her tall husband as she spoke, disappearing into the cool of the Snug.

Theo smiled lovingly after her, at the same moment as a muddy little girl spotted her father, and screeched his name

"Papa!"

"What were you saying about perfect ladies?" Theo winked at Billie. She chuckled.

Theo strode out over the garden to his daughter who was smiling up at him angelically from a very grubby face, her arms held out indicating she wanted picking up.

"You will make me very dirty, Bea." He admonished.

His four-year-old daughter looked at him, assessing how serious he was, her head tilted in exactly the same way her mother's did when she was ruminating over a sticky problem.

Theo's breath caught, and he sent up a silent prayer of thanks for this, most unexpected, gift. He still found it hard to believe Grace had been delivered of not one but two healthy children and that, most importantly, she had survived.

Beatrice Willow Elliott was her mother's double in almost every respect, down to the same fathomless gaze which could reach inside his very soul.

Theo had been thrilled when it was clear his daughter's hair would be the same burnished auburn as her mother's, but rather than amber, her eyes were deep blue, and she had her father wrapped around her chubby little finger.

Neither Grace nor Theo expected to be twice lucky but, a little under a year ago, Grace again discovered she was increasing. The birth of their first child had been worrisome, but Theo consulted the best doctors he could find and, between them all they minimised the danger to both his wife and unborn child.

After several examinations, they concluded that while,

yes, Grace had suffered trauma during the birth of the child she lost, it was not as bad as first suspected, and all agreed she was at no greater risk than any other expectant mother.

Thus, when Grace informed him of her condition, although he experienced mild panic — accepting, even with the best care, there were no certainties when it came to childbirth — he covered it well, ensuring every precaution was taken throughout her pregnancy.

Hannah Alicia Elliott entered the world just over three months previously on a cold dark day at the end of February after a very short confinement, and her tiny features already resembled those of her father.

She had little hair, and her eyes were still baby blue, but Grace was positive Hannah, would have brown eyes and hair the colour of dark straw. Nothing Theo said could convince her otherwise.

Between the arrivals of Beatrice and Hannah, Billie gave birth to a daughter of her own. Vivienne Elizabeth Grace Trevallier was a very independently minded, nearly three-year-old, who led the other two children a merry dance.

Neither Grace nor Billie engaged a nanny; each relishing the role of motherhood, and their children accompanied them everywhere including the schoolroom.

Grace had waited too long to relegate any child of hers to a nursery. As she had declared to Billie, they were her children, she knew best how they ought to be brought up. Should a little assistance prove necessary, both of their homes offered plenty of willing helpers.

Beatrice had decided being muddy was about as good as it got, and presumed her father was teasing. She grabbed him by his hair and planted a sticky kiss on his mouth, earning her a merciless bout of tickling. Beatrice was chortling with glee, when a bellow from Max announced the presence of Giles.

The earl had ridden over on Bronte, leaving her in the meadow with the other three horses — not to mention goats and chickens — and was entering the garden through the gate in the wall.

Giles swung Max up onto his shoulders, ignoring the mud clinging to his son's boots, which splattered all over his pristine riding jacket.

"Elliott! Well met." Giles grinned.

"Winchester! Glad to see your stewards released you," Theo replied nodding at his friend, knowing Giles had been caught up in estate business for much of the day.

"For a while it was debatable, until I pointed out we really needed to make a decision as I had an important dinner to attend, and it would be unconscionably rude should I arrive late. At that they, literally, shoved me out of the door."

Giles laughed at the memory. Theo joined in and the two enjoyed a brief discussion on the outcome of said meeting.

Of late, it had become a pleasurable habit for the two couples to take it in turns to host dinners. Tonight, Grace was entertaining, and she had already commented it was a good thing no one stood on ceremony, for any plate of food was likely to be accompanied by a side dish of soil.

Bored with adult conversation, Max was starting to fidget.

Theo waved his hand in the general direction of the house, saying, "Billie has just gone in to put Vivienne to bed, or maybe to bath her, again. Regardless, she is upstairs, you know where to find her."

Giles thanked his friend and, pulling the muddy boots off his son's feet, piggybacked Max upstairs in search of his wife.

Grace came back outside, Hannah in her arms, the babe drowsy now after satisfying her hunger. Walking over to her husband, Grace stretched up to kiss him, admiring the way the late afternoon sun highlighted the angles and planes of his face.

Theo smiled down at Grace and snuck a quick a kiss on Hannah's downy cheek.

"Don't you wake her, Theo Elliott, or you will be the one to settle her," Grace tried to sound stern, failing dismally.

Theo, wholly unrepentant, untied the ribbon of her hat and pulled it off her vibrant hair, kissing the tip of her nose as he did so. Cupping the back of her head, he drew her close.

"I promise, Grace Elliott."

She chuckled and leant into his shoulder, Beatrice nodding sleepily on his other.

Grace and Theo stood together in gentle light of the balmy evening. Their two daughters snugly tucked into their parents' arms; gales of laughter floating down from the guest bedchamber — where no doubt Max was running his parents ragged.

Theo kissed his wife with infinite tenderness, the caress of his lips laden with promise.

Grace felt warmth suffuse her as she gazed up at her husband. The depth of her love for him clear in her beautiful eyes, which glowed like molten brandy in the dying rays of the sun, holding him spellbound.

There was nowhere she would rather be than wrapped in Theo's embrace.

~

Rosie Chapel lives in Perth, Australia with her hubby and three furkids. When not writing, she loves catching up with friends, burying herself in a book (or three), discovering the wonders of Western Australia, or — and the best — a quiet evening at home with her husband, enjoying a glass of wine and a movie.

Website: www.rosiechapel.com

A Christmas Prayer *with Ashlee Shades*

The Lady's Wager

Winning Emma

A Love Impossible

Unravelling Roana

<u>Fairy Tale Romance</u>

Chasing Bluebells

<u>Contemporary Romances</u>

Of Ruins and Romance

All At Once It's You

Cobweb Dreams

Just One Step

His Heart's Second Sigh

The Pomegranate Tree

Hannah's Heirloom - Book One

Hoping to trace the origins of an ancient ruby clasp, a gift from her long dead grandmother, Hannah Wilson travels to the fortress of Masada with her best friend, Max. Strange dreams concerning a rebel ambush begin to haunt Hannah and following a tragic accident, she slips into the world of Ancient Masada.

A woman out of time, Hannah must rely on her instincts and her knowledge of what will befall this citadel to survive. Will she escape, or is she doomed to die along with hundreds of others as Masada falls – and what does any of this have to do with an ancient ruby clasp?

Echoes of Stone and Fire

Hannah's Heirloom - Book Two

Pompeii - a vibrant city lost in time following the AD79 eruption of Vesuvius. Now rediscovered, archaeologists yearn for an opportunity to uncover the town's past. Some things, however, are best left alone - revealing the secrets hidden beneath the stones could prove perilous. Hannah and Max are brought to Pompeii by a surprise invitation to join an excavation team who are trying to uncover the city's long history.

After entering an excavated house that bears a Hebrew inscription, Hannah's two worlds collide, and she falls back through time to ancient Pompeii. A place where her ancestor is a physician to gladiators engaged in mortal combat, where riotous mobs run amok and where a ghost from the past returns to haunt her.

Will Hannah and her loved ones manage to escape the devastation she knows is coming, before the town is engulfed in volcanic ash?

Will she ever find her way back to Max the love of her life, waiting not so patiently millennia away? Or will echoes be all that remain?

Embers of Destiny

Hannah's Heirloom - Book Three

AD80 - Hannah and Maxentius must embark on a new journey to Northern Britannia. This harsh frontier is far from the comforts of Rome and danger lurks where least expected; a garrison of soldiers, some unhappy with their isolated posting; local tribes, outwardly accepting of their Roman occupier, but who may still resent the seizure of their lands.

Millennia away, Hannah Vallier finds a familiar item while working in a museum near Hadrian's Wall. It is the pomegranate; carved by Maxentius on Masada. Before Hannah can discuss it with Max, disaster strikes! Believing her husband has been killed, Hannah retreats into the past, her soul melding with that of her ancestor, but with little idea of what they could face. Is the risk from the conquered tribes, or much closer to home?

As rebellion threatens to shatter a fragile peace, Hannah's heart whispers that just maybe Max isn't dead and that he is calling her home. Can she trust her heart, or will she remain caught out of time, her destiny floating away like embers on a breeze?

Etched in Starlight

Hannah's Heirloom - Prequel

Maxentius - a Roman soldier fresh from the battlefields of Armenia, arrives to take command of the military outpost of Masada, Herod's isolated citadel in the Judaean desert. A seemingly mundane posting after years of warfare, Maxentius finds it more challenging to maintain a focused garrison than to face the wrath of the Parthians across a disputed frontier.

Hannah - a young Hebrew physician spends her days dealing with injuries from street brawls, deprivation, disease and loss. As her beloved Jerusalem plunges into chaos; her brother — who belongs to a band of rebels determined to drive out their Roman occupiers — tells her of their plans to storm a desert fortress and steal the weapons stored there, persuading his reluctant sister to go with him.

Masada - following the ambush, Hannah finds and treats three badly wounded Roman soldiers. In the aftermath and against impossible odds, Hannah and Maxentius realise that they are more than healer and captive, their fate already etched in starlight.

~

Prelude to Fate

For Lucia, staring into the jaws of an horrific death, escape seems impossible.

Rufius Atellus, a veteran Roman soldier, is appalled when he recognises one of the victims about to be executed. Surely this is a ghastly mistake?

A ferocious she-wolf, anticipating a tasty meal, suddenly finds herself under a human's control.

In an unexpected twist, and as danger threatens, the lives of all three become inextricably entwined.

Was it chance brought them together in that theatre of bloodshed, or simply a prelude to fate?

~

Once Upon An Earl

Linen and Lace - Book One

When Fate saw fit to intervene in the life of Giles Trevallier, the very respectable Earl of Winchester, by dropping a female — soaked to the skin and with no memory of who she is or how she came to be there — literally at his feet, no one could have predicted the outcome.

While uncovering her identity, Giles realises he is falling hopelessly in love with his mystery guest, who unbeknownst to him, is succumbing to similar emotions; but, when the heart is involved, a thoughtless word or gesture can thwart even Fate's best-laid plans.

Faced with misunderstandings, whispers of scandal, secret documents and foreign agents, their chance at a happy ever after seems elusive, but fairy tales often happen when least expected, and love — however inconvenient — usually finds a way to conquer all.

To Unlock Her Heart

Linen and Lace - Book Two

Abused by a duke, and shunned by Society, relief seems at hand when Grace Aldeburgh is bequeathed a house in a small village, far from malicious gossips.

Once there, a tentative friendship blooms between Grace and Theo Elliott, the local doctor, who has already resolved to be the man to unlock her heart.

Just when happiness appears to be within her grasp, her erstwhile tormentor once again stalks Grace. After a failed kidnap attempt, the duke's quest culminates in an acrimonious confrontation, and the reason for his venal pursuit becomes agonisingly clear.

Love on a Winter's Tide

Linen and Lace - Book Three

Every day, Helena disappears into a world few acknowledge, helping the poor, downtrodden, and abused. A husband is the last thing she can be bothered with.

Busy managing his shipping line, Hugh Drummond sees no need for a wife, whose only joy is dancing and frivolity. If — and it was a huge if — he ever married, it would be to a woman as capable as he, not some giddy society Miss.

Then, Hugh meets Helena and despite their resolve, fate, it seems, has other ideas. As their attraction deepens however, treachery threatens to tear them apart. Will they uncover the perpetrator in time, or will their love be swept away, lost forever on a winter's tide?

A Love Unquenchable

Linen and Lace - Book Four

Jessica Drummond, a bright and cheerful young woman, rarely gives romance, let alone love, a thought. Long hours working in her brother's shipping office affords little chance of her ever meeting an eligible bachelor.

Duncan Barrington, veteran of the Napoleonic Wars, believes himself wounded in both body and soul. He has no intention of inflicting his demons on anyone, certainly not a beautiful and, in his opinion, irresponsible city lady.

One cold and snowy morning, the plight of a bedraggled puppy throws Jessica and Duncan together and, as a spark of something indefinable yet wholly unquenchable begins to burn, it is unclear who rescued whom.

A Hidden Rose

Linen and Lace - Book Five

After witnessing his mother's grief at the loss of his father, Nick

Drummond resolved never to cause someone he loved such distress. Even the happiness of his siblings would not sway him – until he met Rose.

Rose Archer was almost content assisting her doctor father in a tiny fishing village in the north of Yorkshire. To experience the world beyond, a tantalising dream – until she met Nick.

Unexpectedly, the impossible becomes possible, and the renounced – desired above all things, but the shipwreck that brought them together, may yet tear them apart. Will Nick learn to trust his heart, or will his love for Rose remain forever hidden

The Daffodil Garden

Horrifically scarred during the war, William Harcourt - Marquis of Blackthorne - prefers to spend his days in the quiet of his daffodil garden; plants do not pity, turn away, or judge.

Lucy Truscott, whose life is far removed from that of the *ton*, has no idea that by saving the life of a young woman, to whom she bears an uncanny resemblance, her own will be placed in mortal danger.

A chance encounter leads to something more. William begins to trust that Lucy sees the man beneath the scars, while Lucy is persuaded that love might actually transcend status.

Unfortunately, before their courtship has really begun, someone has every intention of ending it - permanently.

The Unconventional Duchess

Refusing to suffer the humiliation of her husband flaunting his mistress at Society events, the newly married Duchess of Wallingstead, Ella Lennox, takes control of her life. She leaves London for the family's country seat in remote Yorkshire.

A woman alone, Ella spends the next four years turning a cold, grim house into a home, and transforming the fortunes of the estate. Not afraid of hard work, she soon earns the respect of those around her with her determination and unconventional attitude.

Out of the blue, the duke arrives. Resigned to another arduous visit, Ella is stunned when it seems he is attempting to court her.

Impossible!

Could her dream of a happy marriage be about to come true?

Everything hangs on a snowstorm, a herd of cows and an uninvited guest!

~

Rescuing Her Knight

The de Wiltons - Book One

A story, invented to keep a little girl distracted, marks the beginning of another tale. One destined to remain unfinished for nearly twenty years.

Against her better judgement, Kitty de Wilton is persuaded to help Adam Marchmain banish his demons. This requires a subterfuge which, if discovered, might shatter more than the bonds of friendship forged two decades previously.

To Kitty, determined to break through the shield Adam has erected, the risk is worth it.

To see his smile and hear his laughter.

To rescue the knight of her childhood.

Just when a fairy tale ending is within her grasp, Kitty is threatened by the man who murdered her husband. In a cruel twist the tables are turned, and Kitty is the one who needs rescuing.

~

His Fiery Hoyden

A Novella

Livvy has no respect for the nobility; they let her down when she most needed them. Why should she accede to their demands now?

Philip, Lord Harrington, is stunned to discover the young heir to the dukedom lives a stone's throw away in a ramshackle cottage, and resolves to restore the child to his birthright.

They meet in a clash of wills, but just when it seems Livvy might surrender, the victory Philip desires, may not taste all that sweet.

~

A Regency Duet

Luck be a Pirate

Luck wasn't something retired pirate Kennet Alexson believed in – good or bad. However, even he had to concede that landing a job at Trentams shipyard, and meeting Lynette Collins, was more than coincidence.

Fortune it seemed, was smiling on him for once.

As Kennet adjusts to life on dry land, his friendship with Lynette deepens into something far more enduring, and what once seemed elusive now becomes possible.

Unfortunately, fate has other plans, and Kennet's good luck is about to run out.

The Highwayman's Kiss

Surrendered Hearts – Book One

Nothing exciting had ever happened to Juliette St Clair. Her days were spent assisting her father or calling on friends, wandering art galleries, taking constitutionals or, and more preferably, escaping into her books. Her evenings her evenings — an endless round of balls, where she preferred to remain invisible.

Until the day she was robbed by a highwayman.

A Regency Christmas Double

Heart Rescued

Four years since Jasper lost the woman he was hoping to marry. Four years since he closed his heart and withdrew from Society. He has no idea his reclusive existence is about to be shattered.

Enter his sister's best friend, Harriet, a flame haired beauty, who needs his help.

Reluctantly he agrees and as they spend time together, it is clear their feelings run deep. Although Harriet affects Jasper in a way no woman ever has, he believes her to be out of his league ~ but it's Christmas and she might just be the one to melt his frozen heart

Catch a Snowflake

Romance often blossoms in the most unlikely of places - but in a ward full of wounded soldiers - surely not?

When Lucas Withers comes face to face with Jemima Parsons - a young woman who blames him for her brother's injury - falling in love is the last thing on their minds. What neither of them anticipated, was the magic of snowflakes.

Fate is Curious

A Novella

Happily, ever after? No such thing! Bereft, following her beloved husband's sudden death, Lady Charlotte Sherbrooke has lost her belief in such romantic nonsense.

Successful shipping merchant, Zacharie Romain, is no stranger to loss; his business can be hazardous. Moreover, his wife died in childbirth and even though it happened a decade ago, he has no mind to expose himself to such sorrow again.

They meet in less than joyful circumstances but, as the year turns and grief diminishes, the woes of a small boy become the catalyst for something wholly unexpected. Can Charlotte and Zacharie trust what Fate has in store or will past heartbreak prevent them from taking a chance on love?

∼

A Christmas Prayer

with Ashlee Shades

A Short Story

An entreaty from a frightened child.

Orphaned and only nine, Caroline Thorne has to grow up before her time. She is doing everything she can to keep what is left of her family together and out of the workhouse but is terrified her prayers are not being heard. Or maybe they are…

A petition from a woman desperate for a family.

A chance meeting with three orphaned siblings, tugs at Elizabeth Barrington's heart strings. Thus far, she and her husband have not been blessed with children and, as Christmas approaches, a plan begins to form - one which might just be the answer to her prayers.

Two Christmas prayers, as different as they are the same.

Will they hear and, more importantly, heed the answer?

∼

The Lady's Wager

Surrendered Hearts- Book Two

A Novelette

Ged Mowbray will do anything to avoid being married off to the suitable prospects his parents insist on parading in front of him.

Melissa Bouchard is under no illusion her sizeable dowry is the attraction to suitors, not her.

An overheard conversation leads to an offer too good to refuse, but what happens when a lady's wager, becomes a gamble on the happily ever after, you did not even realise you wanted?

~

Winning Emma

Surrendered Hearts - Book Three

A Novelette

Randolph Craythorpe — earl, covert operative, and occasional highwayman — believed his dalliance with Lady Felicity Hartwich would lead to marriage. It did, but not to him! The arrival of an unwelcome guest, however, provides the perfect opportunity to indulge in a little retaliation.

Emma Newbury accompanies her cousin, Lady Charity Anscombe, to London for the Christmas season. Once there, she comes face to face with the three men who witnessed the humiliating aftermath of her father's disgrace — one of whom, to her irritation, has taken up residence in her dreams.

Their infrequent encounters only serve to confuse but, while winter tightens its grip on the city, what was inconceivable becomes the one thing for which they both yearn, yet bound by Society's rules, cannot admit.

As the snow falls, Randolph begins to understand that to win Emma, he will have to surrender.

~

A Love Impossible

A Regency M/M Novelette

Tasked with investigating a heinous crime, Edward Lindsay travels from London to Dublin — a city which holds too many memories — in the guise of guardian to his sister. He knew it could be hazardous, and relished the challenge, but that wasn't what caused his stomach to tighten as they approached landfall.

Dublin held more than just a murderer.

There was also Aidan.

While attending a party, Aidan Griffen is astonished when he comes face to face with a man who fled Dublin two years previously. A man he has desperately tried to forget.

As Edward closes in on his quarry, a fire, deliberately extinguished, is rekindled. But what of it? Edward and Aidan share a love impossible, and to acknowledge their feelings — more dangerous than confronting a killer.

Is there any hope of a happily ever after?

Unravelling Roana

Tired of being ignored by her husband, Roana Dumont, Countess of Brooketon does the one thing guaranteed to get his attention. She runs away… to Venice, leaving behind a set of riddles for him to solve… *if* he feels their marriage is worth saving.

Gideon Dumont, 6th Earl of Brooketon is flabbergasted when he discovers his wife has apparently vanished off the face of the earth. A series of puzzles, the only clue as to her whereabouts.

The question is… will he unravel them?

Chasing Bluebells

A Novella

Once upon a time, somewhere in France, there was a man whose reckless obsession led him down a dark path — one which, ultimately, cost him his life. That ought to have been the end of it. Regrettably, as is so often the case, those who least deserve it, suffer for the actions of others.

A decade after being sent away, Sebastien Daviau returns to the little village where everything began. Hoping to lay the ghosts of his childhood to rest, he studiously ignores the possibility, he might run into Charlotte de Montbeliard.

As luck would have it, Charlotte is the one who runs into him… well, his horse… and although the brief encounter leaves a lasting impression, neither recognises the other.

A name revealed causes a freak accident, catapulting Sebastien's past into his present, and bringing him face to face with a man whose reputation would intimidate the most ardent of suitors.

Can whatever is blossoming between Charlotte and Sebastien survive the challenge imposed, or is their happily ever after about to fade as quickly as the bluebells they loved to chase?

Of Ruins and Romance

While escorting a group of tourists around the ancient Roman port of Ostia, Kassandra Winters bumps into someone she first met in less than auspicious circumstances two years previously. The encounter leads to a job offer - to be the assistant guide for a three-week tour of ancient sites in and around Rome. Unable to resist such an opportunity, Kassie agrees.

Kassie has intrigued Gabriel St Germain since he accidentally knocked her flying outside her university professor's office. Her face haunts his dreams, yet he never expected to see her again. So, he is surprised when she appears, as though destined to do so, in the middle of a ruin, and he concocts a plan to win her heart.

Gabriel's old-fashioned courtship touches something deep inside Kassie and, although struggling to believe someone as handsome as Gabriel could possibly be interested in her, she soon realises she has fallen irrevocably in love with him. However, just as Kassie shares everything of herself with Gabriel, her world comes crashing down. Can their romance survive, or will it fall in ruins, like the relics of antiquity that brought them together?

All At Once It's You

When Alex arrives in the small village of Rosedale Abbey, to take up a position as a research assistant for a renowned archaeologist, the last thing she is looking for, or expects to find, is love.

Jake was perfectly happy with the status quo. When it came to relationships, he didn't do committed or long term. He called the shots, and if his current flame didn't like it, she knew what to do. A philosophy, which served him well - until he met Alex.

Romance blooms, but even as the untamed wilderness of the North Yorkshire moors weaves its spell, a long-buried secret might yet jeopardise their happily ever after.

~

Cobweb Dreams

A Novella

A holiday on the Scottish isle of Mull was just the break Chloe Shepherd needed, an escape from her boring office job and her complete lack of anything resembling a social life. Romance, it seems, isn't on the cards and, although Chloe dreams of finding her soulmate she is beginning to believe love is like cobwebs — spun overnight, only to vanish in the early morning breeze.

Under sufferance, Dominic Winters makes a flying visit to Mull to check on a rental property owned by his family. He hasn't got time for this — so indulging in a holiday fling is the last thing on his mind.

A lamb stuck in a bog proves a most unexpected matchmaker and, while Mull weaves its magic, Chloe wonders whether those fragile cobwebs might be far more stubborn than she thought.

~

Just One Step

A Short Story

In the aftermath of an horrific car accident, Daisy Forrester travels to Italy - hoping, so far from her memories, she might begin to heal.

Archaeologist, and single father, Adam Willoughby is too busy looking after his young daughter to give romance let alone love, a thought.